WAYFARERS

WRATH OF BLACKFANG

Miles Jackson

Wayfarers: Wrath of Blackfang.

© 2023 by Miles Jackson

Dedicated to my loving and supportive family

TABLE OF CONTENTS

PROLOGUE

M y mentor once told me the best way to truly be remembered for your deeds is to record them yourself so all who discover my findings know my tale and who I was. He told me our very lives are stories just waiting to be written and every choice we make adds to that growing tale. As a boy my ambitions were never grand and my desire to understand the world outside of my home was nothing short of vague curiosity. Never did I wish to explore this vast world of ours, meet new and interesting people or accomplish great feats. I craved a mundane life but despite my best efforts to ignore the call to adventure fate would set me down the path regardless of what I wanted.

During my extensive journey throughout the sacred forest, we call home, I have slain dangerous beasts twice my size, fought in great battles, seen wonders and horrors alike that no ordinary mouse could fathom. Yet despite the numerous perils I faced I still lived to tell my tale. Though now my body has grown old and frail, I am preparing to make one final journey to parts unknown. Once I depart, I know that I will not return. Before I embark, however, I wish to write down all that transpired that led me to this moment. My name is Tybalt Shortwhisker and the story I am about to tell you is a thorough collection of my adventures and of my companions.

I was born in the Southern region of the Hallowed Forest and lived in a secluded clearing away from monsters and other dangers along with my family. My parents had carved out a home for their litter within a stump of a fallen oak tree. Born into the world with four other siblings, I was the second oldest and had most of the responsibility along with my older brother Nathaniel. Our mother mostly raised us on her own as our father had long since passed due to an unfortunate encounter with a falcon. Our younger siblings Olivia, and the twins Carter and Lucy were quite rambunctious, but I loved them all the same.

I was never the most social nor the most popular amongst my kin as Nathaniel was often looked to as the leader amongst us not just due to his age but his maturity, strength and courage. Not that I minded of course, it gave me more time to myself for more reading and writing. We were not a wealthy family mind you, but the clearing we called our home was plentiful with food and other necessities to be foraged from the land. There was little reason for us to want to leave our humble home other than acquiring goods we couldn't craft ourselves, but only Mother would leave the clearing to accomplish this while we were forced to remain home. Though most of my siblings had decided that once they had come of age they would depart and seek out their own future I had already decided to remain with mother until she passed on while looking after the house should my kin choose to return home. In hindsight it was quite naive of us to try and plot out our futures while boldly believing that nothing could ever alter our plans.

We were still young after all and were barely aware of the world outside of our home. I remember the day that changed my life vividly and the events that served as the catalyst to my life as an adventurer.

1

THE BEGINNING

My story and the events that led me down this path began nearing the end of the year 410 AE(After Exodus). It was a warm and breezy summer day and after I had finished all my chores, I would go to my favorite spot in the clearing to relax. We had already begun to see changes in the season, as the leaves began to fall from the trees and turned to a lovely shade of orange while being accompanied by a light chill in the air. Wanting to make the most of what remained of my summer I intended to capitalize on my break and rest in my private hiding spot. My little hideaway was on the hill overlooking our home and was situated at the base of a massive oak tree with a patch of brown mushrooms that I had fashioned into cushions along with some shady leaves overhead which shielded me from the sun. It also gave me a fantastic view of our home as well as the freshwater pond near it, making it all the more tempting to come here and rest.

Though it initially served as a place for me to express myself creatively in solitude I would often come here to get away from my siblings and other petty squabbling that made it difficult for me to concentrate. Unfortunately, I often accomplished very little reading in this area despite being its intended purpose as I would usually doze off not long after opening my favorite book. On this day however, peace and quiet was something I wouldn't be privileged to...

The sound of snapping twigs immediately placed me on high alert!

"H-Huh? What?" The abrupt sound woke me from my peaceful afternoon slumber. I glanced around my surroundings and tried to see who or what had come to invade my hideout. Was I just hearing things? Perhaps it was merely the wind? Though my suspicions were confirmed when I heard the same sound a second time. It was clear I wasn't alone." Wh-Whose there? Show yourself!" I demanded while quickly reaching for my book to serve as a makeshift weapon while sliding off my mushroom cushion." I said, reveal yourself, coward!" I cried out in a less than threatening tone of voice while brandishing my encyclopedia on flowers as though it were a sharpened blade." L-Last chance! I'm warning you! I-If you don't come out of there, I'll—"

Suddenly a pair of gray and white blurs emerged from the tall grass surrounding my hideaway and rushed right towards me! "BOO! FOUND YOU!"

"AHHH!"

Before I could even react, I was tackled to the ground by my assailants with my "weapon" being knocked free from my grasp!

"N-No wait!! Please! Don't hurt me! I—"

Right before my brief existence could even flash before my eyes, I realized just who exactly these intruders were. The pair of mischief makers gazed down at me and burst into laughter.

"So, this is where you've been hiding, big brother!" Lucy said with a smile at Carter.

"Hehehe, you look like you're about to soil yourself, Tybalt," he said with a teasing look.

The twins, Carter and Lucy, had been a constant thorn in my side due to their troublemaking antics. While I enjoyed their jokes from time to time, I was growing weary of becoming the butt of them. The pair were perfectly identical and the only way we could tell them apart was the blue bow we tied to Lucy's tail. They always found a way to get their garments filthy, much to Mother's dismay who frequently sought to keep them clean and out of trouble.

"Carter! Lucy! You little imps!" As much as I loved the pair, they were part of the reason why I chose to step away from the house every now and again.

I would push the pair off me and rise to my feet. As I began to dust off my shirt I'd ask," Why are you two pestering me again? In fact, how did you even find me? No one should know about this place but me!" The twins looked at one another before Lucy spoke up," Nathaniel said, he always sees you go up the hill at the end of the week, so we figured you'd be here today..." Then Carter continued with," ...and Mother's been looking for you. She says she needs help with something." I let out an annoyed grunt. Having already finished my chores for the day I was hoping to not have to help with dinner." Ugh, oh very well. I'll make my way back soon." I said before going over to my discarded book to retrieve it." Please don't tell anyone about this place! I'm trying to keep it a secret!" I told them while dusting off the encyclopedia." Now go on! Shoo!" I would cast a stern look at the twins which served as a clear signal that I was done with their tomfoolery. Once more the twins let out a unified giggle before scurrying back down the hill. " See you at home!" The pair would shout out as they departed. All I could do was sigh and watch them leave knowing well that my secret hideout would become known to everyone in the family if not the entire forest before the week had ended." So much for peace and quiet..." I muttered before collecting my belongings and storing them in my pack." ...oh well, I better go see what Mother needs."

Despite my grumblings, I was determined to heed my mother's call and scurried back towards the stump. Upon approaching the front door I'd see my brother Nathaniel sweeping away dirt and debris from our doorstep with a broom. Hearing my approach, he turned his gaze towards me with a smile.' Well now, it seems the twins have found my reclusive little brother after all." He chuckles and pauses his brooming. Out of all my siblings Nathaniel had the closest resemblance to father, at least according to Mother. He was the largest mouse in the house as well as the strongest. He had a brownish gray coat of fur that reminded Mother of a close relative of hers, but she never said who they were. "Indeed, they did." I replied and flashed him an annoyed look." For what reason did Mother need me again? I've had my fill of cleaning for one day." My sibling simply shrugged." I haven't a clue, when I asked, she refused to tell me and told me to leave." He rolls his eyes," You know how difficult she can be when she's in the kitchen." Nathaniel then reaches for the door to open it and steps to the side for me to pass." Anyway, best not keep her waiting." With a nod and a groan, I would go through the door and into our cozy wooden home." Mother?" I called out while setting my things down near the door. Though not long after entering our home my senses were graced with a savory aroma of mother's famous wild nut stew. A personal favorite of mine and something she only prepared during the changing of the seasons.

"I'm in the kitchen, dear. Please hurry!" She called out in a frantic tone.

Fearing that mother may have injured herself, I scampered into the kitchen to find her tending to a boiling pot of stew. Thankfully, she was unharmed apart from appearing a bit agitated." I was worried something happened to you. Is everything all right?" I asked as I gave her my undivided attention. My mother, Lara Shortwhisker, was a shrewd gray mouse hailing from the far east of the Hallowed Forest. She told us that she left her home and family to live the life of an adventurer along with Father. Though with his unfortunate demise Mother was left to raise a litter all on her own. Despite this tragedy my mother remained steadfast in her duty as leader of our family. She was often quite stern with us, but we all knew it was out of love. "I need you to go out and fetch some brightleaf for tonight's meal." Mother ordered while methodically stirring the stew pot." I'm quite certain I told you to go out and pick enough to last us two weeks and yet I've not seen one since I started cooking this morning!" She gives me an irritable expression as if I had disobeyed her.

"B-Brightleaf?" I repeated with a dumbfounded look on my face as I knew for a fact that I had done what Mother had asked of me the previous day.

Brightleaf was an herb that could usually be seen around the outskirts of the clearing. Mother would use it quite frequently in her cooking so making sure we were always stocked with it was paramount.

"That can't be right. The herb pouch should be bursting with brightleaf! Where is it?" I asked while turning towards the shelves and frantically opening them to see the supposed empty pouch myself.

"With your sister, Olivia," Mother answered. "She's the one who told me the pouch was empty to begin with and even volunteered to go and refill it herself since you couldn't be bothered with it."

"What?" I was baffled by what I was hearing! Olivia found the pouch and saw that it was empty. Something was surely amiss here. "Mother I know for a fact that I—"

"Hush, boy! I'll hear no more of this!" Before I could even begin to defend myself, Mother silenced me." I'm not interested in your excuses, Tybalt. I need you to go and check on your sister. She's been gone much longer than expected and I'm starting to worry." Though I was frustrated with Mother I wasn't about to disobey her. "Yes, Mother." I muttered, before making my way out of our home and towards the outskirts of the clearing where I would hopefully find my younger sister.

Truthfully, my relationship with Olivia was a bit strained at the time. We got along well when we were much younger but as we grew older and our ambitions as well as our personalities became more defined a growing rift between us became more visible. As I grew more interested in reading and writing she favored practicing swordplay with Nathaniel. While I was comfortable with the way we were living, Olivia wanted nothing more than to see the Hallowed Forest in its entirety. Given the many tales of adventures told to us by Mother it came as no surprise Olivia would become obsessed with venturing out on her own. As she grew older her curiosity and wanderlust grew stronger. Olivia frequently questioned Mother about the rest of the forest, the place she originated from and everything else the young mouse could think of. Mother often avoided answering her questions or would tell her to wait until she was older much to Olivia's frustrations.

Unfortunately, Olivia's impatience and the lack of sufficient answers from Mother would sow the seeds of rebellion as she grew older. Olivia became even more frustrated as I expressed no desire to leave our humble home despite her wishes for us to travel together. Hearing this seemed to wound Olivia and for a time she held a grudge against me over it. I then made my way to the closest patch of brightleaf that my family usually went to for harvesting, thinking that my sister would be there." Olivia?" I called out to her but saw that no one was there. Though when I arrived a swelling fear began to build within me as I found the herb pouch idly left on the ground and still filled to the brim with brightleaf but no sign of my missing sibling. Had something happened to her? Did something or someone take her? As I scurried further through the brush, I could feel my anxiety building with these questions buzzing through my mind, longing to be answered. I've grown to despise straying too far from home as the unknown dangers of the lands beyond terrified me. I would pause as I reached the peak of a large, slanted stone jutting from the ground and tried to gain a sense of my surroundings.

" Olivia? Olivia! Where are you?!" I cried out desperately but could only hear the sound of a nearby stream of water in response and the sight of the vast wilderness around me." She could be anywhere..." Now growing desperate, I was preparing to return home to seek out Nathaniel and ask for his help in searching for our missing sister until I heard some strange noises not too far from where I was. Hoping this might be my chance to find Olivia, I made my way towards the noise all the while attempting to approach the area discreetly in case, I was approaching a monster. Drawing nearer to the source of disturbance would lead me through a secluded thicket. Despite my hesitation I navigated through the brush which would lead me into a small hideaway where I would find none other than my missing sibling!

" What is she up to?" I muttered quietly to myself as I observed my younger sister from the bushes. From where I hid, I could see my sister appeared to be quite winded, but I couldn't understand why." Had she been fleeing from something?" I wondered. It was at that moment I saw the true cause for Olivia's weary appearance. In her paws Olivia would hold aloft our father's longsword, an elegant weapon kept in pristine condition thanks to the loving care of our mother who sought to preserve his memory as we were unable to locate his body to give him a proper burial.

The sword had an unusual design as its blade was as green as grass, was engraved with bizarre symbols and had a golden hilt long with a small gemstone at the end of it. It was then that I noticed the makeshift dummy positioned in front of my sister. It appeared to have been crafted from fallen plant foliage. She took a deep breath and checked her feet." All right, let's try that again..." I heard her mutter. Olivia then began to sweep and slash the blade as if she were sparring with the dummy. The manner in which she wielded the blade wasn't done childishly but in a way that mirrored a fledgling warrior readying herself for battle. As she swung the sword, she couldn't help but let out a series of audible grunts as she wasn't fully accustomed to the heft of the weapon. Even an inexperienced youth such as I could easily see that Olivia was still a novice despite her honest attempts to hone her skills. I wasn't sure of what to make of what was going on, but I was determined to get answers. I emerged from the brush and made no attempt to hide myself from Olivia as the sound of leaves rustling and twigs snapping took her out of her trance. She gasped and turned in my direction with the blade raised in a defensive manner.

"Wait! It's only me!" I shouted, wanting to calm my armed sibling down before she did something reckless.

"Tybalt?" Olivia immediately lowered the sword and looked at me with a confused expression." What are you doing out here? How did you even find me?!"

"I couldn't at first, but you were making such an awful racket while you were swinging that weapon it didn't take me too long to find you..." I told her as I brushed away any dirt and leaves from my fur that still clung to me." ...and I am out here because Mother told me to come and find you after you told her you couldn't find any brightleaf for tonight's dinner." I folded my arms and eyed my somewhat younger sibling incredulously.

"Strange, I could've sworn I gathered quite enough brightleaf only a few days ago and suddenly all of it disappears." I can see Olivia squirm under my gaze as she grits her teeth. She flashes me a glare before averting her gaze. "Well? You found what you were looking for, didn't you? You can leave now." Rudely she then begins to turn away as if to say she was finished with our conversation." Forget you saw me and be on your way."

"I'm not going anywhere until I get a proper answer!" I shouted and made it obvious I wasn't just going to let the matter be. She turned back to face me now, appearing even more annoyed with my intrusion.

" You lied about the brightleaf and stole Father's blade from Mother's room! You were even willing to let me take the blame for your deception and now you don't seem to care!" I continued, while growing more frustrated with my sibling." I expected this sort of behavior from the twins, but you? What could possibly be the reason for you to cause all this mischief?" A look of frustration could be seen on my sister's face as she turned her gaze downward. For a time, there was only silence between us before Olivia spoke up again and revealed the truth. "I'm leaving tomorrow night." She'd answer with an adamant tone as if she had already made up her mind. Once more silence fell between us as Olivia's words took a moment to fully sink in. Olivia had made such bold declarations before about leaving home when we were younger, but I could tell by her expression alone that this time she meant it." You're serious, aren't you? You actually plan on leaving us." The anger and irritation in my voice faded as the fear of losing my sister took hold over me.

"I have to, Tybalt. She keeps us here like we're her prisoners and I'm tired of it!" She shouted.

"Prisoners? You don't mean that. Mother loves us! She's done everything in her power to make sure we are safe and happy." I replied.

"Is that why she never lets us leave?" Olivia argues." Mother won't even take Nathaniel and he's the oldest! There's something she isn't telling us, and you know it. I'm tired of her secrets. I want answers!"

Deep down I knew Olivia was right. For as much as Mother talked about her adventures there was always this feeling, I had that told me that Mother was withholding the full story. "Surely you can wait at least a few more seasons, sister. A-At least until it's warmer—"

"A few more seasons?! You can't be serious!"

"I mean it, Olivia! Summer is ending and Fall is practically here." I gesture towards the fallen leaves around us." For only a moment please use your head! It'll be colder and likely more dangerous to travel now. You shouldn't risk it."

"No!" She replied with a fiery expression." I will not wait until I am old and senile to begin my journey! Nor will I wait for Mother to give me her blessing! We aren't her weak little pups anymore. We can fend for ourselves! "She then holds out the fine blade once wielded by our father." If anything does try to do me harm, I will happily use this on them. I've been practicing with Father's sword for some time now. I think I've got the hang of it."

"If you truly believe that then you've already sealed your fate." I told her." You can't solve all your problems by swinging around a sword! Please Olivia! Don't do this!"

"Then why don't you come with me?"

"W-What?" My sister's question catches me completely off guard.

"I want you to leave with me, brother. We can go together! See the world! Meet new people! Doesn't any of that interest you even a little?"

At first, I believed the offer was some sort of jest at my expense but seeing the change in tone and demeanor in Olivia I could see that her offer was genuine. She truly wanted me to leave with her." You've always been a studious sort, Tybalt. I'm sure hearing fairy tales from Mother is all well and good but wouldn't you want to see the world for yourself?" Olivia plants the sword in the ground and walks up towards me. For the first time in what felt like months she smiles and offers her paw to me." Of course, it won't be easy, but I think if we stick together, we can make this work. What do you say? Are you with me?" Looking down at Olivia's paw, I couldn't help but feel a growing temptation swell within me. In secret I did want to see what was out there and the thought of exploring alongside my sister did sound appealing to me.

"Please Tybalt. Come with me...I know we can do this together." There was a sense of urgency in her eyes. She truly wanted me to go on a journey with her like our parents had done in the past. Despite all my claims of being comfortable with the way I currently lived my life something about my sister's plea to accompany her nearly compelled me to take her up on that offer. Nevertheless, I would bury my own hidden desire for adventure and steel my nerves before speaking again." It's...getting late, Olivia. We need to go home.' I turned away from her." You know Mother will be worried about us." While I didn't see Olivia's expression her silence alone spoke volumes and I couldn't bear to face her. Already I began to walk back in the direction of the clearing only to stop and glanced back at my sister whose saddened demeanor seemed to sap her strength for the moment.' Coming Olivia?" I called out to her.

Olivia didn't answer; she simply got down on all fours and scurried ahead of me. At this point the rift between us had quickly become a gaping chasm. With a defeated sigh I tightened the herb pouch around my waist and made my way home. At the time both our minds were so lost in thought that we had neglected to remember one of Mother's most important rules, to always cover our tracks. A broken rule that would cost us dearly soon enough.

2

THE FEAST

By the time Olivia and I could even see the front door of our home the sun had already begun to set, basking the clearing in its golden glow. Still, we hardly had any time to enjoy the beautiful sight as Mother was still waiting for our return as well as the brightleaf she intended to add to tonight's meal. Upon our arrival we'd be greeted to the sight of our worried mother and older brother speaking to one another." Where could they be? I didn't think it would take them this long." Mother frowns with a troubled look on her face.

" Don't worry, Mother. I'll go look for them." Nathaniel replied then as he was about to begin his search only to let out a sigh of relief and smile as he saw us approach. " Oh, there they are!" Though Nathaniel was happy to see us, Mother didn't appear to be in the best of moods.

She storms right up to us and says," Oh thank goodness you're unharmed. Where have you two been?" She questions while looking at us both with suspicion." I sent you, Olivia, to go pick up more Brightleaf and I sent you, Tybalt, to go find your sister. It shouldn't have taken you both this long! What sort of mischief have you pups been up to?" She folds her arms and taps her foot as she waits for a reasonable answer for our lateness.

Olivia tried to speak first. "Well we I... uhm..." though she didn't really seem to have an answer knowing that the truth would certainly get her into trouble. Her voice soon trails off as she lowers her head, unsure of what to say without revealing her true plans. Initially I was plotting to reveal everything that Olivia was hiding from Mother. The lie about the brightleaf, the theft of Father's sword and her little secret training spot yet something compelled me to hold my tongue. Olivia could be very difficult to deal with at times, but she was still my sister and my friend. With haste I thought up a lie to protect her.

"Well young lady? I'm still waiting for an answer and your mumbling will not suffice." Mother would say as she was visibly growing impatient.

"......."

"S-She was stuck in a thorn bush!" I said abruptly.

Mother then turned her gaze towards me." A thorn bush?" She repeated and looked to me to continue the story.

I nodded and pushed my spectacles closer to my face." Yes she...she was caught while picking from a fresh patch." I was trying my best to hide any clear telling's that I was fibbing to Mother." It took me forever to get her out, but she seems to be all right." Olivia was surprised that I would attempt to cover for her after our earlier conversation. She blinked at me with a confused expression, but I continued to weave my false story to mother." She was so embarrassed that she wanted to keep it a secret." I stifled a forced chuckle though Mother hardly seemed amused. She appeared quite skeptical of my tale at first and for a moment I believed that my lie didn't work.

" A thorn bush. Hmm..." For a moment she stood there in silence before shrugging her shoulders with a more relaxed expression." Fine then, but please be more careful in the future. I don't know what I would do if something happened to you both." Mother then opens the door and steps to the side to let us in." Now then, off with you! All of you! I want you dirty pups cleaned and ready for dinner!" She said with a soft smile while removing the herb pouch from my person and sent me off. As we entered our home to clean ourselves and prepare for dinner I looked to Olivia, hoping to get some form of response to my sorry attempt to cover for her, but she simply ignored me and went about her business.

I knew she was still upset with me, but I had hoped this would help me get back into good favor with my younger sibling only to no avail. My intention was to speak with Olivia again the next day before she attempted to leave but for the moment my focus was on preparing for dinner. By sundown everything for tonight's dinner was ready. Mother had prepared an excellent spread of sweet roasted nuts, savory berries and of course her famous mixed nut stew now with the appropriate amount of brightleaf applied to the dish. I could see my siblings salivating at the sight of the scrumptious meal and eagerly took their seats at the table.

Mother then stood up and smiled at her litter," Before we eat, I just want to thank everyone for all of your hard work." There is a proud look on Mother's face as she speaks from the heart." Foraging for food and collecting enough fresh water can be a difficult task not to mention keeping this old stump clean and most importantly stable. Yet despite these troubles you've all pushed through it and kept our home functional and prosperous. Well done, children. I couldn't ask for a finer litter. With the cold season upon us we'll have to work twice as hard tomorrow to prepare for the worst but for now eat, drink and be happy. You've all more than earned it."

With Mother's blessing, my siblings and I all began to take part in the bountiful feast prepared for us. Eagerly I began to prepare a plate of stew with mixed nuts and happily consumed my meal with my kin. For me, the day never truly came to an end until I had savored Mother's delicious meals. While feasting on our harvest I glanced around the table to see how everyone else was enjoying the meal. The twins as well as Nathaniel seemed quite satisfied and hardly spoke a word as they gorged themselves.

Then I took notice of Olivia who had yet to touch her food and wore a troubled expression on her face. Rather than eat her food she simply picked at it with her utensils. While unknown to the others the reason for this was obvious to me. Our conversation from earlier still troubled her to the point that she couldn't hide her inner turmoil from the rest of the family, least of all from Mother. It didn't take long for her to see that something was wrong and immediately voice her concern.

"Olivia?" Mother said after taking another bite out of her stew." What's wrong, dear? You've barely touched your food." Olivia is brought out of her stupor at the sound of Mother's voice." It's...fine Mother. The food is great..."

"It's not too hot, is it? Did I burn anything?" Mother would ask with visible concern.

"No Mother. Not at all. The food is fine it's just..."

"Just what?"

Olivia pauses as if she was taking a moment to muster the courage to speak." ...Mother, a new season is upon us, and we are growing older and stronger. Though we are still young we aren't the helpless pups you brought into this world anymore."

Mother turns her full attention away from her meal and towards her daughter. She frowns as she listens to Olivia and already seems to know what she was about to ask.

"Perhaps it's time we learn more about—"

"No." Mother answers with a firm tone." My answer remains the same, Olivia. You will be told more in time but for now let's focus on enjoying our dinner."

At that point I assumed that things would quiet down and return to normal, but Olivia had grown stubborn and refused to leave the matter be." You always say that..." Olivia replies with a defiant expression." ...you always say that we aren't old enough. We're not children anymore. Why do you insist on keeping the truth from us?!" Olivia raises her voice, grabbing the attention of everyone at the table with her outburst. I had hoped this tension would pass but Olivia once again felt bold enough to press the question. A silence had fallen over the rest of the family as Olivia and Mother's argument took our full attention." Young lady, we've talked about this quite extensively already. What more is there to understand?"

"*Everything!*" My sister replied, no longer attempting to hide her resentment of Mother's rules." You've told us *nothing*! You refuse to let us even go into town with you! Mother, don't you see? You're treating us like prisoners!"

"Prisoners? Do you even hear yourself? Do you realize how overly dramatic you're being?" Mother narrowed her sights onto Olivia as she continued to argue." I have raised you all by myself for the majority of your lives. I have done everything within my ability to make sure you are all safe, fed and happy. Yet for some reason it is never good enough for you, Olivia. All I ask is that you be patient! I am trying to protect you!"

"Protect us from what?" Olivia questions.

Mother holds her tongue as if she were on the cusp of revealing something. She falls silent for a moment and appears distressed. "Well?" Olivia says, refusing to drop the subject. "Enough, Olivia." Mother then finally says.

"Tell us!"

"I said enough!" Mother angrily shouts and gives Olivia a furious glare that causes my bold sibling to shrink down to her seat with a defeated expression on her face. Mother's booming voice startles us as well as the twins and Nathaniel freeze in place. Even to this day the sound of Mother shouting remains a frightening reminder of a parent's authority.

After taking a moment to compose herself, Mother says, "If you'll excuse me." She then rises from her seat and leaves the table before promptly retreating to her room. After Mother leaves our visibly frustrated sister also rises from her seat only to exit through the front door of the house.

"So much for our family feast." Nathaniel sighs and slouches in his chair. He was looking forward to the feast and spending some quality time with us and was quite tired of Mother and Olivia's bickering like myself. The twins were left quite unnerved after Mother and Olivia's squabble.

They seemed unsure of what to do with themselves as their youthful exuberance had diminished after witnessing such a heated argument. "What do we do now?" Carter asks while looking towards me." Is Mother going to be, okay?" Lucy would ask as she turned her question towards Nathaniel. I took a moment to think about what we could do to help this situation but before I could answer Nathaniel was already two steps ahead of me, as always.

"You both need to finish your meals, first of all. Then I expect you both to prepare for bedtime." Our older brother ordered while getting up from the table.

"What?!"

"Aww..."

"None of that tonight, you two. Straight to bed as soon as you're done." Unsurprisingly the twins weren't very eager to go to sleep, but it was likely for the best they did turn in a bit earlier than they usually do." Everything will be all right." He gave the twins a reassuring look before turning his gaze towards me. " I'm going to speak with Olivia and make sure she doesn't do anything reckless. You should do the same with Mother." I nodded and got up from my seat. "R-Right." I was admittedly afraid to interact with our mother when she was upset and usually just left her be. Though after such a terrible argument with Olivia having someone to talk to seemed only natural if not necessary. Upon reaching the door I took a deep breath and braced myself for whatever response Mother had prepared. Finally, I knocked on the door and made my presence known.

"Mother? Are you alright?"

My call was met with silence. Growing concerned I knocked on the door again.

"Can you hear me? I-It's Tybalt."

Still, I heard no response. For a moment I considered leaving her be before finally getting a response from behind the door. "Come in, Tybalt." I heard her say. After once again bracing myself for whatever disposition Mother was currently in, I would open the door. Her room, at least to me, felt like a den of treasures as various souvenirs and trinkets from her adventures with Father could be seen hung up on the walls. One of the most striking things to catch my attention was a single massive fang from a slain monster which hung over her bed. Mother was sitting on her bed with her back facing me, she appeared to be holding something that shined in her paws though instead of asking about the strange object I focused my attention on Mother." Are you all right?" I asked as I approached her.

"I'm fine, Tybalt. I'm just a little tired is all." She turned to face me and despite her attempts to stow away her hurt feelings there was no hiding the fact that she had been crying as tear stains marked her face. Mother had put on a brave face at the dinner table but what Olivia said did hurt her.

"You know Olivia didn't mean what she said." I took a seat next to her on the bed." She loves you; we all do."

"I know." She replies." That girl is practically a spitting image of myself when I was her age. Thinking so much with her heart instead of her head. "Mother wipes the stray tears from her reddened eyes. She smiles faintly before hardening her expression and then saying." She's far too preoccupied with fantasizing about the world beyond this clearing to realize the blessings she already has. Our home is bountiful, safe and secluded. Many would kill to live in a place like this." Mother looks at me with and says, "I swear that everything that your father and I have done for this family has been done out of love. We only want to protect you."

"From what, Mother?" Again, the question would be brought up a second time that night and once again Mother wouldn't reply. For once I was siding with Olivia and wasn't going to accept Mother shutting herself off again. We did have a right to know, and I believed it to be wise to speak to her while we were alone." Mother, you know this is only going to keep happening the older we get. Olivia truly wants to see what's out there and I know Nathaniel has been feeling the same though he's been more reserved about it. No doubt the twins will want to follow suit once they come of age. I understand you want to keep us safe, but..."

"...but you want to know the truth." She'd finish my sentence as she turned her weary gaze towards me." Strange, you're the last mouse I expected to be speaking to about this." Mother pats my head and lets out a small chuckle.

"Y-Yes well...the others seem quite passionate over the matter. I'm just afraid they might do something reckless." My thoughts immediately returned to my earlier conversation with Olivia and her plans to run away from home. I much rather preferred that my siblings had Mother's blessing before going off into the unknown wilderness. Mother takes a deep breath and tries to bring her emotions under control before speaking again.

" Perhaps I haven't been entirely truthful with you and your siblings." She would say. "I loved your father. He and I were like two halves and when he died it has left me feeling incomplete ever since." She looks down at the object in her paw which appeared to be some sort of crest after peering down at it." All I have left of him now are these trinkets and my memories." Mother would avert her gaze once more; she closed her eyes as if to keep her tears from streaming down her cheeks. Very rarely did we ever see Mother cry as we assumed she always wanted to appear strong and fearless in front of her litter." I want to keep you safe from the dangers of the forest but I'm also afraid that you'll all leave me, and I'll be left to die alone." I could see now why Nathaniel was right to send me to Mother. Now more than ever did she need the support from her children. I brought her into a comforting embrace in hopes of soothing her broken heart to the best of my ability. It never occurred to me just how lonely Mother must've felt with Father's passing. To lose someone you truly believed to be your one true love is an excruciating burden I wouldn't wish upon my worst enemy. Mother would release me and once again wiped the tears from her eyes. She smiled warmly at me and said," You've always been a good boy, Tybalt. Thank you. Though now I'm beginning to see that perhaps I have been too hard on you and the others. Perhaps it is time I reveal more about the forest and why I have kept so much from all of you..."

"Truly?" For a moment I wasn't sure if Mother was telling the truth or not but the look of resolve on her face had made it clear that she had already made up her mind.

She nodded." Tomorrow morning we'll all gather around the table, have a nice breakfast and talk. I'll have much to say so I expect you and your siblings to get a good night's rest. Not everything I have to say will be easy to take in but perhaps you are ready to learn. For now, it would be best if you went and got some sleep. You've had a busy day and tomorrow will be even busier for us."

Hopping off of Mother's bed I began to make my way towards the door with a bright smile on my face. While I intended to stay with Mother, I was nonetheless curious about what she had been keeping from us. As I made my way towards the door Mother began to make herself comfortable under her blanket." Rest well, Tybalt. I'll see you in the morning." She said while finally preparing to sleep for the night.

"I shall. Good night, Mother." I would say before leaving her room and shutting the door. In truth I was expecting my talk with Mother to be disastrous and Mother to angrily lash out at me for even suggesting that she be more open with us. Instead, I felt as though I managed to get far closer to Mother than any of my siblings. It felt as though I had left a positive impression on her, which in turn would affect the entire family, hopefully for the better. Not long after walking away from the door did, I began to feel weary as well. After everything that had transpired that day, I felt that a well-deserved rest was in order. I had completely forgotten about Nathaniel and Olivia, but I was already confident before that my older brother would sort Olivia out and keep her from leaving. Despite the blunder that was supposed to be our family feast I believed that my talk with Mother would reflect positively for the future of our family. Little did I know that on the same night my life would change forever.

3

THE NIGHTMARE

Night had fallen over the forest, cloaking our clearing in a tranquil darkness. All of my kin had gone to sleep for the night and were peacefully slumbering in their beds. However, I wouldn't have this luxury. As I slept, I was afflicted with a horrible nightmare that I could scarcely comprehend. I dreamt of a vast wasteland bereft of trees, water or grass.

It was as if the Hallowed Forest had long since died and rotted away leaving behind nothing but a barren land. The clouded sky above was gray and ominous with nary a bird or bug to be seen. For the moment there wasn't a single soul in sight and for once in my entire short life I felt as though I was truly alone. I began to walk through the barren wastes while hoping that I would cross paths with someone who could tell me what had happened here. With each step taken through the desolate lands the sky seemed to grow darker.

I began to panic and called out desperately for someone, anyone to hear me and come to my aid. Unfortunately, I would get a response but not the one I desired. In the distance I could see a large dust cloud building up and could hear the savage cries of beasts that couldn't possibly be other mousefolk. From behind I could see an army of monstrous creatures that were all far larger and stronger than me stampeding in my direction! Keen eyed falcons with sharpened talons, hulking wolves with blood and saliva dripping from their muzzles and ferocious wildcats that snarled and hissed as they gave chase.

Overwhelmed with fear I began to flee from the nightmarish creatures, but the more I ran the less it felt as though I could escape them. There was nowhere to run or hide myself and it seemed as though the beasts were moving closer towards me with each step I took. The twisted flesh of the monstrous aberrations began to fuse into a singular creature, a horrible abomination with the features of various lizards, wolves and birds of prey twisted into an otherworldly entity hellbent on crushing me and devouring my remains. To this day, it's horrible green glowing eyes still haunt me.

The shock of what I saw freed me from the slavering jaws of that terrible nightmare. What I had seen had left me drenched in sweat and my heart racing faster than it had ever done before. As I was sharing the same room with my brothers Nathaniel and Carter, I was surprised that I didn't wake them." Thorns, what a nightmare." I quietly muttered to myself while trying to calm down after such a frightful experience. Nightmares were nothing new to me, but this particular nightmare felt less like a tainted dream and more like a premonition I didn't fully understand. Glancing out of the window near my bedside I could see water droplets splatter against it, a clear sign of a brewing storm. I didn't want to return to bed out of fear that such a frightful nightmare would plague my mind again and instead I planned to get a cup of water to drink in hopes of calming my nerves. Silently I collected my spectacles, left our room and began to make my way towards the kitchen. As I walked through the hallway, I heard the sound of the weathered bark of the stump creaking as the storm raged on. I dismissed the disturbances and continued on my way to the kitchen but the further I went the sound of the wood creaking slowly began to become more audible and distressing. Our home had weathered through harsh storms in the past, but the bizarre sounds I was hearing made it seem as though our home was on the verge of collapsing in on itself! Rushing to the nearest window I peered through it to see just how bad the storm truly was and if I should rouse Mother from her slumber. It was at this moment that I realized that it wasn't the storm causing this disruption because as I peered through the window something else peered right back at me. The side eye of a massive creature lingering outside our home was the only thing I could see. A chill rolled down my spine at the sight of the beast as it's likeness was identical to one of the beasts plaguing my nightmares." I-Impossible..." Slowly I began to step away from the window while the beast eyed me hungrily before moving away. As it did the audible creaking began to grow even louder to the point that it felt as though our home was on the verge of breaking apart!" Wake up!" I finally cried out." WAKE UP! EVERYONE WAKE UP!" Hearing my cries and the disturbing noises around the house would finally cause my kin to rouse from their slumber and meet me in the hallway. Each one carried a look of confusion and concern which resulted in them urgently looking for answers.

"What's going on? What are those strange noises?" Nathaniel asked as he looked around the hallway and noticed that parts of our home were beginning to snap.

"I-It sounds like there's something out there and it's trying to get in!" Olivia cried out with a panicked look about her.

The twins would embrace each other and shook with fear as they were unsure of what to do.

"Quiet! All of you!" Mother says as she comes bursting out of her room before looking towards me." Tybalt, I heard you call out to us. What's going on? What did you see?" She asked and was expecting a quick and proper answer. Mother's presence brought some small amount of peace among my siblings as they all looked towards me for answers.

"I-I was going to get something to drink when I heard something outside." I explained." Then I saw s-some sort of massive creature peering at me with great glowing eyes. I-It's still here too! It's trying to break our home!"

As I finished explaining I could see the fear in Mother's eyes." It's sounds like some sort of monster." The last time a beast attacked our home was when Father gave his life to save us. Since then, we've known nothing but peace until now. Mother then adopts a look of complete focus and determination as she immediately takes control of the situation." Everyone! Move downstairs to the tunnel immediately! Hurry!" Without a moment's hesitation my siblings and I did as we were commanded and rushed towards the escape tunnels. Mother and Father always feared something like this would happen at some point and made sure to prepare accordingly. Should the need arise, we would use a secret tunnel dug out for the sole purpose of evading a prowling beast should our family ever be discovered, and it seemed like the time had come to put it to use. Unfortunately, as we moved through our once safe and secure home, we began to notice massive cracks in the wood due to the weight of the monster. Our ceiling began to crumble, decorations and keepsakes would be knocked to the ground as the creature was trying to force us out of our home! Splinters rained down from above us with even more deadly splints falling the more the monstrous fiend continued to apply pressure. When we reached the door leading to the tunnel Mother would follow behind us with a distressed look about her. She was carrying with her a twig bow with a quiver full of arrows along with the crest from earlier hanging around her neck." The blade is missing!" She shouted.

"Blade? What are you talking about?" Nathaniel blinked at Mother with a puzzled look.

"Your Father's sword! It's gone!" There was an urgent and distressed look in Mother's eyes." That weapon is our best chance of slaying that beast and I can't find it anywhere!"

"O-Oh no." I heard Olivia mutter from behind me. Glancing back at her I could see a dazed and disturbed expression on her face." What have

I done?" I wasn't sure what was wrong with Olivia until the events of earlier today came back to my memory. Olivia had taken Father's blade and left it out in the woods along with the rest of her training equipment. Then another possibility came to mind, could this monster have found our home because it found Olivia's things? My little sister had broken one of the most important rules that Mother had created should we ever venture too far from the clearing: always remember to cover our tracks. Olivia stood there paralyzed as her fear and guilt overwhelmed her.

"We don't have time to look for it!" Mother then said before moving to open the door to the tunnels and began to motion for the twins to move through first." Quickly, everyone insi—" but as Lucy approached the door a loud, crunching noise would be heard from above us as a piece of the ceiling fell from above! " LUCY!" Acting quickly Mother grabs Lucy and Carter, pulling them out of the way of the tunnel and pushing them towards us before the debris could land on them. While she managed to save her two youngest pups the fallen debris would land on her instead." AAUGH!" Mother cried out as dirt and wood began to pour on top of her! The collapse knocks us to our feet as the twins are practically thrown at us. As the dust begins to settle, we would see our mother on the ground struggling to free herself from the debris.

Nathaniel and I rushed to Mother's aid and to dig her out." Augh! Hurry boys! We need to get out of here!" She shouted while trying to assist us with the pile. There was no ignoring the urgency in Mother's voice. Like the rest of us she was frightened as well but knew better than to let it show and start an even greater panic amongst our troubled family. Our situation had escalated to one of pure chaos in a matter of moments as Mother squirmed helplessly while trapped under the wood and dirt. The twins sobbed loudly as they stood there feeling helpless and confused. Olivia was still paralyzed with fear as the reality of our current situation seemed too much for her to bear now only escalated by the sight of our mother suffering. Meanwhile the beast outside continues to destroy our home and seemed hellbent on bringing the entire stump down upon us.

"I... I have to make this right..." Olivia muttered to herself quietly at first." I have to make this right!" She shouted aloud and then suddenly rushed out of the front door!

"No! Olivia don't go!" I called out to her as I saw her leave the house and out into the storm where the creature was waiting for her!" What is she doing?!Has she lost her mind?!" Nathaniel shouted.

"Tybalt! Quickly go after her!" Mother commanded. Fearing for my younger sister's life I immediately gave chase after my sibling in hopes of stopping her from doing something foolish, but by the time I had left our crumbling home Olivia had already rushed into the forest leaving me standing out in the open. At this point the simple rainfall had turned into a fully-fledged thunderstorm. Once more I felt a terrible chill roll down my spine as I turned back towards the disheveled stump, I called home only to see the horrid nightmare plaguing me in its entirety. The creature had no arms, legs, wings or claws and instead of fur or feathers it had scales as black as night only to be made even more terrifying as the storm raged around us. Both of its eyes were illuminated with a sickening green glow and the horrid beast bared two massive, discolored fangs which dropped a foul acidic venom that burned our home. Despite its lack of limbs, the powerful beast was strong enough to wrap itself around the stump and break the wood with relative ease. The fanged monstrosity turned its gaze entirely towards me as I stood out in the open. I knew that I should've ran but the creatures intense predatory gaze terrified me to the point that I couldn't even think straight. Where I hesitated, the limbless monstrosity didn't. The beast uncoiled itself from around our home and was preparing to lunge at me!

"Tybalt!" Emerging from the house would be Mother, still armed with her bow though now sporting a worryingly bloody stump of a tail. I never learned what happened, but I believe she severed it out of desperation to free herself. She quickly takes aim and fires it into the monster's left eye with skillful precision! It let out a pained roar and began to violently thrash about in response. Hearing and seeing my determined Mother brought me back to my senses. Never had I seen Mother wield the bow before and yet with expert aim she managed to wound the beast!" Go and get your siblings! I'll distract it!" She shouted while preparing to take another shot at the creature. Even from a distance I could tell Mother was in great pain for what she had done to herself as the dripping red stump became increasingly worrying but for her family, she was willing to pay any price to protect us. I wasn't so eager to leave my one and only parent behind even if these were her orders.

"What?!No! That's suicide! W-We can't just leave you!"

"Don't argue with me Tybalt! Just go!" Mother shouted angrily at me.

Though every part of me wanted to stay and find some way to aid Mother I chose to be obedient and did as she commanded. I said nothing more to her and started sprinting back towards the house. With the beast still reeling from my mother's arrow I sought to take advantage of the situation and retrieve the twins and Nathaniel before immediately rushing into the forest in hopes of locating Olivia. Sadly, none of this came to be. Before I could even reach the door, the mad beast had managed to swat me with its tail during its aimless flailing! Never in my entire life had I been struck with such a powerful force that immediately overwhelmed my senses and soon caused me to fall unconscious with the last thing I saw was the creature regaining its senses and refocusing its fury on the one who harmed it. As my thoughts fell to darkness, I could have sworn I heard the screams of my kin. All the horrid things that I had endured that night, it all felt unreal to me. While languishing in my unconscious state I began to deceive myself and believed that everything that had happened was some sort of nightmare. No monster could've possibly found our home after years of isolation and the horrible things that occurred couldn't possibly be real. I was going to wake up in my nice warm bed, go to the kitchen and help Mother with breakfast before we all sat down and enjoyed each other's company. This is the lie I told myself, what I truly wanted to believe. Though as I regained consciousness, I would be brought to the crushing reality of my situation. My eyes slowly opened up to the sight of a gray clouded sky as rain droplets sprinkled the clearing. I awoke on top of a lily pad on the pond feeling disoriented and sore. My nose was bleeding and my body ached. Desperately, I looked for something to grab on to help me steer myself back towards my home. I managed to locate a large splinter of wood drifting by. After seizing it I would paddle back towards home before finally reaching land and stumbling towards the stump. "Mother? Nathaniel? Olivia? H-Hello? Where is—" As I reached the front door, I would be forced to face the truth. Stepping closer towards the house I could see my dropped spectacles lying just outside the door only now it was caked with dirt and rainwater. Everything that had transpired last night was no nightmare. Before me stood the remains of the Shortwhisker family home. Once the resilient remains of a felled oak tree had been reduced to a pile of broken splinters and the scattered remains of my family's belongings. The bow and quiver that Mother was using to fight the beast last night both laid on the muddied ground with its previous owner nowhere in sight. A sharp pang gripped my chest at the sight of my family's humble home destroyed and beyond repair. I dropped to my knees as I had lost the strength to stand, and tears began to swell in my eyes." This...This can't be real. It can't be..." I wanted all of this to be little more than a bad dream instead of the waking nightmare it had become." Mother? Nathaniel? Olivia? Carter? Lucy..." I desperately called out to my kin, hoping someone would hear me, but no response was given in return. My kin were nowhere in sight and the monster that was the cause of all our suffering had long since departed.

"Tybalt?" I heard someone say causing me to immediately turn to face the potential intruder. Though instead of a new threat it would be my younger sister Olivia who had miraculously survived! She had emerged from the ruined remains of our home with a wary and weary look about her. "Olivia!" I cried out while wiping the tears from my eyes and smiled at my sister. "Oh, thank goodness you're alive! I thought it devoured you first!"

Olivia looked at me with a drained and disheartened expression. It appeared that she had already shed her own fair share of tears after this tragedy." It....destroyed everything." She muttered.

"Olivia, where did you go? You ran out of the house, and I tried to stop you but the monster—" Just thinking about the frightful beast filled me with emotional anguish. Wanting to keep my mind focused on the positives I returned my attention back on my sibling. "The sword." She answers while showing the blade to me. "I went back for it. I wanted to give it to Mother but she..." Olivia's voice cracked as she spoke of Mother. Given that her last interaction with her was a fight I could understand why she seemed so regretful. She fought back her tears, refusing to let herself cry.

"...what matters now is that you're all right." I would say.

"All right?" She repeated. "You think that I'm all right?!Tybalt, our family is gone, and our home is destroyed! I'm anything, but all right!!" Olivia snapped.

"T-That can't be true. You survived and perhaps the rest of our fa—"

"They are dead, Tybalt! All of them!"

Like a fool I continued to cling to hope, believing that somehow our family survived this savage attack." You...You don't know that for certain..."

"You idiot, I saw it happen! I saw that monster devour them one by one!" At this point Olivia couldn't hide her emotions any longer. Tears streamed down her face as she looked towards the decimated remains of our home. "That thing took everything away from us. We can't allow it to get away with this!" My sister's grip on the gilded hilt of Father's sword tightened." We have to track it down. Find out where it nests and lop that devil's head off!" Olivia declared as she made her intention of slaying the beast. I understood Olivia's desire to avenge our family, but her plan sounded reckless and would certainly end with our demise. "Olivia, you can't possibly think we can slay such a beast."

"We can and we will! Mother and Father faced monsters like this in their youth. Now it's our turn to do the same." Olivia gives me a look that was identical to our conversation the previous day as she returned the sword to its scabbard. "This is a sign, Tybalt. We are meant to do this. We must!" She hoped that I would see the situation through her eyes and join her. Like before I was almost tempted to agree with her mad quest for vengeance. After everything that we had suffered, slaying that monstrosity could give us some form of peace yet still my conscious would tell me otherwise. "No, it isn't! You aren't thinking clearly Olivia. How would you even slay such a beast?" I asked.

"With this." She then gestures towards the sword." Mother said that this weapon was our best chance of killing that monster. I once thought it was just an ordinary weapon, but perhaps there is more to it. I believe it's the key to ending that abomination so I'm going to learn everything I can about it before wielding it against that beast. "Olivia said with confidence despite not knowing if it really was capable of killing such a monster. "So then, are you with me?"

With a deep sigh and a stoic expression, I would give my sibling an answer. "No, Olivia. We should not do this. This plan of yours is flawed and is destined to get us both killed."

"Then help me come up with a better one! You've always been more thoughtful than I. We can do this together!" Olivia shouted as she hoped to inspire me to action." Please Tybalt. We can—"

"I said no!" I replied angrily. "We've already lost so much and you're willing to gamble our lives away on a hunch and a vague idea of what you're doing. Killing that monster won't bring our family back!"

Olivia fell silent, she lowered her gaze but failed to hide the disappointed look on her face.

"Listen, I miss our family too. I wish I could bring them all back but seeking revenge won't give us anything else but heartbreak. We need to find the nearest town and try to rebuild our lives there. Maybe we can try to learn more about where Mother came from. It won't be easy either way, but as long as we have each other we can get through this." We were all the family we had left, and I was the oldest sibling Olivia had now that Nathaniel was gone. I believed it was time to take charge for once. I knew Olivia wouldn't like what I had to say, but I had hope she would come to her senses and support my decision. Unfortunately, I had underestimated just how troubled and determined Olivia was as her next few words would forever remain an example of her defiance. "Do you know what your problem is, Tybalt? You're a coward!" She shouted with a spiteful look. "You've always been a coward! You never wanted to leave home and were always content with the same old cycle of monotony, but not anymore! Look around you Tybalt! We can't hide from the world anymore! It's found us! Still even after everything that's happened you want us to move on and let the deaths of our loved ones go unavenged?!Go ahead then! Find some other cozy little hole to hide in! You'll do it without me!" My younger sister's scathing words wounded me more than the monster had as my confidence and determination drained from my body the more, she spoke. "Y-You say all of this while preparing to throw your life away hunting down that creature!" I would say.

"I WILL succeed in slaying that monster, Tybalt! With or without you it will fall to my blade!" With that said Olivia would turn away from me. Her gaze now locked on the wilderness leading out of the clearing." Goodbye brother." She then began to walk away with her mind already fixated on the belief that she could best the beast. While Olivia was hopeful, I wasn't so eager to give up on stopping her from potentially dooming herself. " Olivia stop! We are not done here! Get back here this instant!"

Fighting through my heartache I began to pursue my sister and reached out to her. Then suddenly Olivia reaches for the hilt of Father's sword and draws it from its scabbard. She turns towards and points the blade straight at me! The weapon was only inches away from my neck and all it would take was one thorough sweep of the blade to end me. " Olivia, W-What are you doing?!"I staggered back and trembled at the sight of my last remaining sibling threatening me with our Father's sword. She glared at me with a look of pure loathing. "Stop! Please stop! We're family for goodness' sake!" I pleaded, never once believing that I would ever be in such an awful situation. For a time, Olivia remained silent and kept the blade close to my neck as if she were deciding whether to end my life or not. Finally, she would sheathe the blade but continued to look at me in disgust." I won't kill you, Tybalt. Not unless you try to stop me but if you get in my way, I swear I'll bring an end to your pitiful existence." With that said she once again began to walk away from both me and the remains of our home before disappearing into the forest.

"Please, sister! I beg you! Don't do this! D-Don't leave me here alone! Olivia? Olivia!" Desperately, I called out to her repeatedly, even after she had long since departed my cries would continue to fall on deaf ears. It was all gone. Everyone I ever loved and the home I thought to be safe from all harm was now lost to me. For the first time in my life, I was truly alone, and I dreaded every second of it.

4

THE VISION

Every aspect of my life had changed for me that night. In an instant all that I knew and loved was taken from me without a care. Mother, Carter, Lucy and Nathaniel had been devoured whole by the monstrous predator depriving me of having any chance of burying my deceased kin. Olivia had abandoned me and was now hellbent on hunting down the beast that had brought us nothing but strife. I had hoped that my belligerent sibling would come to her senses and return home but after three days passed, I knew she would not return.

She would either slay the creature or join our kin in death and even if she succeeded, I doubted I would ever see her again. Like a fool I dared to entertain the idea that I could rebuild our destroyed home by myself and as punishment I spent an entire day removing splinters from my paws. The once beautiful and lush clearing that had been my home since birth no longer felt safe for me. That monster had robbed it of its tranquility after it departed and left the area tainted. The latter days carried with them the chill of the Fall season and with no proper shelter I would likely freeze or starve to death.

I considered leaving but I had no idea where I was going with no map or direction to guide me. Out of desperation I would return to my hiding spot on the hill and use what little food, clothing and other supplies I could scavenge from the remains of my family's home. Desperately I tried to restore some sense of comfort that I had once had but to no avail. The irony of my situation wasn't lost on me at the time. For so long I craved to have my own personal space away from my kin and now that everyone was gone, I had all the space I could ever want or ask for.

The events that took place that terrible night continued to replay in my mind day after day as I thought about all I could've done differently that might've been able to save at least one of my fallen kin from this disaster.

My isolation slowly began to eat at my sanity as it felt as though I was hearing voices at times or seeing other mice that weren't there. Eventually my food supplies began to run short and my motivation to even continue trying to find some way to survive on my own diminished. Too late did I realize just how much I relied on my family and how much they meant to me. Without them I lost the desire to even continue living and for a time I considered accepting death's embrace if it only meant I could be reunited with my deceased kin once again. Without them I felt hollow, and my energy seemed to drain from me the more I thought about what had been so cruelly taken. All I wanted to do was curl up in my makeshift bed and die in my sleep. My story may have ended there if not for another frightful nightmare not unlike the one I had the night before my family was attacked. This one was just as vivid and unnerving as the first though instead of being trapped in a barren wasteland I found myself in a darkened cave filled with the regurgitated bones of various creatures with me laying on the very top of one of the larger piles. Long deceased mice, birds and even some large monsters could be seen strewn about the cavern floor. My mind could barely fathom what horrifying beast could possibly be capable of such carnage.

Such a sight would cause me to panic and scream aloud though no sound escaped my mouth. Before I could even think of escaping, I soon realized that I wasn't alone. Slithering up the pile behind me would be the very same limbless monstrosity that destroyed my home and my family. With no way to properly defend myself and with not enough time to flee from the beast all I could do was fall to my knees and beg for a quick and painless death as the predator approached me. To my surprise rather than being made into the creature's next meal and have my bones join the other unfortunate souls the beast simply phased right through me as though it were some sort of ghost...or perhaps I was. I then came to the realization that I was merely dreaming but I remained unnerved by the fact that my dream felt uncomfortably realistic. With the predator being unable to harm me I began to make my way down the pile to look for an exit. As I began to navigate through the gloomy cave something caught my eye. What I saw was an unusual green glow emanating from within the skull of a deceased monster.

Though cautious my curiosity would get the better of me and I slowly approached the skeletal remains in hopes of seeing what was inside. I didn't fully comprehend it at the time but what laid within this creature's skull seemed to be calling to me, but before I could fully see what the object was the sound of a terrifying crash shook the chamber! As much as I wanted to keep my distance from the predator, I wanted to see what was going on. Moving in the direction of the monster had gone I had hoped to find the beast had simply knocked something over amongst the bones but instead I found a far more gruesome sight. A group of armed mice and other warriors had come to slay the monster, many of which had already been slain. It was a terrifying sight to behold as they desperately struggled against their foe but were met with no sign of the monster weakening. Though I knew this was some sort of dream I dared not to approach the beast out of fear that somehow it would find a way to harm me. I didn't want to see the monster devour the brave but foolish attackers and planned to return my attention back towards the strange object I took notice of one of the fallen hunters who I immediately recognized. "N-No...it can't be..."I thought to myself. One of the hunters rose from the dirt, wounded and disoriented but still armed and willing to fight." Olivia?" The last remaining sibling I had left stood defiantly against the beast that destroyed her life. She was wounded by the looks of the blood around her abdomen and the bruises on her arms and face. If not through sheer determination she would've likely collapsed by now. I tried to call out, tried to get her attention in any way I could but still I could not speak nor be seen by the snake or the hunters and certainly not Olivia. With the remainder of the hunters either dead or fleeing the limbless monstrosity turned its gaze towards my sister, who boldly brandished her sword at the creature, daring it to come at her. Having slaughtered her allies, it was hardly afraid of my sister's threatening pose and swiftly lunged at her with tainted fangs bared!

"NO!"I sprung from my makeshift bed and tumbled to the cold dirt below me. Quickly I pulled myself to my feet and took a moment to catch my breath and put my mind at ease though after yet another frightful nightmare it was far more difficult to accomplish. "I-It was just like that previous night. Was it a dream? A nightmare? Or something more..." Immediately my mind returned to my first nightmare I had before and how much of a strange coincidence it was for me to dream of a savage horde of monsters only to awake to a terribly similar looking beast not long after waking. I now realized that what I had experienced couldn't have possibly been a meaningless fantasy but a possible vision of the future. How I was able to acquire the ability to do such things remained unknown to me, but the more I thought about what I had seen in my visions the more I began to worry. If what I saw was some potential future, it meant that my sister was rushing to her certain doom.

"No, I can't allow this to happen! I have to stop her!" This terrifying vision had ignited a fire within me. After days of isolation and hopelessness I finally found courage and a desire to save my vengeful sibling from certain death. This of course meant that I would have to leave the only home I'd ever known and venture into an unknown wilderness by myself. I had no idea who or what I would encounter once I departed but if it meant saving my sister then I was willing to risk it. Still, I hadn't forgotten Olivia's declaration that she would kill me if I attempted to stop her. The thought of being cut down by my own flesh and blood troubled me, but I couldn't allow my fear to inflict me with paralysis yet again. Saving my sister regardless of the dangers I would encounter was all that mattered to me at this point. Quickly I gathered what little supplies I could which consisted of what remained of my food, fresh water, my favorite books and some light garments for the cold. Lastly, I decided to bring Mother's bow and quiver with me as well though I had no idea how to wield it properly it would've been foolish of me to go out into the wilderness unarmed." Okay then. Here I go." Once I finished equipping myself with whatever might be useful for my journey, I finally began to make my way to the clearing's exit. Right as I was about to leave, I looked back at my home one last time. Memories of happier times came to mind and nearly brought me to tears. If not for my newfound resolve, I would've fallen to pieces once again. With my family dead and our home demolished I saw little reason to ever return to the peaceful place of my birth. I slowly turned my gaze towards the wilderness ahead of me and finally began to walk westward." Goodbye." I quietly muttered before moving through the brush to truly begin my quest." All right Olivia. I'm coming to get you whether you like it or not."

The first steps are always the hardest and the daunting task ahead of me would be no different. It was difficult enough for me to leave my home behind and as I took step after step farther away from it the more, I began to realize that I could never truly return home. With time I would find my footing and focus my mind on the main goal of my journey to keep me centered. For a time, the first stretch of my journey was quite peaceful while giving me the opportunity to witness beautiful vistas that I had never seen before. Having lived my entire life in a lush clearing had given me an appreciation for nature's beauty which often left me distracted by my surroundings. During my trek I would see towering trees, peaceful meadows and scenic streams. I would also encounter large and strange beasts with hooves and antlers that appeared to have no taste for meat akin to monsters.

Despite my attempts to communicate with these creatures I would often go unseen by them or would be given an inquisitive look before they walked away. Over time my anxiety shifted to boundless curiosity as to what would await me the more, I saw of the world that I had been hiding from. Still my goals hadn't changed, I would continue to seek out my sibling and stop her mad quest to slay the murderous beast. Sadly, for the next two days I would find little success in locating Olivia or tracking where she might have gone. By the end of the second day my progress would be impeded by a broken bridge much to my dismay." This is going to be harder than I thought." I said with a groan before beginning to make camp for the night. My food supply was running dangerously low, and I wasn't sure what was and what wasn't safe for consumption. Already I was beginning to have doubts and desires to return home, but having traveled so far, I wasn't sure if it was worth it. This was a decision I had planned to make in the morning only for my night to take an unexpected turn.

My presence had not gone unnoticed in the area. By the time I had fallen asleep the crescent moon had risen high into the sky. I was comfortable with the hiding spot I had chosen which was within an opening underneath a large tree near the bridge though I still longed to be in the company of my fallen kin. I hadn't encountered any monsters during my travels apart from seeing the occasional hawk hovering above so admittedly I had grown lax with my guard. As I slumbered, I failed to notice the intrusion of two strangers entering my temporary home. If not for one of the intruders clumsily kicking a stone with their foot I may not have heard them at all.

"Hrm..mrgh...what?" Still weary from my travels, my mind wasn't fully focused as I saw two large and odd looking mice approach me."Hmh? Who are—"

Before I could even finish my question one of them drew their weapon and promptly struck my head with it, rendering me unconscious!

"Rot take these cursed spies.."

"Lord Dalton will want to see this one."

5

THE ROGUE

Once again, my life had taken an unsuspected turn as instead of enjoying a well-deserved rest after a long day of traveling, I now found myself captured and dragged off into the night by two strangers. For a time, I believed that the only true threat I would face during my travels would be monsters but after that night it became clear that the Hallowed Forest harbored dangers that went beyond large insatiable beasts.

"Wake up, Scum!"

"GAAH!"I would gasp while being jolted awake by a freezing chill as my captors dumped a bucket of mop water on top of me. In a panic I tried my best to move away from the chilling water only to realize that my paws had been bound. I winced in pain as I felt as though my skull was about to split open with a terrible headache. No longer was I in the comfort of my makeshift camp. I had instead been brought into what appeared to be a resilient stone fortress. The room I was being held within was some sort of chancery.

"Quit you're strugglin' mouse unless you want me to bash ya again!" One of my captors threatened while waiving his club about. The creature bared the traits of a mouse but was far larger and was quite intimidating. He and his comrades were equipped as though they were planning to go to battle at a moment's notice. The one that appeared to be in charge judging by his more extravagant military outfit, was a smaller, scrawny but aggressive looking fellow who was missing half of his fur. He sat at a desk in the center of the room looked up from his papers as we entered. He turned his fierce red eyes towards me. ``What's this? You lot actually managed to catch one without getting yourselves killed this time? Hmph. Bring him here. I want to get a good look at our little "guest". "The guards would move me closer towards their leader as they spoke." We caught this one near the perimeter, milord. Must've thought we wouldn't find him in his little hiding spot. " One of the guards would say.

"Yet another foolish spy attempts to sneak around my beloved garrison. Did you really think you could skitter about without our knowledge?" Their leader rose from his seat and slowly walked around the desk to reach me.

"A-A spy? Sir I swear I have no idea what you are talking about! I had no idea this place even existed!" I finally spoke up while being accused of a crime I hadn't committed. "Perhaps your pitiful lies would fool a lesser rat, but not me. "He lowers himself down to one knee to match my height and leers at me." Do you know who I am, little spy? I am Lord Dalton of the rat kingdom of Vroth and humble servant of the Twin Queens. I do not tolerate worthless mouselings sticking their dirty little snouts in our business." This would be the first time I had ever heard of a "rat" let alone a rat kingdom with not one but two queens. It went without saying that they were making a strong first impression. Despite my puzzled expression Lord Dalton remained unconvinced of my innocence." You can feign ignorance all you want, but I know what you're truly after." He said with a snarl, revealing his crooked teeth. Hoping to convince him otherwise I would say," Lord Dalton, I swear to you that my presence near this place was by mere coincidence and nothing more. I am but a traveler seeking shelter for the night. I meant no harm to you or your soldiers! Honest!"

Dalton scoffed at me. "Honest?" He looks up at his companions and smirks at them. "Do you hear that, lads? He swears he is being honest! Hahaha!" They all burst into laughter at my expense, leaving me feeling quite embarrassed for even attempting to speak up. "Oh dear, the poor fool's all red in the face now." I lowered my gaze as I tried my best to hide my face from the rats. "Please, I'm telling you the truth. I am no spy! You have to believe me!" Suddenly Dalton's mood changes, his laughter ends, and a stern look could be seen on his face. He grabs me by the chin and lifts up my head so that he could force me to make eye contact. "How dare you speak to me like that?!Do you think that you are my superior? That I could simply let you go because you claim innocence?!It matters little where you came from. When you step foot in my territory that means that you abide by my rules!" Dalton then eyes me for a moment while thankfully calming down. "Still, perhaps there is some merit to your words. As far as spies are concerned you are probably one of the most incompetent infiltrator I've ever seen." He then looks to his subordinates. "What did you find amongst his belongings? Any intel?"

One of the guards shook his head before speaking up. "No, milord. Just some ordinary books, clothes, little bit of food and a shoddy mouse bow. No other weapons, poisons or journals, not even a map."

"No map?" Dalton gives me a quizzical look." Were you just wandering about the forest, boy? Do you even know where you were going?"

"W-Well I uhm..."I was a bit embarrassed to admit that I really had no plan apart from some light provisions I could scavenge.

Dalton falls silent and releases my chin. He leans back against his desk as he decides on what to do with me before finally giving up. "I grow weary of this. It's getting late and I need my rest." He stifles a yawn while covering his mouth. "I shall decide your fate tomorrow, little mouse." He looks towards his subordinates again, signaling them to remove me from his office. "If you are a spy, I will make sure you are thoroughly flogged, your limbs removed and every bit of fur on your body is torn from your person until we get every shred of information out of you before the day is done. Then I will have you executed, and your remains will be added to tomorrow night's meal." That Dalton would speak in such a calm and unnerving tone was upsetting. That someone could subject another living being to such torment without batting an eye terrified me.

"A-And if I'm not a spy?" I asked, hoping for some silver lining in this situation.

Dalton merely shrugged. "Well, then I suppose I could use a new slave mouse."

"W-What?!"

"You were expecting us to simply let you go? Such naivety." He gave me an amused look and leans in close towards me." I'm afraid you've seen far too much my little friend and I can't allow you to leave and potentially tell our enemies of our location." Dalton then looked towards his guards. "Throw him in with the other one!" he ordered.

With a salute, the rat guards grabbed me and escorted me out of the chancery.

"Rest well, little one. You have a busy day tomorrow," Dalton said as he watched me being dragged out of the room.

Once again, the fear of death gripped my heart as I was escorted through the torch lit halls of the garrison. My travels had scarcely begun and already it felt as though I had set myself up for a terrible end. Whether I would be tortured and put to death for information I didn't have or spend the rest of my days doing the bidding of another; it now seemed impossible for me to ever find my sister again.

The stone garrison was cold and unwelcoming with its rat warrior occupants being even less than that. They eyed me with disgust while I was being taken to the dungeon and seemed to be hoping for an excuse to cut me down.

As my captors pushed me further towards my cell, I couldn't help but question if I should've remained in the clearing rather than risk a foolish venture into the unknown. We would finally arrive in the darkest depths of the garrison which served as its dungeon. "Get in there!" One of the guards would say while shoving me inside as the other opened the cell door.

"Oof!" I was sent tumbling to the cell's stone flooring and soon heard the door shut behind me while the guard's locked me in.

"See you tomorrow, runt. Can't wait to see what Lord Dalton does with you." The pair of thugs cackled at my misfortune while moving to the exit.

As the guards departed, I could feel the hope and drive that I had built up within me to force myself onto this journey rapidly dissipate. I had no way to escape the darkened cell and even if I had, I doubted I would be able to best even one of the guards in combat should I be caught.

Tears began to form in my eyes. "I suppose this is the end of me..." I softly muttered. "...sorry, Mother...sorry, Olivia..."

I turned back towards my cell to get a better look at my surroundings though with hardly any light it was difficult to see. What I could make out were two piles of grass and old linen that were likely to serve as bedding along with a dampened floor stone floor without a single window. There was absolutely nothing that I could see that would help me escape from this rat-infested nightmare which further drained me of all my hope of escaping my fate.

My cellmate had already claimed one of the beds so I went to my own and tried to dry myself off before attempting to get what little rest I could as that would have likely been my last night alive. It was only by sheer luck that that accursed dungeon wouldn't be the end of me. Not long after I fell asleep would I be stirred awake by a curious noise.

"Mngh...huh?" My vision was blurred and unfocused so one can imagine my shock at the sight of a strange shadowy creature picking at the lock of our cell door.

Upon hearing me the figure turns towards me and places a finger to her lips. "Shh!"

It took me a few moments more to realize what exactly was going on. The moving shadow was actually my cellmate who appeared to be a young mouse wearing a gray mask. She mirrored me in age but had fur as black as the night and eyes that were a striking shade of blue. She said nothing more before turning her attention back to the lock.

In her paws was a small thin piece of metal that she was using to silently undo the only thing keeping us from leaving the cell. Quickly I sprung to my feet as it fully dawned on me that this strange looking mouse could potentially help me escape. The blue-eyed mouse slowly opened the cell door once she finished with the lock and carefully peered out of the cell before glancing back at me.

At the time I wasn't sure if she intended for me to follow her but as soon as she felt that it was safe to do so, she began to make her way towards the staircase leading out of the dungeon.

"W-Wait!" Not wanting to be left alone I tried to hurry after her only to be stopped by the abrupt sound of snoring at the end of the dungeon's hallway.

A large slumbering rat guard resting in a chair with arms crossed and eyes closed remained ignorant of our escape and in it was in my best interests that he remain like that. Silently I crept out of the cell and followed after my cellmate in hopes of formulating some sort of plan with her.

By the time I had reached the top of the staircase the unusual black mouse was already halfway down the unguarded hall. The nimble stranger had stopped to peer over the corner of the hallway as she had done before. Fearing that I would be left behind I thoughtlessly rushed towards her.

"Wait there! Hold on!" I called out to her in hopes of getting her attention before she moved again. She looked at me with an aggravated expression and once I came close enough she roughly grabbed me and pinned me against the wall! I was startled by her aggression and was confused by her actions.

"Ow! Why are yo—"

"Shhh!" She then turned her gaze to the hallway. It appeared calm and vacant until I heard the familiar sound of metallic armor clattering with each step drawing closer and closer towards us.

"Is it just me or was tonight's meal a little bland?" I would hear one of the patrolling guards ask his friend.

"Can you blame the cook? Food stocks are running low, and he don't have much to work with." The other would say with a shrug.

"Hmph, you hear they caught two mouse spies today? Bet they'd make a nice stew."

"Mmmm...been awhile since I've had a good mouse stew."

The two continued their conversation while moving further down the hall and remained completely unaware that me and my cell mate were hiding in the shadows near them. Still it left me feeling quite uneasy just how casually they spoke about eating another person. Once it felt safe enough for us to rest my cellmate released me.

"That was too close. We were almost caught." I would say in a more hushed tone.

"Yes, because of you!" She replied with a glare.

Admittedly, looking back at how I had been behaving I did come off as a bit of a bumbler much to my embarrassment. "I'm sorry I didn't mean to—"

"Hush fool." She peers around the corner once more before speaking again. "Listen well, but only listen. I don't know who you are, and I really don't care, but your very presence is a liability to me and abandoning you will only raise the alarm and get us both killed. If you have any desire to make it out of here alive you will follow every command, I give you. Understood?"

I was in no position to argue, and this mouse seemed far more competent and oddly accustomed to this situation than I was. "Y-Yes of course."

"Good, now before we leave, we need to get to Dalton's office. He has my things. "The black mouse would say which immediately caused me to question her." That sounds rather risky, don't you think?"

"It is, but I'm not leaving here without my belongings." Through her tone it was made clear to me that my opinion didn't seem to matter in this situation. Separation was out of the question as I had no faith that I'd be able to escape that prison on my own. "We don't have time to argue. If we're not out of here before the sun rises, we're dead." With that said she took one more glance around the corner before preparing to make her move again.

"W-Wait one last thing..." I would say before she raced off to the next shadow. She turned to me once more and rolled her eyes. "What is it now?"

I averted my gaze from her eyes and sheepishly rubbed the back of my neck. "T-Tybalt.."

"What?"

"My name is Tybalt. Tybalt Shortwhisker."

The peculiar mouse curled a brow at me as I abruptly and clumsily revealed my name to her. There was a silence between us and for a moment I was beginning to regret even attempting to speak with my unusual savior." ...Blue Eyes."

"Blue Eyes?" I repeated with a confused expression until I realized that she had responded to me with her own strange name. She looked at me sternly as if to tell not to question it any further before beckoning me to follow her. The farther away I was from that cell the better. From shadow to shadow, Blue Eyes and I would navigate our way through the garrison. Initially, it appeared as though the rat guards were a fierce and ever vigilant fighting force who could've caught us with relative ease. Though in truth many of them were quite lazy and often shirked their duties as the guards we slipped pass were usually drunk, asleep or far too busy trying to amuse themselves to notice their only two prisoners escaping. I also couldn't deny how impressed I was with Blue Eyes' agility and felt quite embarrassed that I struggled to keep up with her at times which nearly got us both caught. Even still my heart raced endlessly as the fear of being found out continued to torment me. Thankfully, we arrived at Lord Dalton's office without being seen by our captors. I reached for the handle and attempted to open it with little success.

"Locked tight of course. Give me a moment." Blue-Eyes then retrieved her makeshift tool that she previously had on our cell door. "Keep an eye out for patrols." With a nod I remained vigilant as Blue-Eyes went to work on the lock. Despite being under the constant threat of death I couldn't deny that there was something thrilling about this experience though I knew better than to let my excitement get the better of me. Thankfully I wouldn't have to wait long for Blue-Eyes to unlock the door. "It's done." She says while opening the office door. "Quickly now! Before someone sees us." The black mouse's timing was impeccable as we both heard the casual whistling of another patrolling guard drawing near. Without hesitation I moved into the room and allowed Blue-Eyes to carefully close the door without alerting the passing guard. Thankfully, our presence continued to go unnoticed as the patroller continued his walk. Once we could no longer hear the guard's whistling, we broke our silence and focused on finding Blue-Eyes' belongings. Due to the brutish nature of my arrival, I wasn't really able to get a good look at Dalton's room until that moment. Though all it would take would be a quick glance to see that Dalton was quite full of himself as two large portraits of the lord depicting him in heroic poses could be seen along with decorative weaponry and awards. The room was lavished in needless decadence that could've been used to benefit his soldiers in some way. "Where should we start looking?" I would ask while glancing about the room.

Blue-Eyes gives me a stern look. "Not "we". Me." She looks at the door. " Just stand there and keep your ear out for any trouble. Don't. Touch. Anything." With that said she begins to rifle through Dalton's drawers in search of her own belongings. Though I couldn't deny that I was a tad curious as to what this haughty Rat Lord had hidden in this room, I wanted to respect Blue-Eyes' wishes and allowed her to work without my presence...or at least that was my intention until a familiar sight caught my eye that I couldn't afford to let slip from my paws again.

Stashed away with reckless care would be some of my belongings including Mother's bow and quiver! With my companion distracted I quietly moved towards it and retrieved it from the container that it was holding it." Thank goodness! It's undamaged. "I thought to myself as I gripped the weapon though right when I was about to return to my previous position to avoid attracting the ire of Blue-Eyes a familiar green glint grabbed my attention." It... It can't be..." I muttered while carefully setting my bow aside as I peered back into the wooden container that was holding my weapon.

The only time I had ever seen such a glint was from the nightmare of the cave though I never got the opportunity to see what it truly was I could never forget such a powerful impulse to seize it for myself. It was as if it were calling to me. Only now in the physical world could I finally take hold of it as I retrieved it from the dark confines of the container and held it out in the moonlight illuminating the darkened room. It was a green gemstone with strange runes engraved into it that shimmered in response to my touch. As I held it in my paws it felt as though I was holding the very concept of life itself. The sensation was like nothing I had ever experienced before." Impossible..." I muttered. "This was from my dream, but how could this be real?" Before I could ponder anymore about the stone I was brought back to reality as a sharpened knife was once again inches away from my neck." Drop it." Blue-Eyes had apparently found her things which included a sharpened short sword. She looked at me with a fierce glare. "I won't ask you again, Tybalt. Drop the stone right now. "I would've dropped it sooner but the fear of being cut down paralyzed me once more. Quickly I would do as she asked and dropped it on the ground.

"I told you not to touch anything!" She said with a snarl.

"I'm sorry!" I hastily replied. "I saw my bow a-and I had to get it. I couldn't just leave it here with these thieves!"

Blue-Eyes moved to pick up the stone. "If you know what's good for you, you'll forget you saw this pretty little rock and obey my instructions from now on. "She said before sheathing her blade.

"Y-Yes of course..." I said, showing her that I had no intention of earning her ire. After calming herself down Blue-Eyes looked towards the door." Right, let's get out of here. We've wasted enough time." But right as the black mouse had carefully open the door, she quickly shut it! "Barricade the door!" She says with great urgency in her voice which startled me especially after being held at knife point by the strange mouse. "Is something wrong? What's going on?" I asked. Blue-Eyes locks the door. "Stop talking and do what I tell you!" Blue-Eyes says as she pushes past me and begins to shift Dalton's desk towards the door to block it off!

Then I heard it. Two knocks at the door.

"What's going on in there? Lord Dalton? Is that you? Is something wrong?"

Two more knocks would be heard, and I could hear someone attempt to open the door. "Lord Dalton? Who's in there?!Open this door!"

It was then I understood, we had finally been caught and now were trapped in Dalton's office!" Thorns, why now?" Wasting no more time I began to help Blue-Eyes barricade the door with anything and everything we could get our paws on in the room." What do we do now?!How do we get out of this?!"I asked Blue-Eyes though for the moment I received no response. She appeared deep in thought which seemed like something impossible to accomplish in such a stressful moment. It wasn't long after that the alarms were raised and everyone in the garrison knew what was going on, including Lord Dalton. "Get that door open! I don't care what it takes! Do not let those wretched mice escape!" Unsurprisingly, he was quite furious. I looked around the room hoping to find something, anything that could help us escape. Of course, there was the window, but the fall would've likely killed us and apart from that there was no way out. It seemed it would be the end of us.

"The bow!" She then rushes towards my bow and quiver.

"What? My bow? What about it?" I asked her.

Blue-Eyes didn't respond to me as her mind seemed to be focused on piecing together some unseen puzzle. She took two arrows from the quiver and then goes through her satchel to retrieve some carefully folded leaf fiber rope. She proceeded to wrap it around the end of the arrow.

"Only getting one shot at this..." Blue-Eyes opened the window, grabbed my bow and took aim at a large tree branch outside of the office. She fired the arrow, sending it flying out of the window, and it impacted squarely on the dead center of the branch's bark.

"I'll have the lot of you flogged for this blunder! Get that door open this instant!" I could hear Lord Dalton shout angrily. The guards began to break down the door using their weapons and while the barricade was holding them at bay it wouldn't be long before they broke through.

"Hurry! Grab on to it!" Blue-Eyes said as she gripped the leaf fiber. I wasn't sure what she was planning, did she intend for us to recklessly jump out of the window?!Still there wasn't much time to question her planning as already the guards were beginning to break through the barricade.

"Ready?" she asked.

"Not really," I answered while looking more than a little uncertain of this plan.

"One, two—"

Suddenly the door burst open, sending the pieces of furniture we used to barricade the door flying everywhere! Lord Dalton and his soldiers rushed inside! "KILL THEM!"

"—THREE!" Blue-Eyes then forces us out the window while clinging to dear life to the leaf fiber! We swung through the crisp night air at first until the fibers began to split apart due to the excess weight of both me and Blue-Eyes! We screamed as we fell into the brush below before landing in a bush! It was still dark out and we could hear the alarms coming from the rat's garrison. "B-Blue Eyes? Blue-Eyes! Where are you?" Between the bush's foliage and the now darkened night sky I could hardly see a thing, let alone my companion.

"Tybalt? I can't see you!" I heard Blue-Eyes call out. "Just run Tybalt! Run as fast as you can! I can hear them coming!"

"But what about you?!"I called out in response, but received no reply. Blue-Eyes had already fled. Already I could hear the guards drawing closer towards me and without wasting another second, I began to flee in the northern direction. Following Blue-Eyes' orders I would do everything I could to move as far away from that horrible garrison as fast as possible even as the sound of the guards chasing me became less and less audible. While I was still worried about what had become of Blue-Eyes I knew that I had to keep running. Never again would I ever be held captive in that horrible place.

6

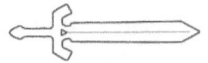

THE AMBUSH

M y journey had only just begun and already I found myself
meddled in affairs far larger than myself merely by accident. My
only intention was to find my missing sister and bring an end to her
obsessive quest for revenge, but instead I would be playing a far larger
role in the future of the forest itself. While fleeing from my captors I
couldn't help but wonder if Olivia was faring any better than I. In time I
would come to learn that her own journey had plenty of its own troubles.
Her first experiences beyond the borders of our fallen home were not
unlike my own.

She was mystified by the sights and sounds of the world around her
just as I was. For so long Olivia had sought her freedom and at last she
finally had it, but the bitter memories of losing loved ones despoiled her
enjoyment. Olivia was curious about her new surroundings but didn't
allow them to distract her from her quest. My sister was hellbent on
tracking the fiendish creature and looked high and low for any traces left
by it. Despite her fervor, Olivia possessed no skill with hunting beasts and
thus hadn't a single clue where it had gone.

She also had no true plan on how to properly slay the creature other than our mother's vague mentioning that our father's sword was the best weapon against it. How any sword no matter how finely crafted could kill such a creature was beyond her yet she clung to this as it was all she had to go by. Olivia was vastly unprepared in regard to supplies as well. In her haste to pursue the monster she left with barely any food or water and spent a majority of her initial days of her journey searching for what little resources she could. Apart from an old brown cloak, the sword and mother's crest Olivia had little else of value.

It had only been three days since Olivia departed and by then she was starving and lost in the wilderness with no sense of where she was or more importantly where the beast had slithered off to. By noon of the third day Olivia had collapse to her knees now regretting her reckless decision to leave home so unprepared. "S-So hungry..."She muttered. "...but I can't give up. I have to keep going....I can't die here." Fueled by her hatred for the black scaled monster, Olivia rose to her feet and prepared to continue her journey only to stop at the sound of rustling in a nearby bush behind her. She gasped and placed her paw on the hilt of her blade, readying it while glancing around her surroundings.

The noise was no trick of the wind, it was obvious to her that she was no longer alone. Who's there? Reveal yourself!" Olivia said aloud but received no response. The forest fell uncomfortably silent around her. For three uneasy minutes she stood still, unsure of what to do." I said show yourself!" Suddenly Olivia would finally get her response only in the form of an arrow being fired at her! Olivia gasps and in her attempt to evade it the arrow's pointed tip grazes and cuts open a wound on her right arm! "AGH!" My sister cries out in pain and falls back to her knees while clutching the fresh cut on her arm.

Just then, three armed rat guards emerge from the bushes in a nonchalant manner. "Take her alive. Lord Dalton will want to see this one." One of them ordered while two of his associates approached my wounded sibling. "Pfft! Don't know why. These worthless mice hardly know anything. We're better off killing them and sticking what's left in the stew. "One of them replies as he approaches Olivia in a casual manner. From my previous experience with these thugs, it was painfully clear that they tended to underestimate us and were not expecting my young, wounded sister to give them anymore trouble.

Unfortunately for them my belligerent sibling wasn't interested in going anywhere with the rat thugs and proceeded immediately to reach for a nearby rock and flung it at the head of the rat guard closest to her!

"OW! Augh! You little rotter!"

Enraged by his injury he reached for his weapon and prepared to strike Olivia! My sister instinctively reached for her sword and unsheathed it, much faster than the rat guard, then promptly thrust the blade into the rat's abdomen before he could even swing at her.

"NNGH!"

As my sister retrieved her blade the rat helplessly fell to the ground while clutching his stomach.

She was admittedly horrified by what she had just done, though Olivia practiced with the sword and fantasized about slaying dangerous beasts they were supposed to be just that. Fantasies. The sight of the wounded rat however felt quite real to her.

"Gotcha!" The other rat guard immediately took advantage of my wounded sister's brief moment of vulnerability by tackling her into the dirt and pinning her down!"Oofgh!"Father's blade is knocked from her paw as she falls! Their comrade being wounded by what they deemed to be an easy capture immediately puts them on high alert and finally began to move with urgency against Olivia! "Little daemon! You'll pay for what you did!" As my sister struggled to free herself from the rat her captor looked back at his comrades.

"See to his wounds! NOW! We're not losin' anyone to some runt! Now then, as for you—"

Though when the guard looked back at Olivia she immediately chomped down on his nose as hard as she could.

"AAUGGH!" The rat guard released Olivia and clutched his now bloodied nose in a panic. Though battered and bruised my sibling was filled with a surge of energy that would be essential to her survival in this harrowing situation. Desperately she scrambled for her weapon and used the pommel of the blade to bash on the rat guard's head.

"AAGH!" he cried while staggering back, too overwhelmed with pain to focus on the belligerent mouse!

Without wasting another moment Olivia ran through the brush as fast as she could in an attempt to escape her pursuers! Though the pain of her wound as well as the lack of food and water slowed her down, she fought through her suffering to escape her pursuers. Despite having wounded two of them Olivia could already hear the rats closing in behind her! They refused to let Olivia leave after all she had done to them and relentlessly chased her through the foliage. She dared not look back at them knowing well that the very sight of her vengeful attackers might cause her to falter. Eventually Olivia arrived at an opening through the forest foliage and towards a decaying bridge made of flimsy wood and leaf fiber ropes that was suspended over a river. Though the sight of it would make her hesitate about crossing she saw no other choice but to take her chances with the bridge. Throwing caution to the wind, Olivia began to make her cross only to be alarmed as yet another arrow flew past her head and impacted against the wooden plank close to her foot!

"There she is!"

Glancing over her shoulder Olivia could see two of the rats from before, one of them still carrying the bruises from her vicious bite and was more than ready to "repay" my sibling for the damage she inflicted on him. Not wanting to be caught again, Olivia attempted to rush across the bridge but only made it to the very center of it before an arrow sunk into her left shoulder.

"AAGH!" Olivia collapsed down to the rotted wooden planks beneath her and writhed in pain. Tears of agony streamed down her cheek as she struggled to muster the strength to rise and continue fleeing.

Already she could hear one of the guard's approaching her from behind and if he succeeded Olivia knew it would be the end of her.

Desperately attempting to escape, Olivia would make yet another reckless decision.

She mustered what little strength she had left and readied her sword, but not to fight back against her pursuers. Despite the fact that both of her arms were in incredible pain she would use the sword to cut through the fiber holding the bridge together! The bridge then began to collapse as it was unable to maintain its form without the ropes to hold them! Fearing that he would fall into the river the bruised guard from earlier scurried back towards his associate right before it all fell to pieces! The bridge was destroyed and what remained of it fell into the rapid water along with my wounded sibling.

Before my sister had even hit the water, she had lost consciousness. After all she had suffered through reaching this point only to be terrorized and forced to fight for her life, Olivia was exhausted. She lacked the strength to paddle or attempt to call for help and was easily swept away by the river. Truly, this should have been the end of her story. As she was wounded, starved and weary from her travels there was hardly any reason for her to survive this disaster. Thankfully the Will of the Woods seemed to have a greater purpose in mind and wouldn't allow death to claim her.

Instead of meeting her end in a cold lonely river, Olivia would awake within the confines of a small but cozy room where she had been placed in a bed to rest and recover.

"What? I...I'm alive?" As she came to her senses and looked around the room for a moment my sister dared to fool herself into believing that everything that had occurred the past few days was merely a bad dream, but in her attempt to move from her bed she'd be stopped by a sore pain in her right arm and left shoulder. Both her arms had been carefully wrapped and seemed to have been properly treated despite the pain she was in.

"Ack! Oh...that hurts! It wasn't a dream. Thorns, I almost died." This sudden realization disturbed my sibling and would serve as a reminder of how difficult this journey was going to be for her. "I need to be more careful, something like that can't happen again, but where am I and how did I get here?" Olivia glanced around the room and could easily see that she wasn't being held captive. While her room was hardly luxurious it was certainly no prison.

Right when she was about to try and move out of bed again the door to her room opened and an older mouse with graying brown fur, a gnarled right ear and long gray whiskers wearing a worn leather hat with a feather inside of it entered while carrying a tray with a bowl of soup and berry juice." Ah good you are awake!" he said with a pleasant smile. "You had me worried there, pup. I was afraid you wouldn't make it. "The stranger sets the bowl down on a dresser. "How do you feel?"

Olivia examined her shoulder and glanced at her arm, wincing slightly as she did." Mostly sore, but thankful to be alive." She then looks at him with a curious expression. "I assume you were the one who saved me? Thank you, sir. I would've surely died in those waters if not for you."

He smiled in response. "Think nothing of it, pup. I'm just glad you're all right. The last thing I expected to fish out of the water was a soggy mouse with an arrow sticking out of her! My name is Walter, by the way. Glad to be of service." Walter tips his hat and bows respectfully earning him an amused smirk from my sister." My name is Olivia, good sir." She replied.

"Tell me, Olivia. What sort of mess did you get wrapped up in to end up in such a sorry state if you don't mind me asking?" Walter asked and made no attempt to hide the concern in his voice. He sat down in an old rocking chair next to the bed. "Looks like you were mixed up in some sort of fight turned bloody!"

"Something like that..." Olivia frowned and laid back in the guest bed."...I've been hunting something, a terrible monster. It destroyed my home, killed my family and now I plan to seek it out and slay it." Walter could see the determination in my sister's eyes. Despite her injuries she wouldn't rest until her foe was dead at her feet. "Such a terrible fate and that it would fall upon one so young is a tragedy. I'm sorry for your loss, pup. No one should have to endure such horrors. Hang on though, how did you get stuck with an arrow then? I can't imagine some monster having the wits to wield weapons like that." He pondered.

My sister shook her head." No, this was something else. A trio of strange looking mice ambushed me. They were far larger and more aggressive looking than any mouse I had ever seen." She said as she tried to describe her attackers." They fired arrows at me and chased me to a bridge! I had to destroy it to save myself. I don't understand, I had done nothing to them and yet they sought to capture me."

Walter grunted and rubbed his chin. "Hmm sounds to me like you had a very unlucky encounter with the ratkin of Vroth." Many of the terms Walter was mentioning were new to Olivia resulting in her giving the older mouse a confused look. "Ratkin? Vroth? I don't understand. I've never heard of any of this." Walter was surprised to hear this as though what he was saying was common knowledge. "Never heard of the Ratkin before? They're distant cousins to us mice, but much larger and at times more aggressive. I get the feeling that the ones you encountered come from Vroth. Never been to that dark city of theirs either but the tales and rumors I've heard are troubling to say the least."

"They...were talking about eating me. That entire ordeal was terrifying."

"From what I know of them Vrothan rats are born and raised to be savage fighters, the males are especially aggressive as they often need to fight for their place in their society. Definitely not the sort you want to start a fight with." Walter would say while leaning back in his chair." Still, not all rats are the same." Walter then frowned and says, "Usually the Vrothans that live in their undercity choose to stay down in their dark little home, but lately we've seen them around the forest, pestering travelers and claiming territory. Very unusual and quite worrying." Olivia wasn't sure how to take this new information. Rats? An underground city? Her goal was to hunt down the vile monster that wronged her and not to meddle in the affairs of others in the forest. "I'll have to be wary of them during my travels."

Walter blinked at the young mouse and looked at her as though she had gone mad. "Now hold on there for a moment. Olivia, I don't think you understand just how close you came to death. I had to summon a healer from the town nearby to save you! If not for her you wouldn't have survived the terrible encounter with those soldiers! One look at you and I can tell you know nothing of hunting beasts and shall surely die out of the wilderness without aid. I suggest you give up whatever this mad quest is and resettle elsewhere. "He advised and for a moment it seemed like his words were reaching my stubborn sibling. Thinking back to how she was faring before her unfortunate encounter with the rats, and she remembered that she was low on supplies while being completely lost in the woods. What chance did she really have to catch this creature on her own? Olivia, however, wouldn't let the obvious dangers of her hunt dissuade her. "With all due respect Walter, but this decision is mine to make. "She narrowed her gaze at the older mouse. "I have already told you that the beast I hunt has taken everything from me. My home is destroyed, my mother and siblings have been devoured and my sense of peace has been taken from me. I will not rest until that abomination is dead and that no other mouse has to suffer from it's vile predation ever again!" Walter clearly had good intentions for my little sister and had no desire to see her throw her life away chasing some monster, but her words seemed to have an effect on him. Though she seemed foolish her intentions were clear. He lets out a sigh and says," Stubborn one, aren't you?" Walter frowned and scratched the fur on the back of his head. "I can't stop you from doing what you're doing, but perhaps I can help you." Olivia quirked a brow at Walter. She was taken aback by how quickly Walter now sought to aid her. "You've done more than enough for me, sir. I'd surely be dead if not for you."

"True, but I think there's a little bit more I can do. There is an old friend of mine that recently came back into the area. I think you both share a common goal."

Olivia seemed intrigued by this notion. Other hunters? Likely more experienced than her.

Walter rose from his seat and walked over towards the bowl of soup he had prepared for Olivia. "Yes, a Slayer as they've been called. Brave or mad hunters of the selfsame sort of beasts you aim to defeat. The one I know of just so happens to be one of the best. I think I can get him to help you, but it'll take some effort. For the moment I think it's best you focus on eating and recuperating. If you truly plan on going out to hunt this creature, then you should at least seek it out once you've regained your strength." Begrudgingly my sister would agree. Despite her bravado Olivia was in no condition to be traveling with her injuries. "I suppose that would be okay." With a pleased look about him Walter offered the soup bowl to Olivia. "Good, good. Now please eat. You need to build up your strength again. "For the next three days Olivia would permit herself to recuperate under the watchful gaze of her savior. She had grown fond of Walter and appreciated his kindness. However, Olivia feared that if she allowed herself to become too comfortable, she may never finish her hunt. By the morning of the fourth day, she was back on her feet and ready to continue her quest with Walter accompanying her to act as a guide.

"So where are you leading me exactly?" Olivia would ask as the two left the small but humble dirt burrow that served as Walter's home." Treefall, my dear. A place not too far from here. That's where we'll be meeting my friend."

"And you're sure this friend of yours can help me?" Olivia asked.

Walter nodded." Positive. The difficult part will be convincing him to help you, but that's why I'm coming with you. I also need to pick up a few things while in town so it's no trouble at all." Walter continued to prepare his things for their walk but not before offering Olivia a familiar weapon and crest." Does this look familiar to you? "Olivia's eyes widened at the sight of the sword being offered to her. "Those are mine!" She quickly took them. "I... I completely forgot! Thank you! These things mean the world to me." He smiled and nodded." The blade and scabbard were a bit murky from the river, but I did my best to clean it up for you. As for that old crest...well it already looked like it had seen better days."

Walter then looks down at the weapon." Strange to hear you claim the weapon belonged to you because I've seen it before and you weren't it's wielder." Olivia blinked at Walter and for a moment looked almost offended. "I assure you, Walter. This weapon belongs to me. I am no thief." Walter waves his paws dismissively. "Relax, my young friend. I wasn't accusing you of anything."

"Then why did you say it looked familiar?" My sibling asked with an arched brow.

"Because the last person I saw wielding it was a mouse named Lara Shortwhisker." He replied.

Olivia froze after hearing that name. "Lara...Shortwhisker?"

"Did you know her?" Walter would ask as he notices that the name seemed familiar to Olivia." She usually comes here from the east to get to Treefall. She often accompanied me on my trips there. I'm not as spry as I once was, and her aid was sorely needed. I haven't seen her in the past few days though and I am beginning to worry. She's never this late. "It had always been a mystery as to where Mother would go from time to time when she left the clearing until now. Olivia fell silent as memories of our slain Mother came to mind and brought her to the brink of tears. My sister turned away from Walter in an attempt to hide her emotions. "She is....was my Mother." Walter gave the young mouse a mournful look. "I'm sorry, Olivia. I didn't know." He moved towards to place a paw on her shoulder. "I see now why you seek to hunt this creature. Your Mother was a wonderful mouse with a kind heart and these woods will not be the same without her." Olivia held the sheathed sword in her arms as it was one of the last pieces of her family that she had left. "Olivia, I know the great pain you have been enduring. Like you I have lost my own family to feral beasts. My wife and children were the most important things in my life and when a vile hawk took them away from me, I spent many years of my life hunting it down, slaying many of its kind in the process. Very rarely would my hunts end in failure and more often than ended with my blade dripping from the blood of my slain prey. Though I saved many lives with my deeds I remained unsatisfied with my kills and desired only to slay the beast responsible for crossing me." Though Olivia remained quiet she would be listening to Walter's tale and wiped the tears from her eyes to glance over her shoulder at him as he spoke." Eventually, me and my companions would find the beast and slay it though it nearly cost me my life." He pulled away from Olivia and gave her a solemn expression." My hatred and lust for vengeance nearly destroyed me, Olivia and I fear you may suffer a similar fate. Please heed my warning and do not lose yourself to the hunt. "Finally, Olivia would break her silence." I will try, Walter. After everything you've done for me the least, I could do is heed your advice."

"That is all I ask of you." He replies. "Now come, daylight is burning, and we still have some time before we reach town. "With that said Walter and Olivia finally began to make their way to the town of Treefall. Olivia's talk with Walter had given my younger sibling much to ponder and even more questions to ask the former hunter along the way.

7

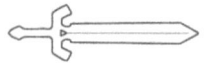

THE VETERAN

During their brief walk to the town of Treefall it would occur to Olivia that she had been quite lonely during her travels as she found herself deep in conversation with Walter. For as long as she was alive, she was always surrounded by kin whether it be Mother or her four other siblings. The past few days, however, had showed her just how much Olivia missed our presence. Thankfully Walter had served as excellent company to Olivia who was sorely in need of both companionship and information about the Hallowed Forest if she truly planned to slay the deadly monster she was hunting.

" I'm surprised that Lara never mentioned that she had children of her own. Your Mother and I were good friends, and one would think she would've brought you and your kin up at one point." Walter said while leading Olivia down the trail he regularly traveled through.

" Mother never mentioned you or anything for that matter that existed outside of the clearing. What little we did know was from the stories she would tell us of her own adventures, but even then, it felt she wasn't telling us everything." Olivia replied. "It doesn't make any sense. Why do all of this? Surely, she had to know she couldn't hide us forever."

Walter took a moment to rest and after brushing away some dirt on a nearby stone would sit on top of it." Perhaps she wanted to protect you?" He'd then say, prompting Olivia to give him a confused look.

"Protect us?" She repeated. " Protect us from what?"

Walter merely shrugged." Simply the wandering thoughts of an old mouse. Your parents clearly went to great lengths to hide and protect you all. You've been living in a part of the forest that has been abandoned by most folk around here who think that area is haunted. Don't know why but it seems like she wanted to hide you from something."

Olivia seemed unnerved by this notion. She remembered asking Mother a similar question the night of the attack but received no answer. Something that continued to bother her. Walter's reasoning was sound and the thought of Mother hiding us from some unknown danger did concern her.

After catching his breath Walter climbed off of the rock and began to walk again. "Never mind it, pup. I'm sure it's nothing." He let out a soft chuckle. "Anywho, we're getting closer to Treefall. Shouldn't be much longer till we see it."

"That's something I've been meaning to ask you, Walter. What exactly *is* Treefall?"

"Ha! If you were anyone else Olivia I'd think you were mad if you didn't know what Treefall was!" Walter grinned as he led the young mouse through the brush. "Come. Why don't you see for yourself?"

And as Olivia steps past Walter her eyes widened at the sight of a massive fallen oak tree filled with other travelers coming and going about their business. Not unlike our former home this fallen tree had been entirely carved from the inside out and served as a massive covering for a bustling town! Within the bark of the tree, Olivia watched with amazement as not one, nor two but hundreds of mice entering the town. She had never seen so many of her kind in one place! With Walter taking the lead, Olivia would be led deeper into the arboreal shelter." Treefall's a busy place, isn't it? For years this mighty oak has been serving as a place of safety for the people of the forest. Over time it became more than that as you can plainly see." Walter told her while gesturing to the busy town around them.

" I just don't understand how such a place could come to be! How was all this made possible?" Olivia asked, still grappling with the realization that such a place could exist. The old hunter shook his head and smiled," Never underestimate the miracles good folk can accomplish merely by working together, my friend. Now come along and stay close. It's easy to get lost in such a crowd."

The two would walk through a vibrant bazaar lined with stalls of merchants peddling various goods, many of which were foreign to Olivia. Though being under the log seemed rather dark at first the town remained illuminated thanks to a strange breed of glowing bugs that clung to the wall and emitted a luminous yellow glow. There were different races among the crowd including rats seen amongst them. Though rather than rudely assaulting mousefolk or talking down to them they treated mice as though they were equals just as Walter claimed. My sister was both intrigued but also overwhelmed by all the new sights, sounds and smells she was being bombarded with. Olivia grabbed Walter's paw. "I must admit all of this is quite uhm—"

"Overwhelming?" The older mouse gave Olivia an understanding look.

Olivia nodded. " Quite." Determined as she was to hunt down a monstrous fiend she wasn't accustomed to dealing with such a massive gathering of people.

The older mouse let out a chuckle." Fret not my friend. Adjusting to this sort of lifestyle wasn't easy for me either. It'll take some time to get accustomed, but you seem capable of adapting. Hurry now, we aren't too far from where we need to go."

"...and where would that be exactly?" Olivia asked curiously only to immediately get her answer as both she and Walter approached a peculiar looking tavern. Like many of the homes and establishments in treefall this one was skillfully carved from the very bark of the great oak tree itself with the name "The Oaken Retreat" hanging from a sign above it. As they approached the establishment the sound of music and boisterous laughter could be heard from within." Here we are, pup. My friend will be inside, but he doesn't know you just yet and he might not be too keen on what I'm about to propose to him without some convincing. It's best you let me do the talking for now." Walter would say though he could see the uncertainty in Olivia's expression. "It'll be all right. I'll be with you every step of the way."

Olivia wasn't in much of a position to argue as whoever this mysterious friend would be the only one capable of helping her hunt down the creature she sought." Okay, Walter. I trust you and I'll follow your lead."

The pair then entered the Oaken Retreat to locate the friend Walter was looking for. Much like the rest of Treefall the tavern was populated with travelers from all walks of life. Whether they be local workers retiring for the evening or wandering adventurers seeking a respite from the dangers of the forest, all would come to the Oaken Retreat to drink, be merry and tell the tallest tales they could. The tavern itself was a cozy place adorned with various cultural knick knacks and hunting trophies from slain beasts complete with a small fireplace for customers to warm themselves. With so many present Olivia wasn't sure where to start looking. " Look at this place! It's absolutely crowded! How are we supposed to find your friend?"

"Not to worry. Knowing him, he's in his usual spot." Walter chuckles. After maneuvering their way through the crowd, the pair would make their way to a secluded corner of the tavern where a single patron, a white furred rat, sat alone near a window. One look at the rat and Olivia could immediately tell he was the one they sought. He had the look of a seasoned warrior and wore armor fitting a barbarous mercenary. A jagged red scar marked his muzzle and the small white beard that grew under his chin was fastened with a small bronze band. The warrior's weapon of choice, an old but sturdy spiked mace hung near his waist and appeared ready to be drawn at a moment's notice should a foe dare to face him.

Two untouched tankards filled to the brim with ambersap sat on the table, one for himself and one for a friend. The white rat then takes notice of the pair after they pushed our way through the crowd to reach him. "So the coward finally shows his face!" He snarls while standing up from the table and slowly makes his way towards the older mouse. "You've got a lot of nerve keeping me waiting, you dusty little runt."

Startled by the hostility, Olivia was about to reach for the hilt of her blade when Walter stepped forward in front of the armed rat and gave him a vicious snarl of his own. "As if a chewed-up waste of space like you has anything better to do!" My sister was terribly confused. Was this really the friend that she had been told about? Another brutish rat thug? An uneasy silence fell between the two that seemed to spread throughout the tavern in anticipation of a fight.

This facade wouldn't last as both Walter and the rat warrior burst into laughter and embraced one another, not as rivals nor enemies but as brothers. "Walter! It's good to see you again, brother!" The white rat warrior would say with a boisterous smile.

"Gareth, my friend. It's been too long. I'm glad to see you haven't been turned into some sorry beast's meal without me watching your back." Walter told him. The two would make their way to the small table and began to chat amongst themselves. Olivia was still trying to process all of what she had witnessed. For a moment she expected to be embroiled in another fight with a rat but then suddenly everything is defused, and she is left in a dumbfounded state with her paw still on the hilt of her sword.

"Olivia?"

"H-Huh? What?"

Both Walter and Gareth gave the younger mouse a confused look. "Something the matter, pup? Come and join us!" Walter said.

"Right, of course." Feeling embarrassed by her behavior she'd quietly take a seat next to Walter. The two friends toasted to one another's health before drinking deeply from their tankard.

"Ahh! That hit the spot!" The rugged warrior said while wiping his muzzle with his right gauntlet. Decided to remember my manners and wait for you this time. You're welcome by the way." Gareth grinned at Walter. "I thank you for that, old friend. As always it's good to see you again."

"Likewise, but I get the feeling we're not here to reminisce on the old days."

"I'll admit. As much as I wanted to see you again there is a reason why I wanted you to be here."

Gareth took another swig from his drink before speaking again. "Wait! Don't tell me! You're rejoining the hunt, aren't you?!" The rat made no attempt to hide the enthusiasm in his voice.

"Wha? No Gareth I—"

"The Wingslasher, The Beak Breaker, The Slayer of Flying Devils! Finally, back on the hunt at last! Ha Ha!"

"Gareth—"

"It'll be just like the good ol' days, brother! You and me against the mangy beasties infested the for—"

"Gareth!" Walter shouted aloud as it was the only way to get his friend's attention. Gareth fell silent after hearing his voice and at first seemed confused until he took notice of the somber look on Walter's face. "I'm sorry, Gareth. I've told you this already. My hunting days are done, and that decision will not change."

Walter's words would deflate the old rat warrior's enthusiasm. He slouched in his seat and was visibly disappointed. "Right, of course. Apologies brother. For a minute there I really got my hopes up." Gareth lets out a defeated huff but respected the decision of his friend." So then, why did you message me? I'm guessing it's a matter of great importance."

"I would ask a favor of you. Something that only you can accomplish." Walter replied.

Gareth appeared inquisitive." A favor, eh?" Gareth seemed less than enthusiastic now but was willing to humor his former companion.

" Do you remember that beast you wrote to me about? The one with no limbs, scales as black as night and a sinister unnatural glow in its eyes?" Walter had peaked Gareth's attention. "What of it? You've seen it around these parts?"

Walter smiles softly and shakes his head." Not I, friend..." He then looks towards Olivia who had remained silent since she took her seat at the table."...but she has."

Gareth turned his sights towards Olivia and looked at her as though he hadn't even realized she was present that entire time. "Is that so?" His red eyes leave Olivia feeling slightly uncomfortable despite Gareth meaning no harm. "Tell me then, girl—"

"Olivia."

"What now?"

"My name isn't "girl", It is Olivia Shortwhisker, good sir." Olivia wanted to be respectful, but she also had no intention of being talked down to. "I know the beast you're seeking because it attacked both me and my family." Thankfully Gareth wasn't bothered by Olivia's blunt correction and if anything seemed more amused with her. "Well then, Ms. Shortwhisker if you wouldn't mind regaling me with your encounter with the beast." Olivia then looked towards Walter to get his approval. He merely smiled and nodded, knowing well that this was exactly what Olivia needed to further her goals. My sister then proceeded to tell her tale of what occurred that terrible night and her desperate journey for revenge against the horrid beast that brought her family to ruin.

"Quite the story, Ms. Shortwhisker." Gareth finally said after hearing Olivia speak. "Sadly, you aren't it's only victim. "The slayer folded his arms and wore a stern expression on his face." This beast you speak of is called a serpent, a vile reptilian creature with no limbs but like many of the feral monsters that infest this forest they are untouched by it's blessing and act only with instinct." Olivia had never heard of this type of creature and now knowing what it was would be a massive boon to her hunt. "Even still this beast couldn't have been ordinary." She replied.

"You're right. It isn't." Gareth then finished what remained of his drink before continuing to speak. "This serpent is like nothing we've seen before. It doesn't attack randomly but has been striking very specific towns and attacking very specific people and from what I've heard from other hunters it's far larger and stronger than the average snake. With scales as black as night and a tainted glow in it's eyes...or should I say eye..." Gareth smirks, remembering that our Mother had left the beast partially blind before her death." ...this is potentially one of the most dangerous monsters roaming these woods in a very long time. Some folks have begun to call it Blackfang and it has already drawn in many would be heroes seeking to claim it's life. Though few have returned from their hunts alive."

"...but how could such a creature exist?" Walter asked. " Occasionally a larger monster will show up around the forest, but from what you've said it seems to exude some sort of power. This is something else entirely."

"It doesn't matter." Gareth then said. " In the end I will slay this creature. I've already made up my mind." Despite the obvious danger, the veteran slayer seemed more than willing to accept the task. "Not without me!" Olivia then shouted. " I'm going with you! My fallen kin will be avenged, and I won't take no for an answer!!"

"Olivia!" Walter looked at the younger mouse as he wanted to stop her from saying something that might cause Gareth to reject her. "Pardon?" The flabbergasted rat would say before looking towards Walter. With a begrudging sigh Walter would speak again." This is what I wanted to ask you, brother. This young one wants to hunt this monster and to do so is to walk the bloody path of the slayer. Just as we did. Please take her under my wing as I can think of no greater warrior to shape her into the slayer she must become." Gareth did not seem fond of the idea despite Walter's pleas. "Walter, I already have a younger slayer in my pack, and I don't need another. Especially not one that is so inexperienced."

Walter was preparing to argue with his former friend and seemed adamant to continue to fight for Olivia only for the young mouse to speak for herself despite Walter's wishes to allow him to speak on her behalf. She stands up from her seat and gives Gareth a hard look before saying, "You will never kill that beast without me." Both Walter and Gareth turn their attention back towards Olivia. Gareth laughs, "Ha! Bold words, Ms. Shortwhisker. Yet you forget that you are speaking to one of the Hallowed Forest's greatest slayers! I have yet to encounter a beast I cannot kill and doubt that this serpent will be any different. What sort of tactic could you possibly have that I don't know of and can't employ against this beast?"

"Simple, I know the serpent's one true weakness." Olivia was bluffing of course, but she needed some way to convince Gareth to let her accompany him. She still held onto the belief that her family's sword was the secret to Blackfang's defeat with Mother's words still echoing in her mind, but Olivia had no proof of this. Nevertheless, she continued to lie to the elder hunter. "You claim that there isn't a beast alive you haven't bested but this is no ordinary beast, Gareth. I can help you kill it and we can share the glory together or you can try in vain and perish like the other failed hunters."

A silence fell over the table from Olivia's bold words only for Gareth to break it soon after. " Quite brash of you, little one. Very bold indeed. You speak with confidence in your words and if what you say is true, perhaps I might be willing to bring you along my hunt. "Rather than feel insulted, Gareth seemed more than amused by the fiery youth. "I'll give this matter some thought and then I will give you my answer." Too often many would think twice before speaking to him in such a manner and Gareth found it refreshing to meet someone with the courage to make such claims. Gareth gave Walter a friendly nod before rising from his seat and walking amongst the tavern crowd.

Walter looked content with how their conversation panned out," Well that didn't go as I planned but I think you won him over." He'd told her. " Good thing too. I was about to start twisting his arm." Walter laughed, but Olivia wasn't certain if he was joking or not. If what Gareth said about the friendly older mouse was true then he was not someone to be trifled with. While relieved that she was able to get into contact with Gareth an important question continued to pester Olivia to the point that she could no longer hold back her curiosity. "Why are you helping me?" My sibling suddenly asked. Walter blinked at Olivia and her odd question. "Why? Why not? It seems like the right thing to do an—"

"No, Walter, I mean.... Why are you helping me do any of this? Why aren't you trying to stop me?"

"Stop you? What are you talking about?"

Olivia felt somewhat frustrated by the older mouse's response." You realize I could perish on this quest, right? You're not even trying to convince me to quit anymore. Walter you're well aware of the danger I could face out there and that I could die if I am ever careless. Don't misunderstand me, I am thankful for all the help you've given me, but I just don't understand why you would go so far for a girl you hardly know."

Walter could see the look of confusion and anguish on Olivia's face. She wanted to hunt down Blackfang, but she knew the dangers could come at the cost of her life. Olivia was so accustomed to others telling her not to do something obviously reckless and dangerous that it felt jarring for her that someone far older and more experienced than her would knowingly allow her to put herself in danger. Walter listened to Olivia and could see the confusion within her and once she had finished, he would finally explain himself." Olivia, my young friend." He placed his paw on her shoulder in a reassuring fashion.".…I am not your father. "He would say. "I am in no way blood related to you. I have no authority over you whatsoever. While you are still a pup in my eyes, you are mature enough to comprehend the weight of your decisions. "He bluntly answered her. "You are right, I sorely wish that you wouldn't hunt down this horrible serpent. If you asked me I would happily help you resettle here in Treefall and start your life anew, but instead you choose to walk a dangerous path that I am all too familiar with."

Walter wore a frown on his face, but he continued to speak his mind. "You may speak boldly Olivia, but I sense fear in you, but fret not as it is nothing to be ashamed of. When I was a Slayer, I felt fear quite often but overcame many dangerous foes regardless of how I felt. In your youthful eyes I see myself and it spurs me to assist. It is why I am giving you my support. I want to see you succeed and return to me as a triumphant slayer. You have the ability to choose your own destiny, Olivia. I simply feel the need to assist you. "Walter's words seemed to touch Olivia. She suddenly embraced the older mouse." Thank you, Walter. I promise to return to you once this is over. "The old hunter wasn't expecting to be hugged by Olivia but returned the affection nonetheless." I know you will."

8

THE SAGE

As Olivia's hunt for the dreaded Blackfang continued, so did my desperate escape from my captors. Heeding the command of my absent savior I fled from the Vrothans and ran as far as my legs could possibly take me. Even long after I could no longer see my pursuers giving chase or their dreaded prison, I continued to flee knowing that if I were to ever be caught again it would guarantee my death. I could only imagine the enraged look on their leader's face as we escaped his clutches and used that fear to urge myself onward. For an entire day I scurried through the forest while ignoring my need for food, water or rest much to my own detriment.

What little provisions I had left had no doubt been taken from my pack and the only remaining thing in my possession was my mother's quiver. My limbs had grown sore while my paws and feet developed blisters and cuts from the brush and rough terrain I ran through. My reckless flight wouldn't last forever and by the afternoon of the next day I finally collapsed to the dirt and lost consciousness shortly afterwards as my sleep deprived body could carry me no further. As I fell into a deep slumber, I soon found myself once again in a vision I had yet to fully understand. Instead of a barren wasteland or a forlorn cave filled with the skeletal remains of the unfortunate I found myself within the streets of a bustling city.

No longer did I feel the burdens of my weary flesh which came as a great if not temporary relief. Rather than wood, the city itself was constructed with strong stone much like the rat's garrison and was populated by ordinary mousefolk merely going about their daily routines. The sight of such a place left me feeling overwhelmed and incredibly curious about my surroundings. It made our humble home seem remarkably insignificant in comparison to what other mice had constructed. Sadly I would be robbed of my opportunity to explore this city and learn more about its people as a familiar feeling of impending dread washed over me.

Suddenly the mousefolk around me began to scream and flee in terror, chaos ensued and engulfed the streets. I was confused as to why this was happening as all seemed normal at first until I saw the source of the abrupt chaos. The dark serpent that brought doom upon my family had come to repeat its crimes upon the poor unsuspecting citizens.

Many fled from the beast and while some guards attempted to fend off the creature, they would accomplish very little as the ravenous serpent devoured them whole with little ease. Their weapons and other defenses made specifically to harm such monstrosities were useless against such a foe. It thrashed about as though it had gone mad with rage, destroying the nearby buildings as if they were little more than playthings for an ill-tempered child.

I tried to warn the brave, but doomed guards but none heard nor saw me in this bizarre dream state. Truly, there was nothing I could do. Perhaps the worst part of these unusual visions that I was receiving was the overwhelming feeling of helplessness. Seeing such evil being wrought and being unable to do anything as innocent bystanders lost everything troubled my soul even if it was only a dream.

As Blackfang finished devouring another guard the devilish creature turned its limited gaze towards me as if it somehow was aware of my presence. Similar to my initial face to face encounter with this fiend I found myself paralyzed with fear and unable to run.

With a savage hiss the serpent lunges at me with fangs bared, completely prepared to swallow me whole like the others.

"AAAUGH!"

The shock from my nightmare would stir me to consciousness only for me to realize that I wasn't alone. A darkened figure was approaching me and I couldn't recognize who or what it was. Night had fallen over the forest and my vision was slightly blurred from my awakening, making it difficult to see who was present.

"W-Who's there? Blue Eyes?" Reaching for my fallen spectacles and placing them back on my face only to see that my "guest" wasn't my former cellmate.

"Found you!" A gravely masculine voice could be heard from the figure before he suddenly grabbed me by the neck, dragging me to the nearest tree and pinning me against it.

My worst fears had been realized as I now saw that my guest was a rat soldier from the jail, the same sleeping guard who was supposed to be keeping watch over me and Blue-Eyes! Despite having completely exhausted myself in my attempt to flee I had failed to evade my pursuers!

"MMFGH! Aagh! S-Someone! Please help me!" I called out while desperately struggling to free myself only to be punished for it with a swift punch to the gut. "Uunf!"

"Shut it, whelp!" he growled and snarled at me. "Nobody is coming to save your sorry tail! It's just you and me out here my little friend." His hold on me tightens as he speaks. "Did you really think you could get away? Do you have any idea the trouble you've caused me and my friends? Lord Dalton was livid after what you did! You made a fool of us mouseling and for that you're going to pay in blood!" He struck me across the face and seemed more than willing to further vent more of his frustration upon me. I felt a trickle of blood drip down from my nostrils.

"Mnnfh!"I continued to struggle but I lacked the energy to fight back against my captor. Even if I did I doubted I could defeat this fiend. "I never meant to cause trouble for you or your people. I-I just wanted t—"

"Stop lying!" The rat guard struck me again, once again aiming for my face.

"Nngh!"

"You and your cohort took something of great importance from my lord. Before I gut you and leave you for the birds you're going to tell me where you've hidden it!" At first I wasn't entirely sure what my attacker was talking about until I recalled the memory of my discovery of the peculiar glowing stone within Dalton's office. "Y-You're referring to that strange rock?"

"Starting to remember now? Good! Now tell me where you stashed it! By the decree of the Queens all Sagestones are property of the royal family and withholding any of them is punishable by imprisonment or death! Now where is it?!"The last time I had seen the stone it was right after Blue-Eyes had held me at knife point and took the stone from me. I had no idea what a Sagestone was at the time, but I recalled how both Blue-Eyes and the rat lord were behaving strangely because of it. All too late did I now realize that I very briefly held an object of great importance in my paws. Of course, I had no idea what had become of the stone or Blue-Eyes for that matter. For all I knew the roguish mouse had perished during our escape or given how elusive she could be was probably far away by now with the stone in her possession. "Why would I tell you anything? You're just going to kill me afterwards." I said to him with little defiance.

The guard gave me a wicked grin. " You're not wrong, but you also haven't considered the alternative." He explained. " Would you prefer that I end your pitiful life here and now or would you rather I drag you back to Lord Dalton and let him take his time tearing you apart piece by piece?" Obviously neither answer agreed with me, nor did I have an answer to give that would satisfy my pursuer. "Well mouseling? The choice is yours." I fell silent as I once again found myself trapped in yet another situation that I was powerless to save myself from.

"Well?!"The guard was growing impatient, but as he was preparing to strike me again he suddenly screamed aloud in agony while releasing me! "NNAGGH!" Still slightly dazed from the rat's thuggish blows I began to crawl away from the wounded warrior. It wasn't clear to me at first what had occurred until I noticed an arrow sticking out of the wounded rat's side! "Filthy rotters! Worthless mouselings!" The rat draws his sword and turns his gaze towards the nearest target for his aggression, that being me. I attempted to stand and force myself to flee, but my legs were still weak and sore! There was no escape for me this time! He lets out a berserker's roar and rushes towards me with his blade raised and ready to strike, but instead of cutting through my fur and flesh his sword would instead clash against another!

"What? "I had closed my eyes, expecting this to be the end for me only to open them as it was my attacker crying out in pain instead of me. To my surprise and relief my former cellmate had come for me right when I needed her most! "You're the other one that got out! You die along with this one!" The rat guard angrily shouted. Blue-Eyes glared at her opponent. "Come and try, cur! You aren't the first rat I've had to gut this day!" Then the two began their duel to which I immediately used what little strength I had to crawl away. I hid myself behind a nearby rock jutting from the ground to cower behind as Blue-Eyes and the rat guard fought!

Between being accosted by my pursuer and now the sound of clashing blades filling the calm night air I was uncertain of what to do next. Fearfully I peered over my sturdy hiding place to watch the two participate in a perilous duel to the death! Sparks flashed as their swords clashed against one another, briefly illuminating the fighters in the darkness. It was then that Blue-Eyes struck, slashing at her foe's paw causing him to cry out in pain while disarming him of his weapon! Despite his size and strength Blue-Eyes had proven that she was far more skilled with a sword.

Unfortunately, this only served to enrage her opponent who promptly struck her with the back of his unharmed paw! "Gnh!" Blue-Eyes was knocked to the dirt with her opponent tackling her to the ground and proceeded to violently grab her neck. " You filthy little wretch!" He shouted angrily, glaring at his struggling foe with unfathomable hatred. "If neither of you will tell me where that stone is then I'll at least have the satisfaction of ending your lives and showing your remains to Lord Dalton! "Much like I was, Blue-Eyes was in no position to escape and all she could do was weakly struggle and attempt to pry the enraged rat's paws from her neck.

The sight of my reluctant savior in peril stirred something within me. After failing to protect those I cared for from Blackfang I refused to sit by and watch it happen again to Blue-Eyes. For once in my meager existence an urge to act drove to me intervene. With no other weapon among my belongings, I retrieved an arrow from my quiver. Then I proceeded to muster what strength I had left to rush out of my hiding spot and towards the rat before stabbing the steel tipped arrow into his back as hard as I possibly could!

"Aargh!" the guard howled in pain, releasing Blue-Eyes while knocking me back as he tried to remove the arrow now lodged in his back.

The gasping mouse recovered soon afterwards once she caught her breath! Blue-Eyes takes advantage of the confusion to drive her blade deep into the rat's chainmail vest and pierces his stomach.

"GARRGH!" He staggered backwards while clutching his wounded stomach.

Unwilling to give the rat even a moment to fully realize what had happened to him, Blue-Eyes lunges forward and slashes her blade at the wounded rat's neck!

"Ghrk!"

Overwhelmed with pain and now unable to speak, the rat collapses to the ground in a bloodied heap. Blue-Eyes stood over the dying rat and stabbed her sword into his heart to end her foe once and for all.

Witnessing such a lethal flurry of actions had left me feeling disoriented yet overall relieved to be alive while being in the presence of a familiar face.

"Blue-Eyes! You're alive! Thank goodness! Another second and I would've been-..uhm Blue-Eyes? Is something wrong?"

As I picked myself up from the dirt and tried to speak to the unusually silent rogue she'd collapse to her knees, dropping her weapon as she did. "Blue-Eyes!"

Without wasting a moment, I rushed to her side to see what had befallen my savior. "What happened? Did he wound you?"

"Ergh...not him. Another rat..." she muttered through her pain while clutching her side where a grizzly blade wound could be seen.

It became apparent that I wasn't the only one who had faced hardships during our escape as my wounded cellmate looked just as worn and sleep deprived as I was. From the looks of her minor injuries, she had encountered more than just one attacker just as she claimed.

"I bested him as well, but he managed to wound me before the end." Once more an overwhelming sense of helplessness came over me as I had neither the supplies nor knowledge to tend to her injuries.

"No! You can't die here! What do I do? H-How can I help you?!" I asked with a look of urgency much to her irritation.

"Be silent, fool! Are you trying to alert even more guards to our presence? Or would you prefer a wandering beast to locate us instead?" Her scolding reminded me that despite my pursuer being defeated we were hardly in a safe place, prompting me to lower my voice. She then gestured towards the slain rat. "Check him for supplies. Look for Brightleaf and find some cloth to wrap this wound. Those thugs usually carry something useful on them." Blue-Eyes had been holding her paw against her bloodied wound to keep pressure on it.

"Brightleaf? What good will that do?"

"Stop wasting time and do as you're told!"

"All right! All right! I'm going!" Not wanting to get another earful from Blue-Eyes as I hesitantly approached the deceased rat guard who lied eerily still.

Never had I been so close to a dead body before, it was just as repulsive as I believed it would be with the very sight of the dead guard causing my stomach to turn. "Urgh... oh my..."

Nauseated by the sight of the corpse, I needed to cover my mouth as I searched through the soldier's belongings that had been tied around his waist. Along with a set of jail keys and a small pack of mixed nuts I found a blood stained herb pouch containing a few clippings of brightleaf within it.

I wasn't sure why such a brute would carry this, but I had no time to question it. The guard's garments were hardly suitable to help cover my cellmate's wound, so I then decided to use the fabric of my cloak to wrap around the bleeding area.

"Here I found some," I said to her as I returned. "The bag's a tad bloody but—"

Blue-Eyes snatched the pouch away and proceeded to chew and swallow every piece of brightleaf in the bag. I was startled by this as I had never seen anyone consume that plant raw, but I didn't waste time questioning it. My attention then focused on her wound as I tied my cloak around her waist and tightened around the wound to stop the bleeding. I knew I would likely never use it again, but it was a small price to pay if it meant saving Blue-Eyes.

"There, how do you feel?" I asked her.

"I'll be fine, at least for a while." Though Blue-Eyes was still in pain, the brightleaf did seem to ease her suffering much to my surprise. I would later learn that the herb had medicinal uses and would often be used for salves but could also be ingested to relieve pain as well as other ailments. She slowly rose to her feet, still clutching her bloodied blade before finally returning it to it's sheath. "We need to keep moving in case there are more of these louts searching for us. There's a village not too far from here. There's someone we need to meet."

"We?"

"Yes. 'We'. You are coming with me." Blue-Eyes slowly began to shamble eastward and clearly expected me to follow her.

"Blue-Eyes, I'm thankful for your help. You've saved my life twice now bu—"

"That's right. I did save your life. That means you're in my debt," she interrupted. "Don't tell me you intended to leave the mouse that saved you to walk back to town on her own?"

"W-Well I uh—"

"Of course not, you have a bit more tact than that or at least that is what I assume."

The rogue wasn't wrong, after all she had done for me, it would be cruel to part ways and leave the wounded mouse by herself in such a weakened state. "Now if you're done being difficult come and help me or would you rather continue to wander the wilderness with no sense of direction?" she asked me in a condescending tone.

As much as I wished to argue with her, I couldn't deny that she was right.

I was alone, tired and had no provisions as well as no idea of where I was going which was only made even more difficult by the darkness shrouding the forest at the moment. With no room to argue I followed after her in hopes of finding safety. Though we were weary and wounded from our escape we knew that to stop and rest would only put us in more danger so we continued our trek towards the town of Treefall long after the sun had risen.

With no food of our own we would sustain ourselves off of what little provisions the slain rat had in his possession. Blue-Eyes sought to mask her injury but over time she begrudgingly accepted my aid to help her walk.

For a time, we remained silent as I was unsure if she was receptive to my questioning. It became obvious to me that my presence had caused a great shift in her plans, and I didn't want to agitate her any further, partially out of respect for all that she had done for me. Admittedly I also feared that Blue-Eyes might consider cutting me down in a similar fashion to the brutish rat guard that attacked me.

"We're almost there."

"W-What?"

After almost an hour of silent walking, I wasn't expecting the masked mouse to be the first to speak. It actually startled me, but frankly that wasn't very difficult to accomplish. "Treefall, it's not very far from here." Her sights remained locked on the path ahead.

"And at this 'Treefall' place...we'll be able to find the help we need?" I asked.

"My contact should be willing to assist us once we give her what she wants," Blue-Eyes replied.

I nodded in response and for a brief moment our silence continued on. Still it wasn't long until my desire to question the odd mouse returned and as the silence between us had already been broken I quickly spoke up again. "Why did you come back for me?"

Already I could see that Blue-Eyes had begun to regret speaking up when she did. "Because you're carrying my contact's item of interest."

"What?!"

"I slipped it into your quiver before we jumped out of the window." Blue-Eyes spoke in such an unusually nonchalant tone that bothered me considerably.

"You do realize that I would've been killed immediately if it was discovered that I had this, don't you?" I asked, obviously not being too keen on being used as a carrier without my knowledge.

"I found you, didn't I? You could at least have some form of faith in me."

"How could I? I know nothing about you!"

Blue-Eyes let out an irritable grunt as we moved through the foliage closer to our destination. "Don't make me regret saving you, Tybalt. I prefer to work alone and *tag-alongs* are usually left behind."

"So then what sets me apart from your usual 'tag-alongs' then?"

Blue-Eyes fell silent for a moment, but not to ignore my question but more to think of a way to properly answer my question. "Let me just say there is a reason why I came back for you and not just because I hid the Sagestone in your quiver. My contact is someone who could be an asset to you after I receive my payment. Whatever questions you may have, save it for her. If not for that, I would have left you for dead."

With that said Blue-Eyes no longer seemed interested in discussing anything further much to my dismay. Despite the numerous questions I had I would honor the wishes of my savior and held my tongue until we arrived at our destination.

Eventually we would reach the great town of Treefall as my sister had done so before me and just like her, I too was overwhelmed by the sights and sounds of such a vibrant town. Sadly, Blue-Eyes had no interest in sightseeing and instead directed us towards a secluded arboreal home carved into the far end of Treefall.

Strange glowing symbols had been carved into the bark of this home unlike the other carved structures with the name "WILLOW'S PLACE" painted on a sign near the front door. Though I wanted to learn more about Treefall I knew that Blue-Eyes was in need of medical treatment for her injuries.

Once we reached the door Blue-Eyes proceeded to pull away from me and would knock on it to get the attention of its owner.

"Willow! Open the door!" The masked mouse's condition seemed to worsen during our trek here and while she attempted to remain unshaken by her wound, I could hear the sense of urgency in her voice. "Willow! Open this blasted door right now!" she said while beating even harder on the door before suddenly collapsing to her knees.

"Blue-Eyes!" I rushed to her side and helped her back on her feet.

"I'm fine, just a tad winded from the walk..." the blue-eyed mouse muttered while gritting her teeth through the pain.

The door to this home then suddenly swung open only for there to be no one present to greet us. "So my little thief has returned? Good,

good! Come in and hurry! Time is of the essence!" an unknown speaker said.

The voice was that of an older female and it seemed to echo through the house. Apart from my peculiar visions I had yet to truly encounter anything of the supernatural until this point which left me feeling quite anxious.

"I..I don't know about this. All of this seems rather strange...w-where is this 'Willow' friend of yours?"

"She is not my friend," Blue-Eyes answered with an aggravated look.

No doubt her wound wasn't improving her mood.

"We are here strictly for business. Once I explain our situation and receive my payment, we'll part ways and hopefully she will be able to help us both. Now stop acting like a frightened child and help me inside."

Not wanting to get another earful from Blue-Eyes I'd help her inside the peculiar home. The front door would shut itself as soon as we entered which startled me much to my chagrin. Moving deeper into Willow's home would shed at least some light as to who she was just by looking at my surroundings.

Much like its entrance, the dwelling had arcane symbols carved into the walls that emitted a faint glow which illuminated the darkened hallway. Massive stacks of strange books could be seen with some of them simply being piled up and pushed against the walls in a disorderly fashion. Peculiar artifacts from other cultures from within the Hallowed Forest would be placed on display as well.

As Blue-Eyes directed me further into the home I was already beginning to piece together who exactly her contact was. The peculiar aura of power exuding from the home itself, the numerous books that littered the place and the obsession with unusual artifacts of which the strange gem that we had obtained from the rats would no doubt be a part of her collection.

My mother had told us stories of strange practitioners of ancient magic known as the Green Sages. They wielded the very power of the forest itself and in return served as its guardians. Often a Sage or two would appear in Mother's tales either to offer guidance or assistance in fierce battles.

When I was younger, I believed in these stories but as I grew older the very idea of some of the feats and powers Mother claimed they were capable of seemed nonsensical to me. Though now walking through such an eccentric and undeniably magically charged home I was starting to believe again.

We then entered what would appear to be some sort of makeshift laboratory filled with bizarre experiments on flora and a plethora of other books same as the ones we saw before. Enchanted notes and regents drifted in the area in a circular fashion near the ceiling. There was even some kitchenware and living room seating present to add even more madness to the room. I wasn't certain if I was impressed by what I was seeing or disturbed by the untidy nature of the place.

"You're late!"

Sitting in the farthest corner of the room would be a peculiar sight, a strange looking brown mouse with mottled fur was jotting down notes on probably the largest book I had ever seen at the time. Once she finishes with her notes, she takes hold off a finely carved wooden staff with a familiar green gemstone as it's tip and approaches us.

The grayish white mouse wore a lengthy brown robe with a pair of spectacles like my own and had unusual runic patterns cut into her fur and flesh. Stranger still were her eyes that had a bright green glow to them as if the very spirit of nature itself inhabited her body. By her demeanor alone I could tell she had little patience for foolishness.

I had questions for this peculiar mouse but before I or Blue-Eyes could speak Willow angrily shouted, "I expected you to be here a day ago! I trust you have a fitting excuse for your tardiness?" She turned her glowing gaze towards me which caused me to shift uncomfortably. "And who is this supposed to be?! This task was entrusted to you and you alone! More importantly where is the Sagestone?! Did you get it?! Did you break it?! I swear if you damaged it—"

"Willow!" Blue-Eyes interrupted Willow's bombardment of questions before they went any further. "If you hadn't noticed, both me and my companion are tired and wounded from our escape. I am willing to tell you everything that occurred after you see to our wounds."

Willow groaned as she finally took notice of our injured conditions. "Yes, yes let's take a look at you." She approached the wounded mouse and carefully removed the makeshift bandage.

Despite our best attempts to treat the wound it seemed to only worsen without proper aid and I wasn't sure what exactly Willow would do to tend to her injury.

With a grimace she said, "Oh dear, that is a troubling sight. You're of no use to us dead so let's not waste any more time." What Willow would do next is something I will never forget. "Put your mind and body at ease. Let the power of the forest mend your battered form." Willow closed her eyes and raised her staff into the air while muttering some form of archaic incantation.

I was unsure of what she was doing at first and how she was going to mend my companion's wounds. Then Willow's entire arboreal home began to creak and shift as she drew forth a luminescent aura from the wood around her and harnessed its magic into her staff. She then held the staff with both paws as if to take full control of the power.

As Willow reopened her eyes the two glowing spheres seemed to have become even brighter somehow. Gently she'd place her paw against the wound which caused Blue-Eyes to flinch in pain for a moment before a look of relief could be seen on her covered face.

The borrowed magic within Willow enveloped Blue-Eyes, mending her wounds while also placing her into a state of blissful slumber. The masked rogue would slump over in her seat as she fell fast asleep. I failed to realize this however and for the moment I believed that she had done something to harm the masked mouse.

"Blue-Eyes?! Blue-Eyes! W-What did you do to her?!" I cried out in a panic.

"Hush boy! Goodness, you make such a ruckus!" Willow snapped, appearing somewhat winded from her spell. "I don't gain anything from doing her harm."

Upon examining the unconscious rogue I could see that she no longer appeared to be in pain and was in fact resting peacefully. I could even see her wounds slowly mend themselves.

After regaining her energy Willow then turned her full attention towards me. She knew who Blue-Eyes was, but I remained an anomaly to her. I am not ashamed to admit that I felt anxious under her gaze.

"Now then, it's becoming clear to me that our mutual friend brought you here for a reason and I would like to know why. The Sage eyed me with a patient expression, but I knew she wouldn't be taking no for an answer.

9

THE REQUEST

To my embarrassment I was anticipating a brutal interrogation from the Sage likely involving terrifying magics unleashed upon me. I soon realized that this was simply my fears and overactive imagination taking control rather than me using rational thought. The peculiar Sage known as Willow the Woodshaper offered her services as a healer to the severely injured of Treefall while also monitoring and occasionally mending any withering parts of the fallen tree. I would later learn that she played a pivotal role in this town's creation as well. Willow, who I previously assumed was a cold, impatient and calculating mouse, revealed her more nurturing side as she personally tended to my minor injuries while I told her my tale with how I came to be in Blue-Eye's company over a cup of honeyed tea and biscuits.

From the destruction of my family to being captured by the Vrothans and later escaping with the help of Blue-Eyes, everything was revealed to her as Willow requested. She took a particular interest in the bizarre visions that continued to invade my dreams. " That you have survived such an ordeal is nothing short of miraculous, Tybalt. Especially with how little you know of the forest and it's dangers." She'd say while applying a rank smelling salve to the cuts on my paws and body. My injuries were minor in comparison to Blue-Eyes so traditional medicinal methods would be used instead of the Sage's healing magic. "I mistook you for some random thug that escaped with our associate here, but it seems you are far more than you appear." I winced slightly as Willow tended to my injuries. "I just wanted to save my sister. I never thought I would get myself embroiled in such troublesome matters."

Willow briefly examined the bruises on my face and said," Life in general often has other plans for us that we are frequently unprepared for. It is unfortunate what happened to you, but thankfully the Will paired both of you together. I doubt you would have survived without her aid." This wasn't the first time that I had heard mention of the Will. Mother spoke of something similar before and how it was some sort of benevolent force of nature that watched over the entire forest. Though initially doubtful that such a thing existed I was beginning to believe she was right after all I've experienced. To survive all that I had endured couldn't have been a mere coincidence or a stroke of good fortune. Still, it causes me to question why this "Will" couldn't intervene with the attack on my family when we were in dire need of aid.

Briefly I glanced back at the sleeping rogue to see how she was fairing. Already Blue-Eyes was looking much better with her wounds barely being noticeable. That such potent methods of healing existed was a marvel to behold. More importantly I felt no shortage of relief to see that she would be okay. Though Blue-Eyes was often short with me and even threatened me with her weapon I couldn't deny that I was slowly becoming fond of her and felt deeply in debt to the masked mouse for all that she had done for me.

"Ahem!" The sound of Willow intentionally clearing her voice snapped me out of my daze. "You seem a little distracted." There was a sly smirk on the Sage's face, one that left me feeling oddly flustered. I wasn't aware that my simple glance had lasted far longer than I expected. She chuckled. "I jest, boy. Be at peace and worry not over that one. She will be fine by the morning." I felt relieved to hear this from Willow, but the more I thought about Blue-Eyes the more curious I became. I knew so little about her and it felt as though she wasn't telling me everything." She has told me nothing of herself and even less of her quest. What do you know of her?"

"Hardly anything apart from that ridiculous name of hers." Willow replied before setting aside her medical goods to take a sip from her tea." No one knows who she is or where she comes from, but she was responsible for a series of elaborate thefts. She has stolen from wealthy denizens as well as my fellow Sages around the Hallowed Forest and developed a bit of a reputation among the simple folk who view her as a rebel against the affluent. She even had the audacity to steal from the Great Sage himself! She failed of course and is being punished for her crimes. She has now been tasked with retrieving relics for my fellow Sages for research."

"You're referring to the Sagestones?" I'd ask her while retrieving my quiver. Blue-Eyes did mention that she had placed the sacred gem inside of it without my knowing and it seemed like the appropriate time to reveal it to the intended recipient. Just as she claimed at the very bottom of the arrow container lied the engraved stone, still glowing with power. I seized it then offered it to Willow who held her paws out to carefully hold the precious rock. She lets out a sigh of relief," Thank goodness it's unharmed."

"What are they exactly?" I asked. " When I held it in my paws even for the briefest moment, I felt a surge of.... something. I-It's like nothing I've ever seen or felt before! "The Sage examined the stone and ran her finger across the carefully etched runes.

As she touched it the soft glow it emanated seemed to brighten for only a moment. Willow then turned her glowing gaze back at me and peered at me searchingly. " Before I answer that, I want to ask you about these visions you've been having." I quirked a brow at Willow before speaking. "My visions? Well, I don't fully comprehend them but the events that I witnessed frighten me. Yet without them I fear that I would have very little to drive me forward."

"It felt as though an invisible paw was pushing you in the direction you needed to go."

"Huh? Erm yes that's almost exactly how I've felt."

A warm smile could be seen on Willow's face." Young Tybalt, there is a reason for this. I now see that our meeting was destined, and you have been chosen to fulfill a higher purpose."

"Are you suggesting the Will had something to do with me being here? I don't understand what you mean by that. I'm no one of great importance."

The Sage chuckled and shook her head. "Perhaps not yet but of what you have told me is true then that may change. Tybalt you bare the power of clairvoyance, a rare ability that is often only seen in those deeply connected to the Will. "Willow's words were met with silence from me as my mind buzzed with new thoughts and questions as she continued to speak," The events you have witnessed must be of great importance. Your sister, the Sagestones...and this serpent creature. All of it is connected." Willow also seemed to have much on her mind after learning more about me. "I would like to make a request from you, but not until the morning. Please try to rest until then."

"Very well, Willow." I said with a yawn as my own exhaustion from my journey finally caught up to me.

My conversation with the Sage had unknowingly lasted for a majority of the day. It had been too long since I had enjoyed a full conversation with someone without having to worry about having my head lopped off that I lost track of time. After everything that had been said between the two of us, I had many more questions of my own, but I also couldn't ignore the fact that I too was weary from our harrowing escape. Once I finished my tea I rose from my seat and went over to the cushioned couch where "Blue-Eyes" was resting and sat next to her. Giving the masked mouse one final look to see how she was fairing I too would carefully set my glasses aside and closed my eyes for a well-deserved nap. That my nightmarish visions was something only Sages could experience would cause me to wonder if I too could learn how to become a Sage.

I wasn't sure how long I slept, only that I would be abruptly torn away from a blissful dream by the sound of Blue-Eyes angrily shouting, "You've lost your rotting mind if you think I'll agree to this!" Startled by the uproar I would tumble out of my comfortable couch spot and onto the floor in a panic! "W-What?!What's going on?!Are we under attack?!" I'd see that there was no true danger, only the disruptive ruckus caused by Blue-Eyes and Willow arguing with one another. Neither seemed to even notice my less than graceful fall to the floor to which I was thankful. "You can't do this to me, Willow! I had a deal with Alden himself!" The enraged rogue angrily shouted. "You got your precious stone already so I've earned my freedom! Now tell me what I wish to know and let me leave!" The Sage gave Blue-Eyes an annoyed glare but maintained a composed demeanor. "You failed to grasp the terms of your punishment, thief. You will not be released from your service until the Great Sage himself relieves you. Until then you are not to defy us."

"You lied to me! You said this would be the last one!"

"It *is* the last one, but that doesn't mean you are free to go and return to your crime spree! Not to mention the fact that you'd likely be dead as of now without my aid so technically you are in debt to both Alden and me. You don't have the power to choose your fate."

"Willow! Blue-Eyes! Please calm down!" After picking myself up while retrieving my glasses, I approached the pair and tried to understand what the reason for all this arguing was. "What is all of this fuss about?"

Willow narrowed her illuminated gaze at Blue-Eyes before turning towards me. "Ah you're awake Tybalt. I've already informed the thief of her next task and I wish for you to accompany her."

"You do? Um to where exactly?" I cautiously asked.

"I am sending you to meet with my mentor, Alden the Evergreen. He is one of the Great Sages, one of the most wise and powerful of all Sages and it is paramount that you speak with him." I wasn't sure how to take what Willow was saying at first. While I was interested in learning more about how the Sages could help me understand my visions, I also still needed to find my sister. "This is...a great honor Willow, but I still need to locate my sister and stop her from confronting that frightful serpent. I'm afraid I can't do this."

"Tybalt, if there is anyone who could help you find your sister it's Alden. His power allows him to see much of the Hallowed Forest and has obtained incredible insight as a result. If you wish to find your kin, then I assure you it is with his help that you will find her." Willow implored me and appeared genuine with what she was claiming about her mentor's power.

Despite my urgent desire to see Olivia again I had no leads of my own and I saw no other alternative at the moment with Willow's task being the only immediate option." Then I suppose I shall seek out this Great Sage and have a word with him." Willow smiled warmly at me and placed her paw on my shoulder. "Thank you, Tybalt. I promise that you are making the right choice. Alden was my mentor, and you will find no wiser mouse in this forest. I see something special within you and I feel that he will see the same."

"Aren't you leaving out some details, Willow? You seem to have forgotten a few things. Like the massive target you intend to paint on the back of our heads!" Blue-Eyes interrupted and was still fuming after being denied her freedom.

Willow's brief smile faded as she shot Blue-Eyes and aggravated expression. "Be silent, Thief! I wasn't finished explaining," she snapped.

I arched my brow at Blue-Eyes before looking back at Willow with a questioning look. "What is she talking about?"

With a sigh Willow retrieved the Sagestone from the prison out of a pouch tied around her robing. "You asked about this last night and I refrained from giving you answers until I was absolutely sure I wanted to do this. Tybalt, A Sagestone is the crystalized magical essence of the Hallowed Forest itself. It is this magic that has altered the denizens of this sacred forest. Without such power we would be nothing more than mindless beasts. Though there are some fools who have tried to wield its power only those with a strong connection to nature and the Will can access its true potential hence why these stones share a name with Sages.

I need you to take this stone as well as the others to Alden. He will keep them safe and put them to good use."

"Others?"

At that moment Willow walked over to a locked drawer and after unlocking it she returned to me with five glowing Sagestones much like the one we found. The stones themselves began to react to each other and radiated with even greater power. My eyes widened with astonishment at the sight of them all. "S-So many..."

"Indeed, and you must bring them to Alden. I fear that they are no longer safe here, especially with another being added to the collection." Willow's expression became stern as she placed each stone carefully in a secure and unassuming brown pouch. "As you might have already guessed, these stones are filled with incredible power, and should they fall into the wrong paws they could cause untold destruction upon our forest home. Both of you must head east to an unsavory part of the forest known as Rotmire."

The name alone caused me to hesitate and immediately ask, "Rot...mire? What exactly is this place? Why is the Great Sage there?"

Willow wore a troubled look on her face as she answered. "How can I explain this? Our forest home has become ill these past few years due to the spread of a foul source of magic known as the Wyther. I know very little of where Wyther comes from, only that it is a vile destructive power that kills or corrupts most things that it touches. The land is perilous for settlers and is known to attract unusual characters or birth disturbing creatures from its vile muck. Alden has been studying that tainted land for years and seeks a way to cleanse it which has resulted in him isolating himself within the mire much to the dismay of his fellow Sages... myself included. He also is there to protect an ancient and powerful tree within that cursed place. The burdens he bears are ones that I wish he would share with me, but he's a stubborn old mouse and I only desire to respect his wishes."

Seeing my hesitant expression Willow then quickly added, "Fret not though, my young friend. There is a shortcut to Alden's home so you will be able to avoid the dangers of the mire. A single Sagestone is all that is required to open the way for you." The Sage then looks towards Blue-Eyes who was purposefully avoiding eye contact with her. " The thief knows the way and will continue to guide and protect you as she has done so already. "I could hear an audible huff from Blue-Eyes in response though Willow simply ignored her. "Listen, Tybalt. I know that I am asking a lot of you, and I would gladly go in your stead to see my mentor, but my duties here at Treefall keep me from leaving. I feel that you must meet with The Great Sage though and I have complete confidence that you will succeed. Please, will you do this for me?" I was still feeling hesitant about all of this.

At first, I was eager to see this Alden but hearing the dangers I would have to face would cause me to think twice. Not to mention carrying several magic runestones with us would potentially attract unwanted attention from brigands and unnatural creatures. Nevertheless, this reclusive mouse maybe the only one who could help me find my wayward sister and I couldn't allow such an opportunity to pass me by. Hardening my nerves, I would give my answer to Willow.

"I'll do it."

It wasn't long after I gave my answer that we began to prepare for our journey. While the Sage couldn't accompany us, she made sure that we were well prepared and would assist us with purchasing supplies. By the time we were ready to begin I would walk away with a new cloak to replace the one that I had used to bind Blue-Eyes' wound, a quiver of refilled arrows along with Mother's bow returned to me, a light brown jerkin and a white long sleeve shirt to offer some minor protection, a small knife, some light material and other necessities. Physically I was still a bit sore from the escape, but I knew that any time wasted on resting would only make the search for my sibling more difficult. Now prepared for the journey ahead both myself and Blue-Eyes would leave out the rear exit of Treefall to begin our quest to Rotmire.

For once I dared to allow myself some degree of optimism. Despite knowing that I was walking towards danger I felt more prepared and confident, especially with Blue-Eyes accompanying me though she appeared to be in a sour mood. As per the usual she remained silent as we made our way east towards our destination. She continued to walk slightly ahead of me as we navigated through the lovely autumn foliage. Originally, I intended to respect her space and remain silent, but seeing as we would be traveling together, I sought to forge some form of camaraderie with the masked mouse.

"So, uhm, Blue-Eyes..." I said while scurrying a bit closer to her as we pushed our way through some blades of grass. "...you've met the Great Sage, haven't you? What is he like?"

My question would be met with silence. Blue-Eyes didn't even glance in my direction. It was impossible for her to have not heard me.

Feeling a bit awkward, I attempted to speak again. "You must know a lot about the forest from your travels. Are there any interesting places you've enjoyed in particular?" Again, nothing.

She even began to move faster, forcing me to chase after her.

"Blue-Eyes?" I called out to her only to be ignored once again.

At first, I was simply going to fall silent, but knowing that this roguish mouse and I would be stuck together for awhile it would be worth getting to know her or at least forging some level of understanding.

I then rushed ahead of her to cut her off. "Wait! Slow down!" I called out as I stood in front of her.

The blue-eyed mouse eyed me with a deadly glare which weakened my resolve. Nevertheless, I spoke my mind, "Blue-Eyes I understand that you never intended for me to accompany you, but what exactly will ignoring me accomplish?"

"It'll give me some much needed peace-of-mind for starters," she finally replied with a snarl. "I should've left your sorry hide with the mangy rats or gut you myself! It's because of you that I am in this mess to begin with!"

"Wha-...t-that's not fair! I made no request for me to accompany you!" I argued.

"And what? You thought you could survive the forest on your own? Spare me, you're a cowardly, clueless little weakling who'd end up becoming some hapless beast's dinner if not for me!" The snarling rogue stomps towards me and jabs a finger into my chest. "I don't need to know your life story Tybalt to see right through you. You have no idea what you're doing.". She was being needlessly rude, but she wasn't entirely incorrect either. Though her words wounded me for once I held my ground as I spoke. "Y-You're just bitter because you got caught!" My words seemed to strike a nerve as the masked mouse became visibly flustered to the point that even her mask couldn't hide her embarrassment. "W-What?I...I have no idea what you are talking about!"

"You can feign ignorance all you wish, but Willow told me all about your schemes and your vain attempt to steal from the Great Sage himself! What possessed you to even do such a thing?"

"That's none of your business!"

Blue-Eyes and I glared at one another and for a moment said nothing. As much as I was in debt to the rogue, I had come too far to be treated like I was some sort of nuisance.

With a sigh I calmed myself down and said, "Blue-Eyes, I know you don't want to do this but I need your help. Assisting me could be the only way I could ever hope of finding the last member of my family. You don't have to like me, but I want us to show each other some level of respect." I then extended my paw to Blue-Eyes. "Are we in agreement?"

The rogue's furious glare began to soften as she appeared to be taking my words to heart but made no attempt to shake my paw.

She turned her head away and said, "My respect is earned not given freely, Tybalt. I will work with you, but I expect you to pull your weight."

I frowned but nodded in agreement. "Fair enough, but as you've pointed out I am not exactly as experienced as you are. I know very little of the Forest and I am not much of a fighter. I'm not sure what I can do to help but I'll try."

"I suppose that is good enough..." She then turned her azure sights eastward. "...now come. We've spoken enough for now and need to focus on crossing the water."

We later arrived at a peaceful creek with a slow current though any attempt to swim across would likely result in a delay in our course. Thankfully a small but worn dinghy rested on dry land not too far from us.

"Right where I left it," Blue-Eyes muttered before quickly preparing it for our use.

I couldn't deny I had some anxiety about crossing the water in such a shoddy looking boat. "A-Are you sure this is safe?"

Blue-Eyes merely rolled her eyes at my hesitation. "Can you pretend to not be a coward for only a few minutes? We'll be fine, Tybalt. Now stop wasting time and get in."

Seeing no other way to cross I carefully climbed into the dinghy, allowing Blue-Eyes to push the boat out into the water. Though I was still feeling hesitant I tried my hardest to keep my mind off of the thought of drowning.

As we continued on our way, I couldn't ignore my urge to learn more about the masked mouse. A game I once played with the twins would come to my remembrance when we were bored with our chores and sought to preoccupy ourselves.

As we began to make progress through the water with Blue-Eyes rowing I asked my question. "Uhm Blue-Eyes?"

Already I could hear her groan in annoyance at the sound of my voice, but I ignored it and continued with my question.

"Would you perhaps be interested in a game? Just to pass the time that is. I could ask you a question and then you answer before asking me a question and then I answer. We do this back and forth until we are satisfied."

"In my line of work Tybalt, it's very unhealthy to ask too many questions." She'd say with a grunt while straining to row. I wanted to assist her, but the masked mouse was reluctant to trust me with the task. "Fine then. Ask your questions..." With a smile I began our little game.","...but I reserve the right to skip a question! That's non-negotiable."

"I suppose that's all right. Hmm..." For a brief moment I thought about what I wanted to ask. I wanted it to be something that wasn't too intrusive, at least not yet. "Let me ask you this, out of all this places you've been during your travels what location has left you feeling awestruck?" My guide fell silent, and I feared that she had changed her mind much to my dismay.

"Auric Falls."

"Huh?"

"Auric Falls. You asked me about a memorable location and that's your answer." Though it took her a moment I would get the answer I sought. With an encouraging smile I'd then ask," I've only heard of such a place in my books. What was it like? What did y—"

"It's my turn." She'd interrupt and kindly reminded me of the rules I already I had forgotten. "Right, my apologies. By all means ask away." I implored her and after taking some time to think she'd ask," What do you do for leisure?" She would ask in a casual manner. " You hardly have the look of a fighter or an explorer. More of a bookish sort than anything else." Blue-Eyes didn't exactly frame her words in a complimentary manner. "Well erm yes I suppose that does describe me. You make it sound like it's a bad thing."

"It isn't, but some of the more scholarly types have a habit of thinking they always know better than everyone else. Those tight robed sages especially. "I quirked a brow at Blue-Eyes while adjusting my spectacles. "You're not very fond of them, are you? What did they do to you?"

"It's not what they've done, more of what they have. They have something I need and believe that I am unworthy of it."

"I-...what? What are you aft-UGH!"

My focus on our exchange of questions was so intent that I had forgotten we were crossing the water and already reached dry land on the other side. Despite being startled by our somewhat rough landing I was relieved to be able to touch my feet on the soil once again.

"We're here. The rest of the way to Rotmire we'll be on foot." Without skipping a beat Blue-Eyes would climb out of the boat and continue on her way. I climbed out of the boat as well though not as effortlessly as Blue-Eyes had done. Soon enough the two of us were continuing our way eastward once more. " You didn't answer my question. "I'd say. Though the little game we played served as a nice distraction from the terrors of traveling across the water I still wanted to continue.

"I'm aware of that Tybalt. Let us stop for now and perhaps speak more later." She said while giving me a curious look as if my existence had finally piqued her interest to some degree. " Come then, we need to keep moving and soon find shelter before night falls. It may appear to be quiet now, but this forest has a way of surprising you when you least expect it." Blue-Eyes said while unsheathing her sword and using it to cut her way through the brushes. With a sigh I would do as my guide requested while feeling reassured that she might be interested in speaking more later. As silence fell between us, I found myself lost in thought while once again admiring the natural beauty around me only elevated by the encroaching afternoon sun. Where the clearing of my birth seemed to still cling to summer, the rest of the Hallowed Forest would submit to the change of the seasons and turned into its gorgeous golden autumn shade. The trees in this part of the wood appeared to stand far taller than any that I had seen from my home or from my travels.

Most notably, a majority of them appeared to have peculiar markings that had either been painted or etched into their bark. They were primitive but undeniably beautiful and left me pondering who had done this. "Such creative patterns..."I muttered while admiring the markings."...Who could've done this I wonder?"

"This is the Tree Dweller's doing," Blue-Eyes answered, no doubt hearing my mumblings. I gave her an inquisitive look.

"Tree Dwellers?"

She nodded. "Surely you noticed some of them back in Treefall. Big as rats but with more fur with even more of it being on their tails. They're quite agile and are more at home in the forest than we are. The Dwellers make their villages in the highest trees in the forest. A place where only they can reach."

I did recall seeing a few of those peculiar looking folk in the market who stood out as one of the many oddities in that town at least to an ignorant young mouse who knew little of the world beyond his home. Many of which looked like primitive but intelligent hunters who wore garments and armor made of pieces of bark and plant fiber.

"Are they friendly?" I asked.

Blue-Eyes folded her arms and appeared conflicted. "Yes and no..." she answered. "There are many tribes, and some are more peaceful than others." She approached the tree and examined the curious markings. "We're moving through the Heartroot Tribe's territory. They shouldn't give us trouble as long as we don't tamper with their trees. All trees are sacred to the Dwellers, and they won't tolerate anyone desecrating them."

"You almost say that as though you were speaking from experience." Blue-Eyes then gave me a look that immediately told me not to press the topic. "Let us continue, I'd like to find shelter before—" She then fell silent as if something disturbed her.

"Blue-Eyes? Is something the matter?"

"Shh!"

Something was amiss and had immediately put the dark furred mouse on alert while I stood by her feeling hopelessly confused. "Hush and listen..." she said at a much quieter tone. At that moment I heard nothing and was prepared to question her until..

"Keep moving, mongrel!"

"Gnh!"

It was then that I heard it. An aggressive and gruff voice would be heard moving on the other side of the marked tree we were standing in front of. She motioned for me to press myself against it as whoever was disturbing the fragile peace of these woods wasn't someone Blue-Eyes believed to be a friend. As we pressed ourselves against the tree Blue-Eyes clutched her sword in her paw and seemed ready to wield it against yet another unlucky foe. Soon I began to hear the rattling of armored footsteps walking from behind the tree and further down a path that we were initially walking through. Fear gripped me once again as I saw just who my guide had detected. A warband of Vrothans, armed to the teeth and walking in unison. I had truly hoped I had seen the last of these thugs after we escaped from the prison. I nudged Blue-eyes and looked to her for orders. She held a finger up to her lips to signal for me to remain silent. Our presence thankfully went unnoticed as they continued on their way.

"Quit dragging your feet! You want another taste of my cudgel?!" The ratkin leader shouted while threatening what appeared to be a young Tree Dweller with reddish fur. The ruthless louts had taken a hostage. "We've got a long way to go before we reach Rotmire, boys. Keep up the pace!" the captain ordered as the group disappeared into the foliage and moved further out of sight.

Once we were certain that the rats were long gone, I immediately spoke up. "What are Vrothans doing here?" I asked. "I thought we had seen the last of them!"

There was no hiding my fear of those thugs as the memory of their cruelty and persistence from our prison escape was still fresh in my mind.

"Well of course not." Blue-Eyes sheathed her blade and rolled her eyes at me. "They have garrisons all over this forest. Of course, it wouldn't be the last we saw of them. What I want to know is why they are going into Rotmire. Surely, they know that entering that cursed place means certain death."

"Mayhaps that young Dweller they were pushing along knows something they don't."

"Regardless, it's none of our business. Come, let's continue and try to move around them without gaining their attention." The rogue then turned away from me and casually began to walk away much to my surprise.

"Blue-Eyes, please tell me you aren't thinking of leaving that child alone with those brutes!"

She continued to walk away from me. "We've wasted enough time with your sightseeing. It's time to make our way to Rotmire. I'll not be putting my tail on the line along with the sagestones just to free some brat."

Normally, I would make sure to avoid danger as much as possible, but something was compelling me not to give up on this matter so easily. "B-But the rats and that child! We can't just ignore this!"

I could tell my continued defiance was beginning to aggravate Blue-Eyes as she turned her narrowed gaze towards me. "Tybalt, I think you have the wrong impression of me. I'm not some fearless heroine who rushes in to save every careless fool who can't avoid a few Vrothan dullards." She walked back towards me as she spoke with a frigid expression on her face. "The fact that you are still alive is only due to me foolishly thinking that it was a good idea not to leave you behind to reveal my escape. If I knew you'd cause me this much trouble I would've gladly left, you to rot in that cell!" The rogue's words were like poisoned daggers stabbing into me again and again.

I had hoped to grow closer to my savior, but I was beginning to believe that such a thing would be impossible. "My blade has tasted the blood of both the guilty and innocent alike. I have lied, stolen and killed to achieve my goals. Your life only has meaning to me because Willow has tasked me with protecting it and once that is done, I wish to never see you again. Now come." Blue-Eyes had said enough she turned away again and prepared to move eastward again, but I didn't follow after her. "Did you hear me, Tybalt? We are leaving!"

"No."

"What?"

"I-I said no!" I shouted angrily and made certain my voice was audible enough for her to hear. "I will not stand by and let this happen!"

Once more I found myself drawing from strength, I never knew I had. Blue-Eyes may not have wished to involve herself, but I wouldn't remain idle much to my guide's ire.

We glared at one another as she began to approach me again. "I'm not risking our quest for the sake of someone we don't even know!"

"You have to do this!"

"Excuse me?" Insulted by my tone, Blue-Eyes snarled at me. "Just who do you think you are?!I don't have to do anything you tell me!" She then roughly shoved me.

"Nngh!" I staggered back before steadying myself.

"I am not some servant bestowed upon you to do as you please!"

"I... I know."

"Yet you expect me to do as you wish even after I told you I wouldn't?!"

"Yes...I do."

Blue-Eyes was becoming increasingly frustrated with me. "Have you gone mad? Are you listening to anything I am saying?!"

"I am, Blue-Eyes, but I won't budge on this matter," I replied. "You are probably the most capable mouse I know but you simply choose to waste your talents on ruthless brigrandry! Even after all the terrible things you've said to me I still have faith in you! You may try to portray yourself as cold, cruel and impatient but I know there is more to you than that! You could've easily left me to die in that prison or left me to be slain by that guard and retrieve the Sagestones afterwards, but you chose to protect me regardless! There is more to you than you think, and I refuse to think there is no good in you whatsoever. Please, help me do this. It's all I ask of you."

Blue-Eyes seemed unsure of how to respond to my words. For the majority of our time together I had obeyed her commands, but this matter was just too important for me to ignore. If that meant incurring the wrath of my guide, then so be it. "Stubborn fool. You truly want this, don't you?" The rogue lowered her gaze and placed her paws on her hips. "Fine then." The masked mouse let out an annoyed sigh. "Come, let us hurry before the trail goes cold. Don't make me regret this Tybalt. "I tried my hardest to hide my joy from my guide as it felt like I actually managed to get through the blue-eyed mouse's frigid exterior at least for the moment. "Let's not waste any more time then...and thank you."

10

THE SLAYERS

Now knowing the name of her tormentor, Olivia was more determined than ever to hunt down and slay the dreaded serpent known as Blackfang. With help from Walter, Olivia would prepare accordingly for her travels.

After saying her final goodbyes to the retired hunter, Olivia made her way to the far end of Treefall where Gareth would await her. "Ah there she is! My Secret Weapon." He let out a hearty chuckle and grins at her. "I trust you've packed accordingly, lass. We won't be seeing this place for a while so it's best you've finished all your business here." Olivia frowned and glanced over her shoulder.

Though her time in Treefall was brief she couldn't deny that she had grown quite fond of the town and its welcoming aura, especially after wandering in the untamed wilderness she escaped from. Regardless, she had a goal to achieve and couldn't allow herself to become too comfortable in her new surroundings.

"Yes, I'm ready to leave when you are," Olivia replied with a determined look about her. Gareth nodded. "Then let's be on our way.

My companions and I have made a camp not too far from here. We should be able to reach it before sundown." He turned away from Olivia and began to walk into the wilderness. Olivia couldn't deny that the idea of giving up the hunt and starting anew in Treefall did feel enticing, but should she allow herself to become too comfortable her already miniscule chances of slaying Blackfang would completely diminish. If my sister wanted to succeed, she would need to change herself entirely, she needed to become a Slayer. "I must admit that I was expecting to be bringing Walter with me for this hunt as were my fellows." Gareth says to Olivia as they navigated through the brush. "Some are a little hesitant about hunting this one and the presence of a slayer as renowned as Walter would've been an encouraging sight." Olivia appeared dismayed by his words and began to fear that she would draw ire towards her for replacing Walter. "I would've figured your presence alone would've been enough. Do they not believe we can succeed?" She asked resulting in Gareth letting out another hearty laugh." Haha! You would think so, but this hunt is quite different, and my fellow slayers are a bit uneasy. Stories of how this limbless devil has been tearing foolhardy slayers apart have shaken them up so their hesitation is understandable." Gareth replied while pausing to glance around his surroundings. " Not that we have anything to worry about. Especially with you joining the hunt." He smirks at her. Olivia seemed confused at first until she remembered her bold claim that Gareth would fail his hunt without her help as well as the knowledge, she possessed concerning the creature's weakness. "Erm yes of course, I'll do my best to aid you and your comrades."

"That's all I can really ask of you. What did you say your name was again?"

"Olivia good sir."

"Right then. I've got a good feeling about you Olivia. Walter is a friendly sort, but he doesn't take a liking to anyone so quickly. He sees something special in you, something that might be just what we need to turn this hunt to our favor." Walter pats Olivia's shoulder. " Shouldn't be much farther now." Truthfully the last person Olivia expected to receive any form of support would be from a rat and yet Walter viewed Gareth like a brother and seemed to have complete faith in the older warrior. Gareth walked with strength and confidence in spite of his growing age, not to mention that despite being a mouse he treated my sibling with respect and dignity instead of something lesser. Olivia hoped that the other slayers who accompanied Gareth would treat her with the same respect and friendliness that the senior slayer had despite the fact that she hardly came close to the level of experience Walter possessed.

As night once again fell over the Hallowed Forest, Gareth had led Olivia to an old stump that was within walking distance of Treefall. The stump itself had some similarities to our former home but it was in a dilapidated state and was blanketed in overgrown moss, glowshrooms and signs of decay. "Is this it?" Olivia asked as she glanced around her surroundings but saw no others present. "Gareth, are you sure this is the right place? It looks like no one is here." Gareth grinned in response while approaching the withering stump. "Looks can be deceiving my friend..."Gareth then pushes aside some of the moss draped over the old stump to reveal a hidden entrance much to Olivia's surprise."...Little hideaways like this exist all over the Hallowed Forest. Traders, Slayers and other travelers built them to serve as temporary shelters during their journeys. Now then, I believe it's time for some introductions." Gareth then enters with Olivia cautiously following behind him.

The stump was entirely hollowed out from the inside, leaving a large open space for its occupants to move about while also serving as a secure covering from monsters. In regard to those particular occupants there were three presents. An intimidating black furred warrior who wore a primitive set of armor made from the carapace of some slain insect, a rat with light brown fur who seemed to be a few years older than Nathaniel and a young female mouse with minor scars on her face and body who wore spectacles not unlike my own but mirrored Olivia in age only with a shorter snout white fur and a gray underbelly. When they entered the occupants turned their sights towards us and reached for their weapons as if expecting intruders before relaxing once they realized it was only their leader returning.

"There you are, Gareth! We were about to send someone to come and find you." The young mouse exclaimed and appeared relieved to see him. "Speak for yourself, girl. The old codger likely needed a nap after such a long walk." The rat said with a laugh as he set his finely crafted bow back down beside him. "Hush fool! Gareth must've had a perfectly good reason for his tardiness." The mouse chided while smiling at Gareth, but then took notice of Olivia. "Wait a moment, Gareth who is that?" It was after this was said that the trio turned their attention fully towards my sibling and noticed that Walter wasn't present. The other rat Slayer gave Olivia a confused expression. "While I've never met the mouse I'm certain that this isn't Walter." As Gareth had mentioned previously, Olivia's inclusion in this hunt would draw some discord towards her. The concerned looks cast upon her made her feel uncomfortable and as if her presence here was a mistake. Thankfully Gareth stepped forward and said," There has been a change of plans. Walter has made up his mind and has decided that his days as a Slayer are over. Therefore, he will not be accompanying us on this hunt. "This news didn't sit well with the other Slayers as a quick scan of their faces showed a mixture of confusion and disappointment. "Fret not, though my old friend may have chosen to retire, it doesn't mean he hasn't sent someone new to go in his place." Gareth turns towards my sibling with a confident smile. "This is Olivia, the newest addition to our little family. Walter may not be with us, but he believes that she'll be invaluable to the hunt which is good enough for me." Olivia could tell Gareth was trying his hardest to make her appear far bigger than what she actually was and could also see that his boasting wasn't convincing his companions.

"All right I'm convinced..." The younger rat then said." ...I'm convinced that we're all going to die." He remarks sarcastically. "This horrid serpent has killed dozens of our fellow Slayers and you expect us to succeed because we have some young and unknown Slayer accompanying us? It's bad enough you've already allowed this little know-it-all to join us but now it feels like you're trying to turn a party of monster hunters into a babysitting service. "He complains while gesturing towards the other mouse in the group.

"Excuse me?" The mouse looked towards the complaining rat and appeared to be insulted by his words.

"Complain if you must but know that I have already made my decision. She's coming with us and that is final." Gareth stated and no longer seemed to care if his allies agreed or not. "If you don't like the way I make decisions then by all means, leave. Go and find another hunting party strong enough to bring down that monstrosity!" Gareth's words would startle the other Slayers and by looking at their faces alone I could tell they wouldn't argue.

The young rat groaned. "If you are truly so hellbent over this girl then fine, Gareth. Do as you please..."

The mouse eyed Olivia with disinterest and appeared to share the same sentiment as her companion. Olivia had assumed that if anyone wanted to have her present it would be another mouse and yet the impression, she received from her would be the exact opposite.

"I trust your leadership. If this is what you think is best, then I'll not argue," she said with a frown.

The strange looking warrior was the only one who had remained silent during this entire situation but simply nodded at Gareth. Unlike her companions she truly didn't mind my presence much to Olivia's surprise. "Good, now if you're done being rude it's time, we all get acquainted." Gareth then left Olivia's side to approach the warrior. "This is Ch'Teka, a dweller warrior and one of the finest Slayers from the savage Deadwoods to the North. I can't think of a greater hunter I'd want by my side for this challenge."

Olivia nodded respectfully at the Dweller who did the same in return. My sister had taken a particular interest in the Dwellers as she had seen a few of them in the Treefall market. The Dwellers weren't just physically different from mice and rats but also culturally. Their devotion to nature and the land around them went far deeper than the average person living in the Hallowed Forest.

My sister was both intimidated and wary but also increasingly curious about the Dwellers though such inquiries about them would need to be asked at an appropriate time. The senior Slayer then walks over towards the mouse who was preoccupied with a strange contraption that appeared to be some sort of peculiar bow.

Save for a dagger and a sling in her possession, she appeared to be the least prepared for combat and appeared more equipped to deal with more technical issues the group would face judging by the tools she had with her. "And this here is Paige, our clever trapper," Gareth said while patting the mouse on her shoulder who smiled warmly at him as he did. "She has a talent for crafting tools and traps to help us slay those monsters.

Since I picked her up near Gladstone, she's been making the chore of hunting all the bit easier with her tricks and traps." Paige made no attempt to mask her pride. With a smug grin she'd adjust her spectacles and said, "I only wish to prove that brute strength alone won't be enough to slay some of the fiercer monsters in these woods."

"And you've done a fine job of that. I can say that for certain," Gareth said as he walked away though much to Olivia's surprise when he turned away from Paige, she glowered at her before turning her attention back to her contraption.

She wasn't sure what to make of the strange mouse but felt that she should be cautious around her. While briefly wondering why she had seemingly earned such a distasteful glance Olivia turned her sights towards the other rat in the group. Just by looking at his lightly armored garments and equipment she could tell he was an archer. Out of everyone within the group he was quite well-kempt in regard to his appearance. His fur had been carefully brushed and his whiskers were stylistically curly. By the way he was dusting himself off, puffing out his chest and posing in a heroic fashion, he was expecting Gareth to speak of his accomplishments and why he was important to the group.

"And I believe that's everyone—"

Gareth's words seemed to completely deflate the swelling ego of the rat archer. "I beg your pardon?!" he shouts while rising to his feet. "Aren't you forgetting someone?!" the archer snaps. Gareth merely shrugs. "Can't say I have, good sir as no one else comes to mind." The younger rat was fuming after hearing this and decided to give his own introduction. "I am Alistair Vandlebane the Third. Expert Marksrat, Sellsword, Tracker and Beast Slayer! I am a proud noble of the people of Ashwen who hails from a family with a storied history! Without my masterful aim and perfect perception, you'd be swarmed by beasts easily! How dare you ignore me?!My work is pivotal for this pack to function!"

"Oh is that what you do around here?" Gareth sarcastically remarked.

"I always assumed his job was to complain and eat all our food," Paige mockingly said while sneering at Alistair much to his ire. "Ingrates, all of you..." he grumbled before reseating himself on his makeshift mushroom chair. Though her time with Gareth and his companions had only been brief Olivia could tell there was a dynamic within the group. Despite their differences both in background and species they worked together to achieve their goals. "Well, Olivia? You've been quiet for some time now. What do you have to say?" Gareth would ask her. By the way he was looking at my sibling she was expected to say something to truly sell her value to the group. Ignoring her hesitation Olivia took a deep breath and spoke her mind, "Fellow Slayers, I know I am not who you were hoping to have with you on your quest, but like you I want nothing more than to see that serpent dead. I am not nearly as experienced as Walter is, nor do I have intimate knowledge of the ways of Slayers, but I am willing to learn. Allow me to aid you anyway I can if it means felling this awful beast."

"Oh, please—OW!" Alistair muttered under his breath before receiving a firm smack on the back of the head from Gareth.

"Well said, Olivia! Well said, indeed. Now then, gather around! It's time we speak of the next step to our plan." Gareth beckoned for all of the hunters to close in, including Olivia, as he removed a weathered map of the Hallowed Forest from his baggage and placed it on top of one of the larger mushrooms in the back of the stump shelter.

Though Walter had purchased a map for her she hadn't taken the chance to glance at it, but seeing it now showed Olivia just how massive their forest home was. Gareth's map was especially detailed with locations of towns, cities and potential breeding grounds for beasts. Most notably were highlighted areas that were marked as locations where Blackfang had been sighted.

"Now then, this limbless daemon has been spotted slithering about all over the Hallowed Forest."

"For a beast with no legs it certainly knows how to get around," Alistair added.

"It's unnatural. Unless it can fly, no serpent should be able to traverse the forest that quickly," Paige remarked.

"How it manages to move from one side of the forest to the next remains a mystery but what we do know is that the beast has been frequenting the Southern parts of the forest recently. A fact that we'll be using to our advantage." All Olivia could see were focused expressions on the faces of her fellow Slayers.

She could tell that these people truly meant to bring an end to Blackfang regardless of the dangers. They were precisely who Olivia had been hoping to find.

"Blackfang attacked my family despite us living in seclusion. We had never seen a creature like it in our clearing," she grimly said.

"All this does is serve as confirmation. The beast is near, and we must discover its location as soon as possible," Gareth continued while tracing his claw against the map towards a set of trees and a strange primitive marking encircling the area. "Tomorrow we'll be embarking towards the tree top village of the Heartwood Tribe to meet with their Treespeaker. Hopefully they can reveal some information as to where our wayward target as slithered off to."

"Are we really putting the fate of this hunt in the paws of crazed Dwellers who think they can speak to trees?" Alistair asked with a dry tone. "Please tell me I'm not the only one who thinks this seems just a tad farfetched."

"For shame, Alistair," Paige chided the older rat. "After all Gareth has done for us, and especially YOU, the very idea of you doubting him should be a foreign concept! In case you have forgotten you'd be nothing but spider droppings right now if not for him! I for one have complete and total faith in his judgment."

Alistair merely scoffed. "Ignoring Paige's brown-nosing, surely someone else has a problem with this. Right Ch'Teka?"

"Do not disrespect the Treespeakers." Ch'Teka said in response, startling Olivia as she did. The Dweller Warrior hadn't uttered a single word since she entered until now. Her voice was deep but feminine and the warning glare she gave Alistair left my sister feeling uneasy. "Oh come now, Ch'Teka. Your people aren't exactly on the best of terms with them. Why do you even care?" Alistair was looking for support from the Dweller warrior, but she too seemed to be against the rat archer. "It doesn't matter what Tribe you are from. Treespeakers are revered by all Dwellers." She replied.

"The Dwellers have a connection to the Forest far greater than most people realize and should surely be willing to assist us due to some prior aid that Walter and I had given them years back. If you don't agree with my plan Alistair, then by all means give us your "brilliant" alternative. "The white rat suggested with a bored expression and knew full well that Alistair had nothing in mind. With all eyes upon him Alistair nervously cleared his throat as he struggled to come up with any idea of his own to locate Blackfang. "Erm..."Unsurprised by Alistair's relative silence Gareth lets out a yawn and says, "Tell you what, lad. You tell me all about your amazing idea in the morning as we walk to go visit the Red Dwellers." He then looks towards the rest of the hunting party. "Get some rest you lot. We make for the Dweller village tomorrow."

"Good night then."

"Rest well."

"Sweet Dreams!"

Everyone then walked away to prepare for the next day and rest for the night. All the while leaving Alistair overwhelmed with embarrassment before he too returned to his makeshift nest to sleep and pretend this little incident didn't occur. Silence fell over the camp as all peacefully slept, all except for Olivia. For at least two hours she spent tossing and turning in her nest. In the presence of far more experienced Slayers, Olivia could feel her opportunity to finally avenge our family drawing near, but she also felt a swelling pressure to perform perfectly not just for her own sake but for that of her new companions. Unable to rest, Olivia rose from her makeshift bed, grabbed her sword and silently left the stump in hopes of clearing her head with fresh night air.

Once outside Olivia gazed up at the night sky above and admired the beautiful sea of stars. Desiring a more comfortable spot to sit, she would then climb to the top of the mossy stump and rest upon its edge. As she attempted to put her restless mind at ease memories of the previous days would begin to plague her. Though it wasn't home the similarities to our former living space reminded Olivia of simpler times before Blackfang brought ruin to her life. After enduring so many hardships since her departure from the ruined remains of our home my sibling now saw the harsh reality of what Mother sought to shield us from.

Olivia finally had the freedom and adventure she sought only to lose her home and family in the process. She longed for the hijinks of our younger siblings Carter and Lucy, the strong but kind heart of our older brother Nathaniel and of course Mother's firm and loving hold on our family. She recalled the last conversation she had with Nathaniel that terrible night and how she planned to leave home with or without Mother's blessing. Nathaniel had agreed to accompany her and the two of them would explore the Hallowed Forest together. A desire that would never come to be. Her thoughts then fell to me and our previous unpleasant exchange that resulted in her abandoning her last surviving sibling to hunt down Blackfang. Olivia didn't believe I was strong enough to survive on my own and thought that I had surely perished. Sorrow, guilt and regret would grip Olivia's heart as the realization that she could never return to her old life became more and more prevalent. Even if she and her new companions did somehow slay the beast, what would become of her then? Blackfang's demise wouldn't revive our family, nor would it restore our destroyed home. Tears filled her vision and Olivia could feel the growing weight around her heart. "What have I done…" She quietly muttered to herself with tears streaming down her cheek. The last thing Olivia wanted was to wake her companions with her sobbing and attempted to bury her emotions.

"Are you well?" The voice of Ch'Teka startled Olivia and nearly caused her to fall off of the stump. She then remembered that as she was leaving the stump Ch'Teka wasn't sleeping with the others but didn't stop to ponder why.

Olivia hadn't heard the Dweller Warrior approach and the presence of the Slayer clad in peculiar armor still bothered her. "Oh! I-It's you." The young slayer sought to hide her emotions from the older warrior. "Nothing is wrong, Ch'Teka, I just wanted to get some fresh air."

"Do you miss your kin?" Ch'Teka abruptly asked.

Initially Olivia seemed hesitant to answer but something about the strange warrior would compel her to speak. "I do," she replied. "I think of them every day."

"And you realize that should you perish; it would be the end of your family." The Dweller's words put the chilling thought of the Shortwhisker family being completely extinct after her death made her visibly uncomfortable.

"Why are you asking me this? What do you want?" Olivia asked with a skeptical look.

The Dweller warrior then told her, "The path of the Slayer is a dangerous one. Many attempt to walk it but many fail and perish because of it."

Ch'Teka's gaze was stern and her voice unwavering. "You are young and inexperienced in our ways. Many like you desire to become Slayers but only find disappointment and death in the end. Is this what you want?"

Olivia fell silent as Ch'Teka's warning was met with no immediate answer. The Dweller looked towards the West. "Treefall isn't far from here. You could return to it if you wished. Our companions still rest, and your absence would only cause a minor stir."

It was at this point that Olivia briefly began to reconsider her decision to become a Slayer. Her initial outing into the Hallowed Forest nearly resulted in her death if not for the kindness of Walter.

Despite surrounding herself with competent warriors who shared her goal there was no guarantee their quest would be any easier and would only become more dangerous the closer they came to Blackfang. That growing temptation to start anew within the safety of Treefall with Walter's aid came to mind once again.

Yet after everything she had endured thus far; how could she turn her back on her fallen kin after promising to avenge them?

"No, I will do no such thing," my sibling replied while narrowing her gaze at the Dweller. "If your intention is to frighten me then know that you have failed. I will not back down, I will kill Blackfang, and I will prove my worth to my fellow Slayers."

Olivia's passionate words served as the answer Ch'Teka sought. "Good, now go and rest. Know that I will aid you in the days to come."

My sibling blinked at Ch'Teka and was uncertain by what she meant. The Dweller warrior saw the confusion on my sister's face, and she then said, "I mean to say that I wish to teach you. Both Gareth and I will prepare you for what's to come. All that we ask is that you heed our advice."

There was something about the Dweller's tone and choice of words that reminded her of our mother. In truth she expected Ch'Teka to be the last Slayer, apart from Gareth, to show her any support and yet her words filled her with encouragement.

"Whatever aid you have to offer me I gladly accept it. I know that I will need your help and that of the others soon enough. Thank you, Ch'Teka. I'll see you in the morning," Olivia said as she bowed respectfully to the older hunter who bowed back in return.

Though thoughts of her fallen kin and previous life still lingered, Olivia's resolve would harden as she returned to her nest to continue resting for the night. She knew not what the future held for her, but whatever would come she would face it together with Gareth and the others. When all was said and done Olivia promised herself to return to the clearing of her birth and properly honor our fallen kin.

11

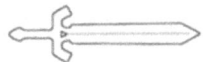

THE QUARRY

At first light, Olivia and her new traveling companions awoke and prepared to embark on their journey to meet with the Red Dwellers. For once, Olivia wasn't trudging through the wilderness by herself and was now in the company of true Slayers. This fact alone reassured her and made her feel far safer than she did when she was traveling on her own. It gave her the opportunity to finally admire the beauty of the forest foliage around her as she and her companions navigated through the tall grass.

"So then, Alistair," Gareth loudly called out. "Have you come up with an alternative to our trip to the Red Dwellers?" he asked with a playful smirk.

Olivia could see Alistair visibly cringe at the sound of his voice.

"As someone with such a complex and tactical mind I'm sure you have something perfect in mind," Gareth continued while glancing over his shoulder. The marksrat wasn't fooling anyone including himself. He had devised nothing since the previous night and wished that everyone had simply forgotten his attempt to challenge Gareth's leadership.

"Ahem! I believe that for the time being your judgment in regard to seeking aid from the Dwellers is reasonable enough, but I reserve the right to announce that I was right all along should it fail," he responded with great 'humility'.

"In other words, he couldn't come up with anything. Shocking revelation to no one," Paige said as she snickered at Alistair while the rat glowered at her.

Olivia could scarcely stifle her own laughter at the archer's expense.

"How gracious of you, Master Vandalbane. Now then, let us press onward," Gareth commanded as the party continued to advance eastward.

Even with the brief amount of time she had spent with these Slayers, Olivia could tell that they had a bond through their experiences and had already formed an effective but comfortable dynamic with their party. Olivia was wondering where exactly she fit into this dynamic. None of them had seen what she could do, nor did they seem to care.

If anything, it felt as though most of them had already written Olivia off as Gareth's "tag-along", something that needed to change. She considered speaking with Gareth but she risked distracting the senior Slayer who seemed more focused on directing the party and remaining vigilant for potential traps or attackers.

Olivia then considered interacting with Alistair or Paige, but she recalled how neither of them seemed to want her present, Paige especially for reasons unknown to Olivia.

"Did you rest well?" Approaching from behind her was Ch'Teka who once again startled my sibling with her presence. Though after their brief talk Olivia was a tad more willing to interact with the Dweller warrior.

"I slept well enough, I suppose," Olivia responded with a polite smile. "I would've preferred a bit more time to rest but I gathered that such a luxury would only hinder the pack. Regardless, I'll be fine."

Ch'Teka nodded in response as she walked along with Olivia. "With time you will adapt to our ways." Once more the Dweller had approached my sister and sought to keep her company.

The warrior's kindness would make Olivia feel quite shameful for her fearful behavior from the previous night especially as the Dweller had done nothing to harm her or even appear hostile.

"Ch'Teka, I must apologize. I hope I haven't given you the impression that I dislike you. It wasn't that long ago that I had no idea who or what a 'Dweller' even was."

The Dweller let out a short chuckle. "I sensed some hesitation from you but worry not I hold nothing against you," she said in hopes of putting Olivia's mind at ease. "Many find my presence and appearance off-putting as my people are rarely seen beyond our lands."

"Your people?" Olivia struggled to remember what Gareth had mentioned about Ch'Teka's origins before it came back to her remembrance. "I don't recall Gareth mentioning your tribe. Are you a part of one?"

Ch'Teka thought about what to say as the answer wasn't so easily explained. "I am, but my kind are different from other Dwellers. What few tribes there are only formed for the sake of survival rather than desiring comradery. They often never last before falling apart for one petty reason or another. Others become raiders and fight for resources against other outcasts or to attack travelers that stray too close to the Deadwood, but most seek to live alone as distrust and greed are rampant among us. Our home, the Deadwoods, are nearly barren with resources like food and water being scarce. Some of the deadliest monsters in the forest make their home there and are forced to contend with them. The life we live is a difficult one, but we endure nonetheless."

Apart from seeing Blackfang, Olivia had yet to encounter other dangerous beasts but to imagine a land infamous for such creatures troubled her. As she thought on Ch'Teka's words the warrior continued to speak.

"Akin to its name, the trees there have no leaves to shelter us and yield far less food than seen here. Every day becomes a battle for survival there, but it has made our people strong in the process."

In Olivia's mind the black furred warrior's answer would paint a picture of what life was like for Ch'Teka and her kin, a very unpleasant and savage picture to be specific. "I see, but how did you meet with Gareth if you don't mind me asking?"

Ch'Teka let out a slight chuckle in response, though Olivia couldn't understand why. "I was on the hunt for a large spider near my home as I needed it's eyes and fangs for an important matter. I wasn't the only one hunting it however. Gareth, Paige and Alistair were hunting the beast as well. They succeeded in finding the creature first...or should I say, Alistair did." She blinked at the Dweller who even with her makeshift helmet could see the trace of a smirk. "Through some manner of misfortune our 'Master Tracker' had been caught in the spider's webs and had stirred both the broodmother herself as well as her hungry children. I had never heard anyone scream with such a shrill voice."

The mental image of the overconfident marksrat squealing like a newborn pup did amuse Olivia. She giggled. "I assume you had some part in saving him?"

Ch'Teka nodded. "It wasn't an easy battle, but we emerged victorious in the end. At first, I wasn't too pleased to share this victory with outsiders, but the foe we faced couldn't have been bested by an ordinary hunter, especially one that hunted alone. Though I am no stranger to battle I realized wouldn't have succeeded without them."

"And then you asked to join them..."

"Actually, it was Gareth who approached me about joining his group." Ch'Teka corrected my sister. "He was impressed with my prowess in battle and gave me the offer. I was hesitant at first as I had never ventured beyond the Deadwoods before, but the allure of seeing more of the forest and hunting new prey enticed me." It was upon hearing this that Olivia believed she had found her kindred spirit as she shared a similar sentiment. "Truly?"

"I had always wanted to explore beyond the Deadwoods when I was younger, but life changes frequently and so did my goals. As I grew older and other responsibilities demanded my attention, I abandoned such ambitions; I focused on surviving and honing my skills." Ch'Teka looks ahead of the group, towards Gareth. "Perhaps it was also my vain attempt to reclaim my fading youth, but Gareth's offer was one I simply couldn't refuse. I had grown fond of him as well as Paige and Alistair though they didn't feel the same initially."

"They didn't trust you?"

"They were wary of me, but through our travels and experiences I have earned their trust." Ch'Teka frowned. "I can't blame them for being cautious. My people have done little to build outside relations. Most brand us as territorial savages who often raid passing caravans as I said before. Such viewpoints are difficult to argue against given our reputation." Ch'Teka then turned to look at Alistair and Paige. "I know that you feel that they may not trust you now, but with time they will see you as an ally. You need only show yourself willing to fight and defend them as I have."

Olivia took Ch'Teka's words to heart and now felt more determined than before to show her new companions what she was capable of. They both then focused their attention on traversing the wilderness together along with the other Slayers to the homeland of the Heartroot Tribe.

By midday they arrived at their destination with little trouble. Olivia quickly took notice of the intricate tribal markings either painted or etched into the bark of the nearby trees which served as an indication of the Red Dweller's territory.

Each of the marked trees appeared to be taller and healthier than any of the others that she had seen at this point of her journey.

"Here at last! I'd say we made excellent timing with this trek," Gareth said before stopping the party right in front of the base of one of the tallest trees in the area.

Alistair looked about with a confused and annoyed expression. "Uhm Gareth? There isn't a single Dweller in sight. I thought you said we'd be going to some sort of village," he complained, much to the annoyance of Paige.

"The Red Dwellers make their homes high in the trees instead of its base. I'm certain we told you about this already," the mouse chided.

Ch'Teka simply nodded in agreement with Paige.

This information wasn't received well by Alistair, though this came to no surprise to anyone. "Please don't tell me they expect us to climb. These immaculate paws of mine weren't made for such hardships." He looked up towards the very top of the tree which towered above him. "Besides, such a climb seems impossible for most of us."

Gareth was taking a sip from his waterskin as he listened to the marksrat complain. "Oh hush! We won't be climbing anything. Be silent and allow me to handle this," he said before searching his belongings and retrieved a small wooden flute that had been crafted with great care. "This shouldn't take long."

Gareth then put the flute up to his mouth and proceeds to play a short but melodic tune. The song carried through the Dweller's homeland. It wouldn't be clear why he did this until a curious skittering sound could be heard from the tree in front of them.

Olivia then noticed a Dweller skillfully climbing down the bark before landing in front of us. Unlike Ch'Teka this warrior's fur was a vibrant reddish orange with distinctly pointed furry ears. He wore a strange set of armor that bared a likeness to what Ch'Teka was wearing though it was constructed from the hardened bark from the tree and leaves.

The warrior looked towards Gareth who eyed him expectedly. "You've come. Good, we've been waiting for you." He then turned his sights towards the rest of the party and examined all of them. "Very odd looking group though, but I suppose that is normal for most of you Slayers. Wait..."

The Dweller readied his spear and narrowed his gaze at Ch'Teka. "You didn't mention you would be bringing one of the Marked with you." The Red Dweller made no attempt to mask his hostility and disdain for Ch'Teka.

Olivia did recall Alistair mention that both Ch'Teka's people and the Red Furs weren't fond of each other. She feared that the Red Dweller would attack Ch'Teka, but she made no attempt to show herself to be a threat. Ch'Teka held her ground and displayed no fear of the Red Dweller.

"How dare you bring this scum to our lands?" he growled with a vicious snarl.

Gareth's patience for the younger Dweller was being tested and he seemed visibly annoyed with his hostility. "That 'scum' is a valued member of my pack," he corrected him. "You needn't worry about her. She will cause you no trouble, but I will take full responsibility should something occur."

The Red Dweller maintained his fierce glare at Ch'Teka before finally being coaxed by Gareth's words. "If what you say is true I will leave it at that."

He grunted irritably at Ch'Teka before turning back to the white rat. "I will summon the lift and bring you to our village. Only you and you alone may come, however. The rest must stay.... the Black Fur is especially unwelcomed."

Gareth nodded in agreement to the terms. "Fair enough." He looks back at the rest of the pack and said, "Hopefully this meeting will bear fruit, but for now I need you to remain here and wait for my return."

While the others simply nodded in response Olivia couldn't help but feel uncertain about Gareth going into this village alone given the unfriendly welcome they just received. She ultimately decided to remain silent and allow the seasoned Slayer to go about his business.

The Dweller guard climbed back up the towering tree and a few moments later would drop the lift down to the forest floor. Gareth then stepped onto the platform and was lifted into the village above.

"I hope he'll be all right..." Olivia said after watching Gareth disappear from sight.

Paige shot a glare at her. "Of course, he'll be all right! Gareth is one of the finest Slayers this forest has ever seen. Only a fool would doubt him!" she snapped.

By now Olivia was beginning to lose her patience with Paige's unearned rudeness towards her, but decided to hold her tongue this time around.

"As thrilling as it would be to stand here and await the return of our *beloved* Senior Slayer. I believe I'd much rather do something constructive with my time...." Alistair walked towards a nearby stone and, after dusting it off, he set his bow and other equipment aside, sat down and rested his head against it. "...like napping."

The marksrat then closed his eyes and attempted to fall asleep as though he didn't have a care in the world. It was at this point that Olivia began to question if the strange behavior that Alistair and Paige displayed was common for Slayers.

Her fellow mouse had been strangely cold towards her despite having done very little to earn her ire while Alistair played the role of a fool almost perfectly. Still the two were her companions and she wanted to try to get to know them despite her reservations.

After Alistair had walked away to find a place to rest, both Ch'Teka and Paige had also decided to preoccupy themselves to bide their time. The Dweller Warrior was inspecting the intricate markings on the Heartwood trees made by the Red Dwellers.

Meanwhile Paige had moved towards a nearby shrubbery and had chosen to make good use of her time by checking the condition of her equipment. Feeling that she had spoken enough with Ch'Teka, Olivia chose to speak with Paige instead.

Despite her fellow mouse's dismissive demeanor Olivia wanted to get to know her better and decided to approach Paige as she sorted through her equipment. "Paige, is everything okay?" she asked.

"Yes."

"Oh, uh, do you require any help with—"

"No."

"Are you sure? I mean I could—"

Paige then finally turned towards Olivia with an annoyed expression on her face. "Perhaps it would be for the best if we stop wasting each other's time and you tell me exactly what you want." With arms crossed and impatient look about her she awaited Olivia's response.

The tinkering mouse's blunt responses were making it difficult for my sibling but at this point she had little reason to deny her true intentions.

"Very well," Olivia replied. "Though we have only known each other for a brief time I get an impression that there is a wedge between us. I merely wanted us to speak and get to know one another."

My sibling gave Paige a friendly smile, but her feelings weren't reciprocated. The brown mouse narrowed her eyes at Olivia, adjusted her glasses and immediately Olivia could tell that Paige had nothing kind to reply with. "No, I don't think I'll be doing that."

Confused, but unwilling to relent my sibling then asked, "Can you at least tell me why?"

To which Paige bluntly answered with, "Because your presence in our hunting party is unnecessary." She made no attempt to mask her feelings especially with Gareth absent. "I don't need to know your little sob story to tell that you haven't the foggiest clue what you are doing and have more potential to be a liability to our group instead of an asset. We may be of the same age, but I have played a pivotal role in several different hunts alongside Gareth. Meanwhile you offer nothing of worth to us."

Olivia was taken aback by the harsh tone of her fellow mouse.

"I don't believe for a second that you have some 'secret' knowledge that could help us slay Blackfang. The only reason you are here is because Walter and Gareth took pity on you and allowed you to join us as a tag-along and nothing more. Unlike you, the rest of us had to prove ourselves to be worthy enough to join Gareth's hunt!" Paige angrily said before turning her attention back towards her equipment. "I will tolerate your presence, but nothing more. Now if you don't mind..." She didn't even bother to finish her sentence as Paige had made her position clear.

Olivia was absolutely livid after hearing this, but mainly because Paige wasn't entirely in the wrong. She was fighting back both tears and her swelling urge not to beat the smaller mouse senseless. My sibling ultimately decided to walk away before she did something she would quickly come to regret.

Whatever desires Olivia had in hopes of forming a friendship with the only other mouse in the group had been dashed to pieces and in its place a growing disdain for Paige took hold. Hoping to distance herself from Paige, Olivia made her way over towards Ch'Teka. "What are you doing over here, Ch'Teka? Something caught your eye?"

Olivia made sure to mask her emotions from the Dweller in hopes of not drawing her concern. The last thing she wanted was her friend and fellow Slayer to see was tears.

"The markings made by the Heartroot tribe. My parents had described them to me, but I have never seen them for myself," she said while she gestured towards them.

Turning her sights towards the tree, Olivia studied the tribal symbols for herself. Among the various illustrations and carvings, the one that seemed to catch Olivia's eye would be a crude painting featuring many different Dweller paws placed upon one another in the form of a circle.

"Strange...wonder what all of this means exactly?"

"Unity, family..." Ch'Teka answered. "Such things hold great value to their tribe. Far more than my own."

My sibling blinked at Ch'Teka with a confused look. "You make it sound like that is a foreign concept to your people."

"In a way it is." The Dweller lowered her gaze. "We consist of outcasts from other Dweller tribes in the forest who broke the ancient laws of our people. All are banished to the Deadwoods and are forced to endure its hardships. Even their children are forbidden from re-entering their former tribes. Our parents are marked with cursed signs that brand us as defilers of the forest, stripping us of the bond we share with it. The mark will carry on to the next generation of Dwellers born from the outcast and carry on to their children after that and those that come after. Forever stained by the sins of their fathers and forefathers."

To Olivia's surprise, Ch'Teka removed her helmet to reveal a white paw print the marked her head. At first it appeared to be paint but Olivia could see that it was indeed apart of her fur, if not only her very soul.

"That doesn't seem right. If your parents committed a crime, why should their children suffer for it?"

Ch'Teka agreed with that sentiment but knew there was nothing that could be done to undo what could be seen as the equivalent of a magic curse. "In the eyes of the other tribes, we are unclean and unworthy of the bounty of their trees. While theirs speaks to them ours remain mute and lifeless." She then looked back towards the tree itself. "My mother was once a part of this tribe, but committed some unspeakable crime and thus was deemed unworthy to remain among them. I probably have family here who will have no idea of my connection to them...or care for that matter."

Olivia had the impression that Ch'Teka's people were different from other Dwellers, but to know that they were outcasts of other tribes marked for their crimes or that of their parents did shock the young mouse. Even more so with the harsh conditions they were forced to dwell in. "Can't your people simply leave? Go and live somewhere else?"

"Some of my kind do leave and become mercenaries or try to begin their lives anew in Ashwen but most fear living outside of our old ways despite everything they have endured. Most of your people mimic the ways of the Giants that ruled this land in ages past only to destroy themselves as a result. We Dwellers fear that you could share their fate."

Olivia didn't fully comprehend what Ch'Teka was telling her but couldn't ignore the faint ominous tone to her words. Wanting to return to what they were previously speaking about, she said, "From how you describe your people, they seem to be little more than crude and violent survivalists...uhm no offense."

Ch'Teka sighed. "Given how ruthless my people can be, it comes as no surprise. I once thought as they did and viewed all outside of our kind as weaklings. In truth we are envious of your prosperity and despise you all for it. My time with our companions has shown me the error of such thinking. There is greater strength in unity and there is wisdom in learning from others who live in the Hallowed Forest. To continue to harbor such hatred will only serve to harm me."

While she could understand what Ch'Teka might learn from Gareth, Olivia struggled to understand what she could learn from both Paige and Alistair. Still Ch'Teka spoke with such conviction that she appeared to truly believe in what she meant.

"My people must change, they must become more than survivors, scavengers or raiders. We are strong, but we could become even stronger if we united. With time I will make them see..."

Before Olivia could ask Ch'Teka to elaborate or ask about her homeland, she would notice the lift begin to shift and lower down to the forest floor. "That must be Gareth."

Both Olivia and Ch'Teka returned their attention back towards the lift where Gareth would be stepping off of it to rejoin his companions. The seasoned Slayer had a determined look about him.

"Gather, friends! We've a task to complete!" Gareth commanded with a booming voice which startled Paige and brought her focus onto the older rat while rousing Alistair from his "constructive" nap much to his dismay.

With a yawn the marksrat rose from his sleeping spot and approached Gareth as he stepped off of the lift. "Back already? What did the Dwellers tell you? Do they know where Blackfang is?" he asked while the rest of the group gathered around Gareth. "They are willing to aid us, but we must aid them first."

Alistair scoffed at this. "If you think even for a second that I'm going to demean myself with tedious chores then—"

"Cease your mewling! They tasked us with slaying a beast, not doing their laundry!" Gareth growled in response. "Apparently, the Heartwood Tribe has been frequently attacked by a pair of winged devils who have made their nest not far from their village. One of them has already been slain but the other remains. A fiend they've come to call The Shrieker. There is a chance it may abandon its eggs with its mate dead, but the

Heartwood want an example made of the devil and want us to take care of it," Gareth explained.

"That seems a bit odd, the Dwellers tend to frown on the services of Slayers and prefer to handle their own problems." Paige says while she folds her arms and eyes Gareth curiously. "Why would they want our help now?" she asked. The lead Slayer merely shrugged and shook his head. "Apparently, they've sent off many of their strongest warriors to the west but wouldn't say why. The tree the winged fiends have made their homes are used for vital food storage for the winter. More importantly, all that matters is that, if we fell this beast, they'll assist us with locating Blackfang afterwards."

"Ah that explains it. Why send more of their own people when they can send some expendable riff raff to do their dirty work for them." Alistair groaned.

"Regardless, we will slay this beast and earn the favor of the tribe. It's the only way we'll be getting closer to locating Blackfang. "From the tone of his voice, the party knew that Gareth had already made up his mind. This would be their latest goal, one that they would overcome like so many others. "The Dwellers will be sending a guide momentarily, but until then sharpen your blades, ready your arrows and steel your nerves! Battle is upon us!" Gareth's words were passionate, inspiring and filled with youthful vigor. His inspiring presence clearly had an effect on the others as everyone immediately began to prepare their equipment for the coming battle. For them, this level of preparation and focus was instinctive. Olivia on the other paw, felt even more like an outsider to the group as she seemed visibly uncertain of what to do with herself.

"Feeling all right, lass?" Gareth asked as he noticed that everyone, even Alistair, was preoccupied with their preparations except for my sibling. "You seem a bit lost." Rather than appear upset with Olivia, the old rat gave her an encouraging look which urged her to speak her mind.

"I'm sorry, Gareth," she said. "As I've said, I know nothing of the ways of Slayers and I'm quite uncertain of what to do with myself." Olivia hung her head. "I want to help but I fear I might get in your way."

Gareth took a moment to ponder the situation and carefully stroked his beard as he thought. "You raise a fair point, but then again I'd prefer if you gained experience with facing these beasts, especially with the abomination we'll be facing once we're done here."

After taking a few more moments to consider his options he gave Olivia a grin and said, "Very well, I'll allow you to make the call. You can assist us if you want but of course that means putting yourself in potential danger like the rest of us, but if you wish you can merely observe us from a safe distance and allow us to face down the beast."

Uncertainty gripped Olivia as she was silently wishing Gareth hadn't given her this choice. Apart of her relished the opportunity to wield her sword against one of the Murderous ferals, but after her conversation with Paige, she wasn't entirely certain she was ready for this and could easily end up putting herself and the other Slayers in danger. Though she couldn't see it, she could feel Paige's judging gaze bearing down on her.

After a brief silence, Gareth asked for an answer. "Well? What will it be?"

"Mayhaps it would be for the best if I were to observe from a distance. I don't want to get in your way." Olivia answered though her response was half-hearted. Gareth seemed disappointed but gave the young mouse an understanding nod. "If that is your decision then so be it. "Once the other Slayers were ready they would rejoin Gareth and Olivia, now properly armed and ready to face their foe." Where's this guide of yours, Gareth? Figured they'd be here by now." Alistair asked though Gareth was beginning to wonder about that himself." A good question." The veteran Slayer was considering returning to the Heartroot Tribe's village to see what was impending to the Red Dwellers from sending their guide. Paige then took notice of a single Dweller emerging from their tree village above to carefully climb down. "Hm? It appears they've finally sent someone. "When the scout joined us at the base of the tree Olivia as well as the other Slayers were a tad confused at who the Heartroot Tribe had decided to send. Before them was a young male Dweller no doubt only a few years older than the twins. Though armed with a spear, by the way he held it in his paws it was obvious he wasn't fully accustomed to wielding it. He wore hardly any armor compared to the previous warrior they had seen. Despite being the youngest present, this Dweller tried to present himself as a brave and competent warrior. He looks at them briefly before asking,"Krrrchakrrr?"The Dweller scout's strange tongue startled Olivia, it was a bizarre mixture of shrill, chittering noises that were completely incomprehensible to my sibling. "Um excuse me?" She'd asked. The scout repeated himself."Krrrchakrrr?"

"Really? They couldn't send someone who at the very least spoke the Queen's Common? And a child at that! As if we don't have enough of those," the annoyed archer complained.

Gareth simply sighed and looked towards Ch'Teka. "You wouldn't mind acting as a translator for a little while, would you?" he asked her, to which the Marked Dweller nodded in response.

As she stepped forward the young scout finally took notice of her presence and immediately the confident look, he wore drained from his face. He gasped and clutched his spear as she approached him all the while shaking like a leaf. Of course, Ch'Teka meant him no harm but Olivia could understand the red Dweller's hesitation.

"Chrrrkarakchrk?" Ch'Teka asked the scout, though he seemed hesitant to speak at first.

"KrachhkChrrkacher..." he'd answered.

"What did he say?" Alistair asked.

"He thinks I am going to eat him."

"I can see that being something to be concerned about."

Alistair was then promptly elbowed in the stomach by Paige.

Gareth then said, "Please try to put our guide at ease. We're burning daylight and I want this beast dead before sunset."

Ch'Teka nodded before turning her attention back towards the young scout. Though at first he was uncomfortable with Ch'Teka's presence he slowly began to warm up to her as they converse in their native tongue. She then turned back towards her companions. "This is Ze'hoz, he says the Treespeaker has chosen him to serve as our guide. He knows where the beast has made its nest and will lead us there."

"Good, tell him we're ready to depart."

Following behind the nimble scout, the Slayers would make their way to where their mark had chosen to nest. Along the way, Ze'Hoz sought to sate his curiosity by asking his escort numerous questions about them and their adventures.

Though traveling to the monster's nesting spot took only a brief amount of time, Ze'Hoz intended to make the most of it much to the annoyance of a certain marksrat. He also spoke of the winged fiend they would be facing and how it had strange feather-like horns, massive wings and talons that could tear through almost anything.

While the Slayers seemed to believe he was exaggerating it became obvious that these monsters had been causing trouble for some time. They eventually arrived at the clearing and more importantly the Dweller tree that the beast now called home. Using the brush as cover the Slayers began to plot their attack.

"There." Ch'Teka gestured towards a large cavity high in the tree above," Ze'Hoz said this is where the monster has made its nest."

Olivia and the others peered upward from the bush they were taking shelter in to see where Ch'Teka was pointing.

"Do you believe our winged host is present?" Alistair asked.

"Possibly," Ch'Teka answered. "I should be able to climb up there and check." She then looked toward Gareth as if to ask for his permission.

He nodded in response. "Do it and be careful."

"I always am." But before Ch'Teka could leave the brush to scout the tree, Ze'Hoz rushed in front of her. "Chakkrrchkcha!"

"Is there a problem?" Gareth asked, to which Ch'Teka looked at him with concern.

"He wishes to accompany me," Ch'Teka replied.

Gareth frowned at this. "That isn't necessary. The boy needn't put himself in more danger. We're professionals, we can handle this," he said, looking to Ch'Teka to translate his words.

She nodded in agreement before turning back to Ze'Hoz who urgently responded. "He says the Treespeaker himself saw a vision of our victory...with his assistance. He claims this is his true purpose for being chosen for this. He not only wanted to show you where the beast made its home, but also to aid us in slaying it."

"Hmph, he neglected to mention that with all of that chattering he did on the way here," Olivia heard Paige mutter.

Though skeptical, Gareth seemed willing to trust the words of the Treespeaker despite his concerns. "Fine then, but keep an eye on him, Ch'Teka."

The Marked Dweller nodded in agreement before speaking with Ze'Hoz who seemed delighted to hear that he was approved to help them slay their winged foe. As the two Dwellers then made their way towards the tree, the other Slayers focused on making their preparations.

Gareth turned towards his fellow Slayers with a focused and determined look in his eyes. "Right then, Paige, Alistair. Ready yourselves! We've faced filth like this before and they die all the same! They think their size and strength alone dictates the outcome of our fates. We will show this monster otherwise!" Gareth spoke with righteous fervor as he readied his mace and shield.

Alistair readied his bow and retrieved an arrow with a barbed tip from his quiver while Paige prepared a well-used sling while choosing the first stone she wished to launch at her foe. "Step one is to draw it out, step two is to clip its wings, step three is to blind it," Paige said with a confident smile while briefly flashing a cold leer at Olivia.

All three bore hardened expressions and showed no fear for the battle to come. Seeing them ready themselves gave Olivia a sense of urgency, but Paige's cruel but truthful words clawed at her. The fear of her potentially ruining the cohesion of this pack had become a constant pain.

A growing sense of shame began to swell within the young mouse as everyone, even their young scout seemed willing to fight but her.

"Olivia?" Gareth's voice seemed to snap my sibling back to her senses. "Everything all right, lass?" He placed a paw on Olivia's shoulder and gave her a reassuring look.

"I...I'm fine," she answered. "I just don't want to be a distraction."

Gareth smiled. "Relax, lass. We'll be done with this beast before you know it. Just wait here and watch us work." With a wink both he and Paige turned their attention back towards the clearing to see what progress Ch'Teka and Ze'Hoz had made.

Suddenly, a sharp bestial screech pierces the air! Worried for the safety of the Dwellers, the party turns their gaze towards the tree. Scurrying down the tree would be both Ch'Teka and Ze'Hoz." I see the Dwellers, but not the beast..." Paige said before gasping and pointing upward. "There I see it!"

Bursting forth from its nest would be the winged fiend they were hunting and despite Ze'Hoz's exaggeration the airborne monster was a menacing sight to behold. A great and terrifying horned avian with massive wings and blade-like talons whose feathers were coated in the yolk that would've become its offspring.

Angered by the decimation of its eggs the beast's furious gaze was fixated on the two responsible for the intrusion. Ch'Teka and Ze'Hoz scurried down the tree and made a mad dash across the clearing, but the two would never reach the brush in time before the beast struck. The winged daemon swooped downward and readied its talons to end the lives of their companions.

Ze'Hoz was lagging behind Ch'Teka and the vengeful bird had its sights on him. Right before it could strike Alistair loses an arrow and lets it fly straight into the avian's right wing! Shocked by this sudden surge of pain, the beast let out an agonizing screech as its flight was disrupted causing it to tumble onto the ground and land in the center of the clearing. It thrashed wildly as it struggled to comprehend what had happened to it.

"ATTACK!" Gareth roared aloud with Paige and Alistair following behind him to commence their attack on the beast.

Ch'Teka and Ze'Hoz stopped fleeing from their pursuer and readied their spears as they boldly charged at the monster. "Quickly now! Break those wings! Make it sorry it was ever born!" Gareth shouted as he violently slammed his mace on the horned avian's injured wing while Ch'Teka and Ze'Hoz impaled the left wing. The creature cried out in pain and confusion while continuing to thrash about.

"Watch those talons! Don't let it get back up!" Gareth commanded as he continued to repeatedly bash the bloodied beast with savage fervor with his mace.

Alistair continued to fire arrow after arrow into the creature's feathery body as Paige launched deadly stones at the fiend's left eye.

Olivia watched as her companions fought fiercely against their foe in astonishment. They continued to take advantage of the downed monsters' deliriousness and for a time appeared to be close to ending the beast's life as they continued to stab and strike at the wounded creature! Then suddenly it let out yet another awful screech and rose from the dirt, knocking back Gareth, Ch'Teka and Ze'Hoz.

"Even after all of that, it's still alive?" my sister said to herself in disbelief.

This vile creature refused to accept defeat though there was no denying that the wounds that the Slayers had inflicted were severe. Its wings had been broken and bloodied by Gareth and the Dwellers, its feather coated body was riddled with arrows and stab wounds from Ch'Teka's spear as well as bruises from the stones launched against it by Paige.

Even after all of this the beast still lived though perhaps not for long. There was a maddened look in its eyes, not only had it lost its children but now found itself becoming the prey of what would usually be its meal.

"Chhrkra!" Ze'Hoz was the first to rise and the first to charge back at the beast as it scrambled to its feet! With his spear in his paws, he hurled it with all his might at that wounded creature, but Ze'Hoz's small form and lack of training with the weapon would only allow the spear to land mere inches away from the enraged avian's talons. All the young scout had achieved was gaining the attention of the beast.

"K-Krchhra?"

In a manner similar to my frightful experience with Blackfang, the beast locked eyes with Ze'Hoz and instilled fear into the would-be Slayer. Once more it shrieks and began to pursue Ze'Hoz, batting away Paige and Alistair with it's bloodied wings!

Paralyzed with fear Ze'Hoz's attempt to flee was delayed right as his enraged pursuer charged towards him. Before he can fully scamper away the maddened fiend lunges for Ze'Hoz's and grabs him by the tail with his beak. "NO!" Olivia cried out as she saw the young scout being violently tossed about! His desperate screams and cries for help rung through the clearing!

Gareth and Ch'Teka pick themselves up from the dirt before rushing towards the crazed animal.

"No! Ze'Hoz!" Ch'Teka cried out in horror as she rushed to aid the red Dweller!

"It's gone mad! Quickly! Bring it down!" Gareth would slam his mace on top of the beast's talons while Ch'Teka flanked their foe on its side and stabbed it with her spear. The beast recoiled in pain, flinging Ze'Hoz away it did! He would be sent tumbling near the brush close to where Olivia was watching.

"O-Oh no!" Olivia looked on in horror at Ze'Hoz as she immediately took notice of half of the Dweller's tail missing, leaving only a gnarled and bloodied stump.

His body was battered and bloody from the violent fall while appearing unable to move. She could hear him whimpering and pleading for help as he squirmed in pain. Already Olivia could see the maddened feral advance towards the wounded youth with reckless abandon!

"It's going for the boy! Kill it now!" Gareth commanded as he tried to jump on the back of the beast only to be thrown off before he could strike it with his mace.

Ch'Teka would attempt to further pierce the dying beast's side with her spear only to be batted away once more with the fiend's wing. Neither bludgeoning stone nor sharpened arrow could cease its assault despite Paige and Alistair's efforts to slow the beast.

"My quiver's empty, Gareth! We can't stop it!"

This bloodied avian was partially blind, riddled with arrows, bruises and stab wounds but despite everything the Slayers had tried it wouldn't be stopped. The beast wasn't invincible as they could all tell that it was dying from its injuries it had sustained, yet it pressed onward regardless.

Ze'Hoz could see the maddening fury in the one remaining eye of the beast and knew it intended to end him before it suffered from its own demise. It was at this point that Olivia could no longer remain idle. She had decided to watch the true Slayers fight the beast, but now it was her turn to step onto the battlefield. Without wasting another moment, she draws her father's blade and rushes down to where Ze'Hoz laid, placing herself between the young Dweller and the raging beast.

"Y-You'll go no further daemon!" Olivia shouted as the beast screeched and seemed more than willing to devour my sibling as well as Ze'Hoz. The mere sight of this bloodied monster terrified her, but her desire to save one of her companions overruled her fear.

Though right as the enraged mother drew near, the etched markings of the blade began to glow brighter and brighter to the point that Olivia had to shield her eyes. The blinding light of the runes engulfed the blade with the very sight of it blinding the bloodied beast as it came within arm's length of Olivia only to have its reckless charge stopped.

The sword's glow began to dim shortly afterwards allowing Olivia to see her wounded foe. The avian was blinded, stunned and vulnerable to attack and my sister didn't waste a single moment to take advantage of its weakness.

In place of fear, a rising fury swelled within my sibling as she rushed towards the beast to drive father's sword deep into its heart. It cried out in agony as the resulting strike would once again force it on its back.

Olivia withdrew the blade, now coated in the blood of her enemy, before moving towards the monster's head and ruthlessly slashing its neck with all the force she could muster! "DIE MONSTER!"

Olivia had sealed the fate of the dying beast; a pitiful squawk escaped it as it weakly struggled to move before finally falling silent. At last, their foe had been slain and with it's one remaining eye partially opened, my sister could see the life and fury fade from it's eyes as its body grew cold and still.

The rush of energy coursing through Olivia would be replaced with an overwhelming exhaustion and numbness. She fell to her knees on top of the bloodied beast's feathery bosom and clutched her rapidly beating heart.

"Olivia!" Gareth shouted as he and the other Slayers rushed to check on her and see to Ze'Hoz's injuries. "You all right, lass?" he asked with an urgent look about him.

Olivia had begun to calm down as it fully set it in her mind that the battle was over. "I-I'm fine Gareth." Olivia glanced back at Ze'Hoz who was being cared for by Alistair and a very concerned looking Ch'Teka which came as no surprise to Olivia.

Despite being of two different tribes the young Dweller had quickly grown fond of Ch'Teka and vice versa. The sight of the injured child was devastating for her. Climbing down from the beast's body, Olivia's gaze briefly caught the look of both astonishment and envy on Paige's face before she storms off.

My sibling wasn't sure of what to do with herself after this as her senses felt overloaded and her mind felt foggy. Despite only joining the battle briefly at its conclusion, Olivia felt as though she had faced the dreaded avian alone. Gareth smiled and helped her steady herself.

"G-Gareth, this feeling... this rush..."

"I know, lass. I know. You'll grow accustomed to it in time," he said with a knowing smile. "Congratulations, you're one of us now."

12

THE RESCUE

espite her initial resistance Blue-Eyes agreed to assist me in rescuing the Dweller child from the Vrothans. Thankfully it wasn't too difficult for us to find them as my guide easily discovered their trail in spite of their attempts to hide their tracks.

By the time we had located the kidnappers, night had blanketed the forest in a shroud of darkness which would serve as a perfect cover for Blue-Eyes and I. We found them gathered around a small fire nestled under a pair of large trees and bushes as they had prepared their camp for the night. We kept our distance while observing them.

"Yes, they're certainly Unblooded all right," Blue-Eyes quietly spoke as we spied on our foes. "Lower caste warriors deemed unworthy by their superiors. They aren't battle hardened and usually never become anything more than fodder due to their inadequacy. Dull-minded and lazy, they're looked down upon amongst their fellow warriors. The Vrothans send them out as scouts or as a distraction while their more competent soldiers are dispatched for more pressing objectives."

Recalling our escape from the prison, I noticed how lazy and incompetent the guards were when not being scolded by their superiors. "I'm guessing the Vrothans we faced in the prison were similar."

The masked rogue nodded. "Indeed." She carefully examined the rat troops as they ate, drank and sung off tune Vrothan melodies. Her eyes then looked towards their dweller captive who had been bound from head to toe in an effort to prevent any attempt of escaping to the trees around her. "Still, there's certainly enough of them to give us a hard time. I doubt we could simply sneak in and free the captive without being caught. One of them is bound to notice us and raise the alarm." Blue-Eyes looked towards me. "How many do you think you can pick off with your bow?" she asked me, which in response she received a stupefied expression from myself.

"Oh err I uhh...I-I don't actually..."

"You can't be serious..." Blue-Eyes leered at me and struggled to keep her voice low to refrain from alerting the Vrothans. "...you've been carrying around that bow this entire time and you don't even know how to wield it?!"

"It was on my list of things to learn, but I never reached that point!"

"Please tell me you didn't recruit me for this suicidal mission because you were expecting me to single handedly solve all of your problems."

"Of course not! How could you even suggest such a thing?" Blue-Eyes was sadly correct, much to my shame. Though I was armed I had no idea how to properly use a bow or any weapon for that matter.

In hindsight I probably should have put more effort into devising a decent plan of rescue.

"Well now what do we do? Though the Unblooded are fools they are armed fools which in most cases makes them twice as dangerous. I doubt I could defeat several rats on my own," Blue-Eyes complained. "We don't have all night either and I don't want to risk confronting them near Rotmire. Also remember that these wretches mustn't get their grubby paws on the Sagestones. I've seen what their mages are capable of doing with these stones and it's better that they remained in our care."

As Blue-Eyes spoke, I pondered what we could possibly do to solve this problem. Fighting was out of the question and would undoubtedly lead to certain death. Negotiation wouldn't work and would no doubt result in violence given who we were dealing with. The young dweller was also in a difficult position within the camp which made it far too risky for us to attempt to take a far stealthier approach.

It was then that a devious plan came to mind. One that skirted the lines between brilliance and madness. "Blue-Eyes, you mentioned that these 'Unblooded' Vrothans aren't particularly bright, correct?"

She gave me a curious look. "Aye, there's not much between their ears as I said, but unless you plan on defeating them with harsh language, I'm not sure what you have in mind."

"I believe I have a more effective plan, but it is one that will require your total support no matter how strange it may seem. "Blue Eyes was hesitant and wasn't too fond of how eager I was to use her in my madcap plan before even hearing it. "I suppose I've come this far so there is little reason to stop now. Whatever you have in mind I do hope it works. For all our sake."

"It will! Just have faith in me."

It became clear to me that we wouldn't be able to solve this dilemma through violence. I realized that if we couldn't fight them, we could instead outwit them. Moving away from the camp we began to make our preparations. Acting swiftly, I would put to use some of the rope we had brought with us as well as some of the nearby twigs and used it to construct a disguise for Blue-Eyes that would be more than enough to fool our foes. While I knew nothing of fighting, I spent many a night assisting mother with her leisure crafting that we often used to decorate our home. A talent I had no idea would be used to save someone's life this night. Lastly, I would stash away my garments and belongings while covering myself in dirt to appear distraught and desperate. Finally once Blue-Eyes was in place for our little show we'd begin our performance. I ran fearfully into their camp appearing bruised, filthy and terrified. My abrupt presence would immediately cause a ruckus among the rats as many of them were either half asleep or half drunk.

"What th-?!A mouse?!"

"An intruder!"

"A-Alarm! ALARM!"

"What's happening?!Are we under attack?!" The rats were in a frenzy as they scrambled for their weapons. "Who are you?!What are you doing' here?!"One of the rats would approach me with a sword drawn. Just by looking at him it was obvious he was the captain and appeared to be far more seasoned than the other soldiers though he too seemed to be a bit tipsy. I wasted no time in weaving my tale. "Please you have to help me!" I begged the rat as I dropped to my knees. "I-It's after me! It killed my whole family and won't leave me be!" My terrified appearance baffled the captain and seemed to unnerve his subordinates. This worked to my favor as the captain had yet to consider if he should kill me yet. "What are you blabbering about, mouse? What's after you?"

"I-It's some sort of bird! A massive monster larger than life itself! "I cried out with tears in my eyes. "The Monstrous.... the Vile....the D-Dreaded...Dreaded....err...uhm... "Suddenly I began to truly panic as I had neglected to give my fictitious monster a name.

"Dreadwing?"

"Y-Yes! Dreadwing! Dreadwing is coming! RUN FOR YOUR LIVES!" Thankfully one of the fearful rat warriors would give me just the name I would use to instill terror among them. Already murmurs and panic would be heard amongst the soldiers as they seemed unsure of what to do.

"What do we do? We've never fought a beast before!"

"We've never fought anyone before!"

"I think my friend's cousin's brother was eaten by a Dreadwing..."

"I've heard that monster has the wingspan the size of a mountain!"

"A wretched beast with tattered wings, a crooked beak and an ear piercing shriek."

"It'd be impossible for us to slay such a beast!"

"Silence! All of you! "The captain shouted angrily though he too seemed a bit uncertain of the current situation. All that needed to be done was place the idea and fear of a terrifying monster in their minds then allow the intoxicated lay-abouts to do the rest of the work. "Imbeciles! There is no "Dreadwing"! This is obviously some sort of trick! I-It must be!" The captain was trying his hardest to maintain control of his subordinates while also attempting to poorly mask his own growing anxieties. Admittedly it was nice to see the thuggish rats being fearful for a change after all the suffering they caused both me and Blue-Eyes. Still, I knew that if we were going to pull this off they needed to see the "beast" itself.

"Wait! Quiet! Do you hear it?" I rose to my feet and looked around with a terrified look about me. "I-It's coming! We're doomed!!RUN FOR YOUR LIVES!"I shouted which served as the signal for the "monstrous creature" to strike! "L-Look! Up there!" One of the guards fearfully pointed above them as the shadow of a flying creature swooped down from above! The squad of Unblooded were terrified at the sight of the strange "creature" and the camp erupted into full blown panic!

"Run for your lives!"

"Every rat for himself!"

"Not me! Please not me! Eat them, not me!"

"What are you idiots doing?!Form ranks! Get a hold of yourselves! FIGHT DAMN YOU!" The captain tried to bring his troops under control but the sight of the "monster" swooping at them again and again was too much for them to handle.

They fled into the forest in random directions in hopes of evading the vile Dreadwing!

"Where are you going?!Come back here and fight you... y-you..."

For the briefest moment the rat captain caught sight of the beast and proceeded to let out the most feminine shrill I've ever heard! Like his subordinates he fled into the darkness of the forest! Clutching my chest, I let out a sigh of relief.

"Thank the Father. It actually worked."

Once I was certain that the rats had dispersed, I dusted myself off and immediately went over to check on the Vrothan's captive near the campfire. The dweller had fallen unconscious, no doubt weary from her travels, but I knew she couldn't rest any longer.

"Wake up friend! We need to get out of here!" The young dweller slowly opened her eyes only to be startled by the sight of me. "Don't be afraid. I'm here to free you," I said while attempting to cut through his bindings with an abandoned knife I saw on the ground.

"Krrrchrk?" the child chirped.

"Pardon me?" The girl's strange dialect was unfamiliar to me. Never had I heard anyone speak in such a manner until then.

"Krrchrk?" she repeated as he looked at me curiously.

"I-I'm sorry I don't understand," I replied.

"She's asking for your name, Tybalt," Blue-Eyes said.

At that moment I recalled that I had forgotten to check on my *beastly* guide. The rogue now dangled helplessly above of the camp while wearing a hastily crafted set of leaf wings and a makeshift wooden mask shaped similar to that of a bird of prey.

"As amusing as all of this has been I would like to be let down."

"Oh! My apologies, Blue-Eyes. Give me a moment..."

After helping both Blue-Eyes and the captive Dweller, we three pilfered what useful supplies the rats had in their possession before fleeing. With Blue-Eyes acting as a translator, we learned that our new friend was named Vi'Hra and had left her village to search for herbs and berries to help tend to her ailing sibling. We offered to help her return home, but she refused and seemed confident that she could find her way home safely without being captured again. Instead, she sought to return her gratitude by revealing a hideaway that her people would use during foraging trips that had been hidden at the base of a tree and covered with a large bush in front of it. Once we said our farewells and parted ways we began to settle in for the night with unusually high spirits.

"This place appears secure enough..." the rogue said as she placed her belongings as well as the things she had pilfered from the Vrothans' camp against the walls of our wooden shelter.”...I wasn't expecting Vi'Hra to be so generous. The Dwellers are often quite secretive with their little hideaways. ”Dirt and twigs still clung to my fur much to my dismay.

As I attempted to remove what I could I replied, “My Mother would always say that one good deed deserves another. The kindness Vi'Hra has shown us this night is merely an example of that belief in action.”

Never had I felt so sorely in need of a proper bath though that was just an inevitable fate of those seeking to travel the forest. Nevertheless, I attempted to make myself comfortable in our temporary shelter.

“I must say, I wasn't expecting your little plan to work,” The rogue said. “I expected those louts to draw their blades and attempt to strike you down the moment they laid eyes on you.” Though the rogue's bluntness perturbed me I could at least respect her honesty. “However, I admit I was wrong and I had the honor of frightening several spineless rats as a result. It was.... fun.” Blue-Eyes gave me an approving smile. “Well done, Tybalt. Well done indeed.”

Something about the masked rogue's compliment would cause my heart to flutter while I fought off the urge to grin from her approval. My words clumsily fell from my mouth before I immediately took time to calm myself down and speak in a more coherent manner.

“Ah y-yes well... I'm glad you enjoyed yourself though it would likely be for the best that we do not make a habit of these sort of schemes as I highly doubt it will work a second time.”

She nodded in agreement before turning her attention towards a small stack of papers she had taken from the ratkin's camp. “Rest well, Tybalt. We won't be reaching the mire for a few more days. Though we won't be entering it entirely we'll need our strength for the journey ahead,” Blue-Eyes warned to which I nodded in agreement and chose a comfortable spot to rest my weary body for the night.

With a yawn, I bid her a good night before drifting off to sleep. Given all the hardship we had endured a well-deserved rest was sorely needed. At dawn, Blue-Eyes and myself continued to travel eastward now with us both fully focused on our goal. Much to my surprise traversing the forest began to feel more natural to me as my paws and feet didn't ache to the same intensity as they did when I first began traveling. I was even able to keep pace with the nimble rogue as we darted through the grass to evade the hungry gaze of prowling monsters.

Blue-Eyes also seemed more receptive towards my presence as well when originally, I appeared to be little more than a burden to her. Finally Blue-Eyes had stopped treating me as an objective for her to complete and more as a companion. She still remained her usual reserved self but seemed more willing to speak with me and even take my opinion on certain matters.

Slowly I begin to tell her more about myself and my quest to save my sister to which Blue-Eyes had quietly grown more curious of. The masked mouse would even take time to teach me how to properly use the bow to an extent. I had many questions for the rogue, but I figured it would be better if I respected her privacy and hoped that with time, she would open up to me.

For awhile, I found myself in much higher spirits, but this wasn't meant to last. As we drew closer to the mire, I immediately took notice of the concerning changes to my surroundings. The lovely autumn foliage that I had grown accustomed to seeing appeared to wilt and turn a sickly grayish color the closer we came to the mire.

A growing silence filled the air as we could no longer hear the chirping of birds around us or for that matter any other animal present in our surroundings. The sky grew darker even during broad daylight and an ill wind blew through this part of the woods where once a cool autumn breeze filled the air. Probably what troubled me the most was how Blue-Eyes was reacting to all of this.

Where once the rogue walked with unshakable purpose and confidence, she now appeared fearful with her paw never far from the hilt of her weapon. It was as if she were anticipating something to attack us at any moment. Quite often my companion needed to rest and distanced herself.

Whenever I offered aid, she merely refused it before moving forward. Something about this place was affecting Blue-Eyes in a manner that I couldn't fully comprehend and seeing her in such a sorry state left me feeling uneasy. She no longer seemed interested in casually conversing with me and only spoke when necessary. Her condition only seemed to worsen at night as she struggled to fall asleep.

I began to wonder what exactly was Rotmire and why did such a horrid place exist in the Hallowed Forest? At the time I was only comforted by the thought that we wouldn't be truly entering the mire and braving whatever horrors lay within. As our journey seemingly came close to its end Blue Eyes would thankfully catch her second wind.

She sprinted further into the murky mire forcing me to give chase unless I wished to be lost on the very edge of Rotmire. Staring into its vile murk was not unlike staring into the mouth of a ravenous beast waiting for us to step into its mouth.

"B-Blue-Eyes? Blue-Eyes please slow down!" I called out to her as I pursued her as fast as I could while just barely being able to make out the sight of her tail and cloak through the fog.

She didn't seem to hear me or seemingly ignored me and kept up her pace. She'd eventually lead me up a large hill where the grass and other plant life appeared unusually healthy than what we had seen on our way here. Rows of large stone pillars with familiar arcane markings carved into them created a pathway up the hill for us to follow.

"At long last, we've arrived!" she exclaimed and finally took time to rest and collect herself. Blue-Eyes seemed uncharacteristically overjoyed by this as she fell to her knees in front of some peculiar stones at the top of the hill. "This nightmare can finally end!"

"Then perhaps you can now explain to me what is going on with you," I said after finally catching up with Blue-Eyes. "You've been behaving very strangely ever since we first entered this part of the forest."

"There's no time to waste. The way must be opened," she replied as she rises to her feet. "Tybalt, give me one of the Sagestones," she ordered and made no attempt to hide the urgency in her voice. "Quickly now! The sooner we get to Alden the better for the both of us."

Reaching into the pouch I was given by Willow I'd retrieve one of the sacred stones and handed it to Blue-Eyes who immediately snatched it away.

"We'll be out of here soon enough."

I wasn't sure where exactly Blue-Eyes had in mind as there was no visible way this hill led anywhere but over a cliff. I was about to question if this was truly the correct way to reach Alden until I took notice of the ground below my feet.

More of the arcane symbols had been etched into the grass and dirt and a large circle of stones sat in the very center of the hill, each bearing the same markings on the ground as well as the ones on the pillars we passed on the way up the hill.

Blue-Eyes had walked towards the very top of the circle and had inserted the sagestone into a slot that was intended to hold it. "To me, Tybalt!"

Though slightly confused I'd join my companion in the center of the circle. "I'm not sure I understand what's happening. Is this the right place?"

After making sure she had properly inserted the Sagestone, Blue-Eyes turned back to me and said, "It is. This is a waygate constructed by the Sages."

Feeling safer and appearing assured that this was the end of our journey her demeanor seemingly returned to what it was before we entered the mire. "It's some sort of magic device that can teleport you from one place to another. This is how I was originally able to enter Alden's home though this time we have proper permission to do so. Any moment now we'll be on our way..."

Just then the inserted Sagestone began to glow brightly, illuminating the area as both its light and power began to spread to the other stones in the circle before spreading to the rows of stone pillars down the hill. A soft hum could be heard from them that grew louder the longer the Waygate remained active.

"Brace yourself, Tybalt. This may feel a bit strange," Blue-Eyes warned me.

Readying myself for whatever was to come next, I closed my eyes and expected to be magically transported from the vile mire to the home of the enigmatic Alden. Right as the waygate appeared to have become fully powered however, the lights as well as the magic within them dissipated and returned to its dormant state once again.

The unusual humming noise the stones were emitting had fallen silent and as I slowly opened one of my eyes, I could see that nothing had happened, and we were still in the mire.

"I-It didn't work?" Confused, I turned towards Blue-Eyes for answers, but she seemed just as baffled as me.

"This doesn't make any sense." She looked back towards the Sagestone she had used as a power source and saw that the magic within it had also fallen silent. Blue-Eyes then removes it and idly tosses it aside. "Give me another! Now!" the aggravated rogue said to which I immediately retrieved another stone and handed it to her.

Same as before the stones around us responded to the power of the Sagestone only briefly before once again falling silent.

It was obvious something was wrong with the waygate, but Blue-Eyes refused to accept this. "Another NOW!" she commanded.

"But Blue-Eyes—"

"ANOTHER!" She shouted angrily while casting a threatening glance if I were to question her again.

Not wanting to incur her wrath any further, I did as she asked, but the result remained the same. I could see my companion begin to panic once again as the realization of our situation became evident.

If the waygate wasn't operational then we had only two choices: to begin the long journey back to Treefall to speak with Willow or to brave the dangers of Rotmire to find Alden's home. No doubt Blue-Eyes understood this and liked neither option.

"No, no, no! Why won't it work? Why is this happening to us?" Frustrated, Blue-Eyes slammed her fist into the dirt.

While admittedly afraid of my troubled companion lashing out at me I swallowed my fear and spoke my mind. "If we can't use the Waygate then we must enter the mire ourselves."

Blue-Eyes rose to her feet and didn't even bother to look back at me as she replied, "You know not what you say, this is one of the most dangerous places in the forest. I have no idea what we will face in there if we entered apart from death itself. We're returning to Treefall to speak with Willow. Surely, she has something else in mind."

Blue-Eyes had already made her decision. I didn't need to be a seasoned explorer to tell that Rotmire was a dangerous place. Of course, I was frightened of what horrors we would encounter, but each moment wasted only harmed my chances of finding my sister and stopping her foolhardy quest to slay Blackfang.

If I needed to do this alone I would, I couldn't afford to waste time. "I-If you wish to leave...then go and do so. I have to find Alden and if I must traverse this cursed ground to do so then so be it."

"You're mad!" she exclaimed while finally turning her troubled sights towards me. "If I don't stand a chance against the horrors that lurk within that place then what chance could you possibly have?"

There was no denying that Blue-Eyes was right about the possible dangers of the mire and a small part of me did wish to be rid of this place, but I had come too far to back out now. If Alden had the answers to my problems I couldn't risk turning away.

"Then what do you suggest we do, Blue-Eyes? Returning to Treefall would be a waste of time. I must save my sister and if that means going into the very heart of Rotmire then so be it."

Already I began to walk back down the hill after retrieving the discarded Sagestones. While Blue-Eyes seemingly had already made up her mind so had I. For a time she remained silent as she watched me once again to foolishly walk towards danger. She appeared to be in shock that her timid charge had chosen to defy her once more.

Rage began to build within her as she rose to her feet and stomped after me, only to turn me around to send her fist straight into my stomach. "Idiot!"

"Hrrk!" The blow forced air out of me as I fell to my knees before the angry rogue.

I had hoped she would respect my decision especially after the goodwill we had built between us during our travels, but it seemed as though being in proximity of Rotmire had left the usually calm and collected mouse in an emotionally unstable state.

She grabbed me by my shirt and glared at me. "Will you stop and think for a second, Tybalt?!" Blue-Eyes shouted. "Come to your senses, fool! This isn't like that ridiculous trick we pulled on the Vrothans. The mire will be the death of us both if we take a single step inside of it! You're recklessly throwing your life away for what? Some siblings who threatened to kill you if you came after her? Is this danger truly worth risking your life?"

Though her words were spoken with anger I could see the fear in her eyes. Not just for her own sake, but for mine as well.

After letting out a hacking cough and sucking air back into my lungs I answered my question with a definitive, "Yes, yes it is."

She seemed confused by this, but I continued to speak regardless.

"I failed her, Blue-Eyes. I failed my family. When Blackfang struck I was helpless to do anything against it and as a result I lost everything that I ever loved. Not a single night goes by that I don't think of them and what I might've done that could've saved even one of their lives. Now the last of my kin rushes off on a reckless quest for vengeance and will soon join the rest of our loved ones in death." As I spoke from my heart, memories of those I had lost gripped me. Tears began to swell in my eyes and my voice cracked with emotion. "If anyone should've died that night, it should've been me! I would've gladly perished in the stead of my mother or siblings, but alas I still draw breath. I have to live with this guilt, and it eats at me despite my best attempts to hide it."

Blue-Eyes loosened her grip on me and remained oddly silent as she listened.

"Olivia and I haven't always seen eye to eye, but we are kin nevertheless. Nothing, not monsters, nor Vrothans and certainly not some festering swamp will keep me from making sure she's safe!" Wiping the tears from my eyes, I recollected my belongings and dusted myself off. "I will not force you to join me, but understand that I will do this regardless of what you think, Blue-Eyes. The rogue and I stood in uncomfortable silence for a time before she lowered her head in a shameful fashion.

"I'm sorry," she said. "There is something about this place. It's affecting me in ways you can't understand. We haven't even fully entered the mire and I feel it's tainted power baring down on me." This I already knew from how different Blue-Eyes had been behaving the closer we came to Rotmire, but still had no answer as to why.

"Please, Blue-Eyes. Tell me what is troubling you. There must be something, anything that I can do t—"

She dismissively shakes her head in response. "My affliction is something you could never fix." She then turns away from me, her sights now set on the mire. Even from the hilltop our eyes couldn't penetrate the unnatural gloom clouding the area. "We both need to go and brave it's dangers. I know this. For your sister and for my freedom...but I'm not sure I am strong enough to do this." She wrapped her arms around herself and to my surprise I could see the rogue trembling. "I...I can't do this." Seeing the mouse who had been guiding and protecting me, albeit reluctantly, since our initial encounter at the Vrothan's garrison now appeared meek and feeble. It was an unnerving sight and weakened my own resolve in the process. Still, my mind was already set, and I intended to commit to it. "You must, Blue-Eyes. You'll never be free if you don't. "Looking to encourage my companion, I approached her from behind and placed my palm on her shoulder. "I'm not ignoring the fact that this won't be easy, but I believe we can overcome this. We've come this far together and now stand at the precipice of our goals. Please, friend. Don't let all that we've endured to reach this point be in vain." Blue-Eyes didn't respond at first and I feared as though my words had all fallen on deaf ears. Then suddenly she slowly rose to her feet and gave me a weary but determined expression. "We're so close..."She'd say.".....we'll keep going. Alden can help us...he must." With an encouraging smile I'd nod at her and we'd both begin to make our way down the hill. We'd return to the path we were following before, the path that would lead us into Rotmire. Blue-Eyes wasted no time in drawing her sword, knowing full well that we would likely encounter some sort of danger though she knew not what that might be. "Let's go, Tybalt. Quickly, while I still have the strength."

Making use of one of the torches we "liberated" from the Vrothans I'd ignite it and use it to light our path as we moved further into the darkness of the mire. "I am ready when you are. " With that said we began to enter the mire though scared and uncertain we wouldn't allow our fears to take hold of us, not with victory so close we could grasp it in our paws. Whatever dangers we would face in this godforsaken part of the forest, we would face it together.

13

THE MIRE

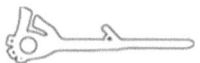

By now one might assume that given all that I have endured since the night Blackfang had attacked my secluded home that I had seen the worst of my journey. Admittedly I too had chosen to deceive myself with this wishful thinking only to be shown the truth of my reality as Blue-Eyes and I took our first steps into Rotmire.

From the moment we entered, a nearly overwhelming sense of dread fell over us as we knew the land, we were entering would be far more perilous than anything we had faced thus far. There was no need for you to be a world weary traveler to tell that the place we were traversing was dangerous. The mire was a festering, fetid swamp cloaked in an eerie black mist that even when fully entering the mire remained difficult to see through. Even with the torch I was carrying we struggled to pierce the unnatural murk of the mire.

What little we could see were the infected flora around us which appeared to be in even far worse condition than what we had seen previously on our approach into the mire. The trees shrubbery and even the ground beneath our feet were being strangled by red vines that tightly clung to them. I had seen nothing akin to them since the start of my journey and neither had Blue-Eyes who had seen far more of the Hallowed Forest than I had.

The ground itself was uncomfortably moist and the air had a bitter taste to it while bereft of the cool, fresh autumn breeze that I had grown accustomed to. Though there were plenty of bodies of water seen within the mire most of if not all appeared to be unsanitary and unsafe to drink from. We also weren't alone in this twisted reflection of our forest home.

Just as Willow had mentioned, bizarre and disturbing creatures lurked within this foul domain of rot. From large lumbering beasts slowly navigating the swampy waters to smaller creatures that matched the size of a fellow mouse, rat and even dwellers could be seen slowly shambling in the distance.

Wherever these creatures lingered we made sure to keep our distance with Blue-Eyes often demanding that I douse the torch to avoid their detection. As much as I detested the mist cloaking this forsaken part of the forest there was no denying that it played a pivotal role in masking our presence as long as we didn't draw too close to the "denizens" of the mire. It was as if the vile Wyther from the mire had seeped into every aspect of this part of the forest.

The air, the plants, the water and even those who called this cursed place home. Nothing was exempt from its touch, and no one was safe. As we traversed the swamp in search of any signifier of where Alden might be there was very little said between myself and Blue-Eyes as our focus remained on our surroundings. Not only were we wary of any sign of potential threats or other hazards but Blue-Eyes was still grappling with an unknown affliction that she refused to speak of.

Often, we needed to find cover in the mire's foliage for her to rest, but soon even that wouldn't be enough to ease her pain.

"Blue-Eyes..." I said to her, breaking the long silence between us. "...we can't continue like this. We must find shelter."

The stubborn rogue shook her head. "No, we keep going. W-We must..." The sickly mouse fell to her knees and dropped her sword.

Without hesitation I rushed to her aid to help her back on her feet.

"...we can't stop now..." Her voice lacked the commanding strength it once had and from her appearance alone I doubted that she would be able to protect us both if we were to be attacked.

"No! This can't continue, you're in no condition to travel." It was clear that I would have to take control of the situation with Blue-Eyes being in such a weakened state.

Peering around my surroundings I had hoped to find some place that could serve as a temporary shelter for the night, but my eyes could see little with the mist obscuring my vision which seemed to have thickened the deeper we went into the mire.

Initially I was about to suggest we hide ourselves in the nearest bush only for me to just barely see what appeared to be a small, short and hollowed out log that was covered in the same strangling red vines I had seen everywhere else.

Though I feared potentially coming in contact with some ghastly horror I was more afraid of Blue-Eyes losing her life should her condition go untended. With haste I would place my companion's arm over my shoulder and pulled her blade from the dirt. We then hobbled over towards the log with me praying that our shelter wasn't occupied by another.

Thankfully our weathered shelter was seemingly vacant though given its decrepit state it wasn't surprising as to why. At the very end of the log, I could see an opening on the other side which also showed no sign of another traveler or wayward creature being present.

For the moment this would be as safe as it could possibly be for us, and I immediately took the opportunity to carefully set Blue-Eyes down against the inner bark as well as our other belongings before shifting my full attention towards tending to the rogue.

"W-Why are we stopping?" she muttered weakly and seemed to be struggling to breathe. "We can't stop, we...we have to get out of here." Blue-Eyes tried to stand to her feet, but she lacked the strength to do so.

Taking a moment to see the full extent of her condition I realized that she was suffering from a terrible fever with a worryingly high temperature, chills and aching muscles only worsened by heavy sweating. Whatever was causing this affliction had sapped her strength almost entirely and threatened to consume her life.

While I recalled a remedy in the form of a meal Mother would make involving Brightleaf I lacked all the necessary ingredients to create it. Instead, I searched my belongings for the last few drops of clean drinking water we had along with the last of the Brightleaf, hoping that eating the prime ingredient raw would aid my friend.

"Here, please eat and drink this. It should help..."

Being in no shape to fight me on this Blue-Eyes consumed what was given to her before closing her eyes to finally rest. Though I let out a sigh of relief as Blue-Eyes finally began to rest the reality of our current situation began to plague my mind.

In her condition, Blue-Eyes was in no shape to defend us or herself and I lacked both the knowledge as well as the medical supplies to cure what ailed her. It certainly wasn't helped by the fact that we were hopelessly lost in the mire with no visible way back from where we first entered.

Not only that but we hadn't a single inkling as to where the Great Sage had made his home. Even if my guide was in a healthier state Blue-Eyes had never entered Rotmire until now and knew nothing about traversing it and its treacherous terrain. I couldn't help but blame myself for our predicament as it was I who convinced Blue-Eyes to brave through the horrors of the mire after all. It was naive of me to believe that we could simply weather the dangers of Rotmire and hope for the best.

"I've doomed us both..." The words left my lips in the form of a pitiful murmur. For all my chastising of the recklessness of my sister I couldn't deny that I had made the same mistake. "...it can't end like this. We've come too far to fail now."

I took a seat beside my ailing companion, struggling to think of something to solve our predicament while dreading what would become of us if I failed to do so. For what felt like hours I sat and thought about my options and because of the unnatural gloom of the mire I couldn't tell whether it was night or day.

Over time my own exhaustion began to eat at me, causing my body to crave sleep after braving the dangers of the mire. For a moment I was close to surrendering to it until something caught my eye. At the other end of the log, I caught a glimpse of a floating light that immediately drifted away as soon as my sights turned towards it.

"What was that?" I muttered. "Blue-Eyes, did you see—"

My words fell on deaf ears as Blue-Eyes was deep in her sleep and given how much she was suffering I saw little reason to wake her up. At this point my curiosity got the better of me and I decided to investigate the strange sight on my own.

"I'll be back. Rest well..." I said, despite knowing she wouldn't hear me.

Beginning to make my way to the other side of the log, I briefly paused as I heard what I could only describe as an uncomfortable skittering noise above me, but as I turned my sights towards the top of the log, I saw nothing but darkness due to the lack of light as we had used the last of our torches already.

"Must be imagining things."

Ignoring whatever I thought I heard I continued onward to the other side of the log. Cautiously peering out of it I looked to see if I could spot the strange light I had seen before.

"How could something so bright ever exist in such a gloomy place?" I wondered.

At first, I saw nothing and began to believe that it was my imagination attempting to distract me from the dangers around me, but then I saw it again. The light was lazily drifting further into the mire's mists...

"At least I'm not losing my mind, but what on earth is it?"

Once more my curiosity had gotten the better of me and after making certain that there weren't any of those horrid creatures present, I would pursue the strange light. It wasn't long afterwards that I would see the wandering light again, only to discover that it had led me into a very grim location.

"Goodness, what is this place?"

At that moment I stood at the very entrance of what appeared to be a village or what remained of it. This location had long been abandoned and not a single soul could be seen. The entire village had fallen to ruins and was now in the tainted grasp of Rotmire.

"A village in the mire? What madmice would settle in this cursed land?"

Taking a step further inside my foot unknowingly brushed against something causing me to step back and look down at what it was. It appeared to be a waterlogged wooden sign with the faded text "WELLSPRING" barely visible to me.

"Was that the name of this place?"

Chills ran down my spine as the very thought of what might've become of the town's former residence. Despite this I fought the growing urge to flee from this place and slowly began to make my way into the empty village. There was no ignoring the eeriness of this location as abandoned homes and shops could be seen all around me.

I recalled Willow mentioning that the Wyther had only taken hold in the recent years which meant that this town if not the entirety of Rotmire wasn't always like this. Perhaps if things had been different Wellspring would've served as a welcoming respite for two weary travelers such as myself and Blue-Eyes. I couldn't help but imagine the two of us resting in the town's collapsed tavern, relaxing and enjoying each other's company.

The very thought of this potential occurrence never happening saddened me, but I knew I couldn't afford to allow this to slow me down. At first I was prepared to turn away and return to Blue-Eyes as I saw no sign of the light that I was pursuing or anyone present within Wellspring, but a thought did cross my mind.

"What if there's something of use to us of here? Medicine and food perhaps?"

Though it felt a tad disrespectful to loot this fallen village like a scavenger, we were in a dire situation, and I could only imagine Blue-Eyes agreeing with this idea given the circumstances.

With haste, I scoured the town's few standing structures for anything that might be useful. Each home and shop I entered seemed to paint a sad tale of what the residence of this fallen village were like before disaster struck.

One was the home of an avid writer, one who sought to spread their tales across the forest only for some terrible calamity to leave this poor soul's dreams unfulfilled. Now only a few scattered notes and torn illegible remains of their writings are left. Another appeared to be a long abandoned smithy, it's anvils no longer sung with the sound of hammer striking steel while its fires had long since died.

The once finely crafted armaments as well as other forms of metal craft that lined the walls had rusted save for a single short blade that I decided to take for myself. There was little point in leaving it to decay with the rest of it. Many of these homes had been reduced to shambles but to my surprise one of the remaining houses shared a faint resemblance to our own as it too was carved from a stump while the other homes were constructed with stone.

What lay within showed me that its denizens had a love for cooking and would've certainly gotten along well with Mother. Still this location was also abandoned and from the look of it whoever called it home had made a hasty attempt to depart. Ingredients had been laid out as if in preparation for a meal including foul spoiled fruit that was left on a cutting board.

Most of the food I found had long since spoiled and were unsafe for consumption and what medicinal concoctions there were appeared to have expired from what I could tell of the foul shade of color they had taken that seemed to be similar to that of Wyther. This was a bit of a disappointment but not unexpected given the state of the village.

Thankfully I was able to locate a few untainted scraps of food and even a barrel of what was likely the only clean water that I had seen since entering the mire. "This isn't much but at least it's something I suppose."

Once more I began to prepare myself to depart but then an idea came to mind. I recalled seeing an old pot and firewood in one of the abandoned homes. "Perhaps I can make a hearty soup for Blue-Eyes," I thought. "That should surely help her regain some of her strength."

The more I considered this idea the more tempting it sounded. Making my decision to stay and prepare a meal I would return to the house where I initially found the old iron pot. After giving it a thorough cleaning to the best of my ability I began to prepare one of my favorite meals, wild nut soup.

Though it was lacking a few ingredients, namely the last of my Brightleaf I had given to Blue-Eyes earlier, I made do with what little I found. "It won't be as good as Mother's but I'm sure Blue-Eyes will enjoy it all the same."

Lighting the kindling underneath the pot would illuminate the abandoned home and gave it a comfortable glow that was sorely needed. With great care I began to prepare the soup, but as I did my mind began to recall past memories of myself and Mother cooking.

"Careful with the spice," she'd always said. "Too much and you'll overload the broth with that flavor." Mother valued careful precision and that value would be passed on to her children as well.

Preparing this meal would only stand to make me miss her more and long for the days when the most troubling thing I had to worry about were my chores. Never in my lifetime did I believe I would end up in a situation like this, so far from home and in search of my last surviving sibling. Having endured so much hardship and danger all I could wonder was how did this become my new life?

My body was experiencing a level of exhaustion that it had never endured before and my well kempt appearance in regard to my clothing and fur had long been tarnished by my travels while only worsening in the filth of the mire. Scurrying from one danger to the next in what was beginning to feel like a fruitless chase to find Olivia?

"What if I never find her?" I fearfully thought. "What if I'm too late? Goodness, what has become of my life?"

No visions had invaded my dreams since I embarked on this journey and while it made my sleep more peaceful it did make me feel that I had already failed to save her.

"N-No, I mustn't give up hope. I've come so far...Alden, he will help us. He must."

Though still frustrated with my situation, it wouldn't impede the process of finishing the soup. I taste tested it myself and was satisfied with how it turned out in the end.

"It'll never be as good as hers, but I pray that it helps."

Seizing a bowl from the cupboard I would fill it with the wild nut soup and began to prepare it for a brief travel. My plan was to bring the soup to Blue-Eyes and feed it to her to help the ailing rogue regain some of her strength. Then I would help move both her and our belongings into Wellspring and take shelter to here as it seemed to be a more suitable place for us to rest given that it was abandoned. What would become of us after that I still wasn't sure yet, but at least it would be a start.

All of this planning would be for not in the end as a sharp screech would pierce the air causing me to pause. "W-What was..." My heart began to race as a horrifying realization came to me. "...Blue-Eyes!"

Abandoning the disheveled house, I rushed out of the town and back towards the log that we were using as shelter. With haste I made my way towards the far side of the log where I had left my companion to rest.

"Get back!" she shouted in desperation.

"I'm coming Blue-Eyes! Hold on!" I called out to her in hopes of reassuring her that help was on the way.

Drawing closer to the log revealed a terrifying sight as a large insect-like creature with a multitude of legs snapped and lashed its sharp appendages at my weakened friend. Immediately I recalled Blue-Eyes describing these creatures to me in the past though I had hoped that I would never encounter a spider in my entire life.

Blue-Eyes was in no condition to fight, and it showed as she desperately swung her blade in a reckless fashion as opposed her more focused swordplay.

"You stay away from her!" Without wasting another moment, I drew my bow and pulled an arrow from my quiver. With what little practice I had I would use it to take aim and attempt to attack the beast from behind. "Over here!"

The beast ignored my attempts to get its attention and instead focused on knocking my enfeebled friend to the dirt.

"I said leave her alone!"

Despite my unsteadied aim my arrow found its target and sunk into the thorax of my enemy. It cried out in pain and briefly halted its advance towards my downed comrade.

"I...I hit it?"

For a brief moment I relished the fact that my training appeared to have paid off, but then the rotting beast turned its sights towards me and let out an enraged screech. The terrifying visage of the red spider was that of a twisted monster with its multitude of glowing eyes and two sets of jaws dripping with venomous saliva would cause me to pause with fear.

"Oh dear..."

It then dawned on me that I hadn't exactly planned for what would happen next once I got the creature's attention. The best idea that I had in mind at the time was to lead the beast away from Blue-Eyes but that wouldn't be the case. Instead of pursuing me for attacking it, the twisted beast twitched and quivered in a disturbing fashion until three small forms crawled out of its orifices. They appeared to be the monster's corrupted offspring which were no doubt eager to consume whatever their mother had decided would serve as their next meal.

In this case, that meal would be me. Skittering off their mother's body they began to make their way towards me!

"S-Stay away!"

At first, I thought to nock back another arrow and take aim for the head of the beast itself, but the rapid approach of her hungry children would have me alter my aim! Though it was smaller than I was, much like their mother, they appeared just as ravenous than her if not more so given their young age.

Once more I fire a shot and in spite of my fear, I would manage to land another, this time killing one of the spider's skittering spawns. It led out a pitiful "Screep!" as the arrow sunk through its body and pinned it to the ground. Though, despite slaying one, two more continued their advance and had taken advantage of the opening I had made.

Acting quickly, I batted away one of them with the bow alone, but I still sought to ready another shot before it could strike again. This opportunity never came as before I could retrieve another arrow from the quiver the spiderling lunged at me! Desperately I used my bow to block its sharpened fangs.

While small its bite was powerful and much to my horror it was strong enough to bite through the bark of the bow, splitting it in half!

"NO!" I cried out as one of the last effects belonging to my deceased Mother was reduced to splinters.

The spiderling that had destroyed it was struggling to spit out the splinters from its maw while the other surviving spider spawn had recovered and once began to skitter towards me in search of its next meal. Losing Mother's bow felt like a blow aimed at my very soul.

Though I was no master archer it went without saying that it was a treasured piece of Mother's past, one that I wouldn't be alive without it. In a way it felt as though I had lost her all over again, once more being just as weak and powerless.

Rage, like never before, swelled within me as tears trickled down my cheek. I would wield the shortsword I had found in Wellspring and with a vengeful cry swung the metal down on top of the spiderling that was charging towards me.

With my rage still not sated I struck the corpse of the young spider again and again before directing my fury towards the spiderling still spewing what remained of the bow out of its mouth only to now be forced to swallow steel as I drove my blade through its body. Though I knew nothing of swordplay, very little was required to dispatch such base creatures.

With my sword now coated in the blood of my defeated foes I gripped it in my paws and set to wield it against the spiderling's mother......only to see that it had already departed.

"What? Where did it go?"

Racing back towards where I initially saw the creature. Regardless of my attempts to thoroughly search the area there was no sign of where the spider had gone. It was as if it were never there to begin with.

"But it was just here. How could it—"

Finally, a terrifying realization had dawned on me as I noticed that my ailing companion was also absent.

"Oh no, Blue-Eyes? Where are you? Please come out! I-It's safe now!"

With hope in my voice, I pleaded for my companion to reveal herself, but I was only met with the distant sounds of the mire around me. My rage turned to fear as I desperately searched the area for any sign of Blue-Eyes, but to no avail. Though I considered widening my search it was suicide to wander the mire with no sense of direction. She was gone and something told me the spider had taken her during my struggle with its spawn.

Repeatedly I called out her name, pleading for any sign that she was nearby and more importantly alive but still no response was given. This realization of my latest failure drained me of my strength as I dropped my blade and crumbled to my knees.

My fear would then turn to despair, an all too familiar feeling that I suffered from after losing my family and being abandoned by my sibling. Once more, I had failed to protect those close to me, once more I was alone in some forsaken part of the forest.

"This is all my fault," I told myself. "She knew something like this would happen here, but I ignored her. Why did I ignore her?"

My memory of her giving a furious argument against the very idea of venturing through Rotmire only for me to selfishly think only of us achieving our goals instead of our own well-beings. We had overcome so many dangers and hardships together that I felt that we could brave through whatever horrors Rotmire had in store for us. Too late did I realize just how much of a fool I was and how at the time I had doomed both myself and Blue-Eyes to a terrible fate for my overconfidence and recklessness.

Ignoring the obvious dangers of the mire had cost me my friend, the last thing I had to remember my mother and my only chance of finding Olivia.

"I-It's over. I've failed..."

With no foreseeable way of locating Blue-Eyes or even escaping, I gave in further to my grief and could only imagine that it wouldn't be long before the horrors of the mire consumed me. Feeling defeated and exhausted I fully collapsed to the dirt and slowly closed my eyes.

"Nathaniel, Lucy, Carter, Olivia, Mother...please forgive me. I've tried so hard, but I can't do this anymore. I am so tired and just want to rest. I just want to see you all again. I don't want to carry this burden any longer."

Once more I believed this would be the end of me and that despite all that I had overcome it wasn't enough to succeed. This should've served as the end of my tale, but the Will had another plan for me. So lost in my own self-loathing that I neglected to notice a familiar illuminating presence hovering over me.

Turning my gaze up from the dark and tainted soil I could see the luminous creature that had lured me away from Blue-Eyes. It was some sort of moth, one that glowed with a pure light. I looked up at it in wonder and confusion as unlike before it didn't flee from me and instead flew closer. It was almost as if it wanted me to touch it.

"Its you! I thought I was imagining that-...w-what are you?" I muttered and regardless of my hesitations cautiously reached my paw upward towards the illuminated creature.

The white moth made no attempt to flee or avoid my paw as I touched its fluffy abdomen but as I did a strange sensation washed over me. The moth's presence brought with it a form of reassurance that lifted my spirits just enough to remind me of my purpose for going on this journey. It was as if for the briefest moment my mind and that of the white moth had become one.

Though it couldn't speak, it's intentions were made clear to me. The moth sought to guide me to safety to someone who could help me. Immediately, I was wary of the creature as it could easily be some form of trap meant to disguise itself as a luminous savior in this murky place. Not to mention I found it hard to believe that a strange insect could offer any sort of substantial aid.

Still, the more I thought about my situation the more I realized that I didn't have much of a choice.

"I'm still not sure if this is some sort of trick, but I'm willing to trust you..."

As the glowing moth prepared to fly off in hopes of leading me to whomever it sought to take me to, I spoke up once again.

"Wait! Before you take me, I must ask for your aid in saving my friend first," I pleaded. "I'm not sure where she is, and I fear that the longer it takes to find her the less of a chance I have to save her. Please, I can't leave her to die in this cursed place."

14

THE TREESPEAKER

Olivia and the Slayers had accomplished a great feat by slaying The Shrieker. The Dwellers would finally be able to take back their territory and regain some semblance of peace in their home. However, this victory had been soured by the one and only casualty of the battle, that being the young, injured scout Ze'Hoz. What should've been a time of celebration was now one of great concern as the group was uncertain of how the Heartroot Dwellers would react to seeing one of their young now wounded by the beast. After removing the monster's beak and eyes along with a few of its feathers to serve as proof of their kill, the Slayers returned to where the Heartwood's village was located to reveal the outcome of the battle to its people, both the good and bad.

"Surely you're not thinking of telling them what occurred..." Alistair would say as he carried the grizzly remains of the slain owl's beak in his arms. "Just say that the boy suffered from a bad fall or something of the like. There's no need to go into details."

"No," Gareth answered. "There is little reason to try and deceive these people. One of their own came to harm under our watch. There is no avoiding this fact." The older rat had a tired look about him. "As leader, the responsibility falls onto me. Whatever happens I will take the full blame." Gareth had already made up his mind.

Though Alistair was relieved to not be held accountable for this incident he couldn't help but be worried about what might become of Gareth. Still, he knew better than to argue when the old hunter had already made up his mind.

Meanwhile Olivia and Paige carried the eyes of the beast, much to Olivia's dismay. She had never carried such a grisly item before and felt uneasy as it still felt as though the beast was glowering at her long after it had died.

All the while she could feel Paige glaring at her as well but for a reason she didn't know. The mouse held her tongue at least for the moment, after all that had happened a bit of silence was needed. Ch'Teka took up the rear as always but now carried the wounded Ze'Hoz in her arms. It was no secret that she had grown fond of the young scout despite her brief time with him and no doubt felt responsible for what became of him as well.

Ch'Teka did all that she could to treat his injuries and now he slept peacefully in her arms as though she were his mother. Olivia wanted to speak with Ch'Teka but after everything that had happened, she chose to give her space for now. The pack walked in continued silence as the sun finally set over the forest. They would thankfully arrive at the base of the Heartwood tree village not long after, but they would see that they were being expected.

The same guard from before, flanked by several others watched them as they approached. He stepped forward as they came near.

"We could hear the shrieks of the beast from here and judging by the trophies you carry the beast is slain?" he asked.

Gareth nodded grimly.

"The deed is done. The nest has been destroyed and its eggs demolished," he reported.

"Excellent, the Great One was right about you—"

"Wait. There is something else."

Ch'Teka stepped forward with the injured young Dweller." He fought valiantly. He still lives but has suffered greatly."

"Hmph, I see."

To Olivia's surprise the guard wasn't upset by the sight of the injured youth and simply ordered one of his fellows to take the young Dweller.

"We will take the trophies as well to show the Great Sage. They will serve as proof of your victory. We ask that you wait here until we have spoken with him."

Gareth was also unsure of what to take away from the unusual stoicism of the Red Dwellers after seeing one of their own in such a terrible state. "Very well."

With that said the Red Dwellers began to either climb up the tree themselves or returned to the lift to move Ze'Hoz and the trophies safely. As the Dwellers retreated to their home a brief silence fell over the group as they were uncertain of what would happen next.

To no one's surprise, it was Alistair who broke the silence. "I don't know about the rest of you but I dare say that went rather well," he remarked while giving the situation an approving nod. "The Dwellers have their dead bird and didn't fill us full of spears and arrows once they caught sight of Ze'Hoz. I call that a win."

Ch'Teka glared at him. "How can you be so pleased with yourself? Ze'Hoz was hurt!" she argued.

Alistair rolled his eyes. "Let's not fool ourselves here. Ze'Hoz knew the risk of joining us and had many an opportunity to leave. What happened to him was unfortunate but at least he gets to live another day. Tail or no tail," the rat said with a shrug.

"No! I—We should've done more," Ch'Teka argued, though deep down she knew Alistair wasn't wrong. Alistair frowned. "Come now, Ch'Teka. You don't seriously hold yourself accountable for what happened do you? We all fought hard for this victory—"

"Hmph. Some more than others..." Paige would add before casting her gaze towards Olivia." ...maybe if someone had done more during the battle. Ze'Hoz might've ended up in better shape."

It didn't take long for Olivia to speak up and defend herself. Her patience with Paige was reaching its end. "Excuse me? Are you holding me accountable for what happened to him?"

Paige folded her arms and gave my sister an incredulous expression. "Oh please, you hid in the bushes while the rest of us fought and right when you felt you could gain the most favor with the group you *heroically* emerged from your hiding place to show off your fancy glowing sword and play *hero*. All at the expense of Ze'Hoz!"

My sister wasn't afraid to speak her mind and though she had wanted to treat the slayers with respect, Olivia wouldn't tolerate being accused of such selfish actions. Now enraged by Paige's words, Olivia no longer felt the need to hold her tongue.

"The only reason I didn't participate was due to your *Sagely advice* that I shouldn't interfere in the affairs of *true* Slayers," my sister proclaimed aloud and angrily. "You're right, Paige! I should've done more during that battle, and I'll be sure to ignore anymore of your worthless drivel! Thank you very much!"

Olivia's defiance seemed to strike a nerve with Paige and at that moment it seemed as though the two were dangerously close to coming to blows with one another. Thankfully, Gareth intervened before anything of the sort occurred.

The older rat came between the two and shouted, "Enough, both of you! I don't know what this is about, but I won't tolerate infighting within my group. Our fury is to be directed at the beasts and NOT at each other!"

Though neither mouse seemed to have respect for each other they still held Gareth in high esteem. Both Olivia and Paige parted ways in a bitter fashion, with Olivia doing her best to keep herself from lashing out at the other mouse. She felt foolish for allowing the rude remarks from Paige bother her and keep her from helping the others.

An uneasy silence fell over the group after this. Olivia and Paige were still fuming at one another while keeping their distance. Gareth was lost in thought as today's events gave him much to think about and Ch'Teka appeared to be in a gloomy mood with her mind still on the injured scout. None but Alistair were willing to speak. Of course, that didn't stop him from making his voice heard.

"Ugh, this is getting awkward and increasingly dull. How long are those Dwellers going to take?" Alistair complained, much to the annoyance of Gareth, if not everyone. "I'm tired and it's growing late. I'd prefer not to dawdle out in the open."

Gareth was about to tell the archer to shut his mouth when he noticed the lift once more come to life. "It seems our wait is over. Let's hear what they have to say and be on our way," the seasoned slayer replied.

Unlike before they wouldn't be greeted by the same Dweller guard, they met earlier in the day but instead an older female Dweller wearing the garbs of some sort of priest. "Gareth Redscar, you and your companions have been given permission to enter our village. The Treespeaker wishes to see you all and properly reward you for your efforts."

Gareth was caught off guard by this as it was very rare for outsiders to be invited into the homes of Dwellers. "This is an honor, of course. One that we shall treat with respect." Gareth gave the guard an affirmative nod.

The priestess smiled. "Then please come and join me on the lift. Once we reach the top, we will immediately make our way to his chambers."

Gareth signaled for Olivia and the others to join them on the lift. While obedient, Olivia was admittedly a bit intimidated by the thought of going up so high. Still my sibling couldn't allow her fear to keep her from achieving her goals otherwise she would've never left home in the first place.

With everyone in position, the lift creaked and lightly swayed as it came to life once more. Olivia let out a small fearful gasp before feeling a reassuring paw on her shoulder.

"Easy there, lass," Gareth said. "It takes some time to get accustomed to, but it's not so bad. Especially not with that view."

Olivia, regardless of her fear, couldn't deny how stunning the forest looked as they moved higher up the tree. Even with its dangers the Hallowed Forest was a sight to behold. The lowering sun would bathe the forest in a glorious amber glow as it slowly prepared to trade places with the rising moon.

The veteran slayer gave Olivia a reassuring smile which did well to ease my sister's nerves while unknowingly drawing more ire from the envious Paige. They eventually arrived at the very top of the massive tree and were in awe at what they were seeing. The Red Dwellers had constructed an impressive home for themselves the likes that Olivia had never seen before. The Dwellers were truly at home in the trees to the point that they had crafted comfortable dwellings within its crevices.

To Olivia's confusion she noticed that none of the wood used to create their dwellings and shops had been carved or cut but instead appeared to have been magically shaped in a way that allowed the Dwellers to move about without damaging the tree. Bridges made of branches and vines connected the Heartroot Tribe's main tree to several other nearby trees, expanding their comfortable dwellings.

"Welcome to Arborhearth, mighty hunters. The Treespeaker wishes to meet you all and personally thank you for your heroism," the priestess said. "Please follow me."

There was little time for sightseeing as they were led deeper into the home of the Dwellers. They of course would attract a few onlookers who likely weren't accustomed to seeing outsiders within their homes. Thankfully their reactions only amounted to curious stares and murmuring in Chitterspeak. The Slayers were brought through the heart of the Heartroot Tribe's village and guided through a heavily guarded door.

Several Dweller warriors, all far more armed and intimidating stood firmly in front of the door, only moving once the priestess had spoken with them and signaled for the Slayers to follow inside.

"Before we enter, I must ask you all for your weapons."

This request caused a brief stir of confusion within the group, Olivia especially seemed hesitant about parting with the family sword.

"Rest assured, they will all be returned once your business is concluded with the Great One," the priestess said calmly.

Unlike the rest of the group Gareth showed no hesitation in handing over his equipment to the guards. "Do it," he commanded. "You lot can go at least a few minutes without your precious killin' tools," Gareth said with a huff. "Where we're going, we won't be needing them."

Despite the hesitation, Olivia and the Slayers would relinquish their weapons. To Olivia's surprise she felt quite vulnerable without her sword but knew that this would be for the best if it meant bringing them closer to finding Blackfang.

"Thank you but also, I should make you aware, not all of my kin are capable of speaking your tongue. This includes the Treespeaker so I shall act as a translator," the priestess said before leading them through the narrow tunnel's staircase. Olivia was growing increasingly antsy at this point; she had heard the Dweller's refer to their Treespeaker many times and in high regards. Now finally she would get a chance to meet him.

"I believe it goes without saying that I expect you lot to be on your best behavior," Gareth said much to the annoyance of Alistair.

"As if you need to say something like that at all. We're not children, Gareth."

"With you Alistair? I sometimes wonder."

Olivia was no historian but even she could tell that they were entering a part of the tree that could be described as nothing short of ancient. More of the strange markings from before could be seen scrawled on its walls with some giving off a faint glow. What Olivia hadn't realized is that what she was seeing shared similarities to what I had seen at Willow's home much earlier during my own journey. A clear sign that they were entering a place of power with deep connections to the Greater Will. Eventually they would reach the very bottom of their destination which led to a hidden chamber. "Unbelievable..."Olivia muttered as she stood in awe of the room she had entered. Vibrant plant life surrounded the room and a small but tranquil pool of glittering tree sap. It was as if she had entered the very heart of the Dweller's great tree itself!

Resting above the pools would be some sort of wooden creature. His flesh, if it could even be called that was not unlike tree bark. As he moved his body loudly creaked like a tree being blown by a strong gust of air. Olivia almost confused him for some sort of monster if not for his undeniable Dweller like appearance. He wore little save for some tattered, wholly cloth that partially wrapped around his body and the air of one who had abandoned all desire for material things. The strange Dweller was somehow capable of levitating above it and appeared to be in a meditative stance. A soft amber colored glow surrounded him as he remained in his peaceful stance only for it to fade as he sensed their approach. Detecting the Slayers' presence the elder Dweller slowly opened his eyes, revealing a similar amber glow within them."Krrchakrakrrachk!" He says, his voice was dry and raspy, but seemed to be welcoming them judging by the warm expression on his face.

After respectfully bowing to her elder, the priestess briefly speaks in their native tongue with the Treespeaker before turning back towards them. "The Great One, Treespeaker Vi'Zhan, greets you all and thanks you for slaying the monster that invaded our territory. You have done us a great service." The priestess would translate. Vi'Zhan himself bowed his head slightly in respect to the Slayers. Gareth bowed back in return. "Our duty as Slayers is to keep the forest safe from these monsters, Treespeaker. It was our pleasure. " He would say. "I only wish that Ze'Hoz didn't come to harm in the process. For that I take responsibility for what became of him." Olivia noticed Ch'Teka shift uncomfortably at the mention of Ze'Hoz, as she also blamed herself for his fate. The priestess turned to Vi'Zhan to translate to which he would give the veteran Slayer an understanding nod before speaking once more to the priestess who in then turned back to them. "The Great One asks that you not feel responsible in any way for what became of the young scout. For he foresaw that harm would come to him should he try to face the beast. He warned young Ze'Hoz of what his fate might be, but it was ignored."

"What?" Gareth exclaimed. He as well as the other Slayers were all shocked to hear this revelation and were confused as to why Ze'Hoz refused to reveal this. "He knew this would happen? Then why would he do this? Why put himself in harm's way?"

"Ze'Hoz had lost his older sister to the winged devil's mate. She was a brave warrior who slew the owl but succumbed to her injuries shortly afterwards. He grieved for her and sought vengeance though the Great one advised him otherwise. While he was choosing a scout to accompany you, Ze'Hoz deceived you and claimed to be the one chosen for this task." The Treespeaker let out a weary sigh and shook his head. He spoke briefly to which the priestess continued to translate. "Rest assured, we will do all we can to tend to his injuries but for now let us focus on your reward." Olivia could see that Ch'Teka wished to speak but held her tongue. The Treespeaker then return to his meditative stance, his peaceful aura engulfing him once more." The Great One will commune with the trees of the Hallowed Forest and gain their insight. Through the eyes of the forest, the answer you seek shall be revealed to me."

"Bah, nonsense..." Alistair quietly said, still unmoved by the very notion of "treespeaking" being a reliable way of tracking their quarry. All his remarks would gain him however would be a swift elbow to the ribs from Paige.

In the beginning they failed to see any form of progress with what the Treespeaker was trying to accomplish, but then the illuminating glow around him began to grow brighter, the very tree they were situated within reacted to his search for answers and in response softly vibrated while an otherworldly hum filled the air. It was a startling thing to experience, to say the least as none of them were uncertain of how to react.

Vi'Zhan, now filled with the power he requested from the very forces of nature itself, directed his wooded paws towards the pools beneath him which caused the sap to give off a luminescent glow. We all needed to shield our eyes from it before the light died down.

"There, the Great One has communed with the tree and it has spoken with its brethren. He now possesses the knowledge you seek." The priestess translated while gesturing towards the glowing golden pool of tree sap. "Behold, this is where that cursed creature has gone." It was as if they were witnessing a vision come to life as images of places Olivia had yet to venture to slowly became clear within the sap. They peered into the vision pools in both astonishment and curiosity. Even the doubting Alistair was left speechless.

"Your quarry has traveled further eastward."

"Eastward?" Gareth repeated with a worried expression.

"D-Does it mean to attack Gladstone?" Paige made no attempt to hide her fear of the very thought of Blackfang assaulting her home. The priestess held up her paw, hoping the slayers would calm themselves and be patient. "Be still, the pools shift once more. "The mystical tree sap continued to show new locations, but the more they watched the more concerning the situation seemed to become. From what they were shown, Blackfang had slithered its way further into inhospitable territory as the lands displayed to the Slayers became more and more dangerous. Finally, the last thing seen within the pools before the magic faded was the foul beast slithering its way deep into the bowels of Rotmire. There it disappeared from sight into what appeared to be its den which was situated within a tar pit deep in the mire. An uncomfortable silence fell over the party after the magic within the sap faded.

"I am sorry, brave hunters. It would appear that the beast you hunt has hid itself within the festering wound known as Rotmire." Olivia, still inexperienced in regard to traversing the Hallowed Forest, failed to understand why her companions now appeared uneasy. Even Gareth appeared gravely concerned with the situation. "Well then what are we waiting for? Let's hunt the beast down and end it once and for all!" Olivia then said with determination that wasn't shared with her fellows much to her confusion. "Rotmire is a cursed land that only the brave and the foolhardy dare to tread. It is filled with strange and hostile creatures as well as other dangers. "The priestess warned. "Those who have attempted to brave its dangers in search of treasure or power usually succumb to the evil of the mire. "The Treespeaker spoke once more, and the priestess would speak for him." Blackfang is a tainted creature and a mockery of nature. The Great One advises against seeking out the beast as traversing Rotmire alone could mean death for you all. Though if you still wish to continue this endeavor, he is still willing to assist you. The Treespeaker shall have proper lodging prepared for you all to rest for the night and make your final decision in the morning." Gareth respectfully bows to Vi'Zhan. "Then we'll take our leave of you. Thank you for all of your help, Treespeaker." With the Treespeaker's blessing given, Olivia and her companions were finally able to rest in more comfortable accommodations instead of sleeping in the wilderness. They would rest within one of the larger knotholes of the Red Dweller's trees, one that was furnished and reasonably cozy. However, the Slayers would find it difficult to relax after witnessing the visions of the Treespeaker. They now knew where Blackfang was, the problem lied with reaching it and then somehow learning how to slay it which now felt like an even more daunting task.

The Slayers were now left with a choice, to brave the dangers of Rotmire to slay the beast or give into their fears and abandon the hunt. Given what Olivia was told during their meeting about what sort of place they would be entering it was understandable that there were some with second thoughts about this hunt. To no one's surprise Alistair was the first to make his thoughts heard. "Well my rugged companions, I don't know about you all but I think this is where our hunt ends." Alistair would say once they were all situated in the guest quarters. "We've had our fun, we've laughed and cried but I believe I speak for all of us when I say that seeking a conclusion for this tale would be suicidal to say the least." He'd say earning him the usual annoyed glance from Gareth. "What a surprise, the "Valiant" Alistair Vandalbane the Third doesn't want to continue the hunt."

Alistair glared at the older rat. "Don't you dare mock me! You know that those who enter that cursed place either come out tainted or not at all! We wouldn't even see that abomination before being set upon by whatever other creatures lurk within the mire! It's madness and I'll have no part in it!" Paige was unusually silent during this heated exchange, where usually she'd rush to speak her piece, often in Gareth's favor, but now she too looked hesitant. Ch'Teka also seemed even quieter than usual, either because she was still thinking of Ze'Hoz or the potential dangers they'd face within the mire. Olivia had come to admire the bravery and skill of the Slayers so to see them so fearful was a great concern to her. "We can't all be the ever heroic and ever fearless Gareth Redscar! My apologies for that good sir." Alistair responded with heated sarcasm which only served to infuriate Gareth. "You daft fool of a rat! You think that I have no fear? That I am immune to such an emotion? Of course I am scared you , imbecile! We all are!" He shouted angrily. "I am not blind to the dangers we could possibly face. We've all heard the stories of Rotmire and its perils, but that doesn't mean we should give in to our fears!" At this point Gareth was no longer just speaking to Alistair but to the pack in its entirety. "Have you forgotten what we have overcome? The constant dangers we have endured to make it to this point? That should even one of you consider turning tail and running is appalling! To turn back now and ignore all of the sacrifices we have made to reach this point would be an insult to ourselves and every fallen Slayer who sought to kill the beast. We are the ones who will fell this abomination and I won't be convinced otherwise." The red eyed rat's gaze met with each and every other Slayer in the room before finally stopping at Alistair. His fury and passion slowly subsided and for the briefest moment the hunter appeared old and tired. "There's no shame in feeling fear. It's whether we choose to give into our fears or face them head on is what defines us." Frustrated and weary Gareth walked away from the party to lie himself down to sleep for the night on one of the beds prepared for them. Olivia and the other Slayers would follow suit soon after. With all that had occurred that day I imagined that none of them had the strength to argue.

15

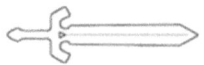

THE HERMIT

O livia and her companions were facing a similar dilemma to that of what both myself and Blue-Eyes were experiencing. To enter Rotmire would be to court death and welcome insanity. Both our parties knew the risks, but if it meant achieving our goals it would be worth it. At least that is what they told themselves in a manner that any sane person would deem as foolish. When dawn broke over the Hallowed Forest the Slayers would reconvene with Treespeaker Vi'Zhan and despite their fears all agreed to continue their hunt for Blackfang even if that meant drawing close to Rotmire. Though still concerned for their safety Vi'Zhan was willing to help the Slayers by sending a guide who would reveal a secret passage to reach their destination sooner. Apparently, the Heartwood Tribe occasionally explored this area to acquire reagents for their rituals, so they possessed some degree of knowledge in regard to Rotmire. Before they departed the Dwellers expressed their gratefulness to the Slayers in the form of lavishing them with gifts and supplies for their journey to which Olivia and the others gladly accepted of what little they could bring with them. Given the dangers they were preparing to face they would need all the help and encouragement they'd be willing to receive.

The Slayers then continued their hunt, now traveling eastward with a scout guiding them. None would say it, but Gareth's words stirred something within them, urging them to fight on for better or for worse. As they walked, Olivia would finally attempt to speak with Ch'Teka who had been distant since the battle with the Shrieker. Like before, the Gray Dweller took up the rear, spear in her paws with a vigilant look about her. She'd turn her attention away from the forest however as she noticed Olivia moving to the back of the group to approach her. "Good Morning,Ch'Teka."Olivia would say to her. "We haven't spoken much since yesterday. I do hope that you've been feeling well." Ch'Teka gave Olivia a somber look with a nod. "I am fine, my young friend." She'd reply. "Please forgive me if I seem distant. I haven't been feeling like myself lately." Olivia knew the reason why she was behaving like this and made no attempt to avoid the truth. "Because of what happened to Ze'Hoz?" Ch'Teka wouldn't deny the truth. "Yes." She answered. "Still I wish I had done more to protect him." Olivia also wished that the battle with the owl had been different as well, but Vi'Zhan had told them this outcome was inevitable should Ze'Hoz ignore his warnings. "What happened to Ze'Hoz was unfortunate but he knew the risks and was willing to fight regardless. You can't blame yourself for that, Ch'Teka. It isn't fair."

"You're right, my young friend. I am sorry, I wasn't expecting to care for the young warrior in such a short amount of time." Ch'Teka turned her sights up towards the trees. "He reminded me of someone close to me, both in appearance and in spirit. To see him come to harm troubled me to no end. It came to the point that I decided to visit him last night as you and the others slept. "Olivia blinked at the Dweller warrior. The Heartroot Tribe were already leery of the Marked Dweller, to do something like this was a tremendous risk. "Do not worry, none but him and now you know of this. I doubt the Heartwood would take kindly to me exploring their village without a "guide"."

"And what of him? How is he?" My sibling would ask.

"He is fine." She'd say with a look of relief about her. "In fact he is in good spirits despite losing most of his tail and nearly perishing. He wanted to continue journeying with us, but I managed to talk him out of it." Olivia smiled at this. Even after enduring such a savage attack the scouts will still remained strong. "That's good to hear. I'm sure we will see him again." My sibling's expression darkened as she'd be reminded that they were approaching a part of the forest that only the brave and foolish dare to tread. "Do you think we will succeed Ch'Teka? Can we actually kill the beast?" Olivia asked the older warrior. Ch'Teka gave her an inquisitive expression." I am not sure why you are asking me. You are the one with our "secret weapon". "She gestures towards the sword at Olivia's side. "That weapon you wielded protected you and Ze'Hoz. I can't say that I have seen anything like it before. I could feel the strength of the forest itself within that blade as you struck down the Shrieker. "Olivia had been so distracted with her frustration towards Paige and the fate of Ze'Hoz that she had completely forgotten the bizarre power her sword contained. From the many times she wielded in secret she had never seen it behave in such a way. "That glow.." She muttered."...what was it?"

"Whatever it is, we will need it for what is to come."

Olivia now knew that there was more to the blade than meets the eye, but there simply wasn't enough time to study it. With hardened expressions the two set their sights back on the path ahead. For the next few days, the banter within the party was kept to a minimum as they focused their full attention on the arduous task ahead of them. Just as we had experienced, the forest around them became more difficult to traverse and signs of decay were becoming more visible all around them, but still they pressed on until they nearly reached their destination. The uneasy silence between the Slayers amplified by the eerie absence of life in this forlorn part of the forest made their journey all the more unpleasant. Yet even with all they were preparing to face an air of grim determination urged the Slayers onward. Guided by one of the

Heartroot's more seasoned scouts the Slayers would be swiftly guided to the outskirts of Rotmire.

"We are here." He would say much to the dismay of the Slayers. Though they were only on the very cusp of this tainted land they could tell they would find no rest nor sanctuary here." So, this is Rotmire." Alistair said. "I-I must say, it's not exactly an ideal place for a vacation. A pity." He lets out a nervous chuckle. The scout guides the group towards a pile of old thin branches and withering leaves before beginning to move them out of the way.

It was then revealed to the Slayers that a hidden passageway underground lied underneath the debris. "This way will take you deeper into the mire." The scout explained." There is an underground cavern down this path that some of our scouts use as lodging. There is an opening in it that will take you deeper into the mire...and closer to your quarry. The serpent's hiding place shouldn't be too far from there." With that said the scout places an engraved stone in his paw before continuing," Speak with the Dwellers within and show them that stone. They will know you have the Great One's blessing and will assist you. "He then begins to move away from the Slayers and back towards the way they entered. "As for me, this is as far as I will go. The others within will assist you with your hunt. "Gareth nodded in response. "We can ask no more of you or your people. Thank you for your help and if possible, give the Treespeaker my regards. "

After bowing to the Slayers, the scout then swiftly departed from the mire, leaving Olivia and her companions to their own devices. "So this is it, our time to face the beast is nearly upon us." Paige remarked. "Not yet, friend." Gareth said as he examined the opening made for them before looking back towards his companions. "We still need to plan accordingly if our hunt is to succeed. We've come this far, but we can't let our guards down. Not only are we in hostile territory, but we'll soon be facing the scaly fiend itself before we know it." Gareth then lit a torch and took the lead as he ventured down the tunnel. The others followed suit though Alistair seemed to be dragging his feet. Ever since they arrived in Rotmire he was on edge and concerningly skittish. While Olivia hadn't seen him like this before, likely the other Slayers were accustomed to this behavior. The tunnel itself was narrow but well-constructed and large enough to accommodate them all. Olivia was reminded of the escape tunnel in our old home, only this was made with far greater care and detail. At first, she pondered who might have been responsible for constructing something like this as she had never seen Dwellers take an interest in being underground, but then she noticed Gareth signaling for the group to stop.

"Gareth?" Olivia said as she wasn't sure why they were no longer moving down the tunnel. "Hush." Gareth replied before turning his nose up and sniffing the air. Olivia turned to see Alistair and Ch'Teka doing the same. Neither appeared pleased with the scent. "O-Oh no...G-Gareth maybe we should...go back." Alistair suggested while appearing unsure if continuing was a good idea.

"No." He sharply replied. "We keep going." Gareth draws his mace. The wary stance of the seasoned slayer now left the entire party concerned. Olivia already had her paw on the hilt of her blade with her companions already preparing their own weapons. Once the Slayers had reached the bottom of the tunnel, they would be stopped by a battered door that was partially off its hinges. A troubling sight. Without hesitation Gareth breaks down the door and steps inside the room only to be horrified by what he saw. Olivia and the others soon followed afterwards and were also caught off guard by the horrors within. They were all told that they would find sanctuary in this cursed place through this tunnelway but instead they found only death. The mossy cavern was in a state of disarray as destroyed supplies and many bodies lay strewn all over the cavern floor. They not only found the deceased Dwellers who were intended to assist them but also the lifeless bodies of slain rat and mousefolk.

"Spirits, have mercy..." Ch'Teka muttered.

"So many slain," Olivia said, visibly disturbed by such a startling sight. She had not seen so much death since that terrible night with Blackfang and even still that paled in comparison to this slaughter.

It took all the courage Alistair had not to flee this nightmarish place as he walked through the carnage, carefully avoiding contact with the bodies. "I-If this isn't a sign that this hunt is now cursed, I don't know what is." He then looked to Gareth who seemed dismayed by the nightmarish sight they had just entered. "Gareth, please see reason—"

"Search the bodies," he said. "We need to understand what happened here." Gareth looked back at the others but was specifically looking at the frightened archer. "That means you, too Alistair. Get to it!" The veteran slayer commanded and wouldn't take no for an answer.

Despite his hesitation Alistair remained obedient and began the grim work of examining the bodies.

"How do I get myself into these messes?" he muttered with a shaky tone in his voice.

The younger rat would've preferred to be just about anywhere else at that moment instead of in that corpse filled cavern. The Slayers began to investigate their surroundings in a cautious manner and the answers they found both disturbed them while also giving them even more questions that needed solving.

Ch'Teka had recognized a few of the slain warriors who appeared to have died fighting as fellow Slayers they had encountered at some point before meeting Olivia. Alistair noticed that none of the warriors suffered from wounds that could've been inflicted with the use of weaponry.

There was no blood present anywhere and the slain seemed to be smoldering from some sort of fiery blast while others appeared to have been drained of their very life essence, leaving them as decrepit corpses. Gareth noticed that the exit to the rest of the marsh had been barred by strange thorny reddish pulsating vines on the other side of the cavern showing that there was no escape apart from the way they entered.

From how the way the door was nearly broken down none were able to escape this massacre. Lastly, Paige grimly noted that a majority of the mice present were actually from Gladstone and bore the armor as well as the tabard of their knights. The sight of one of the deceased warriors shocked her as she fell deathly silent afterwards.

Unbeknownst to her companions she had walked over towards this fallen warrior and taken some of his belongings. None of these findings were received well by Gareth.

"But how did this happen?" he questioned after hearing everything that was said. "It doesn't appear that they were fighting each other. If anything, this lot was rallying to hunt down Blackfang themselves, but someone or something struck first. Not to mention they died without suffering from any ordinary wounds."

"Gareth, this place isn't safe," Ch'Teka spoke, which was often rare unless she truly needed to speak her mind. "I doubt our quarry was responsible for what happened here. Dark magic is at play here and I think it would be best if we leave for now."

Olivia then stepped forward appearing visibly disturbed by the sight of this carnage. "I second that idea, I want Blackfang slain as much as anyone else, but something doesn't feel right."

There was no hiding the conflict within Gareth. Even before Olivia had joined, he and the other Slayers had overcome so much to reach this point. To take even a single step back from their progress felt as though they were taking a massive blow.

Gareth frowned and slowly nodded in agreement. "I suppose you're right. I'm sorry if I seem stubborn. We're so close to achieving our goal and the fear of allowing it to slip away would kill me. We'll leave for now and hope the serpent doesn't move from its home."

"And pray tell, what exactly do you intend to do then?" a new voice asked.

Approaching the Slayers from the vine covered entrance of the cavern was a rat, far older than Gareth who slowly shambled past the corpses while clinging to a withering staff. He wore little save for a tattered gray robe that shrouded his face and clung to his body, hiding his decrypt and nearly furless form from the Slayers. The sight of this strange old hermit would startle them all, especially as it was seemingly impossible for anyone to enter the cave through that direction.

"Who the devil are you and how did you even get in here?!" Alistair exclaimed and immediately drew his bow.

It went without saying that this strange old hermit emitted an ominous aura that made the fur of the Slayer's stand on end and eye this newcomer with caution. Ch'Teka's grip on her spear tightened and she watched the old rat with suspicion. Olivia kept her palm on the hilt of her blade as a feeling of uneasiness washed over her while in the hermit's presence.

The hermit ignored Alistair and continued to question the Slayers. "You have come to harm the serpent, haven't you?" he asked as if already knowing the answer.

Gareth too was suspicious of the rat and maintained a tight hold on his weapon.

"Indeed, we are Slayers and we've come to end the monster known as Blackfang." He narrowed his gaze at the hooded ratkin.

"Of what concern is that of yours, kin?" Gareth asked.

The hermit snarled at Gareth. "That beast is sacred. It is not to be harmed by anyone. Least of all the likes of you." He then gestured to the poor slain souls that laid strewn about the cave floor. "Let those who lay before you serve as an example of what happens when you threaten one of the Mother of Rot's sacred creations," the mad hermit spoke as he pointed his staff towards the dead. "So, you admit it then? This was your doing?"

Paige, who had fallen eerily silent ever since she caught sight of that particular mouse warrior turned towards the mad rat. In her paws, she gripped a masterfully crafted sword that she had taken from the fallen warrior.

"T-This slaughter of noble and heroic souls...you killed him? You killed all of them?!" she shouted angrily with tears streaming down her cheeks.

The young mouse was crying but Olivia didn't understand why. Without a shred of remorse, the hermit's gnarled teeth formed a sickly grin.

"Yes, child. Those that perished here fell because of me," he proclaimed with twisted pride. "Fret not little mouseling. You and yours will join them soon enough."

It was at this chilling admission that the Slayers finally acted. They readied their weapons and prepared themselves for whatever the twisted hermit might use against them.

"Alistair!" Gareth called out and knowingly the marksrat drew and arrow, took aim and let it fly in nimble fashion towards the head of this hostile hermit.

However, before the arrow could impact against the hermit's frail form, he'd hold up his callous furless paw which began to emit an ominous glow before being fully consumed by it. The hermit vanished from sight and the arrow harmlessly flew past the place where he was previously standing, implanting itself in the far wall to the back of the den!

Everyone was shocked by this, especially Alistair who had missed his shot. "How the—?!Where did he go?" the flabbergasted archer exclaimed. Though the hermit could no longer be seen his mad cackling echoed throughout the cave.

"Coward! Reveal yourself!" Paige shouted angrily. "Face me!" The demented rat's voice only served to fuel the fury within the young Slayer.

"I see your hearts! I know you will not be swayed by Her truth. Your lives have no meaning, but in death you shall become apart of something greater."

The cave began to shake and crumble as the dastardly rat began to cast a wicked spell. The scent of death seemed to grow even stronger and tainted magic arced around the room like lightning, striking the corpses in the process!

"Everyone out! Now!" Gareth shouted, to which everyone began to flee for the presumed safety of the tunnel.

"There is no escape, insects! You will all die here!" The hermit wouldn't allow them to leave so easily and as they began to approach the way from whence, they came a new obstacle presented itself.

The same prickly vines that had blocked the entrance to the cave had now sprouted upward and barred their exit as well.

"W-We're trapped!" Alistair cried out fearfully. What little bravery the rat archer possessed now seemed to have left him as he began to panic. "We're all doomed! This is it! We're going to die here!" he cried out with a look of wide eyed terror all over his face.

Seeing the once proud and skillful (though quite boisterous) archer be reduced to a blubbering coward was an uncomfortable sight for Olivia to behold.

"Alistair, come to your senses boy!" Gareth shouted, now aggravated by the continued show of cowardice from the young rat. He then attempted to burn the vines with his torch but the unnatural plant life refuses to catch fire. "Vile sorcery!"

The frustrated Slayer turned his attention towards his irate companion. "Paige! See if you can find a way to clear this! We need to get out of here!"

"NO!" Paige replied with fury in her eyes. "I won't leave until that murderous fiend is slain. Justice must be dealt for what he's done!"

This startled the other Slayers and Gareth, especially as Paige rarely showed defiance towards Gareth and in such a rude manner. "Have you lost your senses, girl? We stand no chance of besting this fiend!" Gareth argued, but the enraged mouse refused to oblige.

"Honor demands that we face this murderer in battle and bring him to justice. Anything less is cowardice!" The cave was shaking, the slayers were bickering or panicking and to make matters worse they were now trapped.

As my sister helplessly watched her allies fall apart a new horrifying sight caught her eye. One of the mouse warriors that had been slain by the hermit slowly rose to her feet and uttered an unnatural groan. Her dull, vacant eyes carried a sinister glint as she loosely gripped her weapon and turned towards Olivia and the other Slayers.

Slowly, one by one the fallen rose from the dirt, brandishing weapons with soulless eyes.

"Everyone look! They're alive!" Olivia exclaimed, gaining the attention of her fellows but as the slain warriors began to shamble towards them it was clear that something was very wrong.

The bodies of these fallen warriors had begun to decay and rot while making no attempt to speak with them as they continued their slow but unnerving advance towards them.

"No, no there not," Gareth remarked with a disgusted expression. "Ready yourselves! These poor souls have long been dead! Show no mercy to these husks!"

One of the withering dead, a former knight of Gladstone recklessly charges towards Olivia with a short blade in his paws. He tried to impale my sister who was paralyzed with fear only for Gareth to intercept the blade's strike with his shield.

He then proceeded to bring the full weight of the spiked weapon down on top of the skull of the now twice slain warrior. Olivia flinched at the sight of this which would cause Gareth to snap at her for her hesitation.

"Didn't you hear me? Fight for your life before these puppets claim ours!"

Olivia nodded and readied her blade, knowing well that she couldn't afford to make the same mistake again. The other Slayers would also prepare themselves for battle as the undead warriors were soon upon them, forcing them to slay the ones that would've been their allies.

Despite his age Gareth showed no signs of weakening as he easily dispatched their rotting foes while bashing his foes with each swing of his mace.

"Stand fast, friends! This isn't the end of our tale!"

Ch'Teka also fought fiercely while launching her spear towards her foe, the force of the weapon knocking an undead Dweller to the ground. However, as she went to retrieve the weapon her adversary rose from the ground once more, plucked the wood and bone spear from his chest and snapped it in twine!

Shortly afterwards another fallen Dweller would rise to strike her along with his fellow. Ch'Teka, now disarmed, briefly searched for a new weapon to wield only to find a discarded greatsword that had been left in the dirt. She immediately lunged for the blade, grabbed it by the hilt and swung it at her foes which would cleave both of the decaying warriors in twine.

Meanwhile, Alistair had finally worked up the nerve to draw his bow again. He fired many of his new Dweller crafted arrows but most if not, all would miss their mark despite his attackers being within close range of him. Fear still gripped the archer's heart much to the detriment of his near perfect aim. It came to a point that he would empty his quiver of its supply of arrows once again, leaving the frightened fool to swing his bow at the staggering warriors attacking him. In his desperate frenzy he failed to remember the short sword at his side.

"Away with you! I'll not die here! Not like this!" He struck one of his attackers with all of his might, knocking the monster to the dirt but not without breaking his heirloom bow in the process.

Unable to concentrate on fighting, Alistair fled and cowered from the very sight of the slow shambling horrors. Though where Alistair would cower, Paige recklessly charged into battle with the sword in her paws. Still enraged by the hermit's atrocities she aimed to defeat her undead attackers and provoke the twisted hermit to reveal himself and duel her.

"Your tricks won't save you from me! I won't stop until you're brought to justice!" Paige shouted angrily as she struggled to wield the weapon and attack one of the undead.

Sadly, the weapon was too large for her to handle, due to her weak physical body. Paige was never one to rely on her strength to solve her problems but her own intelligence though in her current state she was unable to see the truth of her situation through her blinding rage.

No matter how hard she tried to swing the weapon it wasn't enough to bring down the fallen warrior who then proceeded to batter her face with his shield.

"Nnf!" Paige was knocked back and sent tumbling to the ground with the sheer force of the blow.

With ease she was swatted away like a pestering insect. The resulting blow had rendered her unconscious and vulnerable to attack. While Alistair was the closest to her, he was still grappling with his overwhelming fear. Thankfully both Gareth and Ch'Teka would intervene, smashing apart the mindless cadavers.

Despite the fact that they weren't fighting to their full capacity the Slayers were holding their own against their mindless attackers. Unfortunately, more undead warriors began to rise and join the battle.

"They just keep coming. We can't keep this up forever," Ch'Teka said as she drove her blade through the body of another mouse knight.

My sister, who refused to be caught unaware by her enemies again cut through her opponents with relative ease. Not only because their undead adversaries were completely thoughtless in regard to tactics but also because Father's blade appeared to have a strange effect on them.

When the other Slayers attempted to strike down their foes most would require additional effort to fully be brought down only for some to rise again shortly afterwards to continue the fight. Olivia wouldn't be hindered by this dilemma as the magic infused sword she had been wielding cut through the rotting flesh of the fallen warriors with relative ease and permanently put an end to their suffering. The other Slayers continued to fight valiantly but it wouldn't be long before they grew tired and were overwhelmed.

"We have to get out of here, but how?" Olivia pondered as she readied her sword for two more attackers shambling towards her. "Those strange vines couldn't be burnt; they probably couldn't be cut either. It must be some sort of wicked sorcery," she thought to herself. "...maybe I can fight magic with magic?"

An idea came to her head just in time before one of her larger adversaries attempted to cut her in two with a battle axe. Strafing out of the way of the chopping blade, Olivia immediately rushes back towards the vines that block their way to freedom.

Without hesitation she cut through the unnatural foliage, reopening the exit. Olivia's hunch was right and now the Slayers have a chance to survive this nightmare.

"It worked!" she exclaimed. "Gareth! The way is clear! We can get out of here now!"

Gareth had just finished putting down another foe when Olivia called out to him. "What? How did you...never mind! Everyone out! Ch'Teka, grab Paige and go! I'll be right behind you!"

As the realization that the way was clear the Slayers moved into action. The terrified marksrat didn't hesitate, he rushed past the others and immediately began to make his way up the tunnel. Ch'Teka cleaved through one last risen cadaver before swiftly picking the unconscious Paige along with her hefty belongings and leaving back through the tunnel.

With Ch'Teka through Gareth and Olivia would do the same though not before seeing the hermit reappear in the far end of the cave with more undead horrors following him. Gareth hurled his torch back at the monsters as they pursued them in hopes of setting a few of them ablaze as they escaped.

Unsurprisingly the hermit wasn't very pleased with this as he hadn't expected Olivia to possess a weapon capable of harming his barbed plants.

"No! No one leaves! You will not escape your fate!" they heard him shout.

As the Slayers fled, they could feel the tunnel becoming increasingly unstable with more thorny vines forcibly sprouting from the tunnel's walls in an attempt to stop their progress! The Slayers rushed back through the tunnel as quickly as they could with the vines lashing out at them and attempting to ensnare them.

Fate would thankfully be kind to my sister and her companions as they made it out of the tunnel alive. This, however, wasn't enough for them, each and every one of them ran as fast as they could out of Rotmire as they refused to let their guard down and give the hermit a chance to find them and attack them once again.

Even as Olivia moved farther away from the mire, she could still hear the demented cackling of the Hermit in her dreams for the next few nights. Though they would live to tell their tale this was a night that the Slayers would never forget.

16

THE ATTACK

S till reeling from the ambush laid by the strange hermit, Olivia and her companions returned to the closest Dweller hideaway they had slept in the previous night. The Heartroot scout that guided them to Rotmire had revealed this place to them which laid on the outskirts of Rotmire.

By the time they returned night had once again fallen over the forest. Later I would learn that this was the same place Vi'Hra had shown us after we had saved her from the Vrothans.

Once they were all safe inside and were certain that they weren't being pursued, Gareth attempted to make sense of what occurred. "What the devil happened back there?" He set his mace and shield against the bark of their shelter but remained restless and began to pace the floor. "Everything was finally coming together and just when our goal was in sight disaster strikes!"

Feeling frustrated, the old hunter slams the brunt of his fist against the wall. "Thorns, we were so close!" He then looked towards his companions, all of which appeared tired and shaken by the frightful experience to some degree.

Ch'Teka sat calmly by the exit as she usually did but appeared winded from their escape. "I am just grateful that we are all alive. As you should be," she told him in hopes of calming him down but would have little success.

Olivia sat on the ground near Ch'teka and wasn't fully paying attention to what Gareth was saying. She had turned her full attention towards our father's sword. Twice now it had saved her from certain death and left her wondering what else it was capable of.

Alistair had regained his nerve but was still shaken by their harrowing experience in the mire. "I-If anything this should've served as an omen," he said, his voice still shaky. "This hunt is cursed, and we should just abandon it altogether while we're still alive. I d-doubt we'll be nearly as fortunate next time."

Gareth glared furiously at the younger rat. "You don't get to speak, fool!" he snapped. "You completely lost your nerve back there! Screaming and begging like a frightened child. You should be ashamed of yourself Vandalbane," he chided while storming up towards Alistair who flinched at his approach. "Paige was almost killed because of your cowardice! I should lop off your tail for your incompetence!"

Alistair didn't even try to argue as he knew he was in the wrong. He could come up with a thousand excuses, but none would fool Gareth or any of the other Slayers. Certainly not himself.

"H-Haven't I endured enough? My Grandfather's bow was destroyed because of me. What else must I suffer?" he meekly replied.

Gareth scoffed at Alistair's pitifulness. "Cease your blubbering. You brought only shame to your family name today."

Alistair fell silent and hung his head. He said nothing more for the remainder of the night.

"You knew the dangers when you agreed to become a Slayer. If you are so hellbent on abandoning us, then by all means leave. I'll find someone else to take your place. Someone with an actual backbone." Gareth then turned towards Paige who also had a shameful look about her after the way she had behaved.

Her anger had long since subsided and instead of fury she seemed almost entirely drained of emotion. The blow she took had thankfully not done any permanent damage and merely gave her a bloodied nose along with a bruise on her right cheek while cracking the left spectacle of her glasses.

"And as for you..." he said as he stood before the mouse while gazing at her sternly. "...when I give an order, I expect you to follow it. No exceptions!" he shouted. "I know what we saw down there was a lot to take in, and facing your deceased kin was no simple task but to lose yourself to your rage at a time like that is no way to behave! I never thought I would have to tell you this, but I'm incredibly disappointed in you."

Something about that last part seemed to cut the mouse deep enough to bring her to tears.

"What do you have to say for yourself?" Gareth asked with his arms folded. He had the look of a scolding parent but given how close he was to Paige it was no secret as to why.

Paige took off her glasses and looked up at Gareth with tears in her eyes. "Gareth, I'm so sorry," she said. "I tried to stay calm, but—"

"But what?"

Paige seemed almost hesitant to answer at first before finally speaking again. "Some of the warriors that were slain were from Gladstone..." She took another moment to reel in her emotions once again. "...among the dead was the Lord of Gladstone....my father."

The room grew still after Paige made this revelation known to the others.

Gareth's rage and disappointment turned to that of pity and concern upon hearing this. "Are you certain of this?"

Paige nodded grimly. "We were told that he was traveling to the capital to discuss matters with the Queen. Why of all places did I find him in that awful place?" Her voice cracked as she spoke as the very process of simply speaking of her father would bring her to tears. "All I have left of him are some trinkets and his sword. I can't even give him a proper burial now."

While Olivia still had her issues with Paige, she couldn't help but feel sympathy for her as she also knew what it was like to lose a parent. Likely if it were her father or mother who had died in that awful place instead, she'd too would have flown into a blind rage.

"Father had always spoken against the use and exposure of magic. I assumed he was exaggerating, but today I see what he meant."

The rat warrior got down on his knees and embraced the young mouse who hugged him back while sobbing into his shoulder. "What we witnessed today was the insidious power of Wyther magic," Gareth said to the rest of the party. "A foul source of magic that exists to cause naught else but suffering. The one wielding its power was no mere hermit but a practitioner of those tainted arts, a Defiler. A very powerful one at that." His eyes darkened and he made no attempt to hide the disdain in his voice.

Olivia did find it strange how Gareth, a warrior who didn't appear to employ any form of magic whatsoever, understood the type of powers they witnessed. However, my sibling would try her best not to recall what she saw down in that terrible place much like the rest of her companions.

Simply thinking about all the unfortunate travelers who had been slain before even seeing Blackfang aggravated Gareth. If they still lived there was a chance, they could combine their efforts and face Blackfang together.

"Mad or not, that strange rat knew exactly what he was doing. He killed all of those people to protect that cursed serpent. Why? What does he gain from saving that monster? What if he has been helping it move about the forest so quickly?" Olivia asked, now sensing that there was more at play here than they originally believed.

Gareth seemed to agree with what Olivia was thinking as he appeared even more troubled than before. "The more I hear about this, the more worrying this hunt has become," he'd said while tugging at his beard. "I fear that we may be dealing with something far more sinister than some wild beast. I'm beginning to believe that we may not be properly equipped to kill this creature." The troubled Slayer began to pace the floor again. "There was no mention of a hermit following the beast from the reports we received. Has he always been involved with it, and no one has seen him? Bah! There is too much to ponder for one night."

He then looked back at his companions. "Rest up, all of you. We've endured much today, and a good night's rest is sorely needed."

Disheartened by the day's events the Slayers ate their meals and went off to bed shortly afterwards. The events of that day had taken a toll on their hearts and minds. It wasn't strange for a Slayer to experience bizarre happenings during their travels as leading a life of adventure tends to invite such events. Still, what they had witnessed had disturbed them all with none of them truly getting a good night's sleep. The dawn of a new day would come sooner than they would've liked but the brave Slayers stood ready to face it regardless.

Sadly, Gareth was still uncertain of what their next move should be. Though he knew of some people that could possibly help them he doubted they would reach them in time before the serpent and its master would move again.

While Gareth and the others remained undecided on what their next move should be, Paige did have something in mind and thus made a request. She wished to return to her home, a city to the North of the mire known as Gladstone.

As she was the only member of her family with current knowledge of the demise of her father, she would be saddled with the grim task of delivering this news to her kin. There was hardly anything worth burying with the deceased lord save for a few small keepsakes as well as the sword she had taken from his corpse. An unfitting end for a ruling lord.

This was only worsened by the fact that Paige had apparently ran away from home and that her family would no doubt have questions about where she had been and what she had been doing. The likelihood of this being the end of her career as a Slayer was one that she didn't relish.

Nevertheless, the Slayers began to make the journey to the north to reach Gladstone. The Slayers didn't have to travel far as the city was at least a two day's trip away from Rotmire only accelerated by the road constructed by its denizens making it easier for them to traverse.

The Slayers were still coming to terms with what they had witnessed in that wretched swamp and spoke very little. Olivia felt no shortage of relief being away from Rotmire which seemed to be a sentiment that was shared with her companions. Though she sorely wished to sink her sword into the monstrous serpent's scaly head, it was obvious that they weren't ready to face it again.

"Something on your mind, lass?" Gareth's voice brought Olivia out of her pondering just in time before she walked headfirst into a tree. He chuckled and said, "You nearly got yourself a face full of bark."

Olivia smiled weakly at Gareth. Where Olivia was usually taking up the rear with Ch'Teka she unknowingly had walked ahead of her and everyone else to where Gareth was leading the group. "My apologies. Everything that has happened thus far has been an experience like none other. It wasn't that long ago that I was doing chores around my home, now I'm hunting dangerous beasts and fighting off undead. It all feels so surreal."

Gareth nodded and gave Olivia an understanding look. "Well, I can say this isn't something we've dealt with on the regular, dealing with the strange and dangerous is a common part of being a Slayer. Really, you've adjusted to this life well enough."

Though Gareth gave my sibling an encouraging smile Olivia frowned and looked away. "Only because of the sword I wield. If anything, it feels almost as if I am cheating my way through this journey," she said, still partially thinking of what Paige had said on their way back to the Red Dwellers' village.

At that moment she wanted nothing more than to slap her, but given the fact that she just lost her father she wasn't sure how to feel towards her. In a way, the two weren't so different, only Olivia wished that her fellow mouse would treat her with more respect.

"This sword has saved me thrice since I began my hunt. I feel as though I rely on it too much and I wonder how capable I would be if I didn't have it with me."

"And you actually believe that nonsense? I know reaching this point was a trial in itself, but you would have preferred to have struggled even more during this journey?" Gareth questioned. "That sword of yours is special, there's no denying that. I don't think I've seen one like it during my travels. Still to deny the wielder any credit seems a tad extreme don't you think? After all, not just anyone can wield a sword properly. I can tell you've done some practicing." With a grin he nudged Olivia with his shoulder. "You are more capable than you think. You still have a lot to learn and at some point, you and I will need to work on your skill with a blade, but for now there's no denying that Walter had the right idea to bring you to me."

The seasoned Slayer's words did help alleviate some of the fear she held in regard to her purpose in the group.

Olivia nodded and said, "I believe I see what you mean and yes I would like to learn how to properly wield my sword if you are willing to teach me."

"All in good time my young friend. Now come we're almost there."

My sister and Gareth continued on their way with Olivia feeling notably more upbeat after hearing Gareth's kind words and promise to aid her in honing her gift with a sword. As they did Paige eyed the pair with envy.

"We don't need her..." she thought to herself. "...we never needed her. All of this is her fault." She began to direct even more of her animosity towards Olivia.

While the young Slayer continued to grumble to herself, she failed to notice Alistair who had walked up beside her. "Are...you well, Paige? You seem upset about something," he asked her. She was briefly startled by Alistair before returning to her dour demeanor. "I'm perfectly fine, Alistair."

Paige then eyed him with suspicion. "Why do you care? What exactly do you want from me?" she asked.

In truth, Gareth's scolding from the previous night still troubled him especially in regard to him nearly getting both himself and Paige killed. "N-No reason," he replied, feigning a lack of interest. "I was merely curious about Gladstone and I was wondering if you could tell me a bit about it."

Paige scoffed at him. "Hmph, as you say." She narrowed her gaze at him briefly before looking back towards the road. "If you must know, Gladstone is probably one of the most secure cities in the Hallowed Forest. One that rivals even the Boldarean capital. A sturdy stone city that is home to some of the bravest mice this forest has ever known." She made no attempt to mask her pride. "Boldarean's have always had a knack for combating the monsters that infest this forest since the Great Exodus, but we Stoneglories are legends for it."

Alistair was fighting off the urge to roll his eyes. "...and yet your proud kin appeared to be quite close minded. Almost to an obsessive degree if you don't mind me saying." The rat archer's words would pierce through the young mouse's pride.

"I-Indeed," she replied. "My kin have always had a distrust of magic and the other races within the forest. They barely even tolerate mice that aren't Boldareans."

"So, in other words, we will only be able to see the outer walls of your precious Gladstone before we get chased away by your 'kind-hearted' kin."

Paige frowned deeply as she was being reminded of part of the reason she ran away from home. While Paige did care for her people, she was strongly against their prejudice towards almost everything that wasn't Boldarean. She said nothing more to Alistair and resumed her focus on reaching their destination though her mind remained burdened by thoughts of her father and how her family would react to both her disappearance along with the grim fate of the now deceased lord of Gladstone.

They eventually arrived on a hill overlooking the city and just as Paige had described, it was a grand sight to behold. To protect themselves from the slavering beasts that prowl the Hallowed Forest, most mousefolk hide themselves in stumps, under rocks or construct underground burrows. However, the Boldareans built their homes and cities out in the open for all to see.

Taking inspiration from the ancient giants that once ruled this land, Gladstone, like most buildings in Boldarea, were constructed with resilient stone and iron. Each rooftop was fitted with deadly spikes and siege weaponry to fend off both beasts and foreign invaders. The architecture shared similarities to the Vrothan prison that I escaped from.

What really grabbed Olivia's intention was the massive oak tree that the Boldarean's had built their city near its base. The towering tree's vibrant green leaves remained unchanged despite the approach of the fall season with barely a single leaf falling from its branches. It bared a similarity to the Heartroot Tribe's tree. Most notably were the familiar Dweller symbols etched into the bark. This was something even Ch'Teka would take notice of but held off on the idea of investigating further unless she wanted to earn the ire of the Boldarean's living near it.

There was no denying its formidableness that likely could withstand attacks from any savage beast or invading army. Though Gladstone was built on the very edge of Boldarea's civilization, it was nonetheless vital to the protection of their homeland. For years it had stood as a shining example of the Boldarean's ability to endure the harshness of the forest.

Despite this, the Slayers didn't dare draw any closer to the main gate which was being overseen by two armed guards at the front gate and two archers upon the battlements. Gladstone was a home for Boldareans and only Boldareans.

"We're here," Paige said with a mournful look. She had hoped to return to her home some day as a heroine of great renown to equal that of her ancestors. Instead, she would be remembered as the runaway who returned with news of her deceased father. "I suppose this is goodbye then. Truly, I wish you could join me in the city but the last thing I want is to get you lot in trouble," she said to her companions. "I wish I could be there when you finally face down that serpent, but it seems fate has decided against it." Paige lowered her gaze towards the ground, but Gareth stepped forward and places his paw on the young Slayer's head.

"We'll meet again some day, Paige. I know it," he said to her. "You'll be sorely missed, lass. You've been an asset to our group, and I doubt we would've accomplished half of what we've done so far without your aid."

Paige glanced over at Ch'Teka and Alistair who agreed with Gareth's words though she made no attempt to acknowledge Olivia's presence.

"Be strong, Paige. Like you, I know the pain of losing a loved one. You've proven your resilience before. Now do it again for yourself and your family," Ch'Teka said to Paige in hopes of lifting her spirits.

"I suppose you played no small part in some of our victories. Traveling through the forest won't be the same without you. If your kin ask where you've been, simply tell them that you were kidnapped by dastardly but attractive bandits. I'm sure that will convince them," Alistair said and appeared to be only partially jesting in regard to his suggestion much to Paige's slight amusement.

As my sibling was still relatively new to the group, she didn't share the same experiences and emotions the others may have towards Paige. What little time they did spend together was anything but pleasant to Olivia. Really, she wasn't all that upset to see the other mouse go but remained respectful to her companions.

"If anyone can best that snake it—"

It was then that a great shift in the atmosphere was felt as an unnatural hum filled the air. The ground shook soon after and the sound of a great explosion was heard. All of these disturbances seemed to emanate from within Gladstone and it wasn't long afterwards that the terrified cries of its citizens were heard as they fled their city.

"Oh no..."

The moment Paige saw smoke rising from her home as well as terrified mousefolk fleeing for their lives she didn't hesitate. She quickly threw off her hefty belongings and scurried towards the front gates of the city to see what was causing this disturbance. It wasn't long after that the mouse disappeared into the crowded chaos. Even the guards watching the main gate had been called away to tend to deal with the danger within the city.

"What a disaster," Alistair remarked. "Let's be on our way before we get swept up in this chaos, or worse. Be accused of being the cause of it."

The bowless archer had already begun to turn away and walk back through the path where they came from when he noticed that none were following him. Gareth wore a stern expression as he contemplated the situation briefly before deciding what the party's next move should be.

"No," he told the younger ratkin. "I'm going after her."

Alistair wasn't too surprised by this answer but was still just as annoyed as ever for what he assumed was reckless heroism from their valiant leader. "Truly? You mean to brave through that mess? Gareth you've lost your senses this time!" He flashed the old rat an aggravated look while gesturing to the increasing concerning number of fleeing mice streaming out of the city. "In case you've forgotten we are in Boldarean territory. These mousefolk have no love for our kind and could easily accost us and brand us as invaders!" he reminded Gareth. "We are Slayers, Gareth! Not some roaming heroes! Our job is to slay monsters as we are hired to do so. Not to go running to aid every whimpering call for help that we hear! There is nothing to gain from this reckless endeavor."

"Then stay here!" Gareth angrily replied, which startled the younger rat. "I'm not asking you or anyone else to follow me. One of our own just ran headfirst into danger and I have no desire to see her come to harm because of it."

As Gareth began to walk out of the cover, they were hiding behind he paused and looked back at his companions but seemed to be looking at Alistair specifically. "I don't need to gain something to do the right thing. You've journeyed with me long enough to understand that or at least that's why I hoped."

Gareth said nothing else as he made his way towards the city. Though not long afterwards both Ch'Teka and my sister followed after him. The two had long since made up their minds on what they wished to do in that situation.

Alistair stood baffled with all of his companions rushing into danger for the sake of others while he was left by himself. Though it wasn't long after that the archer himself braved the panicked crowd to join his friends both due to the fact that he feared the worst fate may occur for his companions and also that he didn't want to be left out in the wilderness by himself.

Once inside, Olivia and the other Slayers would bear witness to why the Boldarean's were fleeing for their lives. They were walking into what appeared to have been a lively marketplace filled with bustling shops and merchant stalls. Most of which had been damaged and left in ruin due to whatever had attacked Gladstone.

Windows had been broken, entire streets had been damaged by some great force and the injured could be seen all around. The city was a marvel of expertly crafted stone buildings that towered over them, and a proud culture of valorous heroes were now being defaced by an unknown threat. Where usually the sight of a ratkin and a Dark Dweller would cause a stir, it was clear that something else had already done that and left the streets in disarray. None of the mice fleeing the city paid them any heed as survival was their top priority.

"Such destruction..." Ch'Teka muttered as she noticed the signs of battle could be seen in the streets.

Many of the buildings had been laid to ruin. Deceased guards laid strewn about all bearing the same armor and weapons of some of the undead warriors they had faced in Rotmire. Strangely enough there were also some large beetles that were also among the dead. All of which had saddles with light armor as if they were some sort of Boldarean mount.

Olivia had never seen such creatures before, but she had little time to study them given their circumstances. Worryingly, Olivia couldn't shake this overwhelming sense of dread that she had felt before that now permeate the streets of Gladstone. Some manner of beast was responsible for this mess but where and what it was remained to be seen.

"There's no sign of Paige in this chaos," Gareth said before looking over his shoulder to see Alistair breathlessly coming up from behind to join the group.

"T-There you are! I thought I'd never catch up to you," he said after taking time to catch his breath. Gareth simply grinned at the younger rat.

"Vandalbane! Was wondering when you'd join us."

Still appearing annoyed, Alistair prepared to say something witty in response only to be interrupted by another explosion that shook the very foundation of the city. Buildings buckled into one another, nearby friction would ignite growing fires and the air was filled with the scent of fear.

"Argh! What could possibly be causing this madness?!" he exclaimed while picking himself up from the dirt. As Gareth did the same, he helped Olivia back to her feet. "We'll not learn a thing from just standing around here. Follow me!"

After picking themselves up the Slayers moved deeper into the city in hopes of finding one of their own. It wouldn't be until they arrived at the heart of the city that they find the sole cause of this destruction if not the very goal of their hunt.

Olivia now realized why she felt this dread eating away at her as the murderous beast that destroyed her home and family was now wreaking havoc in Gladstone. A monstrous black serpent had wrapped itself around the statue of a great Boldarean hero and under its crushing grip even the masterfully carved stone began to crumble.

The beast's mouth was slicked with blood from his slain prey mixed in with its own venom. Gladstone's courageous knights were attempting to fell the beast with blade and bow alike but none could harm it. There was no mistaking what this creature was as Olivia recognized it by it's one missing eye, still blinded by our mother's arrow.

"Blackfang..." My sibling's voice was filled with hatred for the beast as the very sight of the monster that took her family away from her served as a never-ending reminder of her inability to save them. Her fear soon turned to fury as she glared at the snake with violent intention.

"It's here? How?!" Alistair exclaimed. For the other slayers this was their first time laying eyes upon the beast and as he bore witness to it he now knew the same dread Olivia had grown accustomed to.

"I should've known it was too much to hope that the beast would stay put," Gareth muttered under his breath in frustration.

"Gareth, look!" Ch'Teka shouted before pointing a claw through the chaotic fighting around the beast.

At first it wasn't clear what she was gesturing towards before Olivia could vaguely make out a young mouse desperately trying to pull one of the wounded guards away from the fighting.

"It's Paige!" she exclaimed before rushing to the aid of her young companion.

Gareth paused before speaking as he considered their next move. He surveyed his surroundings, saw the destruction all around him, he took note of Paige before setting his sights on their quarry, Blackfang. The valiant Boldarean's soldiers fought fiercely but none seemed to even be able to wound the beast.

It hardly even acknowledged their existence as a threat as it finished reducing their city's statue to rubble only to finally continue attacking the brave defenders to sate its unnatural hunger. Gareth knew the mice of these lands were competent fighters and were no stranger to slaying beasts on their own. What was worse is that he couldn't locate the hermit they encountered in Rotmire but he knew for a fact that he was somewhere in the city. To see the knights fail with an army of their fiercest fighters was a worrying sight. If they stood no chance against the serpent, what could the Slayers possibly do? He then concluded that grieved him to admit.

"We aren't ready," he begrudgingly muttered.

"What?" My sister looked back at the seasoned slayer with irritation. She was expecting Gareth to signal them to attack Blackfang only to receive the exact opposite.

Much like Olivia, Gareth's heart was set on slaying the serpent, but he wouldn't allow his drive to hunt cloud his judgement.

"I said we aren't ready," he repeated bitterly. "We're in no shape to fight and if even these folk can't fell Blackfang I doubt we'd stand much of a chance. Don't worry, we'll find a way to best the beast but for now our lives are more important than its demise. For now, let's help who we can, grab Paige and leave this place before it's too late."

My sister didn't respond, and Gareth mistakenly took this as compliance with his command. Gareth was in the right, but Olivia failed to realize this. The moment her eyes laid upon the beast it became her sole focus as it was from the very beginning. The very reason she embarked on this quest was to end that monster's existence and with it being so close to her it was all she could think of.

Still wearing our Mother's crest around her neck, she briefly took hold of it and squeezed it in her paw. Flashes from that terrible night came to mind and added fuel to the fiery hatred within my sister. "No...No more running."

It came to a point that Olivia would unknowingly block out all "distractions". While Gareth and the others sought to aid Paige as well as the wounded, Olivia slowly began to approach the serpent.

Ignoring the danger around her she placed her paw on the hilt of her sword and had her sights fixated on Blackfang who was currently gulping down a defeated guard. The only thing that came to my sibling's mind was our mother's words, that the weapon she now wielded was the only thing that could slay the beast.

At that moment Olivia became as cold and predatorial as the serpent itself as she ignored the suffering around her while slowly approaching the scaled monstrosity.

"No more..." she told herself. "...no more death, no more destruction...your reign of terror over me and this forest ends here!" the reckless mouse shouted.

After swallowing yet another mouse it finally took notice of Olivia as she approached it and seemed to have already chosen her as its next victim. Blackfang, with lethal swiftness, lunged at my sister with every intention of devouring her with little trouble only for Olivia to draw forth her sword.

Much like with the Shrieker, the sword of our Father glowed brightly to the point that it blinded the serpent forcing it to reel back. Though instead of briefly stunning the beast the sword itself seemed to cause the serpent pain just by being in close proximity to it. Blackfang began to writhe and thrash in its agony, violently striking its surroundings with its massive tail as it did.

The monster's flesh burned when exposed to the pure light emanating from the weapon and pieces of its flesh began to fall from its body. My sister relished the sight of her quarry in such terrible pain. It appeared that the weapon was even more effective towards Blackfang than it was with the owl.

After all the sleepless nights and the guilt that weighed on her very soul, she eagerly wished to share a fraction of what this abomination had forced her to endure. "You won't hurt anyone ever again!"

With the beast now weary and weakened from the sword's power Olivia then rushed towards her foe to stab the glowing blade into the serpent's scaly underbelly! Though before she can reach it a familiar foe appears before her and unleashes a blast of tainted flame that knocks Olivia back and forces her off her feet in the process. The strange hermit from the mire stood before Olivia with his attention now eerily focused on my sister.

"Now I understand," he said. "You and your companions shouldn't have been able to escape me and I couldn't understand how you accomplished this until now."

Olivia scrambled to her feet with her sword back in her paws. "You?!Why are you doing this? Why are you protecting this monster?!" she cried out, but the Defiler ignored her and continued to speak. "That blade carries *His* tainted power, it is the only reason you still live. No ordinary weapon could match Mother's magic. I will not make this mistake again," the old ratkin declared before raising his staff into the air, charging it with some form of power before slamming the butt of the staff on the ground.

Whatever spell he had casted resulted in both him and the serpent disappearing entirely, leaving Olivia dumbfounded at what she had just witnessed. "No! I won't let you leave!"

Briefly believing the hermit and the serpent had turned invisible, she rushed towards where they once stood only to sweep her blade at nothing but air. The sacred glow that emanated from the sword had diminished and the realization that she had once again failed to slay Blackfang fully sunk in.

"Gareth!" Olivia then heard Paige's voice as she saw her as well as the other Slayers rush to the aid of their leader who now laid on the ground unconscious and injured while being covered in dust and debris.

With the serpent gone, Olivia regained her senses only to see that she had only made the city's situation even worse. The destruction Blackfang had brought only appeared to have been enhanced due to her meddling.

She was about to rush to join her companions when a startling command would cause her to freeze. "You there! Halt!"

Approaching her was a Boldarean soldier flanked by several others. Judging by his appearance and the way he carried himself Olivia wasn't dealing with some low ranking grunt.

"You and your companions are to surrender your weapons. You are all under arrest and I suggest you come peacefully as we will not hesitate to use force."

Olivia made no attempt to fight as she dropped her sword and placed her paws behind her back. She lowered her head submissively to the guards to show them that she would obey their commands.

Given the mess she had made there was little reason for her to cause anymore trouble for the people of Gladstone. "I surrender."

17

THE SPIDER

There was no time to waste as any moment used for rest could cost Blue-Eyes her very life.

Led by the light of the white moth I braved through the murk of the swamp in hopes of finding any trace of my missing companion. Out of fear I called out to Blue-Eyes knowing that I risked detection from the other creatures, but no matter how much I yelled there was no response. Constantly I fought with myself in an attempt to control my pessimistic thoughts as I refused to believe that Blue-Eyes was dead.

Much like the hope that my sister was still alive I would also choose to keep believing that my guide still drew breath as well. Regardless of how unrealistic it seemed given our situation. Thankfully this search wasn't particularly lengthy as the reason the spider was able to escape and hide itself away so quickly was due to the fact that its nest wasn't that far off from the rotting log or the ruined village.

This, however, didn't make the task of saving Blue-Eyes any simpler, especially when I arrived at what I feared to be the spider's nest. The moth had guided me to the mouth of a medium sized hole on a nearby hill. Peering down into the hole I could see nothing but utter blackness and heard no sound from within. It was a foreboding sight, one that I would have to brave through if it meant Blue-Eye's survival.

"A-Are you sure this is the place, little friend? I was always told spiders tended to make their homes out in the open to catch their prey in webs. A hole seems like the exact opposite of where the beast and Blue-Eyes could be."

Though the moth couldn't speak, its gestures were painfully clear as it hovered over the hole, illuminating it slightly only to reveal strands of webbing within the inky darkness. There was no mistaking it, this was where I needed to be, but this meant braving what could possibly be one of the most dangerous places in the mire.

"T-Then there's no other choice than to go in there," I asked, looking up towards my new temporary guide. "It's terribly dark down there isn't it? Please, will you lend me your light?" I asked, to which the moth responded by flying closer towards me.

While it couldn't communicate verbally, I was thankful that my glowing guide was able to understand.

"T-Thank you."

Shamefully, it took me far longer to enter the hole as I steeled my nerves before forcing myself to step inside.

"F-For Blue-Eyes..." I told myself before finally taking my first cautious steps into the spider's domain.

Thankfully there was a slope leading into the hole so there wouldn't be any need to climb up or down just in case a swift escape was necessary. Still, this didn't bring any ease to my mind as I ventured further into the hole which appeared to have been altered into a spacious home for the spider and her young. The ground underneath me felt moist and sticky with thick strands of webbing crossing over each other.

With my short sword I cut through countless strands of webbing that hung from the ceiling with some of it covering my spectacles the deeper we moved in. The light of my insect friend was the only light available in that forlorn place. Only a creature truly warped by the mire would ever call such a place its home.

The further I went in, the more unnerved I became as the silence within this darkened place was practically deafening.

"A spider's burrow, but not a single spider in sight. M-Maybe she left to go hunting again."

Finally reaching what I could only assume to be the central chamber of the spider's home my glowing companion would carefully fly around the room illuminating it and revealing some unnerving things. The victims of the spider were wrapped in thick webbing that covered them from head to toe.

A plethora of them either hung from the ceiling or clung to the web covered walls, all of which were motionless. The sight of this gave me a nauseous feeling but I would persevere for Blue-Eye's sake.

"She can't be dead. I...I refuse to believe it."

The very thought of her being among these unlucky souls troubled me. This was also made even more difficult by the sight of stray bones from the spider's previously eaten prey. Another matter that still concerned me was the noticeable absence of the spider or its offspring. I was expecting to cross paths with at least a few more of those horrid spiderlings but saw none.

All of this felt wrong to me, and it only hastened me to search for my friend and escape that horrid place. "There are so many of them, but which one is Blue-Eyes?" I wondered while fearing that the conveniently absent spider would return at some point.

Thankfully the white moth continued to act as a blessing to me as it hovered towards one of the wrapped up victims.

"What is it? Did you find her?"

The moth guided me towards one of the many web-covered bodies on the far end wall to the north.

Upon approaching it I couldn't help but notice a faint reddish glow emanating from where I imagined to be the head of the cocoon. While cautious at first, I began to doubt that I would be able to find Blue-Eyes amongst the seemingly endless number of captured prey.

"I hope you're right, friend. I don't know what I would do if harm came to her."

Once more I put the sword I found to good use and carefully severed the web strands connecting the captured prey from the wall. Without wasting time, I dragged it to the center of the room and began to carefully slice open the top while praying that this really was Blue-Eyes and not a desiccated corpse or some horrid creature from the mire.

Carefully I cut the webbing to see if this was my ailing friend. "B...Blue-Eyes?"

What I saw next startled me and nearly caused me to stumble back. This was indeed Blue-Eyes and yes, she was thankfully still alive, but something was off about her. The young mouse's eyes flickered with a reddish glint, and she twitched uncontrollably but most concerning of all was the tear in her mask.

The tear was large enough to reveal some sort of mark that had been carved into her forehead, one that emanated an ominous red glow. It was some sort of arcane symbol of the likes that I had never seen before and while I didn't understand it's meaning the very sight of it left me feeling uneasy.

"That spider couldn't be responsible for this. Who would do something so awful?" I questioned while trying to finish cutting her free. "J-Just stay with me. We'll get out of this together. I promise!"

Blue-Eyes remained unresponsive and though this concerned me my main focus was getting us both out of there.

Right as I had nearly finished freeing her a terrifying voice echoed throughout the cave. "Poor little morsel, wandering this part of the forest wasn't a wise decision. Tsk Tsk Tsk."

Immediately I rose to my feet with the shortsword gripped in my right paw. My eyes darted around the room in the vein hopes of seeing where it was coming from but with this choking darkness and my moth guide being the only source of light I was left in a hopeless state.

Once more I tried to calm myself and imagine what Blue-Eyes would do if she were conscious.

"W-Who is there? Reveal yourself!" I demanded while attempting to silence the tremble in my tone.

"You already know who I am, little morsel. For you stand in the midst of my home." The voice spoke calmly as if not offended by my intrusion.

It was then I realized who I had the misfortune of speaking with, the bizarre spider that had taken Blue-Eyes in the first place.

"T-The spider..." I softly muttered while swallowing a lump in my throat.

It then dawned on me that I had walked right into a trap! Why else had the spider kept Blue-Eyes alive if not to serve as bait? With me playing the role of a gullible fool desiring to be a hero who would then meet an untimely end for his foolish and reckless decision.

Though I couldn't see the spider I knew she was watching me from the shadows. Hoping to gain more time to help plot our escape I spoke with the creature for what good it would do me. Slowly I began to move Blue-Eyes to the center of the room during my distraction.

"H-How is this possible? I thought your kind was incapable of speech let alone rational thought."

The spider chittered in a way that sounded almost like laughter. "'Tis true," she said. "I was once like you, little morsel. Small, weak and pathetic. My fate was more akin to yours as well, to be eaten by something larger and stronger than I. This magnificent mire has altered my fate, however. It changed me and made something much greater."

Just then I heard something drip near me, some sort of acidic water that burned at the touch as it splattered onto the web covered floor and dissolved both the web while singeing the dirt. The spider was salivating at the thought of consuming me.

I moved away from it and looked upward only to just barely see my foe skittering further into the shadows. She was getting impatient it seemed and it wouldn't be long before she was upon me.

"You claim to be intelligent and yet you'd eat another sentient creature? It makes you no different from your kin," I said in hopes of buying myself more time or potentially negotiating our freedom though I doubted that it would be possible.

For all her boasting she was still a slave to her animalistic urges. It laughed at me again. "You presume to be my equal when we both know that isn't true. You and your little friend exist to nourish me and my children. Nothing more," she told me. "I have watched your kind, mouse. Pretending to be the inheritors of this land in some vein attempt to tame nature itself. Ha! What a farce! You will share the fate of those you imitate...extinction." The spider spoke in an ominous tone. "You ask many questions for an invader attempting to steal my meal. It is only fair that I ask one of my own," she said in an amused manner. "I am quite curious as to what drew you to the mire? Most of your kind have enough intelligence to see that they could never survive here. What prompted you to make such a costly decision?"

"Me? Well I...I'm looking for someone. Someone who lives in the mire."

"And who might that be?"

Admittedly I was hesitant to answer as I could potentially be putting Alden in danger, but I wanted to keep indulging the spider before she decided to strike. "A mouse named Alden. He is a powerful Sage an—"

The spider once again laughed at me. "A sage? In Rotmire? Foolish mouseling!" she said, "There are no living Sages in this mire! Whoever informed you otherwise has led you to your doom." The spider's insidious words began to worm their way into my mind and plant the seeds of doubt inside it. "Once the Sages tended to this land but no longer. If you are seeking a Sage all you will find are their remains."

"T-That can't be true. You're lying!"

"Do you not have eyes, little morsel? Have you not seen what this part of the forest has become? THERE. ARE. NO. SAGES!" she shouted while seeming to delight in my turmoil and the belief that she was right... "I am beginning to believe that you have deceived me, my prey."

"D-Deceived you? I don't know wha—"

"You claim to come in search of a Sage that doesn't exist, but we both know the truth. You didn't come here seeking a Sage. You came here seeking death."

Slowly I began to feel the way I did at the start of my journey, the overwhelming sense of hopelessness and dread that haunted me for many days. "N-No I-..I came here to...t-to..."

"To die, little morsel. That is what you mean to say." The spider enjoyed twisting my words, making it seem as though I had come this far to fail. Her words were as venomous as she was. "You came to this blessed place to fulfill your kind's true purpose. To sustain beings much stronger than yourself. That is why you were created my little morsel...to feed me..."

At this point I had stopped looking for the spider and slowly began to accept my role as this monstrous creature's meal. After all, what hope did I have of escaping this place? Not just from the spider's nest but from the mire itself. I could feel her drawing nearer as she couldn't hold back her desire to feed much longer.

"There is no hope of escaping this mire. Not for you or your little friend. Accept your fate and embrace it with open arms," the spider whispered.

I could feel it's putrid hot breath on my back as it prepared to take a bite out of my flesh. The beast nearly brought an end to me with her poisonous words alone, but while she had burdened my mind with thoughts of failure I was reminded of my heroic mother. She died fighting off a deadly beast far stronger than her if it meant giving her children a chance to live.

To narrowly survive an attack from one monster only to surrender to another would spit in the face of her valiant sacrifice.

Right before the spider could sink her venom dripped fangs into me, I turned to face her with my shortsword and slashed the blade across her face. Whoever forged the weapon did so with great care as it still maintained its sharp edge while cutting into the tainted flesh of my enemy.

The spider creature recoiled in pain and scurried back into the shadows before I could potentially land a killing blow.

"Aaaugh! You wretched thing, you will never leave here alive!" The smug confidence within the spider's voice had shifted to one of blind fury.

As good as it felt to wound the boastful beast it was clear that I had only succeeded in enraging it. The wounded spider proceeded to emit a horrid screech that echoed throughout her nest. At first, I assumed it was merely crying out in pain but while I finished cutting Blue-Eyes from the rest of the webbing I saw the spider's true intentions.

It wasn't wailing in pain; it was calling its hatchlings to feed! The spiderlings were innumerous and were twice as ravenous as their mother. From seemingly everywhere they spilled forth from the darkness in response to the call of their mother.

Among the wave of hungry mouths was the spider herself, now driven mad by my defiance, she too sought to feast upon us. Earlier I was overwhelmed by only a few of the spiderlings and knew that I lacked the skill to fend them all off on my own.

Instinctively I dropped my blade and threw myself over Blue-Eyes, hoping to at least let the fiends feast upon me first before reaching her.

"This is it," I thought to myself mere seconds before the swarm was ready to engulf me. "I've failed. I will die here in this forsaken place. Please, Mother, forgive me. I've done all I could."

Truly I believed this to be the end of my tale and that nothing short of a divine miracle could save us from this onslaught of foes. To my surprise I was wrong, and fate would once again show its mercy towards me. I didn't notice this but before the spiders overwhelmed me, my winged companion that served as my guiding light began to glow brighter and brighter, creating a light so bright that I needed to shield my eyes.

Suddenly the mysterious insect emitted a blinding blast of an illuminating white light that overwhelmed the unnatural gloom of the cave in its brilliance! Between the overwhelming fear of dying and the blinding light coming from the moth I fell unconscious shortly afterward and for the longest time believed that I had passed on to the next life.

Much to my shame I think after all that I had seen and endured I would've gladly welcomed death's embrace. Weary from fleeing and worrying about my life and those I care for I had been longing to have this burden lifted from my shoulders and join my fallen kin in the afterlife.

Though I knew that the spider spoke only lies to weaken my resolve to survive, it wasn't difficult for her to bring me to my lowest point. Still, fate answered with a resounding "no" for my work was far from done.

You can imagine my surprise when I would awake, not only to be away from the infested place but also in the presence of my now conscious companion who looked over me with a surprising amount of concern.

"Blue-Eyes?"

The blurred visage of my companion slowly came into focus as I returned to my senses. "Thank goodness you're all right..." Blue-Eyes said as she helped me stand to my feet. She seemed to be relieved to see that I was unharmed."...you had me worried there. I was afraid those wretched insects had wounded you."

"Worry not, I'm unharmed but really I should be concerned about you." The memory of that terrible glowing scar on the rogue's head still troubled me though the glow had long since diminished. "What happened and more importantly where are we?" I'd ask as I glanced around my new surroundings. No longer did I stand in the midst of a foul spider infested hole in the ground, nor did it feel that I was even in the mire. The flora around me no longer carried the eerie gloom of Rotmire or the sickening signs of death and decay. Finally, I could see the starry night sky above me and taste the crisp cool air without fear of taking a whiff of the mire's rot. In fact, it didn't even appear that I was in any part of the Hallowed Forest that I had ever seen before. Most notably was the strange foliage around us which consisted of strange shades of blues and purples. None of which appeared to be affected by the changing season. It went without saying that magic was at play here.

"No doubt you are familiar with that peculiar moth. That light it produced blinded the spiders and forced them to flee. Living in perpetual darkness had made them sensitive to light. Once we were safe It used its magic to help restore my senses and guided me here," the rogue explained. "It would be an impossible task to carry both you and our belongings, so I had to abandon a majority of our things through the mire. You and the Sagestones were my priority."

There were a few things I would've preferred to have kept but nothing worth getting upset over. "Such things can be replaced; our lives are more important." Then I looked towards the odd moth that had saved us both which had perched itself on the rogue's shoulder and eyed me curiously. "What was that light a-and that moth...what is it exactly?"

Blue-Eyes glanced over at the fuzzy white moth that glowed dimly on her right shoulder. "It's one of Alden's familiars..." she explained. "They serve as his eyes and ears around the forest. It also possesses some of the old sage's power."

The moth brushed back it's antenna's as it listened to our conversation.

"I doubt we would've survived without it." I said while taking another look around my surroundings. "By the way, where exactly are we? Are we out of the mire?"

"No, but we are safe here and that is the most important thing to remember right now."

While I trusted her word, I couldn't help but feel even more curious about our new surroundings. "This is the mire? It seems nothing like that awful place. How can it possibly look like this?"

Blue-Eyes lobbed the sack of sagestones towards me and by some miracle I would manage to catch them. "Questions for Alden to answer, not me. Now come...we're not far." She looked towards the moth which was somehow able to comprehend that we were ready to continue on our way to see Alden.

Once I fixed the bag's strap over my shoulder I would join Blue-Eyes as we began our approach to our final destination. Similar to our initial venture into Rotmire this was a leisurely walk compared to the nightmare we forced ourselves to endure to reach this place.

While it was important to keep an eye out for any beasts that may come to prey upon us, I neither saw nor sensed any sort of danger much to my relief. Peace of mind was something we both sorely needed after our time in that foul place.

We continued to trail behind our winged guide through this strange new place, but I couldn't help but be concerned about Blue-Eyes. Despite her recovery her time in the mire had taken a toll on her in ways that I wouldn't understand. She walked slower than usual and appeared emotionally drained from her experience with her weary eyes focused only on the way forward.

"I'm fine," she abruptly said, which startled me.

"I—what?" I clumsily stumbled with my words.

The rogue looked at me directly and replied, "You've been glancing at me for a few minutes now."

"Forgive me, I'm simply concerned."

"Well don't be. Stop worrying about me and let us focus on reaching Alden."

Blue-Eyes didn't seem to have any interest in continuing discussing what occurred in the mire, but I refused to fall silent. Not after everything we had been through.

"Blue-Eyes, I thought you were going to die!"

The rogue paused after hearing me abruptly shout before turning towards me. She slowly turned to face me with the same weary look as before.

"Just being near the mire seemed to have some sort of effect on you and the deeper we went in the more ill you became. You had shivers, grew weak and could barely see. You came down with a terrible fever and I had nothing to help relieve your pain. Then the moment I leave you to fine anything that could potentially help your condition you are abducted by one of the most frightening creatures I've ever seen, and I was helpless to stop it!"

Blue-Eyes was shocked at my outburst and seemed unsure of what to say in response. In truth even I was surprised at what I was saying, but with all that had happened I couldn't just keep my thoughts to myself.

"And that mark you have, that terrible glow...what is it? What aren't you telling me? When I found you at last, I thought you were so far gone that I couldn't save you!"

Overwhelmed by my own emotions I fell to my knees and lowered my sight to the dirt. Tears streamed down my cheek as I struggled to keep myself from crying. "If not for Alden's familiar I wouldn't have been able to find you, Blue-Eyes. You would've been eaten alive by those abominations, and it would've been all my fault! I was a fool to convince you that we could survive Rotmire through sheer will alone and it nearly cost us everything..."

The creeping guilt that clung to my spirit had finally come forward. Blue-Eyes stood motionless at first as she listened to me before stepping forward and offering her paw to help me to my feet.

Where I expected dry sarcasm and apathy, Blue-Eyes instead appeared sympathetic and hardly upset by all that had occurred. "I'm not angry with you, Tybalt. Trust me, you would know if I was." She appeared exhausted but focused. "Venturing through Rotmire was a foolish idea and if I were in the right mind, I would've never let you convince me to enter it. Still, you meant no harm by this and in truth I actually came to believe we could accomplish this feat same as you. I'm more impressed by the fact that you didn't abandon me when I needed you the most. You could've easily left me to die and allowed the moth to guide you to Alden. What you did was practically suicidal but for me you were willing to take that chance for my sake. I...I'm grateful." She smiled at me and there was a strange look in the rogue's eyes, something that I hadn't quite seen before in her. Admiration?

The rogue's words did lift my spirits as I feared she had begun to think the worse of me for causing all of this trouble. It was as if the very notion of having someone who cared enough to put themselves in harm's way for her was an unfathomable concept to her.

In truth I imagined her being far more furious with me, but the mire had been too taxing of an experience for her to truly release her rage. Though her smile soon faded as she addressed a matter that still had me confounded. The peculiar mark on her forehead.

"In regard to this mark you see...well, it's the reason why I fell ill in the mire and part of the reason why I wanted to avoid entering that dreadful place."

After composing myself and listening to Blue-Eyes speak of her mark I couldn't help but put the question forth, "If you don't mind me asking...how did this happen to you?"

My guide averted her gaze and was hesitant to answer. At first it seemed that she would ignore my question before finally finding the right words to speak.

"I was once a slave to some very dangerous people," she revealed. "They would make me do...things that I would never do willingly and gave me this terrible scar to not only mark me as their property but to control me with magic. I escaped them but the mark still remains and whenever I draw near areas affected by dark magic the mark activates and causes me great pain. Not only that but if I were to ever be found out by my 'owners' they could use their magic to take control of me once more. Ever since then I have been seeking a way to remove the magic and truly free myself."

It was now finally beginning to make sense to me, but the very thought of some sort of sick minded individual would force someone to do their bidding against their will troubled me greatly. "So that's why you were stealing from the Sages. You believed their magic could help you?"

Blue-Eyes nodded solemnly. "Yes, but all I've accomplished is getting myself into more trouble. As if I don't have enough of that."

"Surely you could just negotiate with the Sages, right?"

"It's not that simple. The Sages are a strange and superstitious folk..." Blue-Eyes made no attempt to hide her caution and disdain when dealing with Sages. "I did initially try to speak with them, but they sensed the touch of the Wyther that clings to me and turned me away. They cared nothing for my troubles while branding me as some ill omen. My life is at stake, and I wasn't about to be told 'no' by anyone. That is why I stole from them in case you figured I had done so for the sake of greed."

The rebellious mouse now seemed even more exhausted after telling her tale. She let out a weary sigh and said, "No more questions for now. The Great Sage isn't far from here so let's not delay any longer."

Feeling at least somewhat satisfied with our exchanges I nodded in agreement. "Indeed, we both have much to say to Alden. The sooner we meet with him the better. We've come this far, let us see this through."

Our focus then returned to our task, no longer under the fear of being attacked by vicious beasts, our attention was now on seeing this delivery to its conclusion.

18

THE CHOICE

If you were to tell me that I would ever consider embarking on a perilous quest to deliver magic stones to some sorcerer hermit who dwelled in one of the most dangerous parts of the forest, I likely would've scoffed at you and thought you were telling tall tales. Yet here I was, far from home and its comforts or any form of civilization for that matter, seeking out a Sage who could hopefully help me save my sister. Like my companion, I was exhausted and filthy from my travels but remained determined to see this quest to its end. Despite possibly being one of the safest places in the forest that I had ever seen, Blue-Eyes remained alert with her paw never far from the hilt of her blade. Given that she had nearly just been eaten alive by spiders this reaction came as no surprise to me. We followed the sage's insect familiar deeper into the peculiar starlit woods while keeping a close eye out for any signs of Alden's abode until at last we had arrived.

"There it is." Blue-Eyes points towards a strange looking home as we both emerge from the forest foliage. At first, I couldn't understand what she was gesturing at as it appeared that she was pointing at a strange patch of unusually large mushrooms that lied on a hill ahead of us and being overlooked by a towering tree with branches that stretched out far and wide. It was as if it were shielding the quaint village beneath it. Thankfully, it was untouched by the corruption same as the rest of the flora in this small part of the mire. Upon closer inspection, however, I saw that many of the mushrooms were decorated and fashioned with cozy accessories that only someone who had called such a thing their home would ever do. "It's a....village? A mushroom village?" I'd pondered but didn't take much time thinking about it as Blue-Eyes had already gone ahead. As I ran after Blue-Eyes I took notice of a nearby sign that I assumed would tell the name of the village but instead was so weathered by the elements that it was impossible to comprehend. Seeing that I was wasting my time I turned my focus back to following after my guide. "W-Wait for me!" Once I had rejoined with the weary rogue we moved further into the curious town and immediately I took notice of how eerily quiet it was as not a single soul could be seen within it." Where is everyone?"

"Gone, if you wish to know why then you can ask Alden," she bluntly replied, her mind was solely focused on seeing her job to its completion. "Our priority is seeing Alden, Tybalt. Nothing else is more important."

Dismayed that the rogue wasn't in much of a talkative mood anymore, I followed after Blue-Eyes as we navigated the vacant village. Much like the ruined Wellspring this fungal village appeared to have once been a comfortable place to call home though now nature had begun to take back control of its dominion.

Still, it fared far better than Wellspring, which seemed to have no chance to recover from it's infestation. There was little time to investigate the vacant homes however as Blue-Eyes seemed only interested in making her way up the hill to reach what I could only assume was Alden's abode.

Once we arrived at the top of the hill, we would be greeted by the sight of an enchanting but humble home. Much like the other house in the village it had been hollowed out to serve as lodging though unlike the other homes it was notably larger and seemed to emit a sort of otherworldly presence. This was evident by the strange shade of blue the mushroom top seemed to had taken unlike the other mushroom homes. The glowing moth from before had landed on the front door, prompting us to enter.

As Blue-Eyes approached the door it flew towards me and perched on my shoulder while eying the rogue. Without hesitation, Blue-Eyes knocked on the door. "Alden! I'm here! Let me in!" she called out in hopes of getting the Great Sage's attention. She was sufficiently audible enough for Alden to hear her and yet no response was given.

Once more Blue-Eyes impatiently knocked on the door, but still yielded no response from within the fungal dwelling.

"Perhaps he's sleeping?" I suggested while glancing through the window only to see no sign of the Sage from my point of view. "It is rather late after all."

Just then Blue-Eyes was reminded of Willow's words long before we departed on this quest. She mentioned that she hadn't been able to contact the old mouse for some time now and wasn't sure of what the reason was exactly.

"No, this isn't like him. I think something is wrong. Ready yourself."

Instinctively she unsheathed her sword which served as a clear signal that we may be walking into danger. I was woefully unarmed as I had lost both my bow and the short sword that I found in Wellspring.

Ultimately, I decided to arm myself with the nearest stone I could find and gave Blue-Eyes a signaling nod that I was ready for anything. She merely rolled her eyes at me before attempting to jiggle the doorknob only to see that the door was already unlocked. Blue-Eyes then opened the door entirely and entered with me and the moth following behind her.

Alden's home was not unlike Willow's as it possessed the same furnishings, bookshelves filled with tomes and various spellcasting components albeit it was notably much more organized when compared to the home of his student. It possessed an additional cozy touch that Willow's domain sorely lacked.

There was one thing that really stood out to me however, an odd small pool of water circled by more of the rune carved stones that I had seen on the Sage's waygate. Above it was a closed ceiling window that shone down moonlight upon the small body of water which gave it a slight mystical glow.

"Alden?" Blue-Eyes called out once more as she moved further into the sage's home, now fully expecting trouble. She wasn't exactly in the best condition to fight, but she needed Alden alive and was willing to slay any foe that would stand between her and her freedom. "Remain here, I will check his room," she ordered while slowly approaching the doorway that had been covered with a tarp instead of an actual wooden door.

I nodded to her before she walked off and was about to begin examining the sage's belongings for any sign of what might be the reason for his disappearance when I heard Blue-Eyes cry out in a panic.

"Alden!"

Immediately I rushed into the room, armed with my "weapon", only to make the same troubling discovery my companion had. Blue-Eyes stood before a grayish white mouse with a wizened look about him who had been bound by quivering vines that had sprouted from the ground. It was as if he were in some sort of trance.

He didn't appear to be in pain but even still a multitude of his familiars appeared to be attempting to bite through the thick vines to free him.

"Daft old fool! You had better not be dead!" Shooing away the moths, Blue-Eyes began to hack away at the vines binding the elderly mouse. She eventually managed to cut the sage loose and with my help moved him over to his bed. "Still with us, Alden?"

The elderly mouse was unresponsive at first only to slowly come to his senses shortly afterwards. Alden, the Great Sage that we had been searching for all this time, let out a weary yawn. As he opened his eyes however, I could see that the Great Sage we had been seeing was also blind.

"Ahhh Good morning, Blue-Eyes. I'm surprised to see you again so soon."

The rogue was confused by this. "So soon? Alden, we haven't seen each other in almost a month! And it's exactly midnight!" she exclaimed. "What have you been doing since I left you? Why were you ensnared by those vines?"

Alden idly brushed off what remaining strands of plant fiber clung to his gray robe and said, "I sought to commune with the Will of the forest, though it seems my time spent lasted far longer than I anticipated. The problem with becoming one with nature...is that you might actually become one with nature. I learned much but also have even more questions than ever. Such an odd predicament. Thankfully you two came when you did." He smiled at us as one of the moths from before perch on his right shoulder and observes us. It was as if the moths themselves were lending him their sight as he had none.

"I'm surprised you didn't starve..." Blue-Eyes said to him.

"When your connection to the land is as strong as mine, you have little need for sustenance..." He chuckled but let out a haggard cough afterwards. "...but a cup of hot tea would be nice. If you would be so kind, Blue-Eyes." The rogue let out a weary sigh before walking out of the room to presumably go prepare Alden's tea, leaving me alone with the Great Sage though it wasn't long before he too wished something of me. "And you..."

"M-Me?"

He gestured out of the room. "Please bring me my staff, it rests against the wall near the door."

I nodded and went out of the room to retrieve it.

As I left I heard him call out and say, "When you both return, do come and tell me of your travels. I'm sure we have much to discuss."

We did indeed have much to speak on and as soon as we returned with the requested items Blue-Eyes retold the events of our journey including how we came to meet each other. Alden listened intently to everything he was being told and even let out a chuckle at some of the lighter portions of our tale. He especially took an interest in the bizarre visions that I had seen previously in my dreams.

By the time Blue-Eyes had finished it appeared that Alden had much to think on as well as much to say in response. "By the Father, you two have been on quite the journey, haven't you?" He casually stroked his whiskers as he spoke. "...escaping prisons, rescuing children from Vrothans and even braving the dangers of the mire."

"We wouldn't have had to go through the mire if your blasted waygate was working properly!" Blue-Eyes snapped to which Alden appeared apologetic.

"Forgive this old soul, the waygate is usually left open to those who know how to activate it but my communion ritual lasted much longer than I wished. Without my power to charge it, my waygate becomes dormant and impossible to use by anyone uninitiated in our ways." Alden let out another slight cough but took another sip from his tea and appeared refreshed afterwards. "You have my deepest apologies my young friends. No one should ever be forced to endure the horrors of Rotmire. Especially you, Blue-Eyes. I know it's dark magic has an effect on you."

She waved her paw dismissively. "The less we speak of it the better," she said, showing no interest in discussing her experience in Rotmire any further as the topic brought her only more anguish. Though I remained silent a familiar pang of guilt stabbed my heart. Silently I swore to find some way to make amends to her for my short sighted blunder.

"Very well," the Great Sage replied before looking towards me. "And you...erm....Tybalt was it? How do you fare after trekking through such horrors?" he asked.

"I'm fine, sir. A bit shaken but alive and well thankfully. If anything, I'm more confused about what I saw within the mire. I saw ruins of villages, horrid creatures and plant life that seemed twisted down to its very roots. How did such a horrid place come to be?"

Alden had the look of a mouse who had seen much in his life, perhaps too much. He didn't rush to give his answer as the topic of how

Rotmire came to be grieved him. After finishing what remained of his drink, he answered my question.

"My dear boy. If only you had seen this land before its fall. It was once known as Shadeleaf and it served as a place of gathering for Sages. Under the shelter of a particularly powerful Ward Tree we focused our time on rest and study before venturing back into the Hallowed Forest.

"Over time, strangers from other nations whether they be mousefolk or ratkin with some even being Dwellers would venture to this secluded part of the forest in search of a new place to live for various reasons. At first, we sought to turn them away out of fear that they may ruin the land, but over time we saw the desperation within them and decided to permit them to stay as long as they obeyed the rules, we had given them.

"Those who agreed would remain, build homes and flourish alongside us. Arborhearth was a bounty for those who knew how to survive in the wilds, and we would show them just how to do so. Though they were not Sages themselves they grew to appreciate our wisdom and respect for nature. We would lead them and view them as kin."

Given all that I had seen within the mire it was hard not to believe Alden's story. Thinking back to the ruined village of Wellspring was a perfect example of that. "It all sounds idyllic, Alden....but what went wrong?" I asked in response to which a deep look of sorrow and regret lingered on the aging elder's graying face.

He didn't ignore my question, but it pained him to speak further of the topic. "Rumors of strangers in red robes and masks began to spread through Shadeleaf. Creeping in the darkness of night and conducting disturbing rituals. By morning no trace of them would be seen, as if they never existed to begin with. My colleagues and I foolishly saw this as nothing more than rumors and failed to see the seeds of corruption that had been planted.

"Then came the disappearances, as more settlers came to us in request of aid to help them find their neighbors and loved ones but there was little, we could do. Despite our attempts to search for any sign of them we learned nothing and saw no evidence. Over time more disappearances became known until the entirety of Wellspring Village had fallen silent."

A chill ran down my spine after hearing that the vacant village I had searched through had had its residence mysteriously "disappear" and I wondered that if I stayed any longer would I have shared their fate.

"We had grown complacent, and it clouded our judgement. Many of the settlers lost faith in us after this failure, not that I can blame them when their children go missing and we high and mighty sages can do nothing to aid them. For all our power and all my foresight, we were blind to the dangers this new threat posed to us if not the entire forest," Alden remarked in a grim manner as a look of regret could be seen on his aging visage.

After taking another sip from his tea he continued, "Those that didn't disappear, left and never returned. We failed to see it, but a dark shadow fell over Shadeleaf as an enemy I had foolishly thought had long been defeated would soon rear its hideous face once again. Before we realized what was happening it was too late and the wythering of Shadeleaf had begun. It wasn't long after that the verdant forest around us slowly began to shift into the mockery of nature you were forced to trudge through.

"The Wyther had begun to take over. My fellow sages and I would help those that remained escape while attempting to fend off the bizarre hellish beast that wandered our home. We sought to fight back against the corruption, but in the end, it was a losing battle. Shadeleaf and its people were no more, all that remains now is Rotmire. Ever since then, I have placed a powerful ward around this area using Sagestones to keep the magic charged."

As he finished speaking, the haunting words of the wicked spider echoed through my mind and prompted me to ask one final question of Alden. "And what became of your fellow Sages?"

Alden shook his head with a grim expression. "I am all that remains, we have long kept our vigil, but we have failed in the end. The horrors of the mire consumed them all...leaving me to carry this burden. A fitting punishment for my failure as a leader," Alden spoke with remorse."

"What you see here is all the remains of Shadeleaf, but slowly Arborhearth too is beginning to become consumed by this evil despite my best efforts. If the Ward Tree falls to corruption, I doubt it will ever recover. Trees such as the one outside my home are some of the oldest and most powerful in the entire forest. The magic it possesses keeps the local flora and fauna healthy. Should it be corrupted, it will spread the wyther rather than keep it at bay."

"Which is why you chose to remain here."

Alden nodded solemnly. "Precisely, it has been difficult, but I will fulfill my oath to protect the forest from this wickedness." The Great Sage's recounting of the fall of Shadeleaf troubled me greatly and gave me much to ponder.

One thing that bothered me was why he chose to carry this burden alone. Certainly, other Sages like Willow cared for his well-being. Briefly I glanced over at Blue-Eyes who was leaning against a nearby wall with an impatient expression on her face.

Before I could ask, however, Alden would speak again and judging by his dour mood, he wished to change the topic. "I believe that's enough said about the mire for now, don't you think?" He forced a small smile. "I knew Blue-Eyes would return but I wasn't expecting her to bring a companion. You have my curiosity, Tybalt. Especially when referring to your visions." He eyed me with a look of genuine interest. "Tell me more about what you've seen in these peculiar dreams of yours."

Right as I was about to tell him of the first of my visions, Blue-Eyes interrupted. "Your business with Tybalt can wait, Alden." She moved away from the wall and towards me then proceeded to remove the satchel filled with Sagestones from my person. "Your precious stones, Oh Great One. I have done as you've asked, and all that Willow has requested of me. My duties are fulfilled," she bluntly said before setting the bag on the bed.

Alden eyed her sternly. "You needn't be so rude. I hadn't forgotten about your predicament. I merely wanted to address this matter afterwards."

Blue-Eyes scoffed in response. "No. We'll be addressing it now. Stop stalling and release me from your spell! My days of being one of your obedient familiars are over!"

Despite her brashness Alden seemed to agree with what Blue-Eyes was saying and with a nod he beckoned for her to come forth as he stood up from his bed.

"Very well, you have served us well enough and, in my eyes, have redeemed yourself of your crimes. Come forward and I shall release you from my service." Alden took his staff in his paw and holds out the other towards Blue-Eyes.

Unsure of what would happen I moved away from the two so that they could conclude their business together. Feeling somewhat distrustful she cautiously approached Alden. "No tricks, old mouse."

Appearing somewhat insulted Alden flashed her an annoyed look. "I would gain nothing from such trickery, Blue-Eyes. Now if you're quite finished with your theatrics..."

Similar to Willow, Alden would softly mutter words in a dialect I couldn't comprehend into his paw before placing it on top of the rogue's right paw. At first, nothing seemed to be occurring but then a faint blue glow emanated from their physical contact.

Alden then withdrew from Blue-Eyes. The rogue said nothing, not even a thank you but her expression showed the look of a mouse who had just been relieved of a massive burden. What exactly this spell must have felt like to her was something I could only attempt to comprehend.

"There, you have your freedom again but before you go rushing off to whatever mischief you may have planned, I would ask you to rest here for the night." This offer came as a surprise to Blue-Eyes. She was expecting to be told to leave as soon as possible. "Both you and Tybalt are no doubt weary from your travels. I merely ask that you rest for now. The spare room is at your disposal."

Blue-Eyes stifled a yawn. It was rather late after all, and she would need her rest if she planned on traveling again in the morning. Despite her hesitation she couldn't help but begrudgingly accept the sage's generous offer to remain. "Very well, Alden. I'll rest for now. However, do not think that this means that I owe you for this."

"Of course," Alden replied with a slight smile that irritated Blue-Eyes.

She narrowed her sights at the Sage before looking towards me with a much softened look. "Apologies, Tybalt but this matter was long overdue to be resolved. He is all yours now. Do what you will."

"Rest well, Blue-Eyes," I said in response.

The rogue nodded at me before leaving the room to presumably go and rest. Just by the shift in her demeanor alone it seemed that she regarded me with far more respect than the Great Sage despite the fact that he appeared to be an agreeable person.

As she left Alden then said, "Even though Blue-Eyes had no intention of having you accompany her, I sense that she is grateful for your companionship. The life she lives is perilous and lonely. For a mouse so young, it isn't natural for her to be alone."

A part of me thought of how Alden, who also seemed to share a lonely existence, may have taken a liking to Blue-Eyes because of their similarities but I chose to keep such thoughts to myself.

"Now then, I am sure you are weary as well, but I still wish to discuss these visions of yours if that isn't too much trouble." With my guide's business concluded, I felt fully prepared to discuss the matters of my own journey with Alden.

Regardless of whether I was tired or wounded, my desire for clarity was far more important. "Not at all, Great Sage. Please allow me to tell you more of what I saw..."

For the next hour I went into greater detail regarding my frightful visions as well as my search for my last surviving sibling. The barren wasteland I saw, the vision of my sister in Blackfang's lair, the vile serpent destroying a city that I had never seen before.

None of these were idle dreams but felt like waking nightmares of things to come. The more I spoke, the more concerned Alden appeared which was hardly surprising given that all of my visions depicted death and devastation.

Once I had told him all that I could recall, the elder mouse looked at me with his silvery gaze was similar to that of a mentor would view their pupil.

"Willow was right to send you to me, Tybalt. These visions you've had are very concerning. The picture they paint is not a pleasant one." Alden didn't mince his words and the dire expression he wore was far from comforting.

"Willow said that if anyone could help me make sense of all of this and help me find my sister it would be you. Please tell me she was right, tell me there is a way to save her from being devoured like my kin."

There was no hiding the desperation in my voice as I still had no inkling of where Olivia had gone or if she was even still alive for that matter. I needed answers and Alden was possibly the only one who could give them to me. The Sage appeared thoughtful and was in no rush to answer me and spent a good portion of his time pondering the meaning of what I had told him. Not wishing to interrupt his train of thought I patiently waited for a response.

A few minutes passed of uncomfortable silence before the Great Sage spoke at last. "I believe I understand now," he remarked before walking out of the bedroom.

I trailed behind him out of the room where I found him standing in front of the peculiar pool of moon lit water. "Would you mind pulling down on that lever over there?" Alden asked while gesturing towards a lever near the front door that I had failed to notice until now.

"Oh, uhm...all right?" I wasn't sure what the old mouse had in mind, but I saw little reason not to.

With relative ease I pulled down on the lever only to hear a slight thump and a popping noise above me. Looking upwards I saw that the ceiling window had been opened after I had pulled the lever. Just as I had done so Alden stepped closer into the moonlight and raised his staff into the air.

It began to glow brightly as he channeled yet another spell.

"Come to me my winged friends! Heed my call! Show me all that you have seen!" he commanded, but I saw no reaction to his call.

I scratched my head in confusion at first but then I began to notice the winged moths that had been trying to free their master from before flying towards the glowing light of the staff. They'd cling to it before losing their insectoid shape to take the form of pure magical energy and then proceeding to bond with the staff.

Suddenly a massive flood of white glowing moths would pour down from the opened ceiling window and cluster around the luminous glow of the staff till none remained. Though I knew nothing of magic I could feel a massive influx of power within that staff...and within Alden. The Great Sage's eyes began to glow with the same impressive power.

Alden then placed the glowing head of his staff into the pool of water, causing the water to ripple then shimmer before finally coming alive thanks to the Great Sage's spell. With caution I peered into the waters but struggled to understand what I was seeing.

Images of anything and everything the moths had seen in the entirety of the Hallowed Forest flashed by in the pool in almost an instant. For me it was incomprehensible and disorienting but for Alden, he saw all that he needed to know.

"Yes, it's all becoming clear now. I see what must be done." Alden then placed the head of his staff back into the water and seemed to reabsorb its power into the staff. He began to make his way past me and out towards the front door. "I have good news for you Tybalt. My little friends have seen your sister. She is alive..."

"Alive?!" Words couldn't express how pleased I was to hear this. For some time, I had feared the worst had befallen my sibling and blamed myself. I was relieved to hear she still drew breath and now wanted to learn more. "Where is she? Is she hurt? W-What has she been doing this whole time—"

"Patience..." Alden answered as I bombarded him with urgent questions while we exited his home. Walking towards a cliff to the right of Alden's home the senior sage would once more raise his staff into the crisp night air. "Go now, my friends...and thank you. Please continue your vigil." He'd say as the legion of moths that had granted him the answers, we needed all left the staff and retook their previous forms. They'd disperse into the night sky as they departed and for a time, I believed them to be living stars as the magical moths flew out of sight. "Your sister, Olivia was it? She has been traveling with a group of monster hunters who seek to slay the serpent Blackfang. Your sister has seen and endured much but she is still alive and is currently in the Boldarean city of Gladstone."

"Gladstone? I've never heard of such a place. What is she doing there?"

"I am not certain, but what I do know is that she faced the dreaded serpent there and nearly felled it with the runed blade she carries."

Hearing this news would baffle me as the thought of my sister actually fighting and nearly killing the serpent sounded impossible. It was then that I was beginning to think that I may have underestimated Olivia if she was able to not only nearly kill the creature that took our family away from us but also recruit like-minded individuals to her cause. "I need to find her, before she moves again." I'd say, having already made up my mind.

"Indeed, you do, you must be with her and her companions to help slay the serpent after all." Alden agreed but also had other intentions in mind which immediately alarmed me. "Excuse me? Slay Blackfang? I...no that is impossible. My intentions are to save my sister, not combat the serpent."

"And why not exactly?"

"B-Because that suicidal of course!" I exclaimed in frustration. "Have you forgotten my second vision? The beast can't be slain, and I don't want to lose the last of my family in a reckless attempt to do it."

"So you are willing to allow other families within the Hallowed Forest to suffer the same fate as you? To lose their loved ones while you and your sister run away from danger?"

The Sage's words cut through me like a blade and caused me to briefly choke on my words. "W-What?!No I...I-I didn't say that! That isn't what I want!"

"Yet this is the decision you've already made up in your mind...to flee instead of fight. Did you not hear me when I said that Olivia had wounded the beast and nearly slain it? The serpent is strong, but it can be killed." The Great Sage was adamant about this matter and wouldn't be convinced otherwise. "I can give you what you require to slay Blackfang, but what good would it be if you lack the resolve to face your fears?"

"I don't want us to throw our lives away!"

"You can succeed, Tybalt. You must! The monster has made the mire his home. It has returned here to rest though I don't know where it is. I know it is still wounded from the fight. Now is the time to strike it down once and for all." The more we spoke of the serpent the more it's terrifying visage blinded my vision to the point that I could no longer see Alden. Fear had once again gripped my very being and forced me to my knees." I can't do it! I-I won't do it! It's madness a-and I want no part of it!" I cried out in terror. "You must do this, Tybalt! Your sister will die if you don't. Your visions showed a possible future for her, but it can be changed. You must be there to help her face the beast. It is the only way to save her life!" Alden warned. The memory of Mother fighting for her life and the horrid screams of my kin being devoured plagued me as he spoke. I trembled in fear of what I would face if I saw the serpent again. "Please...don't make me do this. I-I'm not strong...n-not brave enough...the Will was wrong. I-I'm not worthy." I pitifully squeaked in a sorry tone.

I pleaded with my eyes cast to the ground as I no longer felt that I deserved to look the Great Sage in the face. I expected him to be furious with me, to smite me and scold me for my actions but instead the elderly mouse let out a calm sigh and gently placed his wrinkled paw on my head. "That is where you are wrong, Tybalt." He replied with a reassuring tone. "Look at all that you have done to reach this point. All of the trials and tribulations you needed to overcome. No ordinary mouse could survive such dangers and live to have the ability to choose whether to continue their quest or abandon it." Alden's words slowly began to put my mind at ease as I listened to him. As hard as I was on myself, looking back at my adventure thus far showed that despite the danger I still survived to continue my journey. "If I had no confidence that you could defeat Blackfang then I wouldn't be asking you to do this." The Great Sage prompted me to stand and look him in the eyes. He had the visage of what I could only assume what a grandfather would give to their grandchildren when faced with a difficult decision to make. "It is all right to be afraid, Tybalt. Fear is a natural part of life that can't be ignored. It is when we are faced with adversity and are overwhelmed with fear but still choose to brave through danger for the sake of others that true courage shows itself. You have already demonstrated that you are capable of this which is why the Will has chosen you." He then stepped away from me and began to make his way to the front door.

"I can't force you to do this, Tybalt. Though it would be for the betterment of the forest, there really is nothing stopping you from reuniting with your sibling and starting your lives anew some place safer. This is a choice you and you alone must make, but I have confidence that you will do the right thing. Sleep on the matter and give me your answer in the morning." Before re-entering his home, he gave me an encouraging smile before leaving me alone outside with only my thoughts. "He really is serious about this. This is all up to me." For a moment I was about to call him as I was afraid to make this decision alone, but slowly I began to see what he meant. Never before have I felt the weight of such a crucial decision bearing down on my shoulders.

19

THE REUNION

Not until I reached this point in my life would I have a decision weighing so heavily on my soul that I could do nothing but stop and ponder my situation. This would be the first of many that I would need to make but as this was my first it felt far more impactful and, in a way, would help me grow to make better decisions in the days to come.

My mind remained indecisive and as a result I was unable to rest. There was little reason for me to retire for the night because of this so I remained outside of Alden's home. I paced back and forth through the grass as I continued to weigh the potential outcomes of my decision.

A part of me wanted to kick and scream at the futility of it all but that would be childish, and this decision was too important to ignore. I had no desire to burden Blue-Eyes or Alden with their thoughts on my situation as I realized it would be a waste of their time.

In the end I trudged over towards the edge of the hill and placed my back against a large mossy boulder. I gazed out over the side and looked down at the vacant but peaceful village below, hoping that the sight of such a tranquil place would put my troubled mind at ease.

"What am I going to do? Alden expects me to accomplish the impossible. I'm no warrior, I can't possibly succeed against that monster!" I was frustrated and felt trapped by this burdening choice.

If I were to flee from this terrible fate, I may survive but others would suffer because of me. My sister would try to slay the beast again but only to bring my second vision into reality. I would have to live knowing that all of those deaths, including that of my sister, all occurred because I was too much of a coward to act.

"Could I really do such a thing? Leave my own flesh and blood to die when I could have saved her?" I said to myself and cringed at the very thought of it before thinking of the alternative which involved me facing the beast.

Though I would be reunited with Olivia we would be saddled with the terrible burden of slaying Blackfang. While Alden appeared to have some sort of plan in mind, I wasn't sure if it would be enough. There was too much that was left unknown and too much reliance on faith in the Will to carry us through this battle.

Even if we were to slay the monster there was no guarantee that we would survive the battle. We could save many lives and be remembered as heroes, but we wouldn't live to reap the spoils.

"But isn't that what it means to be a hero? To make sacrifices even if that involves putting yourself at risk?" The more I fought with myself over the matter the more mental turmoil I seem to inflict upon myself.

It wasn't until my mind drifted back to thoughts of my mother and father did, I finally reached the answer I needed. My mind couldn't take the thought of the weighty decision any longer and began to reminisce on more pleasant times long before Blackfang brought tragedy upon my family. I recalled watching the snow fall upon the clearing during the winter, playing with Olivia and the twins in the meadow, but most of all I thought of the stories Mother would tell us of her days as a traveling adventurer.

Mother's tales were always filled with heroism and unforgettable battles against fearsome beasts. Yet despite the danger she and her companions would always find a way to come out alive and tell the tale herself. Mother and Father risked life and limb often not for the sake of wealth but because it meant doing the right thing.

But now they were gone and only their last two living pups could tell their stories. It then dawned on me that I now had the opportunity to tell my own story. One that I know for certain needed to be one of a selfless hero and not that of a selfish coward.

"I know what I must do, Mother. Even if I don't have the strength to do it, I'll face whatever comes with courage. Just like you and Father did..."

A gentle nightly breeze blew by and felt as if I was being briefly wrapped in a comforting embrace. With my mind at peace and my decision made I was finally able to rest my weary eyes and fall asleep.

"I promise, I'll make you proud," I told myself before allowing my exhaustion to finally take me.

When next I awoke, the sun had risen over the remnants of Arborhearth and I found myself breathing much easier as I felt the brisk autumn wind blow across my face. Strangely enough, as I began to rise from my makeshift sleeping spot, I realized that I was covered in a warm blanket.

My own blanket had been lost in the mire, so I was only left wondering where this came from and who the kind soul was that had given it to me. Still, I didn't waste much time pondering as I knew Alden was waiting for my answer so I quickly went back inside his home to speak with him.

It came as no surprise that after agreeing to obey the Will of the Forest that Alden would be pleased with my choice. Immediately we began to discuss what must be done to slay Blackfang.

At first, I wanted to wait for Blue-Eyes and hear her opinion, but the rogue was still resting in her bed. I thought it would be best not to wake her given all that she had endured. We sat down at Alden's table while the old sage prepared tea for the both of us.

"Many have sought to slay Blackfang and just as many have failed. The city you saw under attack serves as home to many brave warrior mice and they too couldn't kill the serpent," Alden explained while stroking his whiskers. "Ordinary weapons, no matter how well-crafted, will have little to no effect on a creature like that."

Hearing this concerned me and prompted me to ask, "Then how can it be done? What is Blackfang really if the finest steel can't harm it?"

Alden furrowed his brows as he began to answer at least one of my questions. "The reason so many have failed to slay this beast is because it isn't alive. Blackfang is dead and likely has been for some time."

"W-What? That's impossible! I saw the beast alive and well with my own two eyes!"

"Perhaps I should clarify. Blackfang isn't just dead, it is undead. A creature forcibly brought back to life by wyther magic."

For a brief moment I was beginning to regret my decision as it felt that I was meddling in matters far beyond my comprehension. Regardless I steeled my nerves as we continued our conversation. "So what you are saying is that someone deliberately brought this monster back from the dead."

Alden nodded grimly.

"It would seem so and likely whoever had done this had made this beast far larger and stronger than what it may have been in life. This is by no means a natural occurrence, Tybalt. Another force is at play here and that troubles me greatly."

"But why do this? Why force this creature back into existence only to unleash it upon the forest?" I asked but neither myself nor Alden had the answer to that question, at least not yet.

"I have...suspicions but nothing I wish to declare now, but for the moment our focus must remain on felling Blackfang."

I was curious about what Alden had in mind but held my tongue and allowed him to continue speaking.

"Know that there was a time when I and several like-minded individuals banded together to slay creatures of a similar origin to the serpent. We called them Wytherbeasts, unholy aberrations of necromantic magics that were nearly invincible. Much like Blackfang, these creatures couldn't be felled by ordinary means. The only way to permanently end their unnatural existence was with the power of the Will itself. So, we set about seeking a way to craft weapons that could be infused with this sacred energy." Hearing this from Alden made logical sense. Fighting magic with magic, but the question remained as to how they would acquire such power.

"I don't suppose you have something of the like in your possession, do you?" I would ask, but Alden sadly shook his head. "I do not, such weapons were left in the care of my companions. After it seemed that there was little need for us to continue our hunt, we all parted ways. The weapons are also difficult to craft with most of them requiring a master weaponsmith who is knowledgeable with both runes and weapon craft. The one who originally crafted our weapons was an aloof sort, always in search of new inspiration. I haven't the faintest clue of what became of him...or if he is still even alive. More importantly, we will need to focus on obtaining a Sagestone. Such an item is the Will of the forest made physical and when forged into a proper weapon can become an instrument of justice against those afflicted by Wyther."

A question did come to mind regarding Sagestones which caused me to ask him, "Can't we simply use one or two of the stones we brought with us?"

"I'm afraid not. I will need every single one of those stones if I am able to keep the ward protecting this place active. As I previously stated, it is imperative that it not fall to the Wyther. Its vile influence will spread like a plague throughout the forest should it go unchecked."

While this was dismaying to hear I could understand Alden's reasoning.

Alden took notice of my concern and sought to reassure me. "Fret not, I have something that would suit you far better than any blade." He smiled, which intrigued my curiosity. "Your sister has already armed herself with one such weapon, but you must do the same."

The tea kettle begins to boil.

"Do you mind getting that for me? There is something I must retrieve from my room."

I nodded and we both departed from the table as I went to finish preparing the tea and Alden returned to his room to retrieve something of importance. I couldn't help but wonder what the Great Sage meant to equip me with exactly.

Throughout my abrupt trek through the forest, it became obvious to me that I was no fighter, but Alden was insistent on giving me a weapon of some sort. By the time I had finished preparing our beverages Alden had already returned. He smiled warmly at me.

"And here it is..."The Sage then offered me what appeared to be an unfinished staff. The wood carried a reddish hue, was smooth to the touch but stood a few inches taller than myself. The oddest part of it was the head of the staff that appeared to have taken a form akin to that of an open paw looking for something to grasp. It felt comfortable in my paws and oddly warm to the touch. "I believe a staff better suits you, friend. It isn't much now, it still needs a Sagestone and as you might've guessed they are rare to come by. Without the stone it's merely a piece of wood. Exceptional wood, but wood, nonetheless. What is important now is that we obtain a Sagestone for you. They are made by sages or form naturally in the world, but we lack the time for either option." This now presented a new problem for us that needed to be solved. With no Sagestone I stood no chance against the Wytherbeast.

"But what can I do then? I imagine striking the monster in the head with this won't be enough and I'm not sure where we might find another stone."

"Are you certain?" The Sage asks with a knowing smile." Oh, I believe you do. As you have already seen one within your dreams."

"My dreams? But I didn't—"

It was then that I quickly searched through my memories of the visions I previously had. At first it was to disprove the Great Sage's claims, but the more I thought on it the more I began to recall what the Sage was speaking of. In my second vision I saw for the briefest moment a green glint that lingered within the mouth of the skeletal remains of some dead beast.

It was then that I realized what it was. "There's a stone in Blackfang's lair!" I said.

"Which lies somewhere within Rotmire," Alden continued. "I fear that it may have belonged to one of my fellows who must've met an unfortunate end within the serpent's lair. When you face that beast, you must retrieve it and use its power to slay Blackfang along with your sibling."

Though unnerved by the thought of claiming the belongings of a deceased Sage, I nodded in agreement. This would be no easy task for me, but I knew it must be done. "I will have my familiars search Rotmire for the creature's lair and with luck it will be vulnerable in its resting place. A perfect time for you to strike."

The details were beginning to solidify, and it was clear to me that the time to prepare for my departure had come. "I suppose I should start preparing to leave then. The sooner I am able to reach Olivia the better. Though I'm not sure where Gladstone is."

"I'll guide you there," a voice would say behind and to my surprise Blue-Eyes stood at the door of the guest room already dressed for travel. "I've gotten you this far after all."

I wasn't sure how long Blue-Eyes had been listening in on our conversation, but I refrained from drawing attention to it. As pleased as I was to see her up and about, I also expressed my concern for her health.

"Are you sure you should be up Blue-Eyes? You were exhausted yesterday and honestly; I don't think it would be right of me to ask you to do anymore for my benefit."

Blue-Eyes waved her paw dismissively, she clearly didn't even want to talk about what happened yesterday though that didn't stop me from feeling that same pang of guilt. "I'm well enough to travel. The old mouse has a waygate that can take us close enough to Gladstone so that it would only take us a few hours before we reach it."

WAYFARERS: WRATH OF BLACKFANG

In truth I didn't even want to consider asking Blue-Eyes to help me with facing the serpent. It didn't seem right to rely on her for such a task after all she had done for me, but I could see she was insisting on at least guiding me there.

"If you feel well enough to travel then by all means, do so and be well." Alden didn't seem to approve of the rogue leaving as he too felt that she needed more time to recover but wasn't about to bar her from leaving if that was what she wished. After all she was a free mouse.

"You won't be rid of me that easily, Alden. As soon as we can see the city's gates, we'll part ways and if you'll allow me, I'd like to stay a bit longer seeing as I don't have a place to stay. The last thing I want is for those Boldareans to mistake me for a bandit lingering where I don't belong."

Both Alden and myself were pleased to hear this.

"Very well, allow me to prepare some breakfast for the both of you before you leave. After all you can't be a hero on an empty stomach."

While I shared no common blood with Alden I couldn't help but feel a wave of nostalgic comfort being in his presence. I'm not certain what would've become of us if not for him and I had every intention of repaying his kindness someday.

We ate our breakfast and soon afterwards traveled through the waygate behind his home to leave Rotmire so we could begin traveling to Gladstone. As we continued our travels, I noticed that Blue-Eyes was still a bit under the weather, but I made no attempt to draw attention to it as I knew she would simply tell me to ignore it and focus on reaching Gladstone.

Thankfully, Gladstone wasn't too far of a trek so it wouldn't be overly taxing on my guide. Before long the front gates of Gladstone were in sight, and it was finally time to part ways with Blue-Eyes.

"I suppose this is it then," I said. "After so long, I finally get to see my sister again. Though we now carry a great burden we will be reunited at last. Thank you, Blue-Eyes. I would've died a thousand times before I ever got this far without your aid."

Respectfully I bowed my head slightly to the blue-eyed mouse to which she looked at me slyly. "Indeed, you would've, for the hell you've put me through I should have you pay in coin for my troubles," she jokingly said, though a part of her likely considered the idea. "Still, I will say that having you around wasn't all bad. I admit that it felt nice to have a companion for a change. Now then, off you go. I'm sure your beloved sibling is waiting for you."

This I doubted but I was willing to take that chance. "I pray we meet again someday, Blue-Eyes. Farewell."

"Farewell to you as well, Tybalt...and good luck."

With that said we finally parted ways with me approaching Gladstone and Blue-Eyes moving back into the forest. Much to my own surprise it pained me to part ways with Blue-Eyes far more than I thought it would.

Before I continued on my way I glanced back at the rogue before she disappeared back into the brush. "Goodbye..." I muttered to myself while stowing away my feelings and refocusing my mind on my mission.

Both Olivia and I needed to do this, attempting to ignore this problem would only cause more suffering. For our family and for the good of the Hallowed Forest I needed to succeed. With haste I entered the city that was still left reeling from the attack in hopes of finding the whereabouts of my vengeful sister.

Unbeknownst to me, three days had passed since the dreadful attack on Gladstone. Olivia and her fellow Slayers had been taken into custody by the city guard and escorted to Gladstone's keep where they would be brought before the city's now ruling leader, Lady Ethel Stoneglory. Given that the slayers consisted primarily of non-mice and the fact that Olivia was carrying an illegal weapon Ethel appeared to be prepared to pin the blame of this disaster on them by branding them as invaders. She likely would've thrown Olivia in jail and had the rest of her companions executed or enslaved.

Thankfully this never came to be as her runaway daughter Paige was among them and was able to speak on their behalf. Paige then proceeded to inform her mother of what she had been doing and who her companions were as well as the reason for why they came to help her. Ethel seemed both relieved and livid with Paige but was willing to show mercy to the others until she decided what to do with them.

Olivia, Alistair, Gareth and Ch'Teka would be held as "guests" within the city's keep with Gareth being kept in an infirmary to be tended to. All of their weapons and other personal effects were confiscated, including Olivia's sword which had been taken into Ethel's possession. Lastly there was the grim task of informing her mother of the unfortunate fate that befell her father.

The news of her beloved's fate had left Ethel grief stricken and drove the now widowed Matriarch to retreat to her room to mourn in solitude much to the concern of her family and faithful servants. To only make matters worse Gareth had yet to wake after being injured by Blackfang.

Without their leader the Slayers felt aimless and uncertain of the future. Gareth had acted as a driving force for the group as they prepared to face one of the most fearsome beasts they had ever seen. With him remaining in a coma-like state the future of their pack remained uncertain. As for Olivia, she had been left wracked with guilt for adding to the destruction of the city and the injuring of several civilians and guards, including Gareth.

Such a disaster was never her intention of course but she was to blame regardless even if no one saw her do this amidst that terrible day. Possibly the worst of it all was that she had failed to slay Blackfang with that mad hermit once again interfering with their efforts to kill the serpent.

Olivia had failed to protect those she cared for and even worse put them in even greater danger. It went without saying that a dark cloud had figuratively and literally fallen over the city and its denizens. One that dampened the spirits of the people that resided within its walls as they sought to pick up the pieces of their damaged home as well as their bruised pride.

Every day the Slayers would go to Gareth's room to meet with one another and check the condition of their ailing leader. Olivia, ridden with guilt, would always be the first to arrive with Ch'Teka, Alistair and Paige arriving shortly after her.

"Is there still no change?" Ch'Teka asked as they entered the room.

Olivia shook her head. "No, nothing," she answered in a grim manner. "He yet lives but he won't wake no matter what we do."

Looking at her fellow slayers, she couldn't help but share their melancholy mood. The Slayers had been stripped of all of the equipment they carried with them as the Boldareans didn't trust a group of armed outsiders within their walls. Even Ch'Teka would be forced to part with her armor which carried no small amount of sentimental value.

As a replacement the Slayers would be forced to wear ragged clothing worn by Boldarean prisoners. Just like Alistair predicted, many of the Boldareans began to believe that they were responsible for the attack. In result, their treatment was less than kind despite the fact that they entered the city to aid the troubled citizens of Gladstone.

When they weren't being interrogated, they languished in a dungeon cell while be fed only unappetizing gruel. They would only be released until Paige came for them. A fine example of no good deed going unpunished. Paige especially looked differently as she had her spectacles, tools and whatever oddity she had stashed in her pack taken away. Now she wore an expensive looking green gown that would only be worn by one born into nobility.

"What a fine mess this is," Alistair then said, appearing disgruntled. "The serpent is still out there, we're being held prisoner by the Boldareans, and Gareth is in disposed. What are we supposed to do now?"

No one had an answer it seemed which only began to further agitate the archer.

"Of all the rotten luck..." He looked towards the unconscious white rat that laid peacefully in his bed. "If he were conscious right now he'd probably be scolding us for pointlessly standing about and trying to come up with some sort of plan to get us out and track down Blackfang." The frustrated rat let out a defeated sigh. "What do these mice even plan on doing with us? We already told them everything!"

Paige then spoke up, "Whatever happens I intend to make sure you all make it out of this alive. I promise you will all have your freedom again. Though my uncle is temporarily in charge, the decision will ultimately rest on my mother." Her expression darkened as she thought of her mourning mother and that of her late father. "Given the state Mother is in, I think it will be some time before she is ready to decide."

"And we're meant to patiently wait for her then?" Alistair snapped, which seemed to irritate Paige.

"Until she's emotionally stable enough to continue her duties, yes. This is the safest way," she curtly replied.

Ch'Teka folded her arms, briefly glancing at the unconscious form of her friend on the bed. "Should we not even consider escaping? Blackfang is still out there somewhere. It needs to die before it causes more suffering."

Paige shook her head at Ch'Teka. "I agree with you, but we're simply not ready for it. Especially not with Gareth in the state he is in." The group continued to argue with one another. Without a clear leader the Slayers were left in a state of disarray with no real plans of their own given the circumstances they were in.

Another consequence that my sibling would bear. Olivia quietly exited the room, leaving the Slayers to discuss their future among themselves without her, with none but Paige taking notice of her departure.

"I...I can't do this anymore..." she told herself. "I can't stay here."

Burdened by her sins Olivia had been plotting to escape from the castle while leaving her companions behind. In her mind, she felt that she had failed those close to her yet again and merely remaining in their presence would only cause them more suffering. She wanted to see Gareth one last time, however, holding out some small hope that he would awaken and reassure both her and the others that all of this would work out for the better. That it all wasn't for nothing.

This was just hopeful thinking however as Gareth remained unconscious much to the dismay of his companions. After memorizing the castle patrol patterns and borrowing a few garments that the servants would usually be seen wearing, she prepared to depart from the castle and Gladstone entirely.

Olivia had no plans on seeking out her confiscated sword because she felt that she no longer had the right to wield the weapon. While making her escape she took notice of the lack of focus and growing distress on the guards and servant's faces. Between the attack on their city and the death of one of their leaders, the spirits of the once proud people of Gladstone had been drastically lowered.

"Just keep walking, Olivia. You can't help them. You can't help anyone," she told herself as she fully exited the castle grounds.

In her mind all of this was her fault, same as the terrible fate that befell our devoured kin. A terrible guilt that gnaws at both the mind and soul, clouding judgement in the process. It was unclear to me just what Olivia had planned after this. Much like how Olivia began her hunt for Blackfang, she had little supplies and seemingly no plan per the usual.

I wasn't sure if she was going to relocate to someplace else to begin her life anew or was plotting to slay the serpent again in some suicidal bid for revenge. Thankfully, Olivia's reckless plan to leave everything behind never came to its tragic conclusion.

As she moved further away from the castle and deeper through the cracked streets of Gladstone, there was a chance my goal of seeking and saving Olivia would failed. The Will, however, was kind that day for as Olivia drew closer towards the city's exit she stopped immediately as she caught sight of a familiar face.

One that she thought she would never see again.

Standing before her was a young mouse who wore cracked spectacles with dirtied and ragged clothes and a weary but determined look about him. A familiar mouse who was just as surprised to see her.

"Tybalt?" she uttered my name and looked at me in astonishment. "Is...Is that really you brother?" Olivia fully believed that I had perished not long after she left and to see me alive and well, let alone appearing more like an adventurer came as a shock to her.

I wasn't expecting to locate Olivia so quickly, but I was all the more thankful. Still, I hadn't forgotten my sister's warning that she would end my life if I showed my face around her again, so I was cautious with my words.

"I-It is," I answered. "Olivia, I know you aren't pleased to see me, but I needed t—"

But before I could finish my explanation my sister was upon me. She pulled me into a loving embrace, hugging me so tightly as if she feared that I would disappear from this world if she were to release me.

"Tybalt, I'm so sorry for how I acted. I should've never left you or gone on this foolish hunt! This is all my fault!" Olivia's voice broke as she sobbed into my shoulder. "If I hadn't stolen the sword our family might've still been here! Our home wouldn't have been destroyed. I was so selfish...so stupid! I just wanted to see what lay beyond our clearing. I never wanted any of this!"

My sister's tearful confession came as a shock to me. Fully I expected her to angrily defend her decision, and, in a way, I was prepared to agree with her especially as I expected her to threaten me. Yet here she was, tired, broken hearted and unsure of what to do with herself.

It was a good thing we chanced to encounter one another then and there because I doubted that I would've been able to find Olivia again if she had managed to disappear back into the forest. To the best of my ability, I would try to console my sibling and reassure her.

"Olivia, please dry your tears. I know you had no intention of hurting our family, but we can't separate ourselves like this. No one could have foreseen what happened that night. We are all that's left of the Shortwhiskers and will gain nothing from bitterly parting again. We are family and nothing will ever change that."

My sister began to calm down and slowly pulled away to dry her eyes with her sleeve. "You're right, Tybalt," she replied. "But now what will become of us? We have no home, no goals, what can w—"

"No, we have a goal. The same goal now," I told her, feeling determined as I spoke. "Our goal is to finally end Blackfang. Once and for all."

Olivia stepped away from me and appeared astonished by my words. She eyed me up and down as if to question if I was truly her missing kin.

"I know it sounds strange coming from me, but we have to do this, Olivia. There are matters at stake tha—"

"Olivia!" Suddenly yet another familiar voice was heard but not one that was yet known by me.

Running up next to us while pulling up her skirt so she didn't trip over it would be Paige who glared at my troubled sibling.

"I can't believe you ran off like that! Did you think I wouldn't find out about yo—" Paige's anger then subsided as she took notice of me as well as the unfinished staff I was carrying. "Wait, who are you?"

"My brother," Paige answered. "I...I thought he died but...he's here..."

Paige gave me a strange look as if she were unsure of what to make of me. To my surprise her first reaction of me was actually far more "friendly" when compared to her first encounter with Olivia. In an attempt to alleviate the awkwardness of the situation I spoke up after Olivia. "Y-Yes, uhm hello. My name is Tybalt Shortwhisker. A pleasure to meet you." Judging by her appearance I could tell she was connected to nobility and recalled my mother's teachings to be respectful towards them thus causing me to bow my head slightly towards her.

"Erm Paige Stoneglory...likewise." The mouse even curtsied back in return. "What brings you here exactly, good sir? A-Aside from your sister that is..." She gestures towards the efforts being made to repair the damage caused by Blackfang. "As you can see you've come at a difficult time for my people."

I nodded and appeared remorseful that I hadn't come sooner though I doubted that I would've been able to help without the completed weapon. Making no attempt to hide my true attentions I clearly stated, "I'm here to help you slay Blackfang." This came as a surprise to Paige.

Who eyed me with suspicion and confusion. I didn't exactly have the look of an experienced warrior after all. "Please, don't allow my appearance to fool you because I know what must be done. I know how we can slay that monster once and for all."

20

THE KNIGHT

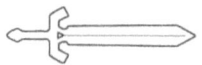   

At long last I had done it! Finally, I had reunited with my sister, but there was little time for us to talk of our adventures. Both of our quests would only be concluded when the ravenous abomination known as Blackfang was no longer a blight upon our forest. A monumental task that I couldn't possibly accomplish alone and required the aid of my sister, her fellow companions and that of the Boldarean soldiers. Paige was initially hesitant, but after some convincing would agree to at least hear me out. We all returned to the keep and met within Gareth's room to explain what I knew and what needed to be done if we had any hope of succeeding. It was safe to say that the Slayers were caught off guard by what I had to say. Though I have written about Olivia's companions this was my first time encountering them in the flesh. It was safe to say they were colorful and diverse if not an unusual sort of people, but I could tell they had good hearts.

"So you're saying that the serpent is already dead?" Alistair reiterated, appearing annoyed by almost everything I told him. "No wonder the Boldareans weren't actually harming that monster. That's foul play if I ever saw it!" Ch'Teka appeared mournful. "How many of our fellow Slayers threw their lives away fighting that miscreation? Not knowing that they never stood a chance of defeating it to begin with."

"All the more reason for us to act now, before this tragedy can repeat itself," I then said with no small amount of urgency.

Ch'teka and Olivia appeared convinced, but Alistair still appeared hesitant to face the beast. After seeing how ferocious it was, he quietly doubted that it could even be killed, magic or not. Paige was even more uncertain of all I had said, but even more so of what my true intentions were.

"So, these magic weapons of yours...are they really that effective?" she asked.

I gave her an affirmative nod. "Without a doubt they are the best, if not only weapons that can be used against our foe. We will only need two weapons thankfully, Olivia's sword and my staff. Still, this isn't something that can be accomplished alone. We need to work together if we have any hope of achieving victory."

"I suspect we would need even more than that," Paige replied. "I could attempt to convince my uncle to aid us and stir the hearts of our knights to face this foe as well as whatever lurks within Rotmire." Knowing little of warfare, I could only assume that Paige was in the right mind when suggesting we recruit the aid of her fellow Boldareans. "That sounds like a great idea—"

"Wait!" she interrupted while looking at me with an inquisitive gaze. "Before I do anything I need to know if we can actually trust you. How do we know you aren't leading us to our doom or working with our enemy?"

"I beg your pardon..." This accusation shocked me and felt rather insulting. I meant no ill will, but Paige still remained unsure. Olivia, who had been mostly silent since her return, rose to her feet and glared at Paige. "My brother is no liar! He only wants to help us!"

Paige looked back at her with a glare of her own. "How can you be so certain that this really is your brother and not more foul magical trickery from that bastard hermit?!" she retorted. "Isn't it convenient for your brother to suddenly appear in our hour of need? The brother you thought had been killed? With our leader wounded and unable to guide us, this mouse who claims to be Olivia's deceased kin reveals himself with all of the answers we need. Doesn't that seem suspicious to any of you?"

Paige's words did seem to start suspicion within the others aside from Olivia who appeared dangerously close to attacking Paige. Olivia knew I was her kin or at least wanted to believe it was me. In this situation all that I could do was speak my mind.

"Paige, I know all of this seems strange and frankly I don't understand it all myself. It wasn't that long ago that I never thought I would be in a situation like this. I'm scared and uncertain if we'll ever succeed but I know that if we don't at least try Blackfang will go on to ruin more lives. I know I have done little to earn your trust, but please give me a chance. I ask that you have faith in my words. That beast ruined my life and took my family away from me. I want nothing more than to see it dead, the same as all of you. Our only hope of succeeding is with your help."

I spoke with utmost sincerity in my voice, even Paige couldn't deny that. The young noblemouse frowned and turned away from us. "I'm just afraid that we will lose someone else," she confessed. "I—We've seen too much death and I don't think I can take another loss."

Ch'Teka moved closer towards Paige and placed her paw on her shoulder. "Slayers can't submit to their fears, Paige. Even under the fear of death. We now have a way to emerge victorious. You know this is what Gareth would want."

Paige glanced over at their unconscious leader before looking back at Ch'Teka then at me. "I will do what I can to help," she finally said, "but I believe that in the end whether we succeed or fail depends on if my uncle is willing to aid us. My words alone will carry little weight amongst my people. Uncle Waylon, however, can sway his fellow knights. They are set to meet later today and discuss what their next course of action is. If there was ever a time to speak with him, it's now." Paige began to walk towards the door before looking back towards me. "It may help if you are there to share your knowledge."

I agreed with her. "Then I'll join you and should the Will allow it we shall convince your kin to aid our cause."

Paige gave me a queer expression after I said this before opening the door and beckoning me to follow her. "Come."

Both Paige and I then departed from the room to seek out Paige's uncle, Waylon Stoneglory, who was currently residing in his own bedroom on the far right side of the keep. Paige informed me that her uncle was the brother of her late father as well as the leader of the Knights of the Emerald Oak, the order that acted as Gladstone's elite defenders.

He was a well-spoken but ferocious warrior with a deep love for his nation and its traditions. Waylon was respected by many including his late brother, but Paige always felt uneasy around the mouse. She claimed that he could be cold and demanding while also detecting a hint of jealousy towards her father.

The two never grew close, which would only make the task of convincing him to help our cause that much difficult. Paige believed that her frail body and smaller size may have played a part in this hostility she received from Waylon. By the time we drew close to Waylon's door I could see Paige was beginning to drag her feet.

"Is something the matter?" I asked with concern. "You still seem uncertain."

"Given who we are about to speak with It's difficult not to be," she replied as we continued to walk. "There is so little that we know and there is no guarantee we will be able to convince the knights. Not to mention that my uncle can be a difficult person to speak with as I have mentioned before."

The potential for all of this to fail wasn't lost on me, but I had come too far to be stopped now. "What choice do we have but to try? There is no harm in doing that at least," I replied. "Don't worry, I don't plan on abandoning you if he doesn't like what we have to say. I'll be with you every step of the way."

Hearing this seemingly renewed Paige's confidence and she once again began to keep pace with me. She approached the door first before glancing back at me as if to silently ask if I was prepared for this. I nodded at her and after she took a deep breath, she'd knock on the door in an attempt to get her relative's attention.

"Uncle Waylon? Are you there?" she said in hopes of getting his attention only to receive no reply. Determined to get a response, Paige continued to knock on the door. "Uncle, please! If you are in there we must speak!" Paige shouted but heard no reply.

She looked back at me with a panicked expression as if uncertain of what to do next should they fail. Much to my shame, I too was uncertain of what an alternative could be in this situation.

"Enter!" we suddenly heard a voice call out to us from within the room.

Paige let out a sigh of relief before opening the door for the both of us to enter. "Uncle Waylon?"

Waylon's room was a comfortable and well-furnished den, befitting of a mouse of notoriety which compared to the sparse bedroom Gareth had been given was a mockery of the injured rat's compact living space.

"Don't dawdle, girl. Come to me at once and speak your piece." Sitting at a desk with his back facing us was a male mouse that I could only assume was Paige's uncle. He made no attempt to stand and greet his kin properly as most of his attention was on what appeared to be a letter he was writing to an unknown recipient.

If anything, it felt as though he was speaking to his niece as though she were a servant. Paige knew this but wouldn't allow it to impede her.

She and I stepped further into the bedroom as she said, "Uncle, we haven't spoken since I returned. I-It's good to see you again after all this time."

An annoyed huff was heard from Waylon. "Enough with your pleasantries, niece. You didn't come to see me out of the kindness of your heart. What is it that you want from me?" The adult mouse spoke with the gruff tone of a soldier, one that showed little patience for false niceties and other flowery speech. Her uncle's response would cause Paige to instinctively flinch at his bluntness and struggled to find the right words. "Well? Out with it!" he demanded.

"We came here to ask for your aid. It's in regard to—"

"We?" he interrupted before finally turning his head towards Paige...and then to me. "Who else have you brought with you?" Waylon rose from his seat and turned to face us. He was at least an inch taller than the average mouse, was middle aged, and had grayish black fur with a gnarled scar on his cheek.

Though he wore the attire of a noble there was no hiding his warrior-like build and demeanor. Waylon eyed me and the staff I carried as if an enemy had just stepped into his room.

"T-This is Tybalt, he is a...friend," Paige swiftly answered to which I bowed respectfully. "He has information on the creature that attacked the city and how to defeat it."

"Does he now?" Waylon's words were spoken in a mocking tone. "Well then why are you still here exactly, Paige?" he then asked. "You've done your part, so there is little reason for you to remain."

Paige was caught off guard by this. She thought that it would be best for her to stay and help Tybalt convince him, but Waylon seemed to want nothing to do with her. "But I—"

"Get out," Waylon commanded.

Paige wouldn't argue and for a brief moment I saw the infuriated expression on her face. She left the room as swiftly as she entered, leaving both me and Waylon alone much to my dismay. I have no shame in admitting that this mouse intimidated me, and it took everything I had not to flee from the room along with Paige.

"Now that the distraction is gone, we have a chance to speak. Tybalt, was it?"

"Y-Yes sir," I responded. Though I didn't approve of the way he was speaking towards Paige, I imagined that I would only anger Waylon by defending her and hinder our chances to convince him. We didn't need to like each other but we needed to work together.

"She claimed that you possessed knowledge that could aid Boldarea in slaying Blackfang, is that true?"

"Yes, sir."

"And how exactly did you obtain this information?" he asked which I was admittedly hesitant to answer.

I recalled that the Boldarean's weren't particularly fond of magic though I saw no other way of explaining how to defeat it. Waylon stood before me briefly before beginning to slowly circle me. Right as I was about to give my answer he spoke again.

"There is no need to speak, boy. "That staff you carry tells me all I need to know," he said coolly. "You are no Boldarean, and I have already seen the mad folk who carry staves exactly like yours before. You're one of the Sages, aren't you?"

"What? No! I-I'm not a—"

"You can deny the truth all you wish, but it doesn't make you any less guilty."

Waylon's increasingly concerning demeanor and skepticism was troubling me but right as I sought to defend myself, I was once again silenced as I felt something sharp and metallic rest on my shoulder and draw close to my neck.

A letter opener, sharp to the touch, now came inches away from slitting my throat. "Sorcery of any sort is forbidden in Boldarea and practitioners who trespass in our lands are to be imprisoned or put to the sword."

I couldn't tell if Waylon was simply trying to extort me for information or if he would really be willing to end my life. Either way, if I failed to please him it would only lead to disaster for us all.

"Tell me all that you know and what becomes of you next will decide your fate," Waylon ordered. Not wanting to waste time trying to think of some way out of this situation I began to speak. "Blackfang, the beast that attacked Gladstone? You won't be able to kill it."

"And why not?" he asked in a frigid manner, bringing the blade closer to the fur on my neck. "The finest soldiers and knights armed with masterfully crafted armaments for the specific reason of slaughtering these oversized monsters and none could harm it?!What sorcery is at play here?" Waylon asked, demanding a prompt answer.

"I-It is sorcery, just as you said. The foulest sort I've ever seen. The serpent is already dead but dark magic keeps it alive. None of your people will be able to slay it."

Something about my answer seemed to anger Waylon as I felt his blade push deeper against my neck, no longer just brushing against my fur but now threatening to cut through my flesh. "And *why* is that young Tybalt?"

I winced in pain but once again answered Waylon. "Blackfang can only be wounded with magic and magical armaments. There is no other way."

Waylon kept the blade close to my neck and remained silent as he thought of what else he wished to ask me while pondering on what I had told him. "You are not one of my runty niece's entourage. I remember seeing two vile ratkin and one of those Dweller savages with some outsider mouse. I know you were not among them so who are you really? Hopefully not a spy for the Sages. That would be quite unhealthy for you," he warned me though I hardly needed a reminder with the blade at my neck.

"I'm no one," I answered. "You are right, I am not one of your people. I lived with my family in seclusion, but Blackfang somehow found our home. It... It killed everyone, my mother, my siblings...only me and my sister survived. She went off on her own to kill Blackfang and I sought to go after her to stop her from getting herself killed. All of this, all that I've done to reach this point was to save her life. If that means dealing with Sages and whoever else to kill that monster, then so be it."

Waylon seemed to be forming an idea of who I was and thankfully moved his blade away from the neck. "Turn to face me, boy. Slowly."

I did as he commanded and met the gaze of the stern senior knight that stood before me. He said nothing at first but stared into my eyes as if searching for some hidden truth. It took all that I had not to break under his gaze.

"You come to me at a very convenient time, Tybalt." Waylon finally set the potential weapon aside on his desk. "My arrogant brother, Dorian, perishes in that gaping wound known as Rotmire, my home is attacked by a seemingly unkillable monster and now I have to deal with my wayward runt of a niece along with her strange companions." He groaned and shook his head. "As you might have imagined, I haven't been in the best of moods these past few days with our fair Lady being of no real help in her current state."

After massaging my neck and making sure there were no "accidental" cuts around my flesh, I said, "Which is why I wish for us to work together. I assure you; I mean no ill will towards you or your people. I believe we can assist one another."

Waylon scoffed at me after hearing this, but it didn't deter me from continuing. "We know it's weaknesses better than you or your fellow knights. Its hiding place is also known to us which is somewhere within Rotmire. With our knowledge and your forces, we could free this forest of a terrible scourge."

In this situation I saw the need to partially lie if it meant gaining the favor of the knight. Apart from being vulnerable to magic there wasn't any clear idea as to how the beast might be weakened or where precisely it even was within Rotmire.

The knight glared at me in response to my words. "Do you even comprehend what you are asking of me? I've already lost my brother and several of my best warriors! You would so nonchalantly wish for us to put even more of our lives on the line against a seemingly invincible foe?"

"I know it sounds difficult, maybe even nigh impossible, but we are fully capable of succeeding. Think of what you could gain from besting the beast!" I exclaimed in an effort to convince Waylon. "Your people's hearts have been dashed by this monster. This victory could lift their spirits, give them the urge to rebuild and become a proud people again."

Something about my words seemed to resonate with Waylon but perhaps not for the right reasons. "On that I do agree with you. It would be a most welcoming boon to show that the good people of Gladstone aren't to be trifled with."

Believing that I was finally getting through to him I would continue. "All that I ask is that you allow myself and Paige's companions to assist in the battle."

Waylon scoffed at me. "Your band of misfits are hardly worthy to stand alongside my fellow knights. Rats and one of those mad Dwellers...the gray ones especially aren't right in the head. Still, I suppose we could use you as fodder. Fine, I will permit this...but only with a few obvious exceptions." This wasn't the answer I was hoping for and immediately tried to convince him otherwise.

"Such as?"

Waylon grunted and shook his head before chastising me with his gruff voice. "Think, boy! One of them is unconscious, he is of no use to us on a battlefield! The same could be said about my runty niece. That girl is far too weak and pathetic. She couldn't even qualify to join her siblings at the academy. Paige would be more of a liability than an asset. I also doubt her mother would approve of her going off into danger and I will not be held accountable for that! She is to remain here while the rest of you accompany us." Waylon wasn't wrong.

Gareth was still unwell, and I knew little of what Paige was capable of doing against such a beast. Still, something did tell me that Waylon was underestimating her, but I was in no position to argue. "Fair enough."

"Once the beast is dead, I will claim its head and mount it above the great hall for all to see. Know that I will take full credit for this victory for news of our triumph won't be enough. My people need a hero in these dark times, and I shall be that hero."

As I sought neither fame nor fortune for felling the serpent these terms seemed fair enough. I could only hope the Slayers and my sister would agree to these terms. "Then we are in agreement?"

"We are," he answered with a respectful nod. "I shall do my best to convince my fellows and rally them to our cause. There is a meeting to be held later today that will serve as my moment to win them over. With luck by tomorrow morning, we will be ready to face the beast and avenge our fallen. I trust you and yours will be ready?"

I nodded back in return. "We shall, but my companions will need their equipment if that seems fair."

Waylon shrugged with a nonchalant expression. "Fine, they'll have their things returned to them." The knight then extended his paw to me to shake in agreement.

"We shall triumph over this beast, sir. Mark my word..."

Feeling that I had accomplished my goal I smiled and reached for the Boldarean's paw who then gripped it so tightly that I feared he would tear it off.

"But a word of warning, boy. No tricks or you and your companions will suffer dearly." Waylon spoke grimly and his grip on my paw only increased. "Do. Not. Cross me."

Finally, he released me, which sent me staggering back as I fell on my tail. My heart was racing and for the briefest moment I felt as though I should be fleeing for my life. Waylon looked down at me in a condescending manner and made no offer to help me to my feet. He made it quite clear that we were not allies.

This was just a matter of convenience for both of us and Waylon wanted to make that clear. "Our business is concluded for the day. Show yourself to the door." Waylon then returned to his desk to finish writing his letter and likely had no interest in acknowledging my presence any further.

Feeling somewhat humiliated but satisfied with our agreement I picked up my staff and dusted myself off before finally leaving Waylon in peace. It wasn't until after I had stepped away from Waylon's door that I dropped my facade and nearly collapsed to my knees.

"Tybalt?" To my surprise Paige had waited for me and shown no small sign of concern as she took quick note of the distress I was in.

"Tybalt, what happened in there? Are you well?" she asked, but I didn't respond, at least not immediately.

My frightening experience with Waylon had left my heart racing and the fear of death clinging to my mind. Once more my habit of brushing with death continued with Waylon nearly taking my life by mere association with the Sages. I had thought my experience with the prison rats, or the spider and her brood was harrowing, but something about this mouse had shaken me to my very core.

Waylon unknowingly reminded me that I was far from invincible and if anything was a particularly lucky mouse to have come this far.

"Remain strong, Tybalt. You must do this..." I told myself as I clutched my chest and tried my hardest to calm down. Even as I continued to try to calm myself, I felt the lingering touch of the knight's letter opener against my neck.

"Please say something! Anything! Do you need to speak with a healer?"

I shook my head and slowly rose to my feet with Paige's help. "No...no that won't be necessary. I-I'm...fine." With my mind at ease, I could once again speak freely. "Come, we must speak with the others. I'll tell you all what was said."

The young noblemouse wasn't convinced but decided to focus on hearing me out along with the others. Upon arrival I began to tell Olivia and the other hunters what came of my meeting with Paige's "dearest" uncle, but I felt it would be for the best not to mention how the mouse held me at knife point for Olivia's sake. Alistair wasn't necessarily pleased with me however.

"Are you daft?!" he shouted angrily at me and seized me by the collar to throttle me. "You told him we would be fine with him taking credit for our kill? Do you have any idea what you've agreed to? Do you understand what we went through to come this far? Who do you think you are? What gave you the right to speak for us? You have no idea what you have cost me!"

Alistair was furious and rightfully so. He and his fellow slayers had been preparing for this hunt for some time now and had endured much hardship to reach this point. I wasn't blind to their predicament but what choice did I have? "Please, sir. Calm yourself. I know this meant a lot to you all, but it needed to be done. Blackfang is a problem that must be dealt with, and this was the price that must be paid."

It was plain to see that Paige, Olivia and Ch'Teka weren't particularly pleased with this news either but weren't as irate in comparison to Alistair.

"That's enough, Alistair. Let him go!" Ch'Teka commanded and separated the both of us.

"Bah! This entire journey was all for nothing. I didn't come all of this way to be denied! I wanted fame and glory, not to play lackey for some *honorable knights* who will steal away what is rightfully ours. I'll have no further part in this! I hope they all get eaten!"

To this I didn't really have anything to reply with. As the only person in the room who wasn't a Slayer, I didn't understand their struggle and goals and began to believe I was a bit hasty with not negotiating with Waylon even if that meant being threatened again.

Olivia refused to sit by, however, and let me be scolded by Alistair. "Did you already forget, Alistair? So many of our fellow Slayers have given their lives to kill this creature. The least we can do is honor their sacrifice by finishing it off. Would you really turn your back on them?"

"S-She's right..." Paige hesitantly added.

While she was never one to shy away from arguing against Alistair's foolishness, she too was dismayed that her opportunity to face the beast was taken away from her by her uncle.

"We... You must go and help them. Blackfang must be stopped. I would proudly go in your place to end that monster, but you must go in my stead and that of Gareth's."

Ch'Teka agreed. "We will not hunt for glory, Alistair. We will hunt for the good of the Forest."

Alistair grumbled loudly; he hated what he was hearing from his companions but knew that they were right. "Why are you all always against me?!This isn't fair!" he complained. "Fine then! You all are so stubborn. I'll help you kill the beast but after that it would probably be best if we searched for jobs that actually guaranteed payment next time."

With a sigh of relief, I directed my attention towards Olivia who I had noticed was unusually quiet. Though she spoke up for me it was clear much was on her mind, but before I could open my mouth to speak, Paige tapped my shoulder. "Tybalt, may I speak with you outside?" she asked.

At first, I was going to deny her, but the urgency in her voice had me choose against it. I nodded and we both departed from the room once again. As soon as we did, she would gesture for me to follow her down the hallway.

"All right Tybalt, what really happened in there?" she asked. "With all due respect it feels that in terms of this agreement we received the bare minimum while Uncle Waylon reaps a majority of the rewards. I agree with your sister that we should do this for all the people that monster killed but it feels more like you are to act as servants instead of allies."

Paige was more perceptive—as well as determined—than I expected and likely hadn't forgotten the look of terror I had as I left Waylon's room. I had hoped she would forget the topic earlier but instead remained persistent. My mind still returned to that dreadful moment when I felt Waylon's dagger near my neck and averted my gaze.

"Your uncle is very...convincing."

She narrowed her eyes. Something about her intense stare reminded me of Mother's whenever one of us had done something wrong and sought to hide their crime. This would actually draw the truth from me.

"H-He threatened me and came close to ending my life. I didn't want to say anything as I feared it would only cause a stir...especially with my sister," I admitted shamefully. "I was in no position to argue and the agreement we made was the best I could do. I'm sorry, Paige. I wish I could've done more for you all..."

Hearing this disgusted the noblemouse and yet it hardly surprised her that Waylon would do this. This was yet another reason for her to loathe her uncle.

"I was a bit cross that you went along with such an agreement but hearing that my brute of an uncle had done this to you doesn't surprise me."

It was then that we heard it, irate shouting coming from down the hallway.

"What is all that noise?" I asked her.

"Likely my uncle and his fellow knights preparing for their 'meeting'," Paige answered. "Hearing them shouting angrily doesn't come as a surprise to me given what has occurred these past few days." She then began to walk towards the hall. "Let us see if my dearest Uncle can succeed in stroking the egos of his fellow knights enough to face this monster. Coming, Tybalt?"

I too wished to see this gathering of knights, hoping that Waylon was as influential among them as Paige claimed. "Very well, lead the way."

21

THE SERPENT

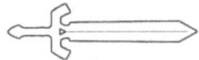 

Wc had barely set foot into the hall before we could feel the anger, frustration and general confusion radiating from the gathering of knights near a large round table. Paige and I chose to remain out of sight on the hall's balcony to avoid causing a stir with our intrusion. Paige watched the bickering noble warriors with great concern.

"The recent events have left our people in turmoil, the knights especially. For years Gladstone has resisted both beast and bandit alike. The destruction caused by Blackfang and the death of my father has left us in a state of despair and uncertainty. We are not a people accustomed to change, Tybalt."

There was no hiding the fact that Paige was affected by all of this as well. In a way I understood the plight of the people of Gladstone as I was familiar with suffering from a swift but destructive blow to my own way of life.

Still, even through the pain and hardship, I needed to move forward regardless of how I felt. Not just for my own sake but for that of my loved ones.

"Change can be difficult, but it is necessary for us to adapt if we are to survive. We can't allow tragedy to slow our regrowth," I replied and offered a sympathetic look to the noblemouse. Partially I was speaking of myself, but I drew no attention to that. "Your people need time to heal and news of Blackfang's defeat will only accelerate that process. For all our sakes your uncle must succeed."

Paige didn't reply but nodded in agreement as we both turned our focus back towards the knights.

The Boldarean knighthood is a crucial part of their people's culture and history which was filled with tales of selfless heroism that shaped their culture to what it is today. With a storied history that dated back to the Great Exodus from the Umbraneath, the Knights of Boldarea have fought fiercely to secure a place in the Hallowed Forest for their people.

A different order of knights would form in this city, however. For the people of Gladstone, they were under the protection of the Knights of the Emerald Oak who proudly identified themselves in forest green tabards with an emblem of a mighty tree akin to the Guardian Tree near their city.

I did find it a tad ironic if not amusing that the people who were so strongly against magic would show such reverence for a tree imbued with magical energy. These knights were known for their resilience, skill in battle and tactical prowess against near impossible odds. It is because of these knights that Boldarean's scoff at the services offered to them by Slayers.

The knights of Gladstone in particular had a history of felling dangerous monsters which had been carved into the walls of their stone structures with well skillful illustrations and immortalized in beautiful paintings that I had seen throughout the castle. Yet now the people's faith in the knights had been shaken. With their lord dead and home assaulted by a seemingly unkillable monster, the once unshakable belief that the common mousefolk would be protected from any and all harm because of their vaunted emerald knights was beginning to waver.

"What are we going to do if that monster returns? We stand no chance against it!"

"If Lord Gladstone is truly gone then so are our brothers and sisters that accompanied him..."

"Should we send word to the capital? Gladstone can't withstand another attack like that."

The knights all expressed their grievances aloud, tossing out questions and words of dismay as they spoke amongst themselves. How could they not when they were dealing with an unnatural foe the likes that none of them had ever faced before?

It was then that Waylon Stoneglory revealed himself, stepping into the Great Hall with a young mouse who appeared to be in her early twenties stood faithfully by his side. She had light gray fur with a fair complexion and might've been mistaken for a maiden if not for the fact that she wore the armor and weaponry of a knight-in-training.

"That mouse next to your uncle, who is she?" I quietly asked Paige to which she answered, "My uncle's squire, Isolda. From what I know, Uncle found her as an orphan, adopted her as one of his own and has been training her to become a knight. From what I've seen of her she is quite talented both as a rider and a warrior."

Waylon made his presence known to his fellow knights. "Brothers and sisters in arms!" he said aloud, his voice so proud and boisterous that it silenced the others. "Once proud and noble protectors of Gladstone and the good people of Boldarea, now forever marked as the weaklings who failed to stop a lowly beast. Are you all done licking your wounds and stewing in your failure?"

Some of the knights looked away in shame at what he was saying while others appeared enraged by Waylon's words. One of the knights, an older mouse with a seasoned look about him glared furiously at Waylon. "Watch your mouth, Waylon! My son gave his life during the attack! You have no right to speak to us in such a manner!" he shouted angrily, the sting of his loss still weighing heavily on his heart. "Are you not the Knight Commander of Gladstone? This failure rests on you as well!"

"This I do not deny," Waylon calmly replied. "I didn't say that I was exempt from this shame that we are all forced to share in. Answer me this my brothers and sisters, does the sense of failure not sting you? Does it not burn at your heart knowing that we all have failed in our duty? I believe it is time to remedy our mistake and bring that foul monster to justice!"

To no surprise of Waylon's his initial call to action wasn't met with valiant cheers and applause, but a grim silence save for one irate knight who looked at him as though he had lost his mind.

"Have you lost your senses? Haven't you heard the accounts given concerning the serpent? We struck the monster with every weapon in our arsenal, and nothing could harm it! You'll have us throw our lives away. Nothing can kill that monster! It has no weaknesses!" the knight exclaimed; her words caused fearful murmurs to be heard amongst the noble warriors.

The uncertainty amongst the knighthood was as clear as day and Waylon sought to use this to his advantage.

"That is where you're wrong, sister. The beast can be killed, and I know it's weakness!" Waylon announced with pride which drew skeptical looks from his fellow knights. "My...informant has discovered vital information of this monster, this 'Blackfang' as they call it. Where it lives and how to kill it. Make no mistake, this is a formidable foe but not an invincible one. It can be slain like every other beast we've brought low in the past. Only I possess the means to succeed but I will need the help of you brave and noble souls to emerge victorious."

Waylon wasn't entirely incorrect, but he was lying to his kin nonetheless. I also noticed he chose to admit the location and the fact that magic would be necessary to kill the monster. At this point, as long as he convinced them to help us, I couldn't care less. The knights were quiet but listened intently as their leader spoke.

"Remember the faces of our fallen. The faces of your loved ones who were lost in the chaos of that terrible day. The innocent commoners, the soldiers who gave their lives, our fellow knights among them...don't you wish to avenge them? Would you truly forsake them? Is it not our duty to deal justice to these fiends?" he asked the murmuring knights. "Normally, I would remain silent as my brother would plot our next course of action, but where is he now? Dead! Along with our fellow knights in Rotmire for reasons unknown. His widowed wife is too distraught with grief to properly lead our people in our darkest hour! Now more than ever we need to stand together! That is why I have summoned you here today! To guide you out of this storm when no one else can and bring us back into a state of peace!"

At last, the knights began to agree with Waylon, and he appeared determined to make a breakthrough with them. They would have justice for their dead and Waylon would give it to them.

"History is about to be made, brothers and sisters! The monster that wronged us all shall be brought to justice by the Knights of the Emerald Oak! Who among you has the strength to ride with me into battle?" he asked his fellow knights with his exuberant call to arms. Without hesitation the knights gave their answer.

"I shall! This crime can't go unpunished!"

"You have my sword, Sir Waylon!"

"I will ride at your side, good sir! For our fallen brothers and our lord!"

"For my city and my son, I shall face this threat with you!"

Even the knights that were initially doubtful of Waylon would have a change of heart. They longed for justice for their dead and to make amends for their failure to defend their city.

"Then ready yourselves! Tomorrow morning, we ride to Rotmire to slay Blackfang once and for all!" The knights cheered for Waylon as he had finally stirred their hearts and drove them to act.

"It would seem that your uncle has won them over," I said to Paige.

"So, it seems..."

While we succeeded in our goal it wasn't hard to tell that Paige wasn't entirely pleased with the outcome. We quietly left out the way we came in and began to walk back towards Gareth's room though even in the hallway we could still hear the cheers. No doubt it wouldn't be long before all of Gladstone was in a fury with preparations for tomorrow's attack.

"You still wish to accompany us," I said to her, figuring that her exclusion from the hunt would play a part in her demeanor.

"Of course, I do!" Paige quickly replied. "I should be there with all of you, not hiding in the keep like some helpless damsel! My father died in Rotmire and I know it had something to do with that mad hermit. Me not being there to help face it feels as though I am doing him a disservice." The frustrated noblemouse looked away from me. "I don't blame you Tybalt, I know how difficult my uncle can be. My only wish is that I could do more to help."

A part of me wished to seek out Waylon and try my best to convince him to allow Paige to join us but I knew it would only end in failure. "Paige, I'm sorry that I couldn't do more, but for now we need to work with your uncle. I promise you that I will do everything I can to aid in defeating Blackfang. For the sake of my family, yours and those that lost theirs to that monster. We shall succeed, I promise."

Paige still longed to join in the coming battle, but she understood that this was simply the way things would have to be. "I will hold you to that promise then," she replied with a small but hopeful smile. "Come, let us inform the others of what occurred."

We then returned to Gareth's room to begin preparations for what I could only hope was the final confrontation with Blackfang. It was difficult for us to sleep that night, knowing the danger we would soon be going off to face.

Just as I had expected, the castle was abuzz with activity as the knights prepared themselves for the battle to come. What were once a disheartened people now seemed enthused at the thought of avenging their fallen.

Everyone in the city did their part, from commoner to noble, donations in the form of food, weapons and other supplies were given to support the effort. Waylon remained true to his words and returned the Slayers' belongings, but little else.

Thankfully, Paige would even make the extra effort to seek out additional equipment and supplies for us. How she managed to get her paws on these things I wasn't aware of and could only hope she didn't put herself at risk for our sake. Though she couldn't accompany us Paige made certain we would be ready to face this threat, especially Alistair.

While Ch'Teka and Olivia armed themselves with both old and new equipment, Alistair stood around looking rather upset. The young Slayer was still mourning the loss of his family bow which he had destroyed in a fit of overwhelming fear. It was a priceless heirloom passed down by a legendary ancestor of his and now It was gone forever because of his cowardice. After all, what was an archer without a bow? This was a problem Paige aimed to fix before they departed.

"Is there a reason why you're pouting and not preparing?" Paige asked as she carried over her belongings that she had been lugging with her for as long as Olivia had seen her, perhaps even longer than that.

Alistair flashed her an annoyed glance. "Begone with you, Paige! Leave me to sulk over my own incompetence," he grumbled, but Paige wouldn't let him be.

"You can sulk when you're dead, but until then I need you mentally and physically ready for the battle to come."

"How can you possibly expect me to fight without my bow?!" he said with a snarl before suddenly panicking at a terrifying thought. "Gracious, I'm going to have to return home and explain why one of the most valuable heirlooms my family possesses has been destroyed! I'm doomed!" The marksrat fell to his knees and is nearly on the verge of tears.

Thankfully Paige was accustomed to Alistair's dramatics by now and simply rolled her eyes at him before setting the hefty backpack she had been carrying down on a nearby table. At last Paige retrieves what she had been tinkering with for countless days and nights from within.

"Dry your eyes, fool, and look at what I have for you." Alistair wiped away his tears to see what exactly Paige was trying to show him.

"What is this thing?"

What laid before him was a curious contraption, a bizarre weapon that shared similarities to a bow but had a far more intricate design.

"It's repulsive! Is this contraption supposed to be some form of bow? What an insult to archery itself!" he exclaimed much to the irritation of Paige.

"It's not repulsive you half-wit! It's called a crossbow! A new weapon that I've been working on for months now. I want you to use it in battle against Blackfang!"

"You expect me to go into battle using this abomination?"

Paige glared furiously at Alistair and his continued ungratefulness before frowning at him, giving him a look of utter disappointment in her companion. "I intended to reveal this to my father once I returned. I wanted to show him I could do more than just remain at home while my brothers and sisters go off to learn and become knights. I sought to prove that I didn't need to be the biggest and strongest mouse to succeed. He will never get to see it now, but that doesn't mean it can't be useful. Please Alistair, I know we haven't always seen eye to eye, but I need you to do this. You always spoke of wanting to be a hero...well right now I need you to become my hero."

Upon hearing this Alistair seemed to change his tune. He wasn't aware of how important this new weapon was to Paige. As someone who knew what it was like to lose a father, he knew what Paige was feeling and why she needed him to do this.

"Well I-..erm...I suppose it's worth at least attempting to use. It's not like I'll be running into battle with those flimsy mousefolk bows your people use." He reached for the weapon and carefully picks it up.

It felt awkward in his paws if not somewhat cumbersome, something he could only hope would fade away as he grew more familiar with the weapon. "Perhaps you could show me to the target range and explain how this bow-cross thingamajig works exactly."

Paige took a moment to calm herself as if she had been fighting off tears. "O-Of course, follow me. I'll show you how to use it properly." She smiled faintly at the marksrat and the two departed to go and practice with Alistair's new weapon.

As they exited the room, Olivia and Ch'Teka were left alone. The Dweller warrior had once again adorn herself in her armor before checking the condition of the great sword she had acquired in Rotmire.

Olivia now wore a set of chain mail under her old garments for protection as well as the old red cloak of our mother but unlike Ch'Teka she seemed hesitant to wield her sword. The memory of her hurting Gareth and others was still fresh in her mind and while she knew Paige had risked much to reacquire her father's weapon for her sake, Olivia still remained uncertain. She gripped our Mother's crests that still hung around her neck and looked at it mournfully.

"Something wrong?" she asked, detecting the hesitation in the young slayer. "The weapon is yours to wield, take it."

Olivia glanced over at her father's blade as it was propped against the wall. She had overcome so much with this weapon and still she barely knew how to use it. "Maybe someone else should wield it," Olivia muttered. "I can carry another sword."

Ch'Teka cast a disapproving look at the young mouse. "You are the wielder of that weapon; no other should hold in it their paws."

"I...don't feel like I deserve it any longer. Not after what happened. So many people were hurt because of my carelessness. What if it happens again?"

In privacy, my sister had informed Ch'Teka of what she had done and expected the Dweller to be furious with her, yet she remained unphased. Ch'Teka walked towards the sword and retrieved it from its resting spot. She partially unsheathed it from its scabbard before offering it to Olivia.

"It won't," she told her. "Do not be sorry. Be better. Very soon our lives will depend on it."

Olivia then took the blade and Ch'Teka walked away, saying nothing more about the subject. Though with what little Ch'Teka had said it was clear to Olivia now that there was no avoiding this. For the good of all

Olivia needed to accept what she had done and move on. This was something easier said than done, but if she was to succeed in avenging our family Olivia knew that there was no other choice but to overcome her fears.

With some lingering hesitation she equipped the weapon to her sword belt and began making final preparations for the battle to come.

The Slayers were nearly prepared for the journey to Rotmire, I was preoccupied with a summons by Waylon who wished to speak with me in private within his quarters. Given how my previous meeting had gone with the knightly mouse I'll admit I wasn't eager to see him again. I would have much preferred to speak with Olivia as we hadn't had any time to ourselves.

Still, I had no excuse, the most I had done to prepare myself for the battle was to equip a new short sword that Paige had brought for me. I decided against wearing any protective armor as I feared it would only slow me down.

Once I was ready and mentally prepared for whatever Waylon had in mind for me, I approached his door. After mustering my courage, I knocked on it only for it to immediately open.

"He's here, sir." Isolda stood at the door much to my surprise.

"Let him in," I heard Waylon say within the room.

Isolda guided me further in where I saw Waylon was already equipped for battle in his knightly breastplate. He was searching through his personal collection of finely crafted swords and seemed to be checking the size as well as the heft of each weapon to see if it was what he wanted to wield during battle.

"There you are, boy," he said in a condescending manner without even looking towards me. "I trust you and your pack of mongrels are prepared? I'll have no layabouts fighting amongst me."

"Yes, my companions are ready to depart when you are," I corrected him.

"Good," he replied. "We leave for Rotmire in an hour. Twelve of our finest knights shall ride with us into battle. The rest of the order will attend to repairs and bolster defense of Gladstone should our other foes catch us unaware. You lot shall take orders from me, and I expect them to be obedient to my commands."

"We will be, sir. I'll be certain to tell them."

In an effort to minimize my time with Paige's "favorite" uncle I decided to keep my responses short and polite. Waylon then retrieves a sword he fancied and examines it.

"Lastly, I feel that it is necessary to have someone with actual skill looking after you. Therefore, my squire, Isolda shall act as your protector."

Glancing over my shoulder at the mouse behind me, Isolda gave me a polite nod but appeared largely uninterested in me. I nodded back before looking back towards Waylon.

"I'm thankful that you care so much about my well-being, sir knight."

This was partially true, but something told me Waylon had assigned his squire to me as a way to have someone spy on me and potentially strike me down if I did anything that might act against Waylon's wishes. With Isolda being Waylon's squire and adopted father I expected her to share the same brutal nature that her mentor possessed. "Be proud, boy. You are about to witness history in the making. A new legend for all of Boldarea to recall in the days to come."

Waylon was right, in a sense. Once we faced the beast, nothing would ever be the same for any of us. It wasn't long after that that the great march to Rotmire began.

Led by Waylon and twelve knights that he personally chose, they rode on beetleback through the streets of Gladstone. These steeds were the finest Gladstone could offer and would have their limits tested in the trials to come. The knights received cheers and support from the citizens who flung flowers into the air as their armored champions rode towards the exit.

Myself, Olivia and her Slayer companions walked behind the mounted knights and were "gifted" with confused stares and ire from the citizens much to our dismay. We didn't appear nearly as organized or well equipped to them, we were mere mercenaries that were needlessly accompanying vaunted emerald oak knights.

Given the fact that we too were going into battle with the monster it would've been nice to have some form of support from the people we were technically fighting for. Nevertheless, we had no choice but to press on.

As we all reached the main gate of the city, the Slayers were allowed to ride with the knights in an effort to save time and reach Rotmire in an expedient fashion. Of course, this was done so begrudgingly as the very notion of riding with a ratkin and Dweller wasn't a pleasant one but the oak knights had little choice but to swallow their pride. We were filled with a grim determination to succeed, fully knowing that the likelihood of us meeting our end within that cursed place was highly probable.

We had our differences of course; it was no secret that Boldarean's had no desire to travel with us but in the end, we needed to stand together to face the coming threat. Normally it would take us at least a day or two to reach Rotmire but on the backs of the Boldarean's favorite mounted beetle, the lumbering but durable, Staghorn Beetle we were able to fly to our destination before the day's end.

In truth I would've preferred to remain a few more days away from Rotmire as the terrifying memories of my previous trip still haunted me. We would set up camp around the entrance of Rotmire, knowing well that entering it could mean certain death without a proper plan.

This was where I, Waylon's "secret" informant, would play my part. Waylon was expecting me to give him information about the whereabouts of Blackfang's lair and given that he had already informed his fellow knights that he knew where it was he was hard pressed to retrieve that information from me.

Unfortunately, I still didn't know myself because I needed to wait for Alden to contact me somehow. If I didn't hear from him soon, I imagined Waylon would take his frustration out on me. Distancing myself from absolutely everyone, I stood at the mouth of the cursed land, attempting to peer through its unnatural murk for any sign of what Alden wished for me to see.

"Please, Alden. I need you now more than ever. Give me a sign, a plan...anything!" I pleaded but would receive no response.

A pit in my stomach began to form as I felt genuinely uncertain of what to do next. I knew Waylon wouldn't be pleased with my silence. The demanding knight wanted results and he would get them one way or another.

As I turned away to return to the camp, something would urge me to stop as an all too familiar presence began to fly out of the mist of the gloomy place.

"Could it be?" I wondered if what I was seeing was real and not some cruel illusion before recognizing the shimmering white light from my previous trip to the mire.

Finally, Alden had come to my aid once again as he sent one of his moth familiars to reveal what I needed to know. The delicate insect then perched itself on my staff and exactly like before I reached out to touch it to once again be gifted with a vision.

It revealed that deep within the mire lied a burbling tar pit with a sizeable patch of land that appeared to be the only place safe from the tar. Therein lied a cave where strange and hostile looking mice and other warriors guarded the entrance. The last thing that I saw was a glimpse of the cave itself which appeared very similar to that of my vision of Blackfang's lair.

What I found strange however was that I saw no sign of the serpent itself but before I could ponder more the vision would conclude. As I returned to my senses and tried to comprehend the vision, I witnessed the moth flutter back into the murk of the mire, no doubt returning to its master. At last, I had the information I needed.

"Thank you, Alden. I'm forever in your debt," I said to myself before returning to camp where Waylon waited "patiently" for my return.

Upon entering his tent, I could see by his expression alone that he needed my answer now. He had been pacing back and forth when he finally looked towards me as I stepped inside. "I trust you aren't here to stall any longer, boy. My patience is wearing thin."

Seeing him in such a irritable mood prompted me to tell him everything he wished to know which improved his demeanor. The tactical mind of the knight already began to form a plan around this.

"So, our serpent is taking a nap after all the destruction it caused? Then this will be even easier than I thought," he boldly stated. "I will have half my knights deal with the deluded fools lurking outside of the monster's lair. We don't need these strangers rushing to the aid of the serpent if they are aligned. Why anyone would be guarding that monster is beyond me but if they seek to protect it then they had better be ready to pay with their lives. Meanwhile, you and your mongrels along with the rest of my knights shall go and slay this monster once and for all."

"A...uhm sound strategy, sir," I said in response to which he scoffed at me.

"Oh, don't pretend that you know anything about strategy, boy. Just go and relay my orders to your little friends and I will do the same with my fellow knights."

With haste he left the tent followed by his squire. For everything that had happened I could only hope that this disrespectful treatment from Waylon would be worth it in the end. I departed from the tent as well to inform my sister and her companions.

Once the situation was explained the Slayers readied themselves for the battle to come. They had been downsized to only three with Gareth still unwell and Paige forced to remain in Gladstone. Yet their confidence and desire to fell the dreaded serpent had yet to waiver.

Ch'Teka appeared as formidable as ever, though I hadn't seen the Dweller fight with my own eyes I could tell from the sight of her that she was a competent warrior and was eager to face the beast. Alistair, still troubled by his cowardly dismay from days ago, now appeared hardened and ready to redeem himself while armed with Paige's strange new weapon.

Despite his earlier complaints he appeared more confident with the crossbow in his arms no doubt thanks to Paige. Olivia also appeared ready for this final confrontation. Slaying this monster was the sole reason she embarked on this journey and now she was about to bring it to its conclusion.

"Whatever happens, I want to thank all of you... I know it hasn't been easy for us but it will all be worth it in the end," Olivia said to her fellow Slayers and myself.

Given that there was a chance none of us would return from this battle, now was the time to speak her mind.

"This shan't be the end of us, Olivia. Watch and see me perform miracles today," the rat happily boasted while checking his new weapon.

"Victory is assured. I see no other way for us," Ch'Teka then said and appeared eager to enter combat.

Olivia smiled at the two of them but quietly longed for Gareth and even Paige to be present. "We shall fight twice as hard for our fellows back in Gladstone!" she declared with pride.

Despite the negative treatment she had received from the Boldareans and their views on Slayers I could see that Olivia's desire to remain as one had yet to be tainted.

As Ch'Teka and Alistair began their last minute checks on their equipment, Olivia turned to me with a hardened expression. "This is it, Tybalt. We're finally doing this. We're finally avenging our family."

I nodded, knowing well what was about to occur. "We'll see this through to the end, Olivia. I'm not going anywhere."

My sister smiled at my words. She embraced me afterwards. "Thank you...for everything."

With that said Olivia walked away to check her own equipment like her companions. To see Olivia like this lifted my spirits and encouraged me to succeed now more than ever. Soon enough, the Boldareans were ready for combat and so were we.

We were to once again fly on the backs of the war beetles to swiftly move through the mire without being bogged down by it and reach the lair of our foe. I rode with Isolda who had proven herself to be an expert when it came to flying.

Before we took flight, she would help me mount the beast by offering her paw to me. "Ready for your second time flying?" she asked while dawning her helmet. "As I'll ever I be I suppose."

Admittedly I had no love for flying, it felt unnatural for a mouse to be in the air like a bird. From what I heard, Isolda's beetle was one of the fastest in Gladstone so it came as no surprise that she would be leading the charge along with myself. "I hope so, you'll be guiding me, and the entirety of our forces and we'll need you at your best."

"No pressure then," I jested, of course but Isolda appeared unamused. She looked over towards the other knight riders and waited for Waylon to give the signal. Riding atop his own mount he stood proudly and readied himself.

"Forward knights! For Gladstone! For Boldarea!" he shouted, spurring his brethren's spirits while signaling for Isolda to fly ahead with me in tow, giving her directions.

Soon the air of Rotmire was filled with the sound of rapidly beating wings as we took flight and soared over the mire. The Emerald Knights stayed in close formation behind us and formed a bird-like V as we flew through the air on the backs of battle-bred beetles. Our presence in this forsaken place was unwanted as the mire's inhabitants hissed and roared in anger yet we flew on in defiance of it.

It didn't take long for us to find Blackfang's lair and thankfully the information Alden's moth had shown me was accurate. Just as planned, we all flew down towards the tar pit with half of Waylon's knights focusing their efforts on fighting the hostile foes guarding Blackfang's lair.

The Slayers, myself, Olivia and Waylon with his knights focused on seeking out Blackfang within its lair and destroying it. While we were dealing with Blackfang none of us would witness what took place during the battle but even from within its lair I could hear the roar of combat raging outside.

For all their faults, I couldn't deny the bravery of the Boldarean knights. Upon flying through the passage leading us into the serpent's home we noticed the cave was unguarded unlike the entrance. This both alleviated us of worrying about fighting more of those strangers but also troubled us as we didn't know why.

Though it wouldn't be clear until we arrived in the heart of the lair that our concerns would only heighten. The serpent's lair was exactly how my vision had depicted; an eerie cave littered with the bones of countless victims of Blackfang. The skeletal remains of mice, rats and Dwellers as well as many other creatures both great and small could be seen. Massive, disorganized piles of the monster's victims filled the deceptively vast cave and served as a grim reminder of how dangerous the fiend we sought to slay was.

Yet despite what we saw there was no sign of Blackfang. "I...I don't understand. It should be here! Why isn't it here?" I questioned as we landed and dismounted our beetles before one of the larger bone piles.

The slayers as well as Waylon with his knight companions landed and were also baffled by the missing serpent.

Waylon especially appeared livid with this matter. "You told us this was where the serpent made it's nest, yet I see nothing here but bones! What are you playing at, boy?" he angrily scolded.

"I-I'm sorry, sir. I don't—"

"I'm not interested in your sniveling excuses! I want—"

Suddenly the cave rumbled to life due to some unnatural tremor causing the bones to clatter violently as we were all knocked to the floor...and then we heard the voice.

"So, you've come, just as she said you would. Such disrespectful children, vile and ungrateful of the blessing she wishes to bestow upon us," a sinister disembodied voice echoed throughout the cave.

There was no sign of who was speaking and neither I nor Waylon knew who this was. The Slayers, however, were quite familiar with that unnerving voice and had already drawn their weapons.

"That voice...i-it's him again!" Alistair said while securing a bolt from his new quiver. Chills ran down his spine, but he fought off the urge to flee in terror.

Ch'Teka growled and her grip on her weapon tightened. "Of course, one monster would be aiding the other..."

Olivia was still furious that the deluded hermit stopped her from finishing off the beast back in Gladstone. No more lives would've needed to be lost if not for him. "Where is he? I don't see him anywhere!" She placed her paw on the hilt of her blade, eager to make amends for her grave error in Gladstone.

"Whose there?! Reveal yourself at once!" Waylon exclaimed angrily and unsheathed his blade, a sentiment that was shared amongst his comrades who also drew their swords. "As a knight of Gladstone, I demand that you surrender yourself for questioning or face justice! If you and your cohorts outside the cave have anything to do with this monster you will answer for your crimes!" he demanded.

"Your people have no power in these lands! Come and try to carve your 'justice' out of me and you will be met with failure." The hermit mocked them from the shadows, only enraging Waylon even further. "I know why you are here. You seek to slay her divine beast like so many others. A grievous sin that shall not be forgiven. Nevertheless, the Mother of Rot is not without mercy. Lay down your weapons and submit to her will and I will let you live only to serve her."

Waylon spat on the ground, disgusted with the hermit's 'offer'. "No true Boldarean would ever submit to such lunacy! As soon as you are dealt with, this 'mother' of yours is next!"

The cave trembled again in response to the show of defiance. "Blasphemers to the end. This comes as no surprise to me. Very well."

It was then that the pile of bones we stood before began to move on its own, as if something lied within the pile of remains.

"It matters not how this ends, whether you slay the beast or the beast slays you."

Then we saw it, a singular glowing green eye, full of hate for all life untainted by the rot. It stared at us with a voracious look.

"The seeds of my victory have already been planted throughout this forest and in time I will reap the harvest..."

Finally, our foe emerged from the pile, sending bones and bone fragments flying everywhere as it revealed itself.

"...for I have already won."

This creature, this abomination was indeed Blackfang though it had been changed. The wounds it suffered from Olivia's sword had left lasting effects on it as its rotting flesh was sagging against its bones while attempting to restore it's withering form with strange dripping tar-like rot that clung to its rotting body. The very sight and smell of it was nauseating and I had to fight off the urge to regurgitate.

The beast seemed to have increased in size no doubt due to the meddling sorcery of the mad hermit who appeared to have departed and left us to the mercy of his monster. It wasn't alone either, as the snake let out an unnatural guttural bellow, the bones of the fallen began to stir, connecting themselves and forming skeletal monstrosities that shambled towards us. They began to arm themselves with discarded weapons that laid on the ground and aimed to use them against us.

Witchcraft!" one of the knight's cried out while readying her shield and blade.

Waylon and his knights had faced dangerous foes before, but never the living dead, let alone anything involving dark magic. Though they held their ground there was no masking the uncertainty on their faces. Now enraged by the hermit's defiance and at the sight of the foulest magic being worked before his very eyes, Waylon held his ground and gave the command to engage.

"*Attack!* For Boldarea!" Waylon shouted while the slayers and his fellow knights clashed with the skeletal monsters advancing towards them.

Isolda was about to join her master when I suddenly grabbed her shoulder much to her irritation.

"Isolda, I need your help!" I said with urgency. "We will never be able to kill Blackfang if you don't assist me. Please!"

Isolda longed to join Waylon in battle but remembered that her mentor ordered her to keep me protected. Begrudgingly she then asked, "What do you need of me?"

"There is an.... object of great importance in the far back of this cave. Without it there shall be no victory for us this day."

Isolda eyed me with a skeptical look before groaning.

"If what you say is true then I suppose there's no time to waste. Quickly now, back on the beetle!"

With haste Isolda re-mounted her steed and helped me back onto it as well. We flew into the air, avoiding the conflict raging below in hopes of swiftly securing the sagestone. Flying above the chaos gave us a bird's eye view of what was going on and how the battle was progressing.

For the moment our allies were holding their own, but we could see an increasing number of skeletal foes assembling themselves in the bone piles throughout the cave. Though Blackfang was moving much slower than before, it wouldn't be long before it too joined the battle.

"T-There's too many of them! Our friends will be swarmed by these monsters! We must hurry!" I urged Isolda who tried to quicken our pace.

As we departed for the far back of the cave my companions and Waylon with his knights continued to fight back the skeletal horrors rapidly approaching them. These creatures were mindless and threw themselves at their attackers with reckless abandon and were easily cut down.

Bound together only by some magic spell the serpent had cast they were easy to break apart. There was a problem with this however, each time they were defeated the bones merely reassembled themselves often using whatever bones were nearest to them to create even more ghastly forms. Waylon continued to hack and slash at every foe that drew near to him while growing increasingly frustrated as he failed to permanently put them down.

"Foul sorcery! These creatures refuse to die!" he shouted while striking down yet another foe.

Some of the other knights began to remount their beetlesteeds and began to use them to ram their opponents into pieces! Ch'Teka swept her sword through the foes attacking her, slicing through bone and marrow alike. Alistair showed off his prowess with his new weapon, proving his skill with each skull penetrated by his bolts.

As for my sister, Olivia had stowed away any hesitation about wielding her sword and unleashed the weapon upon her foes. Unlike the weapons of our other companions the blade not only broke the skeletal fiends into pieces but outright annihilated any trace of them with each one struck down.

With Waylon and his soldiers on the verge of being overwhelmed by the skittering limbs and bone horrors, Olivia along with her fellow slayers fought fiercely to aid them with the young mouse's blade bringing a permanent end to their foes. Waylon and his warriors were astonished by this but instead of wasting time asking questions they joined in her attack to fend off the creatures.

However, this resistance seemed to draw the ire of the wounded serpent who had been eying us as mere prey instead of an actual threat...or at least it did until he took notice of Olivia and the glowing blade she used to cut through its minions. It was as if the beast recalled what Olivia had done to it and was enraged by the sight of her and her weapon. A vicious hiss escaped the rotting wytherbeast as it began to prepare itself to attack!

While the others fought fiercely myself and Isolda flew closer to our destination but there was a problem. Recalling my vision, I remembered seeing what I could only assume was the Sagestone I needed in the skull of a long deceased creature with the stone itself shimmering brilliantly even in a dark and desolate place like this. Yet now, I could see no such light. I was beginning to fear the stone had been moved.

"We must hurry, Sir Waylon and the others will need our help!" Isolda said with urgency. "I-I know, I will only need a moment!" I replied while looking for what I could only assume was the skull from my vision.

"There!" I shouted. "Take me to that large skull! It has to be there."

Cautiously, Isolda lowered us just enough for me to dismount at the top of the pile. Examining it closer I could see that this was indeed the correct place and within the mouth of this deceased beast I did find the object I had sought. At first, I felt relieved to finally hold this powerful item in my paws but then I realized that something was amiss.

"W-What is this? What's wrong with it?!" The item I held was indeed a Sagestone, but unlike the stones that I held in the past it lacked the luminous glow that previous stones possessed. It was cold to the touch, bereft of the comforting warmth of other Sagestones. "This isn't right. I-It's not supposed to be like this!"

At first, I wondered if it simply needed to be connected to the unfinished staff, but the stone remained unresponsive. The sagestone had lost its power causing it to fall dormant and I lacked the knowledge on how to restore it to its former state.

While I panicked and sought to frantically discover a way to reactivate it, my companions continued to do battle with the undead monstrosities attacking them. In spite of their valiant efforts and even with the Will infused sword that Olivia wielded their foes continued their unstoppable advance and grew more numerous as the bone piles began to become more active, no doubt due to the increased power the hermit had infused in Blackfang.

It was becoming more and more clear that fighting undead creatures was nothing like facing a living foe. They didn't tire, or want for food and water, nor did they question the orders given to them by their twisted masters. In comparison, the heroic slayers and knights were beginning to waver and tire from the increasing number of undead attacking them.

At first, they could manage but more and more the knights accompanying Waylon would be overwhelmed. Three of them would be dragged into the approaching mass of undead foes, kicking and screaming, never to be seen again.

"They're too many!" Waylon shouted as he swung his sword through the skull of a skeletal rat. "We'll be overwhelmed if something isn't done!"

Just then Blackfang finally acted and slowly slithered off of his pile of bones to lunge at two of the mounted knights fending off its minions! The heroic warriors were too preoccupied with their undead foes to face Blackfang and cried out in agony as they, their beetlesteeds and even some of it's skeletal minions were swallowed whole!

"NO!" Olivia cried out in horror as she watched the knights perish before rushing towards the serpent, cutting a path through her mindless adversaries to reach the beast before it could strike again.

The monster and its minions would turn their attention towards the wounded and exhausted Waylon who now stood alone with his fellow knights slain by our foes. Olivia wouldn't allow this however as she rushed over to aid Waylon! Same as she had done so before, Olivia held her blessed blade aloft to shine its magnificent light in the face of monster in hopes of burning it alive with its purity as she had done so before.

The runeblade did harm the creature as it recoiled in pain in response to being so close to it, but not to the extent that had suffered previously. The hermit had further empowered Blackfang and just as I had told Olivia before, her sword alone wouldn't be enough to fell this abomination. Enraged by Olivia's defiance it lunges at and only by the Will itself did she narrowly avoid being devoured.

Waylon was sent tumbling back after Blackfang struck the earth, dropping his sword as he flung briefly into the air. The serpent strike pounds the earth was such a force that it shakes the ground.

"Aauh!" Olivia was sent tumbling to the dirt while also being separated from her weapon! The situation was growing more dire by the moment.

Waylon was sent tumbling back after Blackfang shook the entire cave, dropping his sword as he flung briefly into the air. Dazed and exhausted from the fighting, Olivia glanced around the area hoping to see her allies come to her aid.

Olivia could see the weapons and armor of the Emerald Oak Knights scattered across the ground with their owners nowhere to be seen. Ch'Teka was tiring and appeared to be wounded from the fighting but still stubbornly continued to fight against their numerous foes.

Alistair was nowhere to be seen in the chaos and Olivia was beginning to fear that the marksrat's anxiety had gotten the better of him once again and had already fled the battle.

"N-No, not like this. It can't end like this..." Exhausted and sore from the constant fighting Olivia searched for her sword in hopes of wielding it against Blackfang once again. So lost in the throes of combat and the search for our Father's sword that she failed to notice that Blackfang had his sights on her once again. "Tybalt, where are you?"

My sister needed me, they all did. But what good was I without the Sagestone empowered? I could hear Isolda frantically call to me, no doubt in hopes of getting me to come with her so that we could rejoin our allies. I could feel the pile of skeletal remains beneath me begin to stir and in time they would come for me as well. I ignored it all, so absorbed I was into comprehending why the stone wasn't active that I had nearly doomed myself. Right as I was on the verge of once again giving up hope I felt something, or should I say heard something. A voice from within the stone then spoke to me. "Dark days approach, doom for the entire forest is at hand. The strongest of spirits are needed in the days to come..."For me, it was as if time had frozen and all things around me had fallen still. The voice from the stone was all that I could hear. It was dominating, overwhelming...and yet comforting. "Tell me, is your will strong enough?" It asked which replied to it with great confusion. "Who are you? What is happening and what do you mean by "Dark Days?"

"You have already seen what is to come. If you do not act, all will be lost for this forest and what life lies beyond the Green Bastion."

"But what could I possibly do? I am no one. I am no hero."

"That is what you claim and yet you have proven yourself time after time. So, I will ask you again, do you have the courage to save this forest?"

I paused and felt unsure of if I should answer as I knew little of who or what I was speaking to but given the situation I was in and what was at stake I couldn't afford to turn this offer down.

"If it means saving my sister and the forest then I will pay any price."

The voice seemed pleased with my answer. "I cannot promise that the days to come will be easy for you, but I will guide you and give you the strength to prevail."

My desire was to ask this mysterious being more questions but before I could give an answer I returned to my senses and the voice was gone. "W-What? Where am I? What was I—"

It was then that I took notice of the brightly glowing stone in my paw, the Sagestone had reawakened, it's power far greater than any other I had felt previously! It was then that I remembered my situation and knew that time was of the essence.

Without hesitation I placed the stone at the top of the staff and to my surprise the head of the staff reacted to its presence. It twisted its wooden limbs around the sagestone and hardened itself around it, tightening it's hold on the powerful rune. The magic from the stone rippled through the staff and into me, awakening a power within me that I never knew existed.

"Tybalt! Behind you!" I heard Isolda cry out and as I turned to face whatever stood behind me. I saw a hulking skeletal creature climb up the bone pile behind me with several other fiends not far off from it.

Ordinarily, I would have been overwhelmed with fear, but as I held the staff in my paws, I felt neither fear nor hesitation. If anything, I felt empathy for these creatures, knowing that they moved not out of their own wishes but by the cruelty of another.

I pointed the head of the staff towards my attackers. "Please, rest. Suffer no more..."

As if responding to the overwhelming presence of dark magic before it my empowered staff fired off an arcing light that stripped the magic forcing the bones to move on their own. The skeletal fiends collapsed into pieces that tumbled back down the pile. I looked at my staff in astonishment, that I held such power in my paws was something I was unaccustomed to.

Isolda was also in shock, she was planning to abandon me and even still after seeing the magic I wielded. Not to mention that she was hesitant to approach me due to the stigmatism Boldarean's felt towards Sages and magic in general. "Y-You...what are you? Your eyes they...t-they glow!"

"Isolda, there isn't much time. We have to save them before it's too late."

Despite her hesitation she offered her paw to me, and we once again flew towards the serpent and the battle raging around it.

At that moment, Olivia had finally found her blade, but the serpent was once again ready to strike out at her. She made a mad dash for the weapon but as soon as her paw touched the hilt of the runeblade Blackfang once again lunged for Olivia. In my vision, this was where I imagined Olivia meeting her end, but the Will wouldn't allow it.

Right as the creature was about to strike, a single well place bolt flew into the serpent's one remaining eye, fully blinding the beast.

"Oh no you don't!" Alistair smirked while preparing another bolt and firing it at one of the fiends attempting to ambush Ch'Teka from behind.

Both Isolda and I saw the creature writhe in agony.

"It's weakened! Whatever you intend to do Tybalt I suggest you do it now!" Isolda shouted.

"Fly me closer!" I told her while preparing my staff once again. Same as before it crackled with great power. "This madness ends now!"

Once more the staff's power activated and fired an arcing light of pure Will magic that pierced through its withering form. This caused part of the monstrous snake's body to disintegrate from the sheer power contained within the staff.

Blackfang was ill-prepared by yet another overwhelmingly painful attack and found itself in even greater turmoil! It was then that Olivia saw her opportunity to strike, for the nightmares she suffered, for the guilt that clung to her heart and for the lives of all those lost to this creature's ravenous feeding, my sister would end it once and for all!

With a valorous cry she mustered what little strength she possessed to fight through her the skeletal creatures that barred her way to reach the dying monster whose head had clumsily slammed down on the ground.

Seeing this, Ch'Teka would also use what strength that remained within her to assist Olivia in cutting down her foes while rushing to reach Blackfang before it could even attempt to recover again.

Without hesitation or remorse Olivia climbed up a jutting bone in the dirt, jumped at the blinded beast and impaled the sword into its skull! It lashed about wildly tossing Olivia too and fro as it did with her clinging to the hilt of the impaled blade.

Upon doing this, the creature howled in pain which shook the cavern and caused the undead monsters around it to freeze in place before collapsing to the dirt and grime of its lair. This also sent Olivia tumbling to the ground, aching but thankfully alive. Though sore and bruised my sister refused to remain in the dirt with her sword still lodged in her foe. She took a moment to regain her strength and approached the beast to claim what was hers.

As Olivia retrieved her blade the serpent let out one last death howl, startling her right when she believe she had landed the finishing blow. The flesh of the serpent burned away, leaving only the skeletal remains of the monster formerly known as Blackfang.

Isolda then landed the beetle allowing us both to dismount with her rushing to tend to her wounded mentor and me to go and see to Olivia. "Sir Waylon! Are you all, right?" she asked with no shortage of urgency.

Waylon was furious, not only had he been brought low and nearly killed by the undead monsters but those who he thought would be proud to share in this victory, were no more. "This was...not how it was supposed to go." He grimaced while wincing in pain. "Fine their remains, our brothers and sisters will not be left here to rot in this forsaken place."

A tinge of guilt could be seen on Isolda's face, though they were successful in defeating their foe, it came at a high price. "Of course, sir, but allow me to tend to your wounds first," Isloda dutifully said before glancing over at me with a curious gaze before looking back towards the wounded Waylon.

I looked over towards Ch'Teka who thankfully Alistair had to care for her with me immediately rushing towards my exhausted sibling who looked up at me with a look of disbelief. She lay in the dirt beside the remains of the dreaded serpent.

"Brother, did we...did we do it? Is this real? Did we win?"

Olivia was struggling to hold back her tears; she was trembling and could barely hold her sword any longer. I laid down my staff and embraced my sister. "Yes, sister. I think we did. It's finally over." Olivia's hold on me tightened as she wept. At long last our family had been avenged and for a brief moment we finally felt peace.

EPILOGUE

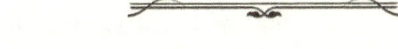

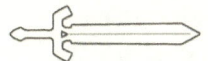 

What I had once deemed to be an impossible task had finally been achieved. The venomous scourge known as Blackfang had at long last been slain. No longer would the beast prey upon the people of the Hallowed Forest and those who had lost loved ones could find peace at last. Yet despite this being a monumental achievement for myself and especially Olivia the outcome didn't bring us the satisfaction that we desired.

Blackfang was well and truly dead, but our home could never be restored and those we lost to the beast would never be returned to us. This truth I already knew of and made no attempt to deceive myself into believing that slaying Blackfang would restore all that had been taken from us. This realization struck Olivia far harder as she found herself in a state of self-reflection and isolation for at least several days once we returned to Gladstone.

For Waylon and his people this victory was also bittersweet, though they were victorious and claimed victory over Blackfang as their own accomplishment many perished in the ensuing battles both inside and outside of the black serpent's cave.

Those that fought to keep the bulk of the monster's horde from rejoining the battle within the cave were forced to fight undead monstrosities as well with some of them even being slain Gladstone knights, including the deceased Lord Dorian.

At the very least the people of Gladstone were able to give their fallen kin and lord a proper burial which brought no small amount of peace to his grieving mate and child. As for the Slayers, all were frustrated with the situation they were currently in.

Despite being pivotal in slaying Blackfang their "assistance" was minimized to bolster Waylon's wild claims of taking the serpent on in single combat. Alistair was still annoyed that they would be receiving hardly any credit for slaying the beast and was eager to depart from Gladstone as soon as Gareth was well enough to leave.

Ch'Teka was wounded during the battle but would thankfully recover. While she would've liked to have her own fame grown with this victory, she saw the necessity in slaying the serpent for the good of all. Paige was pleased to see that we survived the battle and returned with the remains of her Father.

However, she was still upset that she couldn't participate in the fight. With Gareth remaining indisposed the Slayers were permitted to remain in Gladstone until he recovered to which they would then be "escorted" out of their city. They were being treated less as a potential threat and more as exotic "guests" in service to Waylon.

Lastly, there was the matter of the hermit, the one who appeared to be the mastermind behind all that had occurred. Blackfang itself wasn't even a living creature, merely a tool to be used by this sick minded individual.

When the battle ended there was no sign of the hermit present, if he was even there at all. The power that he wielded was considerable and his ominous words before leaving us to face his monster were deeply concerning. We knew nothing about this rat, what his goals were, why he was doing this and what exactly this "Mother of Rot" intended to inflict upon the forest.

Paige especially was aggravated by this and swore vengeance against the hermit prompting Ch'Teka to warn her against doing something reckless. Given the frantic but celebratory state Gladstone was in, Olivia thought it best to pull me away from it all so that we had a chance to be alone. She expressed a desire to return home and to pay our final respects to our loved ones.

With help from Paige, we were able to obtain a beetlesteed of our own and used it to return to the place where it all began. The splintered remains of what was once our quiet little stump. It was around the afternoon when we finally returned.

The clearing still felt off to me as if Blackfang's presence never truly left. The chill of fall hung in the air. Some of the family's old belongings still lay scattered about only now covered by the fall of autumn leaves.

"It feels so strange returning here again," Olivia said. "In a way it almost feels wrong, like we shouldn't be here anymore."

"There's nothing left for us here. No reason to remain...all we can do is give our respects and move on," I solemnly replied. "I still wish I hadn't taken that sword. If only Mother had it. Maybe things would've been different-Agh!"

The young slayer nearly fell over, her injured side was still hurting after the battle and occasionally I needed to come and support her. Olivia was still nursing wounds, but she wouldn't allow her injuries to keep her from returning home.

"At least we did it. This nightmare is finally over, and we could put all of this behind us."

Olivia smiled at me, but she saw that I didn't share her sentiment. "I'm not so sure. Blackfang may be dead, but it's creator that...twisted hermit you encountered...he still lives and is somewhere in the forest. All of this was his doing, even Blackfang was just a tool for him."

Olivia had no sympathy for the snake but understood what I meant. "Well then, what do we do now?"

"That depends on you..." I answered. "I wanted us to begin anew and live somewhere safe and quiet but given all that's occurred during our travels I don't think that sort of lifestyle will agree with us any longer. After all you're a fearless Slayer now, isn't that, right?" My words would cause her to avert her gaze and appear sheepish. "E-Even still, I see that you weren't entirely in the wrong. More times than I could count I nearly perished one way or another. Still, I think I want to remain with Gareth and the others. I've taken a liking to the life of a Slayer."

"And I wish to learn more about this power I possess. Something awoke within me back in Blackfang's lair and I need to learn how to wield it. That hermit is still out there, and I expect him to cause more trouble for the forest in the future. We both need to be ready when he does."

Olivia agreed and placed her paw on the hilt of her blade instinctively. I imagined that with our next encounter with that fiend, we would face him together.

"Regardless of what becomes of us in the days to come. Know that I love you and always will. We are kin after all, and nothing will ever change that."

Olivia smiled at me warmly. "Thank you for not giving up on me, Tybalt. After everything I said, I wouldn't blame you for not wanting to see me again, but you came after me all the same. Mother would be proud of you..."

"Proud of us," I corrected her.

It warmed my heart to know that all my struggles had been worth it in the end. To see my sister's smiling face again was a treasure far greater than anything I ever knew. We then began to construct a small memorial from some of the materials that we had brought from Gladstone and what I had salvaged previously from our home.

It was mostly old belongings like toys that belonged to the twins and a wooden sword that Nathaniel used to spar with Olivia while also including Mother's quiver with the last of its arrows now spent. We used one of the larger splinters as a makeshift headstone and placed these once cherished objects of our loved ones around them.

Finally, with the use of some paint I had taken from Gladstone to let all know what transpired here and to ask those that chose to come here after to respect our fallen kin. For both of us, this process was incredibly painful as we were preparing ourselves to finally say goodbye to our loved ones for the very last time. We needed to do this though, our futures required us to be unburdened with the past.

As we finished our grim task and shed the last of our tears, Olivia then said, "Before we go back to Gladstone, there's someone I want you to meet. I'm sure you'll love him. He's a kind old soul and an amazing cook." Olivia then began to walk back towards the beetle. "Oh very well, I suppose there's no harm in it." I'd say as I began to follow her only to pause and glance back at the remains of our home.

"Tybalt?"

"Y-Yes, I'm coming! Be patient!"

When Olivia and I departed from the clearing, we would never return to it again. This place held too many memories and rebuilding what was lost would be nearly impossible. Though it wasn't as if we wanted to as even the very thought attempting to rebuild felt like doing a disservice to our deceased kin.

We realized that we didn't need a home to be a family, as long as we were there for one another our family would always live on.